"Remarkably fun novel...with nonstop action."
—*KIRKUS REVIEWS*

NOWHERE
TO
LAND

A THRILLER

TERETHA
HOUSTON

D1160282

This is a work of fiction. All characters, organizations, and events portrayed in this novel are either products of the author's imagination or are used fictitiously. Any resemblance to actual persons, living or dead, is entirely coincidental.

NOWHERE TO LAND. Copyright © 2022 by Teretha Houson.

All rights reserved.

Published in the United States of America by Yorkinton. www.Yorkinton.com

ISBN 978-0-9664481-2-2 (trade paperback)
ISBN 978-0-9664481-3-9 (e-book)

For my grandmother, Serleater.
Now that I am older, it all makes sense.

SELECTED PRAISE FOR

NOWHERE TO LAND

"Houston straps readers into a high-stakes thrill ride. The pulse-racing action will keep readers on the edge of their seats. Action and horror fans looking for a thriller with well-rounded characters will enjoy this read. Fans of fast-paced action will rave over this dazzling thriller."

—BookLife Review

"Remarkably fun novel … with nonstop action. Will appeal to genre fans, who may wonder when a movie version is coming out."

—Kirkus Reviews

"A thrilling page-turner with a great cast and compelling twists!"

—Bryan Thomas Schmidt, Hugo-nominated, national bestselling author (*John Simon*, *Predator*, *The X-Files*) and editor of Andy Weir's *The Martian*

NOWHERE
TO
LAND

by

Teretha

Houston

Yorkinton

PART I

SHADOWY FIGURES

CHAPTER 1

To the untrained eye, the Charger parked across the street could pass for a real police cruiser. Quentin had spent four years behind the wheel of an Atlanta PD Crown Vic, and to him the dark blue as fake as Lincoln on a Benjamin. The wimpy-ass bull bar on the front was a dead giveaway. If the driver rammed that piece of shit through anything stronger than a screen door, he'd wind up picking pieces of that Hemi V8 out of his skull.

Quentin and his yellow lab crossed to the other side of Sandcherry Drive, lined with middle-class homes and sculpted lawns. The smell of fresh-cut grass hung in the air. "Slow down, Razor," he said—just a man and his dog out for a casual stroll. He sold it well, which wasn't hard to do since that was his original plan, but the driver might think otherwise about a Black man walking through a mostly white subdivision. He sauntered up to the driver's window all la-di-da and laid-back. "Evening, officer."

"Good evening to you too," the driver said. White male. Late twenties. Short, dark brown hair. Medium build. Dark sunglasses kept his eye color a secret. While the blue uniform looked real enough, it fit too flat against his chest. He definitely wasn't vested up.

Officer, my ass!

"We don't get much police activity in this neighborhood. Should I be worried?"

"Why would *you* be worried? I'm sure you can handle just about anything … Mr. Kane."

Quentin stopped cold. "How do you know my name?" The situation could go sideways fast, and he was standing in the middle of the street, ass out. His piece was locked away four doors down, and Razor was a lover, not a biter. Was this someone he had put in the clink, now out and looking for a little tit for tat?

"We know a lot about you. That's why we're here. But we don't have much time."

Quentin scanned the inside of the car. "We?"

The man checked the street both ways, then glanced back over his shoulder. "It's clear."

A head popped up in the back seat, and the rear window slid down. A white woman wearing a gray baseball cap and a man's oversize, tan hooded jacket looked at him with frantic eyes. "Mr. Kane, my brother is in a lot of trouble." She tucked a wayward lock of long, brown hair under her cap with fingers that poked out of fingerless, black padded gloves.

Workout gloves? That didn't track with someone dressed like a sneak thief riding around in a fake police cruiser with a poser behind the wheel. Quentin leaned over and peered through the window. Her legs were small for her size, probably the result of muscle atrophy. They could be wheelchair gloves.

"Since you're the one doing the talking, I assume this man here isn't your brother."

"No, he's not."

"What kind of trouble, ma'am?"

"It's hard to explain and will be even harder for you or any other sane person to believe."

4

Getting dragged across broken glass seemed more appealing than heading back to his achingly lonely house, once filled with a love and happiness that now only existed in picture frames. But something hard to explain and hard to believe sounded like it had too much stink on it to tackle without a big bowl of alphabet soup—APD, FBI, DHS, CIA.

"I'm sorry, ma'am. I'm not a detective anymore. I think you should go to the police."

"The people he's in trouble with aren't your regular criminals. These people are shadows. They only come out of hiding when they're on the move, and they're on the move tomorrow morning. We don't have time for search warrants and police procedures. If we don't stop them now, no one in the world will be able to stop them. Ever. But you can. Single-handedly."

Tires screeched at the north end of the street. A white van barreled toward them.

"They're coming!" the driver yelled. "Get down!"

She shoved a small, wooden box through the window. "Take this."

"No. Wait. I don't know what you expect me to do."

"Everything you need and need to know is in here. Take it. *Please.* And hide it."

Quentin took the heavy box. It rattled as he jammed it into the inside pocket of his track jacket.

The driver yelled, "Run, Mr. Kane! Run!"

The V8 revved like a horde of screaming demons, tires squealed, and the Charger launched southbound down the street.

"Come on, boy." Quentin and Razor ran north through a cloud of smoke and the smell of burning rubber as the van screeched to a stop in front of his house.

Shit!

It had barely stopped when three men dressed in all black jumped out and ran straight for him. He scaled the fence

5

into his backyard and sprinted onto his patio. Seconds later, they popped over the fence, agile and quick. They had him cornered. Three to one. Big mistake.

The one leading the trio walked right onto the patio and stood there like he was the Big Bad Wolf. A brawny, real tough-looking guy. The kind that brushed his teeth with a chainsaw. When he opened his mouth, Quentin heard the rumble of a tornado. "Where is it?"

"Jumping the fence wasn't cowardice, guys. It was an act of mercy. Now get the hell out of my backyard."

The Big Bad Wolf came at him with a punch that could fell an oak tree. Quentin blocked it and caught him with a reverse roundhouse kick dead in the face. He dropped to the concrete patio floor. Lights out.

Hisssss.

Some kind of spray hit Quentin in the face. Liquid fire filled his eyes. He screamed and threw up his hands. When the spraying stopped and he dared to open his eyes, he couldn't see. His eyelids and most of his face were paralyzed. He waited, listening on a microscopic level, hearing only the birds chirping in his Yoshino cherry trees and Razor barking on the other side of the fence.

"Where is it?" a nasally voice said, two steps away on Quentin's right flank.

Got him. In a flash, Quentin vaulted over and slammed the guy's ass to the concrete with a one-arm shoulder throw. The last man didn't make a sound. Smart move. This guy wasn't going to give away his position so easily.

A sharp pain lit up the left side of Quentin's neck. A needle.

His knees buckled, and the next thing he knew, he was flat on his back and hands were rummaging through his pockets. "Get the f-f-fuck ah me." His tongue weighed a ton, half as much as his arms and legs. A hand ripped the box out of his pocket, and the world faded away.

6

CHAPTER 2

Eden Stone's red Mustang Shelby GT500 shot around a curve, the tall Georgia pines ripping past on both sides of the highway. Straggling in on CP time the first day? No, sir, not when she was sitting on enough horses to pull a train through molten lava. After all the hard work she had done to overcome the "me Tarzan, you Jane" shit she had put up with in her male-dominated profession, no way, not a chance in France.

Shelly wasn't the F/A-18 Eden used to fly, but she wasn't street legal either. The car roared into a deep bend in the two-lane highway as Otis Redding crooned "(Sittin' on) the Dock of the Bay" on the radio. Eden rounded the curve, and when she crested the small hill, the brake pedal hit the floorboard.

Oh no! Water!

Invisible hands crushed her chest as intensely as the force of seven Gs in the Super Hornet had when she was in the navy.

Big lake, little bridge.

Bridge? Dental floss was more like it. Two narrow lanes a half mile long. If she hadn't been about to firewall the gas pedal, she would've had time to stop and turn around. Now she was already on the frigging thing. Some way around Atlanta's I-75 this turned out to be.

An oncoming rusty orange pickup edged over the centerline.

If he didn't get his ass out of her lane …

She hammered the horn, then flashed the headlights. The lake seemed higher than before, an imagination gone wild. The calm water jumped to life with little dancing spouts as the leading edge of the rain stormed in from the west. If she didn't know better, she'd swear the raindrops were wearing cowboy boots and stomping on the roof as they swept over her. She turned on the wipers and throttled those babies up to max power, but the downpour was already blinding and the wandering pickup disappeared between wipes. Guardrails. Someone with a good imagination or a bad sense of humor had the nerve to call them that. More like strips of corrugated aluminum foil.

There's no room for error. That old voice from her navy training days was back. That stalker. It sent her stomach into a tizzy, and the two strips of bacon she'd had for breakfast were playing tennis with the egg. The warning awoke something deep inside her that had been dormant for years. Through the windshield, the two-lane bridge became the flight deck of the aircraft carrier USS *Abraham Lincoln*, and the lake turned into the Pacific Ocean. The sound of the pelting rain became the waves crashing against the hull of the ship.

Please, not now. She forced the images out of her mind and attacked the horn.

Moving back into his lane, the man in the pickup gave her one half of the peace sign, then zipped by.

After a barely discernible bump, it was over. No more bridge. No more water. Just glorious land and lofty Georgia pines again. *Christ's sake!* If that was all it took to knock her off her game, she might as well find the nearest skyscraper and take a long walk off its shortest ledge. The prick's crappy driving shouldn't have bedeviled her so. Clearly, her harrowing past wasn't far enough in the past. It might never be.

Minutes ago, she had been bursting to prove she was up for her latest challenge. Maybe she wasn't. She had been masquerading as the perfect little Black pilot for so long, she had forgotten it was all a façade. Lesson learned.

She glanced down at her new navy-blue suit and white blouse, and that old familiar feeling of being unworthy of the uniform washed over her, the feeling that she had put a gleaming veneer on top of a rotting tooth.

Tough turkey. It was go time. She gunned it toward Hartsfield-Jackson Atlanta International Airport, where her dream commercial aircraft awaited that she would get to fly for the first time. A smile flirted with the corners of her mouth.

Wow! I'm going to get to fly a Combi.

She couldn't let her past rob her of that opportunity. She couldn't let her secret surface. Today or any day. If she did, the FAA would strip her of her wings, and she wouldn't be allowed to jump two feet off the ground without a boarding pass.

CHAPTER 3

Daniel plowed his 4x4 through the muddy, red dirt trail once used by loggers. It dead-ended six miles deep in the woods at a place only he and the other two scientists knew wasn't what it appeared to be or where it was supposed to be. He stepped out of his pickup but kept a hand near the door handle, ready for a quick escape. Ears on high alert.

There were no warning signs. No movement. Good.

The old cabin and everything around it looked like it had been bitch-slapped by Mother Nature. Bears in the thick woods on three sides. Water moccasins in the swampy lake in the back. The early morning air reeked of fungus and dry rot. What a shitpit. The ass end of nowhere. He couldn't stand still ten minutes without kudzu twining up his legs. If the world came to an end, it would be years before this place knew anything about it, but it was one heck of a place to keep secrets.

He opened the door of the cabin. Calling it a shack would give it too much credit. The old wood floors sagged with every step as he walked across a dusty living room crowded with furniture that hadn't been in style since eight-track tapes were high-tech. When he opened the basement door, his heart rate shot up to the stratosphere.

He crept down the stairs nice and quiet, eyes trained on the back of the cage—or rather, on what lay asleep inside it, not that the tranquilizer, still working or not, was any guarantee he would make it back out of the basement with a pulse—or at all.

God, that smell. At least it wasn't *his* flesh that was decomposing. He wrinkled his nose as he walked over to the refrigerated cabinet. He rummaged through the bottles of chemicals and formulas, some familiar to researchers everywhere, some more befitting a witch's brew, and some he wouldn't touch unless he was wearing a hazmat suit. Yet the one bottle that could shut down the gruesome research before it moved into the human test phase was missing.

Ka-thump!

He whirled around toward the cage. From where he stood, he would never make it back to the stairs. He stared through the holes that peppered the edges of the rectangular, steel enclosure. The pencil-size holes lay so close together he could see through them into the dark interior where gator-green hide lay keeled over on one side. Only heavy, raspy breathing emitted from the cage now. The holes were big enough for oxygen to enter, small enough for nothing else to escape—if Professor Ogladorff and Dr. Speck knew what they were talking about anyway. *Ha!*

He glanced down at his watch. Time could be a vicious bastard when it wanted to be. In less than an hour, the other two research scientists would come blast-assing through the door.

His eyes combed the state-of-the-art research lab. A large, brown bottle shouldn't be hard to find. If he could get his hands on a fraction of the money spent on this place, Rachel would be out of that wretched wheelchair. Just a few … hell, the right *one* would pay for his sister's treatment. Banks of DNA sequencers, analyzers, and equipment with lambent lights and flickering panels fought for every inch of the tables and walls and filled the basement with low, steady hums and whirls.

There it is. The bottle of probetalamisol sat on the gray table in front of the cage. He squinted through the holes where the breathing, green hump didn't block his view. *What the—?* It couldn't be. His sight line was too clear. He shouldn't have been able to see all the way through to the table. Unless …

Holy shit! The front of the cage was missing.

Oggie and Speck's warnings flooded his mind. *Never enter the lab alone. This is the deadliest animal ever genetically engineered. Your first mistake could be your last.*

Now he stood ten feet from it, and it wasn't locked in a cage.

With only a few steps to go to reach the bottle, his feet turned to stone. "*Non sum qualis eram. Non sum qualis eram. Non sum qualis eram.*" What had become his favorite motivational phrase worked, but instead of escaping up the stairs, he flew past the cage in the opposite direction, the actions of a lunatic with the Grim Reaper on speed dial, but it had all gone so wrong, there was no other way now.

His head slapped the light bulb dangling from the ceiling. The basement had one pitiful, working light struggling to do the work of half a dozen. The pendulum swung, back and forth, casting an ominous, fleeting light on the shadowy, green figure.

Light … dark … light … dark … light … dark.

A faint slithering sound sprang from the cage.

He shot to the back door, grabbed the doorknob, and stopped.

If he didn't do it, Oggie and Speck sure wouldn't. He had lost count of how many times he had begged their crazy asses to do it. Twenty. Thirty. It didn't matter. They would rather stick their hands in boiling molasses than listen to him until it was too late. With their crackbrained ideas about research, maybe not even then.

Results trump all, Dr. Speck constantly harped like it was a proverb. *Even the law.*

Without a doubt, that "all" included murder. The other two would never let him live if they found out he was the one who did it.

"Non sum qualis eram." He tore his feet from the spot they were glued to and ripped open a drawer. *Where is it!*

He jerked open another. A third. *No, no, no!* A fourth.

No trank gun!

The hell with it.

He yanked out a hypodermic needle with a barrel the size of the Coke can sitting on the table in front of him, then grabbed the bottle of probetalamisol. The urine-colored tranquilizer would take effect in five seconds, ten tops.

Shit! Without the trank gun, he had to get close enough to inject it. So close that in a heartbeat, his flesh could be reduced to half-eaten scraps of offal, clinging to fragments of broken bones. Heaven help his sister then. He filled the syringe with every drop of tranquilizer it could hold. The light dimmed. *Don't do this to me. Not now.* If that lone light went out altogether, his chances of surviving would be slim and none, and slim suddenly hauled ass back up the stairs.

The jerry-rigged electrical system was always somewhere between a hiccup and a fart, which was not a shock considering all the electrical equipment gobbling up power from a system that had been around since Edison.

Why don't you call in a professional electrician, Oggie? Why don't you get the system upgraded, Doc? As if his opinion counted around there. He couldn't wheedle them into calling the fire department, or anyone else with a working pair of eyes, if the place was burning to the ground.

The light brightened again, and then a loud thud came from behind him. What was that? His head whiplashed around so fast that a lightning bolt of pain shot up the back of his neck.

Oh God! No!

Dr. Zebb Speck stood at the bottom of the stairs. Between Oggie and Speck, the more dangerous one had caught him. Dr. Speck was always packing and liked to boast about it. *I got enough guns to start World War III by my doggone self.*

The doc wouldn't need to check the traps in the woods. Daniel was going to be the animal's next meal, murdered and tossed into the cage where claws and teeth would sunder his body and all the evidence would be consumed.

Brandishing his usual condescending sneer, Dr. Speck cleaned his eyeglasses with the tail of his red-and-black checkered shirt.

Had he seen the syringe? No way. Daniel still had a heartbeat.

He eased the needle behind his back and fired a finger at the cage. "It moved! I heard it!"

The doc had the figure of a man who probably buttered his butter with butter. He put his eyeglasses back on and waved a dismissive hand. "Ah, pishposh," he said in a country accent. "The amount of probetalamisol I just shot into that thing would knock out Godzilla. I swear, if you were any more of a chicken, I'd have to pluck feathers off your ass."

Professor Ogladorff walked in carrying a Skil cordless drill. "I found it. Oh, Daniel, you're early."

Daniel's shoulders slumped. "Looks like we all are," he mumbled under his breath. The only thing he could salvage from this fustercluck was that Dr. Frankenfarmer and Dr. Frankenforeigner seemed oblivious to what he had come there to do, a plan now shot to shit. "Why isn't the front on that thing?"

"Well, it would have been if you had gotten your patookus out of bed and been here to help us finish assembling the cage," Speck, the one Daniel called "Doc," answered. "We had to wrangle that heavy animal from the concrete cage to the portable one, just the two of us. We're about ready for the animal cargo company to come pick it up." He lumbered by, his brown, ostrich-skin cowboy boots tapping against the cement floor, then stopped in front of the open cage with his back to it and a dégagé air as if that was safe. "I was so excited that this day had finally come, I didn't know whether to take off running or stand still. I called Oggie and glory be! He was already halfway to my farm, so we got an early start."

Daniel cracked open the drawer behind his back and slipped the syringe into it. "Doc, I didn't see your truck out front when I drove up. Where is it?"

"We took the boat in."

"Why'd you do that?"

"Why are you so concerned about how we got here?" Speck shuffled over to the front of the cage leaning against the wall. "The milk'll turn to clabber waiting on you. Don't just stand there. Grab hold of the other end."

Daniel rolled down his sleeves against the chill, schlepped over, and grabbed one end of the slab of metal. A dark, green leather-covered cushion that was a close match to the color of the animal's hide padded the center of the side facing him. The two of them lifted the slab and sidled over to the cage where Oggie stood ready with the drill. They flipped the cushioned side toward the body of the cage and lined it up.

The animal lay with the rubbery hide of its back separated from Daniel by ten inches of putrid air billowing up from the massive hump inside the cage. "God. That'll blacken your lungs," he said. Compared to this stench, the smell of decomposing animal parts was a field of ripe strawberries. The top of the cage came up to his chin, and he hit the six-foot mark. Cushioning also covered the inside of the other three walls and the top of the cage. "What's with the padding, Doc?"

"If we protect what's inside the cage, we protect everything that's outside it."

"Padding. Hot dang," Daniel scoffed. Nothing could go wrong during that long flight now. They had a razor-thin piece of leather and an inch or two of fluff to save them.

A faint sound arose from the dark lair, the sound of rough hide slithering across taut leather.

"You hear that?" Daniel asked.

Oggie shook his head. "Not so much as an eyelash quivered. I would know. I'm closer to it."

"Yeah, but your ears have thirty-three more years of wear and tear on them than mine."

"You're frightened of the megateratoid. That's all."

"Oggie, frightened is what I was *before* I found out the front wasn't on the cage." Every nightmare Daniel ever had lurked in the darkness of that vile thing, every monster that hid in his closet when he was a child, every steel-cold hand that waited under his bed to grab him by the ankles, and every shadow that came to life by the light of a full moon.

"Daniel, will you stop all this nonsense about the mega-T?" Dr. Speck snapped. "You might as well drag a string of barbed wire across my nerves. The sooner we get this done, the sooner we can go have breakfast. I'm hungry enough to eat the ass end out of a low flying-duck."

Daniel listened. There was only husky breathing now.

Oggie jabbed a Phillips-head bit into the cordless drill and raised it over his head as if the sight of it would spur them on.

Daniel hoisted his end up and got a better grip. "Let's just get this thing attached. The edges are sharp, and it's starting to bite into my fing—"

Green flesh stabbed up through the gap and lashed at his face. He jerked his head away as the flesh whipped by within an inch and fanned his hair back. Dr. Speck dropped his end of the cage. Professor Ogladorff just stood there, frozen. Daniel dropped his end and took off across the room while the loud peal of metal crashing against the cement floor echoed behind him.

"Get the probetalamisol!" Oggie said, coming out of his stupor.

The doc hustled over to the long table in front of the cage. His inner thighs rubbing together sounded like he was sawing down a redwood. He filled a hypodermic needle to a third of what Daniel had filled his. Even from across the room, Daniel could see his hand shaking, a sight he had never seen in the two years he had been working there. The doc leaned down and disappeared. Through the holes in the cage, Daniel could see thrashing shadows and slashing green hide while the sounds of loud rustling and violent slapping against the leather interior billowed from the cage. The sounds waned until …

Silence.

He searched the other side of the cage. There was no sign of the doc and, more importantly, no sign of *life* from the doc.

Daniel edged back over. What remained of the syringe trembled in the doc's hand. All six inches of the needle's steel tip were eaten away except a remnant the length of a pencil tip. The doc laid the needle down on the table but never took his eyes off the cage.

Where was that cocky asshole who turned his back to the cage now? Looked like Daniel wasn't the only chicken in the room.

He tuned an ear to the cage. *Ah.* Heavenly silence.

Oggie laid the drill on the table. "Zebb, we can't go through with this. The mega-T has become too difficult to control, too unpredictable, and there are still far too many unknowns."

Dr. Speck scoffed and shook his head.

"He's right, Doc," Daniel said. "He should know. He created it. And all the others," he added, waving a hand across the room at the glass cabinets that lined the entire wall from floor to ceiling. A creep show. Shelves of glass jars filled with formaldehyde and creatures that gave him the willies. Recombinant DNA research run amuck. Thank God those abominations didn't exist anywhere else on earth. They wouldn't exist *period* without Professor Wilhelm Klaus Ogladorff—one sick son of a bitch.

Jar after jar. From the size of beer cans to beer kegs. All neatly arranged and not a speck of dust on them. It was a twisted man's trophy display, crazy shit *showcased*, no less, in order of creation from top left to bottom right. And each had a pristine, white, laminated label attached with the name Oggie had given it and the date of creation. Not one label had faded or yellowed. The first one read: "SIMBUKTERON, 1981." It looked like someone had zapped a small animal in the microwave until it burst. The label on the second read: "SIMBUKTANNY, 1982." It was similar to the first one and was just as disgusting, but this one showed how much Oggie's skills had progressed in a single year. It was a vast improvement with clearly identifiable features. Four paws. A tail. Teeth.

Every jar showed a quantum leap in Oggie's ability to take fragments of DNA from different animals and combine them to form a new, primogenial creature that had to be an affront to God.

The last cabinet. Man, that thing. Daniel would jump in the slimy water out back, moccasins and all, if he could see that thing sinking to the bottom of the lake. Except for the last one, the one in the cage, he wouldn't have to look at Oggie's newest creatures then, unspeakable monstrosities from the first to the last. A frog with a snake's elongated, serpentine body; a rainbow trout with a scorpion's curly tail; a rabbit with a duck's white feathers and webbed feet; a bird with a piranha's wedge-shaped teeth; a hairless goat with a kangaroo's two short front legs and a pouch; a striped octopus with a tiger's yellow eye and a shark's black eye; and a gray-and-green speckled baby crocodile with a rhinoceros's horn, a hog's feet, and an opossum's tail. On and on. Nightmare after nightmare.

Oggie's last creation—as far as Daniel knew—lay inside the cage, far too big to fit inside any of the jars.

Daniel brightened. "Doc, we should euthanize the mega-T. Administer an overdose. It would die peacefully." If they hadn't come early, the doc would be all weepy at that very moment, moaning about how he had accidentally administered the overdose himself, and Daniel would be so happy he would be laughing out of his ass.

Dr. Speck said, "We *have* to go through with this. Don't forget, I had a hand in this too. If you think I'm willing to throw away all my years of hard work, and all the relationships I've built with Granthom Research Group and everyone else who invested in this research, then there's a hollow space in your head with a sign that reads, "THIS SPACE FOR RENT." My name, my reputation, is on the line."

Ogladorff ran a hand through what was left of his hair. "Zebb, you saw what just happened. Call GRG and tell them it's off. To think it's safe to take the megateratoid out of these woods now, one would have to abandon all common logic."

The doc threw up his hands. "Come on, Oggie. It'll be out the whole time."

"It *should* be in a giant jar of formaldehyde the whole time," Daniel said. "It was supposed to be out a few minutes ago when it came within inches of taking my head off, right?"

"In a state of chemically induced hibernation." The doc hurled an evil grimace at Daniel. "You big baby. Big difference."

"The mega-T can hibernate?" Granted, his field was mitochondrial DNA, not recombinant DNA, but maybe it was time for him to check his master's for an expiration date.

"All mammals have the innate ability to hibernate, Daniel," Professor Ogladorff said. "Even humans."

"I thought you stopped drinking, Professor. You didn't just fall off the wagon; you must have gotten run over by it too." Humans hibernating. Ridiculous. A tall tale of the Rip van Winkle sort. But it had come from the mouth of the man who had collaborated on countless science textbooks that universities used all over the world. Oggie was a sixty-five-year-old Albert Einstein with bad intentions.

"It's true," the doc said. "In 1999, a woman in Norway was submerged in icy water for more than an hour. No heartbeat. Wasn't breathing. Her body temperature was down to 57°F. She lived. In 2001, that toddler in Canada …" Deep ruts appeared between the two gray thickets above his eyes. "… ah, ah …"

"Erika Nordby," Oggie said.

Dr. Speck unfurrowed his brows. "Right. She slipped out of the house in the middle of the night at eleven degrees below zero in just a diaper and T-shirt. Her heart stopped beating for two hours. She lived. And I can't count the times I've seen on the news where someone has stowed away in the wheel wells of an airplane and survived a flight for hours in subzero temperatures."

"What the media proclaimed to be *miracles* was simply hydrogen sulfide," Oggie said in that easy professor's voice of his. "It's found naturally in our bodies, binding to the cells in the absence of oxygen. But with an increase in hydrogen sulfide, the cells' activity practically stops, and that cuts the body's need for oxygen down close to zero. Excess hydrogen sulfide temporarily changes humans from warm-blooded mammals to cold-blooded ones, which is *precisely* what happens to mammals that hibernate naturally."

It could be true. More likely than not it was, with Oggie's academic acuity. Despite that, after the debacle that just happened, neither one of them could sell him a dollar for a dime. Daniel fished his truck keys out of his pocket. "I'm sorry. I can't go through with this. If all the things you two warned me about are true, no one should come within a hundred miles of that thing again." *Until I have a chance to kill it.*

"I guess what everyone is saying about you is true," the doc said.

"No. I am not what I once was. Not anymore."

"You're a has-been who never was." The doc's words were shards of glass that cut to the bone. "Besides, what about your sister, Daniel?"

"Zebb!" Oggie said. "That's low."

Daniel shook his head at Dr. Speck, insensitive son of a bitch. Above him, the bare boards of the unfinished basement resembled giant bones. Fitting. He was trapped in the belly of a mammoth beast in a way. He exhaled a long sigh. "We'd better seal up the cage."

"Good, you milquetoast," the doc taunted in a way that always made Daniel's blood surge through his body in search of a relief valve. "And check for any sign of injury first. You could have cut it when you dropped your end."

Daniel shilly-shallied toward the cage. Why rush? If they missed the flight … yay! Woo-hoo!

The doc's scornful eyes followed Daniel across the room. "This may take a minute, Oggie. I only have two eyes, two ears, two hands, and too little help."

Daniel picked up the flashlight from the table and shined

it through the front of the cage where one color dominated. Green animal. Green padding. Green everywhere the light landed—mostly dark green with a hint of pale green—but there was nothing out of the ordinary. He circled the rectangle and turned off the flashlight when he reached the front again. "No sign of injury."

Oggie rubbed a forearm across the drops of sweat glistening on his forehead. "Good heavens. We must be more careful. Carelessness with the mega-T would be a horrific method by which to commit suicide."

Daniel trudged back to the table. Another rustling sound shot from the cage behind him.

A loud *pop*!

Instant darkness. *Tink, tink, tink.* The sound of fine glass bouncing off the cement floor filled the blackness. The light bulb!

He spun back around toward the cage. Should he stand still or haul ass for the stairs? He would trip and fall half a dozen times in the dark. He kept stone still, ears searching the basement but finding no sounds coming from the cage. Not a peep from where the doc had been standing. Nothing from where the professor had—

He was still holding the flashlight.

His thumb slid onto the switch and froze. If he turned it on, the mega-T might see him before he saw it, and claws would slice him in two quicker than a chainsaw could a toothpick. Coercing his disobedient thumb, he pushed the switch forward and cringed.

"Whew!" Daniel said. It was just Dr. Speck, standing there wild-eyed and mouth agape. He swung the flashlight over to the cage where the mega-T's side rose and fell with each breath.

"Quick!" Dr. Speck barked. "Before it wakes up again. It's going in and out of consciousness."

Daniel laid the flashlight on the table and aimed the beam at the cage. This time he lifted the metal slab by himself. His left foot slid out from under him, and the front of the cage slid down his hand to his fingertips. As he hoisted it up again and reclaimed his grip, he stumbled on something. *Gotta be kidding me. What black cat's path did I cross?* He stepped over it and lined up the holes in the slab with the holes in the body of the cage.

Dr. Speck stabbed a screw into the top left corner and screwed it home with the drill. Ten or twelve screws later, he stepped back from the cage. "Done."

Daniel grabbed the flashlight and pointed it at the floor. "Doc, look!" The slip mark that his foot had made cut through a puddle of blood, and something black lay at the edge of the red circle. He swung the beam over. "Noooo!"

The light rested on the professor's right leg, which was completely severed from the knee down. It was still wearing its shoe, its sock, its pant leg, and probably Daniel's shoeprint now. But the oddest of all was the filament from the light bulb sticking out of the calf. He swept the flashlight left. Right. "Professor!"

Oggie lay in an expanding mere of blood with three parallel gouges running diagonally from his left shoulder down to his right pelvic bone.

The doc ran over and stooped down. "Oggie!"

Oggie gurgled and coughed up a spray of blood as entrails seeped out through the gouges. "Zebb, do what Daniel suggested. You must"—he gurgled again—"kill it. Here. Now. If you proceed … later, it could be just as lethal dead as it is alive. Maybe even more so."

The doc caressed Oggie's head. "You're right. I should have listened to you. This is all my fault. I'll do it, and then I'll call GRG and tell them we're not going to make the flight."

Oggie's eyes closed, and his head thudded against the floor.

The doc stood back up. "Come on. We have to install the crate on top of the cage before Animal Land Aircargo gets here."

He walked out of the beam of light, leaving Oggie lying on the cold floor like his riven partner was nothing more than a broken jar of pickles on the kitchen floor.

"But you just promised Oggie that—"

"Now, Daniel!"

Heavy, raspy breathing filled the cold silence.

"Doc, what did Oggie mean?"

"Get your lazydinkus over here and help me put the crate on. The truck just pulled up."

"How the hell could the mega-T be more lethal dead than it is alive?"

CHAPTER 4

What the hell did I drink? Quentin was still a little woozy, and he couldn't remember anything between the time he'd strapped on Razor's collar to take him for a walk yesterday and waking up on the patio early this morning with his dog's head on his chest and the sound of his open gate clapping against the fence boards in the breeze. His head pounded like there were a hundred tiny men trapped inside his skull, all trying to hammer their way out—busy little bastards. Going on a bender like the one he had yesterday was new territory for him. Sure, he'd tossed back more than his share of the teeter-totter water since he lost his wife and baby girl, a hell of a lot more than his share, but he had never blacked out drunk in his life. *Whatever it was, they should stop making that shit.*

He pried through the hurry-scurry of Atlanta's Hartsfield-Jackson International Airport and arrived at Gate E31. As he weaved around a woman and a little girl standing at the entrance, a redhead caught his attention. The man was stealthy. Quentin had to give him that. Smooth. A real pro. Part of an air marshal's job was to spot odd shit like that. He walked over to the redhead's row with a black leather carry-on bag digging into his shoulder and a cup of perk in each hand. He flopped down directly across from the thatch of curly hair poking above a copy of *The Atlanta Journal-Constitution*. If the man's hair was any redder, it would catch fire.

A *paper* newspaper? Well, la-di-da. It had been some time since Quentin had read a newspaper, printed or otherwise, so who was he to judge?

"You look like you didn't get much sleep last night," Red said without so much as a peek over or around the paper.

How does he know what *I look like?* Quentin stared at the back of the still paper. "I guess I got about a wink and a half." That was his new normal since life did a hit-and-run and left him for dead, although no one could ever accuse him of not doing his part. He was unhappily married to the job and having an affair with the bottle.

"Those two cups of coffee certainly won't help you sleep. Don't count on them to fix that hangover either."

Without a doubt, the aroma gave away the coffee, but how did he know Quentin had two cups instead of one? Screw that. How did the redhead know he had a hangover? He damn sure did, one for the record books, but it couldn't have been that obvious. Covertly studying the passengers waiting to board Flight 1219 to Cape Town was one thing, but now Red was doing the same thing to him. The difference was that, in Quentin's case, not one time did the man move from behind the newspaper.

Quentin examined the back of *AJC's* Monday edition. There wasn't a single peephole. He tossed the first cup of forty weight down his gullet without tasting it and started on the second one.

A bright flash.

It was just the lights reflecting off the corner of a silver briefcase, one of those strong, metal jobs. The pudgy man carrying it walked by in a brown, tweed blazer and brown, ostrich-skin cowboy boots. For a man who had to be on the past-tense side of sixty, he had a head full of hair, silver hair, thick and bristly. He must have a wolf somewhere in his family tree.

"Do I have to do everything?" the man with the briefcase asked. "I only have two eyes, two ears, two hands, and too little help."

The younger man walking with him had the face of a pall-bearer: his ice-blue eyes, distant and solemn; his face, stern. His hand zipped and unzipped the front of his jacket nonstop. When he looked up at the windows, his somber face twisted into a scowl.

"What are you gawking at?" The hairy one looked up, and his mouth dropped open.

The newspaper simultaneously flipped to the next page and moved down enough for two green eyes to get a gander above it at the man clutching the silver briefcase. They paid a blink's worth of attention to it and less than half as much to the man holding it.

Hungover or not, old Quentin Kane saw every minute movement as easily as if the newspaper and the eyes reading it, or pretending to read it, had moved in slow motion.

Still, Red never so much as glanced in his direction. "Do the sleeping pills give you the shakes too, my friend?"

Quentin looked down. His hands were shaking ever so slightly. How the hell did he know that?

<hr />

"Doc, do you see this?" To Daniel, it was another omen. "Where is the mega-T? Is it already on the plane?"

The doc rolled his eyes up to the whites. "There you go again."

"Look at this." Daniel pointed through the light-blue-tinted windows that stretched from floor to ceiling. "How are you not worried? The longer it takes to get the animal to

Cape Town, the more likely something will go wrong, and from the look of things, we're about to get hit with a megaton of wrong." With dark gray clouds hovering above, thunder volleying back and forth, great torrents streaming from the sky, hurricane-force wind buffeting patches of rain one way and then another, the doc wasn't concerned? *Ha!*

"Stop crying, Daniel. I gave the mega-T more hydrogen sulfide than I originally planned. We have to deliver the creature to the Granthom Research Group on schedule."

"You still have confidence in your concoctions? After what happened to Oggie?"

"As a backup, I hit it with a double dose of probetalamisol. Any more and I would have killed it."

If the doc wiped some of that greed out of his eyes, he could see that wasn't a bad idea. "Killing the thing just might keep the runaway death storm from going global," Daniel said.

"There's no runaway anything. I keep telling you Granthom Research Group would never fund—"

"GRG *is* the runaway death storm."

"Ah, pishposh." The doc leaned closer to the window. "This weather is what you call getting the rug snatched out from under you when your britches are down. I didn't reckon on this little surprise."

"Surprise? In the spring, weather forecasters in the southeast have the easiest job in the world. Rain yesterday. Rain today. Rain fill-in-the-blank day. No need for a shower. You'll get one every hour."

"Still, you should have checked the weather before we left. That was Oggie's bit of business. Now it's yours."

There was probably some other little surprise waiting for them that the doc didn't "reckon on."

Dr. Speck looked over his shoulder. "It looks like we'll be boarding soon."

Not from what I saw. Daniel followed the doc's gaze over to the gate kiosk, where two agents had arrived and were typing on the computers.

The female agent pulled the microphone to her mouth. "Ladies and gentlemen, Airland Airlines Flight 1219 to Cape Town, South Africa, has been delayed due to weather conditions."

CHAPTER 5

Ka-bam!

Eden nearly jumped out of her skin. The sound of the deafening clang rang in her ears. Any thunderous crash on an airport tarmac was bad. One on the other side of her aircraft was likely bad, up close, and personal.

From the loud sound, Murphy's Law wasn't done with them. The only thing that hadn't gone wrong was her walkaround inspection of the exterior of the Boeing jumbo jet, and that could change before she finished. Even if it sailed through inspection, what good would it do if they never got off the ground? They were already an hour and twenty-five minutes past the scheduled departure time for a flight that was going to be an ass-numbing sixteen hours long, primarily over a watery hell called the Atlantic Ocean. If they had another delay, they might as well cancel the flight.

She took a shortcut under the belly of her plane. The giant, blue aircraft showed as much wear as a newborn baby, or in this case, newborn conjoined twins. It was a real beauty, stunning, up close or from a distance, with its double deck and elegant humpback. Eden would have leaped at the chance to fly any 747, but for her, the pot of gold at the end of the rainbow was a 747-400M. A Combi. A passenger plane, check.

A freight plane, check. Both boxes ticked with one aircraft. Little fifteen-year-old Eden in her propeller plane didn't know an aircraft with both passenger and freight sections on the main deck even existed. Passengers in the forward section and freight in the aft, basically two planes in one. *Two planes!* Two planes might have crashed into each other on the tarmac. She raced out from beneath the starboard side.

There had been a crash, all right, but not one she ever would have guessed. There sat another Combi, white with a teal vertical stabilizer and a matching cheat line running from nose to tail. The entire aircraft was tilted diagonally with its tail sitting on the tarmac, its nose tilted toward the sky, and its nose landing gear dangling freely in midair. Mystery solved. The crashing sound had been the tail crashing down onto the tarmac. She had seen old pictures of an Air Canada Combi with its tail sitting on the tarmac like this one but never thought she would see it with her own eyes.

Someone was going to get promoted to the unemployment line.

"Do you have bird shit for brains?" a short man dressed in gray coveralls and a yellow, high-viz safety jacket exploded at two men twice his size. "This is a Combi, you assholes. That sixty thousand pounds of freight in the tail should have been loaded only *after* it had been counterbalanced with the weight of the fuel in the wings. Plus, you see that other Combi over there?" He shot a finger at Eden's aircraft. "It has a tail stand under it. You forgot to put one under this Combi."

What could pass for a giant, yellow camera tripod stood under the tail of her aircraft, thank God. In the back, where there was no landing gear, sixty thousand pounds were no joke. No tail stand to shoulder all that weight? *Jeez.* On top of that, no passengers, no cargo in the forward sections, and no fifty-four thousand gallons of fuel in the wings to counterbalance the freight. Of course it was going to end in a disastrophe. They were lucky they didn't get someone killed.

"Here comes a big one," a voice above her yelled.

She looked up as a big, wooden crate with "Animal Land Aircargo" stenciled on it in red rose on a cargo loader and rolled into the starboard, lower-rear cargo hold.

Dexter nudged the wooden crate a tad, then the runners in the floor shuttled it into place at the back of the cargo hold. "You got that right. It *is* a big one. Heavy too." He wiped a gloved hand across his sweaty brow, then frowned. Something clung to his forehead. "The hell is that?" He shed the glove and mopped his forehead with his hand. Slimy, beige gunk clung to his brown fingers. When he fanned them apart, it stretched between them. "Someone blew his damn nose on the crate. A nasty son of a bitch."

Perry scrunched up his nose. "Whew! What's in that thing? It's as funky as a dead woman's drawz." He walked over to a dog kennel, where a Rottweiler with a docked tail lay. The dog jumped to his feet and started barking. "Easy, boy," Perry said. But the dog wasn't barking at him. He was barking at the crate with his eyes fixed on it. Perry stooped down and looked through the bars. A gold nametag shaped like a bone danced from the dog's collar. "Vicious. That's probably a good name for you. Easy, Vicious. Easy, boy." The dog lay back down with his head between his front paws.

"See that?" Dexter pointed at the Animal Land Aircargo crate. "That could be trouble." Vicious released a long, low growl at the crate. With his lips skinned back, he was all teeth now.

Perry walked to the back of the cargo hold, where the reason for Dexter's concern lay at his feet. A cargo net secured the crate to its pallet—almost. One of the net's hooks was loose. He stooped down and hooked it into its pallet ring, then shot back up like he had springs for feet. At the same time, Vicious launched into full-on attack mode, barking and growling. Mad as hell.

"Dex, you hear that?"

Dexter frowned and cocked his head. "Hear what? You and that dog operating on the same frequency or something?"

"Sounded like something was scratching against hard metal, coming from inside this crate. Real soft, but I heard it."

"Come on, man. That crate's made of wood. You're just keying in on that dog's behavior."

Perry pointed to a small, red spot on one of the bottom corners. "Check that out. Looks like blood."

"Or some of the ink they used to stamp their name on the crate. Man, stop bullshitting and get your black ass back to work."

Vicious calmed down for a moment, then cranked up again. This time he went full mad dog, barking furiously, attacking the bars of his kennel with his teeth.

Perry looked over at the dog. "Whatever is in that thing, that dog wants to chew it a new asshole. What do you think it is?"

"Who knows? Animal Land Aircargo is always shipping weird shit. I was working on a freighter one day, and in comes this big-ass, specially designed container. And in it was a live great white shark."

"That's got to be some sort of record, ain't it?"

"That ain't shit. UPS flew in two live whale sharks to the Georgia Aquarium. All the way from Taiwan. Eight thousand miles. Twenty-five thousand pounds apiece. They landed right here at this very airport in two 747s. Now that I think about it, it might have been the same 747 that made two trips. However they did it, the whale shark is the biggest fish in the sea."

Perry's mouth flew open. "Daaamn." Then his eyes met Dexter's, and his mouth got wider. "Ey, man, you a'ight?"

"What you talking 'bout?"

"Dex, you got this purple spot on your jaw, and I know it wasn't there earlier. And you look like you got the pink eye too. They didn't look like that earlier either." A low grunt came from the crate. Perry shot to the other side of the cargo hold.

Dexter, on the other hand, didn't so much as flinch. "Whatever it is, it damn sho ain't sleep."

———�center ornament⟩———

As Eden finished up the walkaround inspection, a piercing scream bellowed down from the same spot someone had yelled from before. "Dex, don't move! Not an inch, man!" A man staggered in the doorway high above her, then fell out of the cargo door.

Eden gasped and clamped a hand over her mouth.

He landed on the cargo loader that was on its way back down. With that kind of luck, the man probably had a praying mother somewhere. A fall all the way to the ground could have broken his neck.

Another man ran into view in the doorway and screamed, "Dexter!" It was the same voice.

A few minutes later when the paramedics wheeled Dexter passed her on a gurney, he sat up, looked directly at her, and screamed, "Cray. Cray." Or maybe it was "Crate. Crate." His brown face, neck, and hands were covered in grape-colored spots, and his eyes were the color of two cherries.

———⟨center ornament⟩———

From somewhere below the main deck cabin, a thumping sound arose. The gray wolf and his pallbearer-faced traveling companion jumped. Quentin heard it. Felt it too. Who didn't? But the sound didn't goose anyon else in the back of the passenger cabin. Then the men he had seen at the gate earlier started a little one-on-one, not a friendly conversation judging by the finger-pointing. The two oddballs made Quentin's rusty old detective antenna spring up from six rows away.

He walked up and slipped into the aisle seat behind the

one with the pallbearer's face. Early thirties. Six feet, six-one. An inch or two shorter than Quentin. About a buck 90, buck 95. Neck and neck with what he weighed. Strong built, but Quentin struck an imposing shadow too. The gray-haired one didn't look like he would be much of a physical challenge if things went sideways. His body overshot his window seat in the exit row and spilled into the vacant one between them.

Thump!

They jumped again, and their whispers and gestures came to a sudden halt.

Quentin could understand why a spooked passenger might be startled the first time, but they should have been used to the sound the second time. The only thing below them was a cargo hold. So someone closed a cargo door. No biggie. The one in his early thirties frowned at the gray wolf, and his face had turned white.

Something is afoul, but I don't see any birds.

The freckle-faced head flight attendant who had introduced herself as Sierra reached the exit row in front of Quentin. "Would you like me to stow that for you, sir?"

The hoary head didn't even bother to look up.

The other one tapped him on the shoulder. "Dr. Speck?"

Sierra reached for something on the empty seat between them.

Dr. Speck yanked his briefcase into his arms. "No, I'll do it."

She jerked her hand back, mouth agape. He babied the briefcase into the overhead compartment above Quentin's head and then sat back down.

Quentin's antenna rose a little higher.

Dr. Speck checked his watch and then looked out of the window on his left for the fifth or sixth time, and Quentin kept studying him. The guy was hiding something, all right, maybe in that cherished briefcase.

Whatever was in it was right above his head now.

CHAPTER 6

Captain Montgomery Locke throttled the engines up, and the Combi streaked down the runway.

At 100 knots, Eden stole a peek through the glareshield, then snapped her eyes back down to the airspeed indicator. The go/no-go speed was coming up fast. Almost there … almost there …

At 150 knots, she said, "V1," remaining vigilant as the next target speed approached. "Rotate," she said when they reached 165 knots.

Monty nursed the control yoke toward his chest and raised the nose 10 degrees positive attitude. The nose lifted off the runway and climbed into thin air. From the start of the takeoff roll until the Combi took to the sky took all of fifty seconds. At 12:50 p.m., Flight 1219 with 157 souls was wheels-up. At 12:51, it looked like that was a mistake.

If Eden was the one making the call, they would boomerang right back to the airport, but she was pilot-not-flying, and pilot-not-flying had better throttle her ass up and take care of her own assignments. Let the captain deal with the threatening sky.

She marched down the after-takeoff checklist, and the world vanished as a cloud swallowed the aircraft in its suffocating dark, gray gloom. Visibility, zero. Lightning stitched a crooked seam across the eastern sky up ahead, and thunder grumbled its disapproval that they'd dared to enter its realm.

Bearing a hint of a smile, Monty glanced over at her. "How's my first officer?" His voice exhibited no sign of concern about the weather. Confidence. That was it. She sure would be glad if some of it rubbed off on her.

"The long weather delay gave me a chance to get rid of the nerves." Good thing she wasn't Pinocchio. Her nose would punch a hole through the glareshield.

"Good," Monty said. "Someone who's been flying as long as you have shouldn't be nervous about this aircraft or that one."

Except for his salt-and-pepper, neatly trimmed curls, Monty, who had to be in his fifties, could pass for a college quarterback, tall and robust with broad shoulders and a tapered waist. She had heard rumors that he was a fearless jet jockey and had been dubbed "Superman in the cockpit."

He sported matching attire, except the epaulets on the shoulders of his white shirt bore four gold bars, one more than her first officer's uniform, and he wore a navy-blue necktie. Hers was a matching crossover tie. She would bet a year's salary that "Superman in the cockpit" didn't think of *his* uniform as "veneer." A cape, maybe.

"Presley, Thiago," Monty said, looking over his shoulder at Captain Aaron Wilcut and First Officer Thiago McGannahan in the jump seats. "You two can thumb a ride home from here. Eden and I can handle it without you."

Aaron gave a hearty chuckle. "And leave poor Eden alone to make sure you fly on the right side of the road? Oh no, no, no." He wagged his finger like a mother who had walked in on little Johnny peeing on the cat.

The good-natured badinage between the two captains was

a soothing balm for the jitters, but handling an 8,439-mile flight without a backup crew was first cousin to waterboarding. The flight was twice as long as the maximum allowed flying time and required two flight crews.

Thiago leaned forward from the seat behind Eden's left shoulder. "Captain Wilcut told me you were in the navy. That you flew F/A-18s off the aircraft carrier USS *Abraham Lincoln*."

An icy gale blew into the flight deck. Monty and Aaron exchanged looks.

They knew. *Shit!* That look they gave each other … They knew! Her anxiety took the express elevator to the top floor, but she manufactured an artificial smile and proffered a gray response. "Yes."

"That's amazing how you can take off and land from the deck of an aircraft carrier," Thiago said, the only one who didn't seem to realize there had been an antipodal shift in the cockpit. "What do you call that procedure?"

"A trap," Eden said.

"A day trap seems difficult enough, but a night trap? In the middle of the ocean?"

Is he messing with me? The navy doesn't turn out any wimps, and if he locked horns with this fighter pilot, he was going to resurrect the fighter. She looked back. He seemed giddy. Innocent. Any second, he was going to float right out of his seat. What she wouldn't give if hers could only swallow her up. Whether he knew it or not, her fellow first officer was doing a real number on her, getting into her head and stripping the teeth off the cogs that were grinding as fast as they could to keep her confidence up.

"I had my heart set on joining the navy straight out of high school."

If Thiago had an "off" switch, she would fight off sharks to get to it. With great effort, she feigned an interest in a conversation that someone should have been merciful and implemented a gag order for years ago. "What happened?"

"My parents happened."

The primary flight display in front of her control yoke and the navigation display to its left suddenly needed her utmost attention. Foul weather painted the ND with green all around Flight 1219, and a patch of red highlighted the upper right part of the screen. Nothing new. She continued the charade of checking the systems and reached up to the panel below the glareshield and turned the ND range selector to 640. The green mass shrank to a few scattered flecks on the expanded 640-naut view. Up ahead, the sky promised to clear. A more extensive report had shown a storm over the South Atlantic, but they would vector around it. More old news. *A ruse by any other name is still a ruse.*

He sighed. "Regrettably, I let them talk me out of it. I'm blown away just watching that on TV. Why did you—?"

"Let her do her job," Aaron interrupted.

Thank you. A few more minutes of Thiago and she was going to need an ejection seat and a parachute.

"She has enough on her mind. Her first 747 flight since she was rated, and she gets stuck with this maniac," Aaron said, jabbing a finger at Monty.

"Thanks for the warning." She faked a laugh and cast a silicone smile back at Aaron as if everything was peachy. Her past remained a tender subject, a scab. And Thiago was picking at it.

The overhead panel emitted a soft ding, and the fasten-seat-belt glyph darkened. Dr. Speck tore off his seat belt and stood up. It wouldn't have surprised Quentin if the strap had left skid marks across his waist.

The captain's voice piped through the PA. "You are free to move about the cabin."

"Excuse me, Daniel." Dr. Speck rushed past him just as a woman sitting across the aisle stood up. A man beside her hooked a hand around her waist and pulled her back. It was a good thing he did, otherwise she would have become a bug on the windshield of that semi. She sidestepped Dr. Speck and walked toward the back of the cabin with the man on her heels. If her dress was one inch shorter, it would have just been a collar, not that Quentin was complaining.

Dr. Speck sprang open the overhead compartment and liberated his briefcase. Quentin had expected that. At least it was no longer above his head. Dr. Speck sat back down and cracked the briefcase an inch or two.

Dang it! It wasn't wide enough for Quentin to steal a peek.

Dr. Speck squinted into it, apparently to survey its contents, snapped it shut, and placed it on the empty seat next to him. Daniel glared down at the briefcase and then back up at Dr. Speck with a furrowed brow. Quentin could glean that Daniel was as perplexed as he was.

Something about these two made him suspicious.

CHAPTER 7

It moved. Of all the beverage carts surrounding Millicent, she could swear that one wiggled. The flight attendant was alone in the galley at the back of the main deck, and there was no turbulence, so she couldn't understand why the cart did a little shimmy.

Okay, girl, you're officially losing it.

Carts and bins overlaid the walls from floor to ceiling on the left and right, except for one missing cart that would have been in the slot next to the one that seemed to move. Two white latches above the vacant slot lay horizontally against the edge of the counter. The ones above the cart that she thought had moved hung in the vertical, locked position. Case closed. It was nothing more than an overactive imagination with el zippo to do until the second leg of the trip when her shift started.

As she popped a meatloaf dinner into the microwave, the beverage cart rocked, barely a quiver but enough to make the miniature bottles of Jack Daniel's, Seagram's Extra Dry Gin, and Jim Beam clink against each other. It then rocked a little harder, and this time the bottles sent out a salvo of little clinks.

Something wiggled on the floor between the two black, rubber casters on the front of the cart. It resembled the tip of a dark green finger.

When she leaned down to get a better look, it wiggled again. She sprang backward. In a flash, it shot from beneath the cart and coiled around her neck, looking less like a finger now and more like a snake that had no end and no head. Every muscle in her body constricted. She tried to scream but had only enough air in her lungs to manage a feeble whimper. Her fingers clawed the cold flesh. It wouldn't budge. She dug her fingernails into it. All for naught.

The front of the cart slammed against the latches while they strained and groaned. One of them shot off, then the second. The cart trundled out from under the counter, and she saw what was behind it.

The shift exposed a five-inch hole in the floor that was filling up quickly as more of the serpentine thing—clearly an appendage of something larger, a tentacle maybe—slithered up through the hole and grew to the size of her wrist. The noose gripped tighter until she could barely breathe at all.

Think!

The curtains ... Not an option. The ones to both the star-board and portside aisles hung closed, and she couldn't reach either pair anyway. The flight attendant's crew rest ... It was next door, but she couldn't alert anyone in it, asleep or not, if she couldn't scream. A passerby ... What passerby? The only thing behind the galley was the freight section, and no one would be going back there.

The *thing* dragged Millicent to the floor, where she had a closer view of the hole. Around the edge, tiny swirls of smoke rose in sinuous tendrils from the strange, light green puddles of liquid that rimmed it. Then the floor beneath melted away, expanding the hole to a foot wide. In a twinkling, it grew to two feet.

With a quick, hard tug around her neck, her back skidded across the floor to the hole. She couldn't let herself be dragged down into the abyss to meet the rest of this thing. Her fingers clawed at the carts on both sides of the hole, but their surfaces were too slick and devoid of anything to hold on to. Her fingernails skated off, and she plummeted into darkness.

⋯⋯

Millicent woke up facedown on the floor in the cargo hold with a dull ache in her forehead and a dog barking in her ear. She had no idea how long the dog had been barking or how long she had been unconscious. She rolled over, clamped her hands onto the cargo nets on the pallets on both sides of her, and winched herself into a sitting position.

The scant light filtering down through the jagged hole in the ceiling rationed out enough light from its shambolic beams for her to get a narrow view through the door of a kennel at the black-and-tan mug of a Rottweiler.

She brushed her hair out of her eyes. *That's not hair.* She held her hand out in front of her, and something dark dripped from her fingers. *Blood!*

As consciousness seeped back into her, she realized she could breathe freely. The noose was gone. Breathing freely came with a lofty price tag. She could also *smell* freely. The cargo hold reeked with a stench like carrion, strong and almost as suffocating as being strangled.

Clearly, she hadn't just fallen. She was ten feet behind the hole, not beneath it. A smudged trail of blood on the floor started directly below the hole and ended in a pool where her head had been when she woke up. For some reason, she had been dragged toward the tail and not killed.

The long, slender thing that had almost strangled her to death stood vertically with its tip beneath the hole. Her eyes traced it down to the floor, where it wended between two parallel tracks of runners and slalomed within inches of her on the way to some point behind her.

Turbulence rocked the plane, and her forehead slammed into the corner of a box, her aching and bleeding forehead. The tip darted from the hole to where she sat and hovered above her. She froze. So did it. Then it descended toward her.

Please! Not again.

It dropped to her eye level and continued its descent to the floor, where it slithered past her. *Thank you!* It snaked to a wooden crate behind her and disappeared in the shadows of the eerie underworld. A few minutes passed without a sound. Maybe it was safe to climb to the top of the shrink-wrapped boxes of various heights next to her and make her way back up through the hole.

Scratch, scratch, scratch. The crate!

It sounded like strong claws gouging a hard surface. Or maybe it was big, powerful teeth. The clawing stopped, but a clapping sound took its place. The crate rocked back and forth against its pallet.

The Rottweiler growled, long and low. Whatever was in the crate growled back even lower than the dog. She had never heard a growl like that. Any animal that could make that sound had to be enormous.

Then came a thwack like the crack of a whip that jolted her into motion. A warning that the container wouldn't hold together much longer. One of the black straps of the cargo net had snapped free from around the crate. She clambered up the stack of boxes, but her left foot slipped through a loop in the cargo net, and her leg lodged up to her knee in the tight space between the net and the shrink-wrap. She yanked her leg up, but the bind only gnawed deeper into the side of her knee.

The clapping stopped.

Something was moving. Shifting … sliding … *coming!*

If her ears hadn't been dialed up to ten, she probably would have missed it—creeping across the floor, cloaked in the shadows. When it stopped, it was directly below her.

44

The dog sprang to life again, barking and chomping at the bars of the kennel. The noise returned, and whatever it was, it lashed toward the Rottweiler, stabbed through the bars, and yanked the kennel into the air. The dog was at a disadvantage inside. If she could, she would set it free and see how the thing liked the chompers on that ticked-off Rottwei—

A roar exploded from the crate.

The kennel pranged against the floor. The thing had to be some kind of feeler or tentacle, and the actual beast was still inside the crate. For the moment.

The Rottweiler whined like it was in pain. The beast had done something to the poor dog. When Millicent looked up, she got a nice surprise. The tentacle flopped around wildly near the hole, twisting and squirming into the light, the end nearly severed.

Good dog!

The mangled tentacle slithered back to the crate, and then a sound like water hitting a red-hot skillet filled the air. A loud bang tore through the cargo hold and echoed off the walls. She jumped. Then a bombardment of hard blows landed on what sounded like metal.

A loud crack!

She had no doubt about *that* sound. If she didn't get out of the cargo hold—and quickly—she would die in it. That was clearly wood cracking. A piece of the cargo net around the crate snapped free. Then another. Double and triple snaps. Then …

The crate stood bare.

A wedge blasted off it from top to bottom, and something shiny glinted through. Metal.

Millicent pulled the strap away from her knee and scrambled up to the top box using the net. The hole in the ceiling seemed a million miles away and had nothing below it. Moving and restacking heavy boxes filled with who knew what without attracting attention was going to be a tall task.

She lay on her stomach and peeked back over the edge. The wooden crate fell away, and a metal cage stood naked. A hole with jagged wedges of metal that flared outward around the rim dominated the bottom right corner facing her, possibly the front of the cage. Metal moaned and strained as a bulge ballooned in the center. From the bottom right corner came more grinding and straining.

Barely visible in the scant light, the front of the cage detached. As the sound of fierce blows filled the cargo hold, the gap widened with each one.

Turbulence rocked the aircraft again, sending Millicent tumbling down the back of the box to the next level. She climbed back up to the top and affixed herself to the net with both hands. When she peeked over the edge, the left corner of the cage had developed a gap as well.

All of the noise stopped abruptly as if it had been severed by a knife. A foreboding stillness took its place, a silence that would register on the Richter scale.

It heard me.

The front and sides of the cage flew off and crashed to the floor. The top collapsed, and a massive arm batted it away before it hit the floor. The thing was free. Clothed in the raiment of darkness, it seemed to move toward her and stand still at the same time. Dark flesh writhed and undulated but didn't move from its spot.

Three long claws jutted out of the shadows and stepped into a shaft of faint light that reflected off a piece of twisted metal. Millicent gasped and ducked from the edge of the box. Something was coming toward her again. And this time it wasn't creeping!

Loud, pounding footsteps tore a path straight toward her. Her ears painted pictures with sound, but she stayed facedown on top of the box.

The sound of a nearby metal bin moaning and buckling reverberated through the abyss. Then the one right next to her—the size of a compact car—slammed against the wall. All the while, the Rottweiler barked out of its mind.

Please be quiet, she pleaded. Ten feet away, the kennel hit the ceiling, then banged against the floor. The stench filled the air. It was getting stronger. Closer. The stack of boxes underneath her ripped from its pallet and smashed against the wall. Whatever it was, it cleared a path through laden metal bins and stacks of cargo with the ease of a sickle through a wheat field.

The top of a green head glided past her. Enormous!

Judging by how high up she was, the animal had to be at least seven feet tall. Maybe more if it was hunched over. Even more than *that* if it was walking on all fours.

The footsteps suddenly stopped. She lifted her head a few inches. Three long claws gouged the ceiling beneath the hole. With each stroke, the hole grew and more light bled into the cargo hold from the rear galley above.

A tentacle leaped up from the side of the box and coiled around her rib cage. Then it yanked her off the boxes and slammed her against the floor.

"Help!" Her voice was a feeble whisper.

The tentacle gripped tighter. If she could only inflate her chest enough to inhale … No such luck. Brutal pain coursed through her torso while rotten breath as hot as the asphalt on the highway to hell blasted into her face.

Her skin was peeling! Cooking!

Giant, yellow teeth plunged down from above.

The sounds all faded: the Rottweiler's incessant barking, the animal's croaky breathing, and the steady hum of the engines. Millicent resigned herself to the fact that the last sounds she would ever hear were these sounds dwindling … dwindling … dwindling to the point that all of them combined were small enough to fit through the eye of a needle.

CHAPTER 8

Thirty-seven thousand feet beloSw, the sun painted the shadow of the 747 on the canvas of an unruly surface. With the sun now behind them, it appeared they were chasing their own shadow across the ocean. Up ahead, as far as Eden could behold, the blue Atlantic stretched out beneath a cobalt sky bejeweled with scattered, fluffy white clouds playing at the southern horizon.

For the next fourteen hours, they would only see the turquoise waters of the Atlantic, as cold and implacable as death, and night would soon blacken their view of it, leaving them cut off from the rest of the world.

⟜⟐⟞

"Stop that!" Dr. Speck said.

It was about time. The noise was getting on Quentin's nerves. If he had to put up with that crap the rest of the flight, he was going to need earplugs.

"Now, Daniel!" This time Dr. Speck's voice was more animal than human.

"Stop what?"

"It's as bad as raking a handful of glass across a chalkboard. Up and down. Up and down." Dr. Speck's hand gestures mirrored his words.

Daniel's wrist moved at blurring speed, zipping up the

front of his black jacket a few inches, then down a few. *Zip, zip, zip.* A pain in the ass.

Daniel let go of the zipper. "I didn't realize I was doing that. Sorry."

Quentin soaked up the glorious peace and quiet. *Ahhh.* What a welcome sight. The snack cart came down the aisle from the front of the plane with Candice backpedaling on the near end and Sierra pushing from the other.

After a bit of hitching and halting, the goodies arrived. "Would you like something to drink, sir?" Sierra asked.

"Coffee. Two cups, please. You know, you could save yourself the trouble. Just hook me up to an IV and connect the other end to a coffeepot."

The purser smiled down at him. When she set the two cups on his tray table, the plane hit a pocket of air and jounced her against his right shoulder. "I'm sorr—" She paused, eyes dissecting something in the back of the cabin.

Candice frowned. "Sierra?" Her tone asked the purser if she was all right. She turned around to see what Sierra was staring at.

Quentin looked back over his shoulder to see for himself. At the back of the cabin, another cart straddled the entrance to the rear galley at an angle with the curtains hanging diagonally, their hems spread out across the top of the cart.

Candice turned back to the head flight attendant. "I didn't leave it unsecured. I *know* I didn't. Maybe it was Millicent."

Sierra shook her head. "She's off duty. Better take care of it. Oh, and when you're done, they can use a little more help in first class."

As Candice started toward the back of the cabin, the cart crawled back into the galley. Quentin didn't know what the conditions were when the cart rolled out, but when it rolled back in, the plane wasn't moving enough to topple a line of dominoes.

Someone had beaten the mess out of the beverage cart and abandoned it in the rear galley. Either that or they had shoved it down a steep hill, all dented and scratched from hither to yon, and if Candice wasn't mistaken, the chassis was slightly twisted. Styrofoam cups and napkins lay scattered on the floor, a meatloaf dinner sat in the microwave, but nothing appeared to be missing. The cart sat cockeyed in front of the empty slot where it should have been latched into place. One of its latches lay on the blue carpet in front of the cart. The other, against a caster on a cart on the opposite wall.

She had better hightail it out of there before whoever did that came back. Shoving the cart back into place was the best she could do anyway. When she spun it around, she saw behind it.

What! As if destroying the cart wasn't enough. Some son of a biscuit had put a hole in the floor. She had to warn Sierra immediately. Better yet, the air marshal. And the pilot.

A muffled grunt—or maybe a growl—floated up through the hole. She inched closer and gasped. A big, black eye gawped back up at her. In one quick motion, something shot out of the hole and looped around her neck so fast and tightly that she couldn't even scream, something dark green and powerful. Cold, spongy flesh yanked her into the air. A tendril or a tentacle. The rest of it was beneath the floor with its huge eye.

Using an upper bin as leverage, she pushed down and stretched her feet toward the floor. Only the tips of her toes touched down, but at least it took her weight off her neck. Something hit her toes. A second tendril! It slithered along the floor, turning one way, then another, while its twin crushed her Adam's apple against her esophagus and yanked her to the floor.

Help, she tried to yell but got only a whisper, a waste of what precious little oxygen she could get. She pushed herself toward the portside aisle, but the tendril pulled her back half the distance in a game of tug of war she couldn't possibly win. But maybe she didn't have to.

She pounded the tendril with her fist. Kicked it. Wrestled with it. Every inch gained was pure torture. Pulling herself free was impossible, but if she could get just a little farther, someone could see her. Summoning all the strength in her body, she made a huge lunge. The portside drapes flopped on her face, and the top of her head crossed the threshold. She flung an arm under the drapes into the aisle and waved blindly. *Please. Someone help me.*

The drapes swept down her face. When her eyes popped open, she was looking up at the exit sign hanging above her in the aisle. The freight section was on her right, and the passenger section was on her left. Everyone's feet pointed forward. No one turned around. No one came down the aisle. Surely, Sierra wondered where she was by now. No, her supervisor expected her to be in first class. Candice tried to scream and got nothing.

A thick book hit the floor beside a pair of pink sandals in the third row from the last. A hand reached down past the hem of a white dress with little pink flowers and picked it up.

Look back! Please look back!

The other tendril slithered beneath the closed drapes, snaked across the aisle to the portside, and stole along the floor toward the pink sandals. A pair of little girls' white sneakers dangled next to them with one shoelace swaying back and forth.

Candice hadn't heard the book hit the floor, but the thing that seemed determined to choke the life out of her must have.

Three-year-old Rona stood up on the seat. Her stupid dog doodie shoelace was untied again. She looked around. "Wow!"

The plane was hugemongous, and there were a thousand hundred people. "Mommy, which one is the flylot?"

Her mother put her finger in the air like she always did when she corrected Rona. "The *pilot* isn't back here, sweetie."

If he can make a plane fly, he must know magic. "Where is he?"

"He's upstairs at the front of the plane."

"The plane has an upstairs?"

"It sure does."

"Ahhhh-mazing!"

The man sitting across the aisle from her mother jumped up with a finger in the air. Her mouth flew open. "Mommy, that man did the bad finger."

Her mother looked up from her fat, grown-adult book she got from her grown-adult school. "He's not giving you the finger, sweetie. He hurt his finger, and he can't close it."

"Ohhhhh, okay."

The man came back later, and she got a good look at his finger. It had a bandage wrapped around it that was the same color as her tennis shoes, and a piece of metal was holding it up. He must have hurt it really, really, really bad. Her mommy was right. The man didn't mean to do the bad finger. He couldn't help it.

She sat back down and started brushing her doll's curly, brown hair, then yawned.

Her mother said, "If you want to take a nap, I'll be right here."

"I hate naps." Rona stopped brushing her doll's hair and looked up at her mother. "And I don't want to go to sleep tonight too."

"That's 'I don't want to go to sleep tonight *either*.' You don't have to take a nap now, but you will have to get some sleep tonight, I'm afraid."

"But I got some sleep *last* night. I'm scared I'll take a nap forever. Like Josh."

"Honeybunch, your baby brother was very sick. You're very healthy."

Rona's stupid eyelids didn't want to stay open. "But he died when he was asleeping."

Her mother put her finger in the air and then put it back down. "Ah, forget it."

Rona yawned again. "I really, really, really don't want to go to sleep, but if I *do* go to sleep, promise you'll wake me up so I don't sleep forever."

"I promise, honeybunch."

While the aircraft rock-a-byed Rona to sleep, Mariana stroked her daughter's hair, cherishing an event most parents wouldn't think twice about, other than to treasure the blessed peace and quiet that came with it. Clearly, she had let it go too far. What kind of mother was she? Rona's eyes fluttered, putting up the same losing battle they had for months. Mariana stretched Rona out across the two seats next to her.

Her now only child was utterly terrified of sleep. She clearly wasn't getting over her brother's death in a normal manner, if there was such a thing, and had probably developed some kind of psychotic malady, bordering on obsession about dying. And she was getting worse.

After three months of seeing Rona in agony before every nap, every bedtime, it was time to make an appointment with a child psychiatrist. "Don't worry, honeybunch. Mommy's going to take care of it."

The plane made a gentle turn to the right. As the turquoise waters of what was probably the eastern Caribbean steadily darkened, Mariana craned her neck and looked through the windows on the other side of the aircraft. The sun slowly entombed itself in the watery sepulcher. By then Rona was sound asleep.

She quietly retrieved a pillow and a blanket from the over-head compartment, then eased the pillow under her daughter's curly, brown hair and covered her sleeveless, springtime-yellow dress with the blanket. The dimple-cheeked angel stirred but didn't wake up. Mariana had to hurry.

There was no way she was going to use the lavatory a few rows behind her seat, where the couple had just spread only God knew what kind of germs. From the look of his ruffled hair, her wrinkled, extremely short dress, and their flushed faces, the two of them had either just joined the mile-high club or renewed their membership.

She rushed up the aisle toward the front of the plane.

＝＝＝●○●＝＝＝

No! Please come back! Candice silently begged, but the pink sandals kept going.

The second tendril sneaked toward the dangling little feet where the untied shoelace on the left foot was swinging again. A small, pink hairbrush hit the floor beneath it. The tip of the second tendril sprang off the floor. Candice screamed in her mind but couldn't get a word out.

The green flesh coiled around both legs. Candice pounded the lasso around her neck. *Focus on me. Not the little girl.* She thrashed around and kicked, yet the coil around the little legs squeezed, then yanked hard.

A high-pitched scream filled the cabin. Tears blurred Candice's view. In an instant, that view changed. The tendril yanked her back under the drapes, and her eyes were looking up at the galley ceiling again.

What was that! She had caught only a fleeting glimpse, but something with a big, black eye was down the hole, scratching and tugging at it. From the sound, it wouldn't be down there much longer.

54

It poked up through the hole again.

They were all going to die. Clearly, the tendrils weren't their only problem. And certainly not their biggest.

Mariana tore down the aisle from the restroom. She could pick out her daughter's scream during the thunderous roll of an atomic blast. A sea of heads and seats blocked her view. "Rona!" She reached their row, breathing for the first time since she'd heard the scream.

Rona was crying with her knees drawn up to her chest, her feet planted on the seat, her wide eyes a mélange of fear and sadness—but, more than anything, a testament of a mother's broken promise. Rona's arms flew up to meet hers. Waking up in an unfamiliar place surrounded by unfamiliar faces sure wouldn't help her fear of sleeping.

She squeezed her daughter tight. "What is it, honeybunch?"

"Mo-na!" her daughter wailed through the hitches in her voice. "Some-thing pulled Mona un-der there." She pointed under the seat. "She's gone. There's something bad … some-thing bad under there."

Mariana cast an apologetic smile over her shoulder at the glaring passengers and sat down with Rona on her lap. "Everything's okay, sweetie. You were just having a bad dream."

"No. I wasn't dream-ing. I wasn't even asleeping when I saw it."

"If it will make you feel better, I will look under the seat."

"No, Mommy! Don't!" She tugged at Mariana's hand. "Something bad. I saw it."

"It's okay, sweetheart. It was all just a bad dream. Sometimes dreams look like real life."

"They do?"

"They sure do. Sometimes it's hard to tell the difference."

"Ohhhhh. Okay." Rona lay down and pulled the blanket up to her chest, then squeezed her eyes shut.

"What are you doing? Are you actually *trying* to go to sleep?"

Rona opened her eyes and sat back up. "I have to go *back* to sleep. So I can go *back* to my dream. So I can get Mona." She waved her hands to drive each point home.

"Mona?"

"Uh-huh. She didn't come back from my dream."

Mariana looked over at Mona's window seat. A little pink hair comb lay on the seat, minus the matching brush. But no Mona. She looked beneath the seat. The doll's hairbrush lay on the floor. And there was Mona, lying on the floor behind the last row and sliding away. The life-size doll wore an identical outfit to Rona's. The money she had spent on the doll's ensemble was money well spent, cheap as far as bribes go. Until someone snatched her doll, Rona had lived up to her end of the deal to be a big girl during the trip. From that far away, it could pass for her daughter's slightly smaller twin sister. The little plastic face stared back at her as it slid to a stop in front of the lavatory across the aisle from the galley.

"Hey! Bring that back. Now!"

———◦———

Quentin turned around to see what all the rumpus was about.

A woman's head popped up from between a row of seats. First, little girl antics, now this. A child that young was going to get into mischief every now and then, throw a tantrum here, have a screaming fit there. Totally expected. But her mother was a whole other nother.

When he was sitting back there, the little girl was nothing less than a little lady. Rona. That was the name her mother had yelled when she blew past him. Something unpleasant at the least was going on behind him, not in front of him. Maybe he had been watching the wrong people.

The woman stood up in the aisle and turned toward the rear of the cabin. "I said, bring it back."

56

A thief. If he had to blow his cover, someone was going to regret it.

The little girl stood up in her seat, facing the back of the cabin, then looked up at her mother with the saddest little face.

That's it. He jumped up.

Sierra rushed down the aisle from the front. When she reached him, she shook her head surreptitiously. Good. She didn't need him. At least not yet. He opened the overhead compartment above his seat and pulled out a pillow, hoping the passengers would buy that as the reason he had jumped up. He sat back down but was damn sure going to keep his eyes open in case the situation behind him deteriorated.

Sierra stooped down in front of the lavatory. She sure didn't want to have a brush with whatever the doll had encountered. "Did you get a look at who took it?"

Mariana shook her head. "All I saw was the doll."

Sierra picked it up by its left shoe and stood up with it between her thumb and index finger. It was heavy and taxing on the two digits holding it. Some slimy substance covered it from its curly, brown hair to its right, white tennis shoe but had spared the left leg from the calf down.

Mariana took the doll. "My little girl is going to have a conniption. She doesn't go to sleep without her Mona." She gagged. "That's disgusting. Look at this." She twirled it around by one of its legs. "What kind of sicko would do this to a little girl's doll?"

"What *is* that?"

"It looks like snot." Mariana sniffed the doll's face. A gob of the thick gunk dripped from the back of the doll's head and puddled on the floor. "This is a new level of heartlessness. If I could get my hands around the neck of the lowlife who did this, I wouldn't stop squeezing until his head popped off."

Sierra pulled a white, plastic trash bag out of her pocket and snapped it open. "Here. I'll take care of it." She grabbed the doll by the other leg and dropped it into a semitransparent bag.

"Thanks. My daughter can't see that. It would break her heart. She thinks of Mona as her little sister."

Mariana walked back to her seat. Sierra waited until she got the little girl to look out the window, then sneaked by. She could have walked up the starboard aisle where the little girl would have had less of a chance to see her beloved doll, but she had a more important reason *not* to.

The head flight attendant, trash bag in hand, stopped in front of Quentin and opened the overhead compartment above him.

A doll? That was what the little girl was screaming about? If he hadn't seen it when he was sitting back there, he might not have recognized it. Only its little feet pressed up against the bag.

Just give it back to the little—

Something slimy covered it and lined the inside of the bag too.

Dr. Speck and Daniel watched it, frozen and eyes wide, then looked at each other. Guilty looks if Quentin ever saw one.

The older one buried his face in his hands and shook his head. He might as well have turned around and yelled, *May I have your attention, please?* right in Quentin's face.

Whatever affliction the gray-headed one had, his younger traveling companion had a much more advanced case of it. He rocked back and forth and once again started toying with the zipper of his jacket, filling the area with the repetitive, annoying sound of the zipper grinding its teeth.

That guy and his frigging zipper. With his luck, they were going to be a pain in the ass the entire flight.

58

Daniel's head slowly sank. The two men were definitely up to something, but Quentin couldn't see how that involved the doll. Neither of them had gotten out of his seat since Quentin moved behind them, and the doll was fine before then. It didn't make sense.

As Sierra pulled a blanket from the overhead compartment, the doll shifted inside the trash bag.

Jesus!

No amount of soap was going to clean it up. No wonder Sierra didn't give it back to the little girl. Rona could never see that thing again even if she lived to be a hundred.

The flight attendant covered the trash bag with the blanket. Thank God!

————◆————

Three gigantic claws jabbed up through the expanding hole in the floor, then disappeared.

An oxygen-deprived brain will see whatever it wants to see. The lie Candice tried to tell herself didn't hold water no matter how oxygen-deprived she was. Traumatized and terrified? Absolutely. Delirious? Absolutely not. No hallucination could toss her around the galley.

The noose around her neck yanked her closer to the hole. Using the little fight she had left, she dug her heels into the carpet. There on the floor! Help lay a few feet away.

Wham!

A dark green paw and its arm or leg punched up through the hole and shot straight up. The mammoth limb stretched from floor to ceiling, where the tips of the claws scraped it and left three parallel gashes. The limb bent at the joint, and the paw slammed down on the floor with an impact that rippled through Candice's body. Her right hand shot toward one of the broken beverage cart latches on the floor. Her fingertips grazed it. Raked it closer.

Got it!

She drove one end of it at the tendril around her neck. No! She stopped. Another inch and anything less than a perfect aim would have severed one of her jugulars. She aimed at the part of the tendril that lay on the floor next to her right hip and drove the jagged end of the latch down hard. The noose only tightened. She was going to lose consciousness any second. She drove the latch into the green flesh again. A long, low growl came up from the chasm below. That wasn't a good sign. She had stirred up the animal's wrath. The paw sprang off the floor and slashed through the air.

The lasso around her neck loosened. Finally! She inhaled her first complete breath since the attack had started. A stench like a three-day-old corpse rushed into her nostrils. Something hit her forehead that barely registered. It was just a light tap. Then a second tap. A third. The claw hanging above her head was dripping with blood.

Three diagonal gashes ran from her left shoulder down to her right pelvic bone.

But there was no pain at all. No pain at all. No pain at—

CHAPTER 9

It had to be a first, a doll that was so important the flight crew needed to see it. Eden couldn't imagine why and didn't have anything in her kit bag to tell her what to do about a doll.

"Good day to you too, sir." Monty signed off from Miami Center, the last air traffic control center before leaving American airspace.

As they headed out into the open Atlantic, Sierra put the trash bag down on the pull-out table next to Thiago, and one of the doll's feet slid down the inside of the semitransparent bag in some type of slimy gunk. As the purser peeled the trash bag down around the doll, Eden craned her neck to get a better look. The hair on the back of its head was matted down with slime.

Sierra turned the doll around. Now, *there* was an image Eden would gladly fly the entire flight to unsee. A crack zigzagged from the crushed nose to the dented left chin. Three diagonal gashes ripped open the front of the doll from the left shoulder down to the right upper thigh. A string of slime dangling from a clump of tousled hair slid down the forehead and disappeared into the crack in the mangled face. Disgusting. Just looking at it, Eden didn't think she would be able to eat for a week.

Aaron shook his head. "That's a twisted, cruel joke to play on a little girl."

Monty slid between the aisle stand and the jump seats over to the doll. He lifted it out of the trash bag by one of its arms, then spun it around. "Looks like it's been gouged with a sharp object." He dropped it back into the bag and went into the crew rest. When he returned, he was wiping his hands on a towel.

Eden couldn't keep her eyes off the repulsive doll. "Perhaps this is something Mr. Kross needs to see."

"Sierra," Monty said, "see if you can get him to come to the flight deck without raising any eyebrows." She hurried out of the cockpit.

"Do you think we should divert to Brazil?" Eden felt like the new kid in school trying to tell the principal what to do.

"If you make an emergency landing because of a doll, they'll take you out of the cockpit and put you in a room with padded walls," Monty said in a voice without a hint of condescension.

A few minutes later, Sierra returned with Ray Kross, a bull of a man, pale with brilliant red, curly hair and big, green eyes. It was a mystery to her how a man who was about as inconspicuous as a flashing, red light in a power outage could work undercover.

Ray brushed a finger across the back of the doll's head and rubbed his fingers together. "It's probably just a mixture of corn syrup, some kind of gelatin, and a sick imagination."

Monty scoffed. "Emphasis on 'sick.' We weren't sure this was an issue for an air marshal, but we thought it best you decide that."

Ray picked the doll up, sniffed it, and spun it around. He stared at the hole in the front of it, brows furrowed. "You did the right thing." The doll's belly popped wide open on a diagonal line. The only thing holding it together now was a slither of skin on its spine. "Whatever cut this doll up this brutally is sharp enough to do the same to one of you. We have a potential problem onboard. We'll keep an eye out for him—or her." He put the doll back into the trash bag.

About time. Eden's skin was crawling.

Monty tossed Ray the towel. "I hope to God I never have to see that thing again."

Eden said, "It's strange hearing my thoughts coming out of someone else's mouth, Captain."

Ray wiped his hands and dropped the towel into the bag with the doll. "Sierra, put the other flight attendants on notice. Inform me or the other air marshal of anything, no matter how small, that seems out of the ordinary. This may only be a problem for the little girl right now, but it could be the jumping-off point for something much more nefarious."

Mariana's heart fluttered a few times, then started going rat-a-tat-tat at the speed of sound. The number one suspect—stress. The long flight was going to be torture when she could do nothing about her daughter's broken heart. When she landed, she would scour the earth to find Rona another doll that looked exactly like Mona.

Her daughter started to cry again, the latest in an endless cycle of loud crying and soft whimpering. At least the piercing wails had stopped.

"It's going to be okay, honeybunch." Mariana rocked her gently on her lap. The crying diminished into a simmering sob, though she wouldn't count on it to last very long. Mariana's condition, on the other hand, was worsening. Her heart raced as if she were in the final stretch of a marathon. She could sure use Ronald's arms around her. The troubles of the world would vanish, and her heart rate would return to normal.

"Excuse me," the flight attendant said, standing next to her. Her voice was softer than when they found Rona's doll.

"The other passengers are a little worried about you. Is there anything I can do to help?"

Mariana frowned up at her, stunned that she hadn't noticed the flight attendant. "Worried about *me*? No. It's my little girl. I'm so sorry. I know they can't help but be annoyed, but I don't think anyone can help other than her father."

The flight attendant leaned down. "What is your name, sweetie?"

"Rona." The name rode out of her mouth on the back of a weak little cry.

"Rona, my name is Sierra. Would you like to go see the pilot?"

"I want my doll."

"He'll show you how he flies the plane."

Rona wiped her eyes. "He will? Is it magic?"

"No, it's not magic, but it is a lot of fun."

Rona sat up straight, and her eyes widened, almost sparkled. That alone was nothing short of a miracle. The flight attendant took her by the hand, and she jumped down off her mother's lap.

Sierra gasped. "Oh my. Your eyes. Are you sure you're all right?"

"I'm just worried about my little girl." Rona was in turmoil over the loss of her little brother. God only knew what it would do if she found out that she had lost what she considered to be her little sister as well. "Oh. You said something about my eyes? What about my eyes?"

"Don't worry. Get some rest. I'll take good care of your little girl."

"You may have to carry her back. When she finally does go to sleep, she's going to sleep like a stone."

Sierra walked up the aisle with Rona in tow and then cast a long look back at Mariana.

Wait. The flight attendant hadn't answered her question. It was weird that someone would be worried about her eyes. Mariana wasn't the one crying. And whoever was worried about her could save it for her daughter.

Rona looked around the cockpit. "Wow!"

Eden smiled. How quickly a child could forget about her problems. What she wouldn't give to be able to do that. She picked the little girl up and sat her in the first officer's sheepskin-covered seat. A disobedient wisp of hair flopped down in front of her face. With a quick toss of her head, she flipped it back and caught a fleeting glimpse of Monty, who appeared to be ogling the wrong two knobs, although she wasn't sure.

Rona gazed at the two screens on the instrument panel in front of her—the navigation display on the left, the primary flight display on the right.

"How old are you, Rona?"

She folded the thumb of her right hand over her pinky and stuck three tiny fingers under Eden's chin. "Three."

"You're a big girl. Have you ever been on a plane before?"

"No. My daddy's been on a plane before. He left on a plane."

"Where did he go?"

"He went to …" The little girl paused. "South Aca … Aca … Acafa."

"South Africa?"

"Uh-huh. Me and Mommy going to see where he works."

"Where does he work?"

"In a horsepital. He's a doctor." She went back to studying the screens. "Your TVs don't work. They just show the same thing all the time."

"They look like little TVs, but they're not. They tell us important things about the plane. They help us to fly."

"Ohhhhh. Okay." Rona pointed at the first officer's control yoke in front of her. "I know what that is."

"What is it?"

"A steering wheel."

"This one does a lot more than the one in your mom's car."

"Look! It's turning all by itself."

"That's because it's on autopilot. The plane is flying itself."

Rona whirled around, mouth wide open, eyes like double zeroes. "All by itself? Ahhhh-mazing!"

An hour ago, the little girl had her mother's eyes. That certainly had changed.

Rona skipped down the aisle in the main deck, towing Sierra by the hand and chuckling her little socks off. Sierra had taken care of the child's problem for the time being but wondered how on earth could she take care of her mother's.

Mariana blinked a few times, then frowned. "Where have you—? Oh. Right. Sorry." Something vaguely similar to a smile happened to her face. "You look like you had fun." The woman's head was shaking slightly.

Something is terribly wrong with Mariana, even more so than when Rona and I left her.

"Mommy, this plane is hugemongous!" The ebullient child was going to pop out of her skin for sure. "And it's flying all by itself!"

"It is?"

"Uh-huh. And they got a thousand hundred buttons. Eeeeeverywhere. They even got buttons in the ceiling. And they got little bitty TVs, but they're not *really* TVs. And they got *two* steering wheels." She held up two fingers.

"Wow." Mariana's head bobbed. She jerked upright and gave one of the most forced smiles Sierra had ever seen. It may have fooled her daughter, but the purser didn't have the naiveté of a three-year-old. At any second, Mariana might fall asleep—or worse.

"Mariana, are you certain you're all right?" Sierra made sure her voice was calm and unalarming to the passengers nearby. She looked around. *Too late.* Every eye in that section seemed to be pointed at the young mother. "Would you like me to get you some water or something?"

"Only if you have a couple of aspirin I can take with it. I've got a pounding headache that feels like it's going to knock my ears off."

Is it safe for me to leave the little girl with her mother or even safe to stand that close to her?

Mariana's eyes were as bloodshot as a lost pothead's, trying to smoke his way out of a ganja field.

<hr />

His eyes! Monty's eyes turned from blue to pink at Mach 1 speed. They were fine a few minutes ago when Eden caught him sneaking a peek at her peaks. *Possibly* sneaking a peek, to give him the benefit of the doubt.

He rummaged through his kit bag, pulled out a bottle of aspirin, and washed two of them down with a cup of coffee. Then he dropped the empty cup inside another empty coffee cup sitting in the cup holder on the worktable to his left. "Presley, Thiago. Eden and I now hand the reins over to you two." He slapped the bottle of aspirin down on the worktable and unbuckled his harness.

Now it was Eden who was taking a peek—at his eyes. "Captain, why do you call him Presley?"

Monty stood up. "Ask Captain E. Aaron Wilcut what the 'E' stands for."

She didn't have to use one brain cell to come up with the answer. She flashed a smile over her shoulder at Aaron.

He hunched up his shoulders and chuckled. "I'm just glad I wasn't born in the sixties when my parents were into the Beatles."

She switched seats with Thiago, and Aaron sat down in the captain's seat.

Monty squinted, looked around, and walked to the back of the cockpit. "I'm going to lie down for a while. See if I can't get rid of this headache." He opened the door—not to the crew rest—to the passenger cabin.

Maybe he had to visit the lavatory before lying down. No, that wasn't it. Not with the way he was just standing there, looking confused and surprised. "Superman in the cockpit" had to know which door was which. Eden stole a quick glance over at the other two pilots. Yep, they were watching. Aaron's thick eyebrows were almost touching, and Thiago's mouth hung slack.

Monty closed the door, looked around, and stopped at the only other door in the cockpit.

The man's eyes! Damn if they weren't getting redder by the second.

He walked over to the flight crew rest door on the portside and went in. Eden couldn't pry her attention from the closed door. All she could do was keep her own eyes open, but there was no way in hell she was going to become bunkmates with a man who exhibited an apocalyptic case of pink eye.

———◦◦———

Eden woke with a jolt. At some point, she had nodded off. It wasn't a catnap either. More like a tiger after a long hunt. She had to find a bed. Either that or a pair of toothpicks to prop her eyelids open. She put on her jacket and walked to the cockpit door. "If you need me, I'll be down on the main deck."

———◦◦———

As soon as the door closed behind Eden, Thiago spun around in his seat. "Okay. Tell me what's going on. When I was talking about her flying Super Hornets, you and the other captain acted like the subject was taboo. Something happened, didn't it?"

A booming thud shot from inside the flight crew rest. Their heads whipped toward the noise.

"Monty?" Aaron called toward the crew rest. There was no answer. "Monty, are you all right in there?" Still no answer. He unbuckled his harness, rushed over to the crew rest, and pressed his ear against the door.

Silence.

Aaron opened the door and gasped. "Monty!"

Thiago shot straight up in his seat. "Captain Wilcut, what is it?"

Aaron didn't answer. He only screamed.

⊷⊶⊷

"A real hottie body," the man in the wifebeater said in a hushed voice, his lustful eyes gawking up the aisle. Luckily, the woman next to him was asleep.

Quentin followed his gaze.

Coming down the aisle from the front of the plane was the female first officer, the crazy-gorgeous first officer. Her honey skin glistened. Her dark brown hair was put up in the back, but a wisp of it bounced rhythmically in the front with every step. Even from a glance, he could tell she had the kind of body that could wear a dishrag and make it look like couture. A real hottie body, indeed. But Quentin's father always preached respect, so he wouldn't be doing any leering.

When she got closer, her hazel eyes blessed him with a glance.

Oh! My! God!

The man in the wifebeater was nearly salivating. His shoulder-length dreads swiveled when she passed, his eyes ogling her from head to toe.

Ogling, my ass! That was an eyegasm.

The woman beside the man with the dreads clenched her teeth and planted an elbow firmly in his side. "Kito, you know better."

69

The first officer walked on toward the back. He would have to be barking mad to think she would ever go out with a man as screwed up as he was. He would have to get his shit together before he was fit to date anyone.

Eden slipped inside the flight attendants' crew rest near the tail. Compared to the pilots' crew rest, it was a spacious hotel suite. This one stretched across the center of the cabin from one aisle to the other like the galley behind it.

One of the off-duty flight attendants was asleep on the top bunk with her back to the door, her long, blonde ponytail hanging over the side. Lauren was the only flight attendant onboard with hair like that.

On the portside wall, two navy-blue seats flanked each side of the only door. Two bunk beds lined each of the other three walls. The five unoccupied bunks still had their folded blankets and pillows neatly strapped to the middle of them. Eden quietly eased under the blanket and looked up at Lauren. The ponytail hadn't moved. Eden closed her privacy curtain and slowly dozed off.

A thunderous crash.

For the second time, she woke with a jolt. Her eyes shot open. Someone should tell the asshole in the galley that people were trying to sleep on the other side of the wall. And what was that loathsome dead-rat smell?

Aaron flew into the flight crew rest. "Monty!"

"Captain, what is it?" Thiago asked. "What's wrong?"

"It's Monty. He—"

Thiago vaulted out of his seat, dashed over, and stopped in the doorway of the closet-size room. The autopilot made a slight banking turn to the right, and the blanket hanging down from the top bunk swayed. On the floor beneath it lay Aaron's friend with his pallid face missing its usual sparkle, his empty, crimson eyes staring up at the ceiling. Large, purple spots covered his forehead and neck. The thud they had heard was Monty falling from the top bunk.

Aaron kneeled down. "Monty!" He put his middle and index fingers against Monty's purple wrist.

"No!"

Against the side of his neck.

"God, no!"

Aaron sank to the floor and buried his forehead in his palms.

<hr />

"What was that all about?" TR asked.

"What was *what* all about?" Ray Kross's tone was distant and hollow. He sat down in his aisle seat in the upper deck cabin, squinted, and cut his eyes across the empty seat at TR sitting next to the window.

TR scowled. "That little visit you paid to the cockpit. Don't try to feed me any bull about going to the lavatory. *Before* you went to the lavatory. I watched you, Ray."

Ray gave the man with gray around his temples, dressed in a tailored, dark gray suit, the once-over. "I'm sorry. Do I know you?"

"Come on. After hours of going back and forth, don't clam up on me now."

"Right. What did you say your name was? Dave?"

"Dave? I said 'TR.' That's nowhere near 'Dave.'"

"TR, I don't mean to be rude, sir, but I'm a little tired, and I have a headache. So, if you don't mind, I'd just like to rest a bit." Ray reclined his seat and slouched down.

A few minutes later, TR started to fidget, then to squirm. Neither earned so much as a glance from Ray. Instead, his squinted eyes glanced around wildly. They shot up to the ceiling, down to the floor between his feet, to the overhead compartment, and came to rest in the aisle next to him.

Sierra came from the back of the cabin bearing a coffeepot. She pulled a bottle of aspirin from her pocket and handed it to Ray. He didn't reach for it or look at it or acknowledge her presence.

She rattled the bottle twice. "Here you go."

He flinched, although his eyes were looking down at the floor, where her navy-blue pumps stood, and she had been there for a few seconds. "Oh. I'm sorry. Thank you." He took the bottle and tore off the top.

Sierra regarded him with a puzzled look. "Would either of you like a refill?"

Ray handed her his cup, then tossed two pills down his throat.

TR waved her off. "I believe I've had too much already." He looked over at Ray, who was wolfing down the beverage. "Well, blessed be me. How can you drink all that coffee and not have to visit the tinkle tank?"

"I've never heard it called that before. I would laugh, but I think my head would split open." Ray sank back into his seat and closed his eyes.

"More coffee, ma'am?" Sierra asked the woman wearing dark shades sitting in front of TR.

After a few more minutes of squirming, TR slammed his tray table up and locked it. "I know something is going on. As much as I hate to leave and have it unfold while I'm gone, my bladder is making a strong case for me to do that. Excuse me." He tapped Ray on his right shoulder. "I need to get out."

Ray didn't answer.

"I really need to get out. Ray? Excuse me. Sir?"

Ray still didn't answer.

TR blew out an exasperated sigh and stepped over him into the aisle. His foot hooked Ray's right leg, sending them both tumbling into the aisle, but only one tried to get up.

"Hey!" TR yelled. "Someone do something. Flight attendant!"

Sierra rushed back down the aisle. "What happened? Are you two all right?"

"He hasn't moved. I thought he was pretending to be asleep." The words flooded out of the thrashing man's mouth. "I think something's wrong with him."

Sierra turned Ray over, and the back of his head flopped down on the floor with a hard, solid thud. A purple spot that started at the left side of his jawline disappeared beneath the collar of his blazer. "Mr. Kross, can you hear me?" She pressed two fingers against his wrist, waited a few seconds, and then her face went sour.

"Is he ... dead?" TR asked.

Her mouth moved, but nothing came out.

"Get this dead guy off me!" TR wriggled out from under the body. Ray's head thudded against the floor again. TR leaped to his feet, dove into the back of the seat in front of him, and yanked out a puke bag. "What happened to him?" He held the bag under his mouth as if he expected his dinner to make a U-turn.

"Probably a heart attack or something."

"Heart attack? Look at him. The man can't be any more than thirty-five. Big, strong, athletic-looking. Hell, the guy looks like he could run in the Kentucky Derby. A heart attack would only piss off a guy like that." He lowered the bag. "What if he died from some communicable disease? Can I catch it?"

He turned his head away from the dead man's face, but his eyes kept crawling back. "What's wrong with his eyes? I've never seen anyone's eyes *that* red in my life."

———◆———

Sierra flew down the stairs, her feet skipping half the steps. Mariana stood at the bottom of the stairs, gazing upward.

Her eyes! Sierra had just seen eyes like that. Ray's eyes on the upper deck, hers on the main deck. Mariana's eyes darted around wildly, seemingly without purpose, and she looked confused.

Sierra didn't slow down. "I haven't forgotten about your aspirin, ma'am. I'll get them for you in just a second." At the bottom of the stairs, she zipped past Mariana and turned toward the back of the plane.

"Have you seen a little girl? Her name is Rona."

Sierra looked back. *Are you kidding me?*

Mariana held her hand horizontally beside her hip. "She's about this tall and has long, curly hair."

The woman's brain had stripped a gear. No ifs, ands, or buts about it.

"I'm sorry. I have to take care of something. I'll be *right* back. Don't move. Stay *right* here. *Please!*" Clearly, the woman needed help, but a more urgent matter demanded Sierra's attention.

———————————————

It couldn't be happening. Not again. Not another nightmare. Another child taken from her. Mariana's precious little girl was missing.

How did she get to the bottom of the stairs? Where was her husband? Where was she flying to? Where on earth had she left Rona?

Oh yeah. She was on her way to see Ronald. That was it. Now where was he exactly?

Ahhh. She had left her daughter asleep ... somewhere.

Someone was turning down the lights. She would have a hard time finding Rona if it got much darker.

Sweat trickled down her forehead and between her breasts. Her head was pounding. To her faltering lungs, the air was molasses. Her heart was trying to take the checkered flag at the Indy 500, and the tips of her fingers, not to be left out, pulsed with a heartbeat of their own.

Whoa! Wait a minute now!

The carpet rippled. Something crawled on the floor … the emergency lights. The stairs stretched upward farther and farther. To forever. The steps grew narrower at the top to an infinitely small point.

The hallucinations were coming in a whirlwind, every one stranger than the last. The walls were darker. No. They appeared that way only out of the corner of her eyes. When she looked directly at the wall, it was light again. She held her hands up in front of her face. They appeared normal, but from the corner of her eye, they were dark and getting darker fast.

Fight it!

For—?

For Rona.

Fight it for Rona! Fight it for Rona! She needs me!

Sierra burst through the curtains at the front of the aft coach section and rushed down the aisle, an "oh shit" look on her face. Quentin braced himself. Given the tension in her body, her rigid arm movements, and her stiff neck, it had to be something bad, something standing-on-a-landmine bad.

She rushed to his row and leaned down. "Excuse me, Mr. Kane." Her sorrowful voice was barely above a whisper, her tone drenched with a palpable dread. "It is imperative that—"

A thunderous uproar suddenly erupted behind him. Screaming. Shouting. Piercing wails. Loud voices. For a split second, he forgot all about her secret. The deafening sounds were coming from the back of the cabin. *All* of the back of the cabin. An explosion of white-hot pandemonium. If there was a sound when all hell broke loose, this was it.

CHAPTER 10

A shadow swept across the portside wall.

The hell was that? Quentin jumped up. There was no way it was human. It was much too tall, too broad, and too deformed. The back of the plane churned with running, screaming passengers. Above them, the shadow disappeared.

It had to be an illusion, nothing more than the cabin lights bouncing off a cluster of passengers running in an odd formation. *Yeah, right.* People don't stampede because of an illusion.

Bright red blood spewed into the air and hit the pale white ceiling. As soon as he planted one foot in the aisle, the front end of a tidal wave of passengers slammed into him and knocked him back to the exit row. Sierra was nowhere in sight. Heaven help her if she hadn't gotten out of the way. He pushed toward the rear of the cabin, going the wrong way on the freeway at the peak of rush hour, meeting passengers head on. A few of them climbed over the backs of seats to avoid the traffic jams in the aisles. Smart move.

The shadow reappeared. Quentin stopped dead in his tracks, eyes locked on the rear of the cabin, breath frozen in his lungs. "Oh God, Jesus Christ, all the angels in heaven." He didn't realize he was speaking until his own voice floated past his ears. It was real, all right.

But a real *what*?

———◆———

Eden bolted upright. She'd had a bad dream and woken up to a nightmare of screaming voices. Shrieking voices amid a deafening commotion emanated from three sides. Only the wall between the crew rest and the galley remained quiet.

Bang! Something slammed against the wall next to her.

Lauren whirled over, and they looked at each other with eyes that asked what was going on. From her droopy yet startled look, the flight attendant had also been jolted from a deep sleep. Something slammed against the door. They both jumped.

Lauren shot up into a sitting position. "What is going on out there?"

"I don't know." Eden leaped off her bunk and flung the door open. A man crashed into the other side, and the door flew back at her with a pernicious impact that knocked her backward a step. Flaming needles shot from her fingers up to her elbow. The passenger ricocheted off the door and took off toward the back of the cabin.

"Bloody hell!" the flight attendant yelled. "He was bleeding."

Lauren missed the mark by a mile. The man wasn't just bleeding. He had sprung a leak. The door couldn't have done all that. Maybe a group of passengers were fighting or a cluster of them were beating the grease out of a would-be terrorist.

Eden stepped out of the crew rest. *All* of them were in a frenzy. She stared up the portside aisle toward the front of the cabin, and a feeling of certain doom washed over her.

———◆———

The silhouette of a cavernous mouth snapped open on the wall on Quentin's right. Two long teeth at the top, two just as long at the bottom.

The ghastly shadow slid down the wall and vanished

77

behind the passengers blocking his view. Blood splashed the ceiling, then the wall. Everything was happening in an instant, a maelstrom of screams and chaos compressed into seconds.

A man sitting in an aisle seat in the center section awoke with a jerk, sending his toupee down over his eyes. He pushed it back, wobbled to his feet, and staggered up the aisle.

A piercing *crack!*

Dark green flesh, a living lasso, whipped through the air, slashing at passengers. Another one, identical to the first, wrapped around a potbellied man's waist, and blood trickled from his mouth. As Quentin headed over to him, a third one snatched a woman backward across the top of the seats. A fourth caught a flight attendant by his leg in midstride and yanked him down. The cabin teemed with long, green lassos. Too many to stop at once.

"Quick!" Quentin waved the passengers forward. "Upstairs to the upper deck!"

Daniel and Dr. Speck jumped into the aisle and joined the stampede. Dr. Speck dropped his briefcase and then pried his way back to it.

Quentin cringed. "Leave it. You're going to get trampled." He directed the frenzied passengers forward while charging hell-bent in the opposite direction, straight for …

What? He would find out when he got there.

A loud popping sound filled the air.

"What was that?" Eden leaned one way, then the other, trying to see around the passengers.

Lauren closed in behind, and her hot breath drummed the back of Eden's right ear. Blood-soaked bodies lay strewn in the aisle and across seats. What could be mistaken for a long snake whipped through the air and looped around a woman's neck. Eden gasped. That was impossible. There were no snakes on the manifest. Many other live creatures, yes—including a few exotic ones and one she had never heard of before—but snakes, no.

A piercing scream came from behind her. Her eardrum was going to explode for sure. When she spun around, the flight attendant's eyes were popping out of their sockets, frozen on something up ahead. She knocked Eden out of the way, shot toward the back of the plane, and disappeared through the galley curtains.

In the portside aisle, ten feet away, stood a four-legged beast more gruesome than any exotic animal she had ever seen, something that could only have been created in the devil's laboratory. Its tentacles clearly weren't its most dangerous feature.

Its head turned. Its eyes focused on her.

If she tried to run now, one of its tentacles would catch her before she took one step. If she waited there—judging from the carnage—she would end up in pieces, strewn all over the cabin. At the time, it would have been smart to follow Lauren. Now that window of opportunity had been slammed shut, nailed down, and boarded up.

The animal reared up on its hind legs in front of her. She tilted her head up to follow it, looked into its steely eyes, and froze.

A green mass soared to the top of the cabin, darted to the left, then to the right. It was some kind of animal. *Good Lord!* It was just a head. The back of an enormous head.

Quentin pulled out his Sig Sauer P229, and a passenger crashed into his elbow. Another darted across his line of fire. He could hit gnat shit on a wall at fifty yards. All he needed was a clear shot for one second. A man's broad chest dashed in the way. As soon as it moved, a woman's blonde head replaced it. *Please!* A parade of passengers' body parts followed. *Okay, I'll settle for* half *a second*. No such luck. The best he got was a flash here and there of something behind the passengers, a glimpse of flailing tentacles, and the left arm and shoulder of a white blouse …

The blouse! It had an epaulet on the shoulder with three gold stripes. The first officer! She stood face to face with the creature, just beyond its flailing tentacles. A row of triangle-shaped plates ran down the center of the beast's back like a stegosaurus.

He took off toward her, knifing his way through passengers, then came to a sudden stop when someone tumbled to the floor in the aisle. The traffic gridlocked, and the first officer was hidden behind it. Or … gone.

<hr/>

A whimper trickled from Eden's lips. Her mouth quivered. The animal's eyes locked onto hers, lips spread, teeth bared. If she was lucky, she would die a quick death. If not, she would spring a leak of her own and suffer a slow, agonizing death. Red streams of blood dripped from long canines, and then its mouth sprang open. Looking into it was like looking into an open grave. By the animal's smell, it could have been dug up from one.

Thick saliva that resembled snot oozed from its lips. In some places, it comingled with the blood and created a nauseating cocktail of horror. Its massive head lunged forward.

Please. No!

Then a forepaw lashed toward her.

<hr/>

Quentin pulled two women off the floor. As soon as he cleared the bottleneck, he caught a flying elbow. Molly-whopped dead in the chops. *Great, just great.* When the passengers started to thin out, he could see no sign of the first officer. Only blood. On the ceiling. On the seats. On the passengers. His heart was in freefall.

Something flashed between two passengers' heads, something white. The first officer's blouse. She was still alive! When he caught another tease of a view, her face and the front of her blouse were soaked with blood and gore, and then she tumbled to the floor.

"Nooooo!"

The beast loomed over her, one of its forepaws dripping with blood from the entrails dangling between three long, hooked claws. A brutal son of a bitch. Not again. The last time Quentin had seen a disemboweled body, it took every ounce of his willpower to stop himself from becoming judge, jury, and executioner. Not this time. First chance he got, he was going to write his name in bullet holes in the animal's big ass. If it cost him his last breath, done deal.

It dropped back down on all fours and disappeared. Only a blood-splattered ceiling hung where the green head had been. Then it popped back up on its mammoth hind legs facing him. The image would forever stain his memory. Hide as armored as a croc's. Head as big as a grizzly's. Eyes as black as an eclipse. It was stooped over, yet its head still scraped the ceiling. It needed at least another two or three feet to stand up straight.

Its mouth flung open, and a bellow tore through the cabin like a lion's roar through the jungle. The deafening sound reverberated off Quentin's bones.

Four tentacles attached to each side of the freak's torso writhed and whipped all around. The two closest to its upper limbs were longer and thicker than the others by far. The end of one hung on by a shred, nearly torn in two, and flopped around like a wet noodle tied to the end of a stick.

He had gotten off to a piss-poor start to taking something that big out of the game, but he would finish it, him and a few rounds of tre five sevens, as long as the shots were straight and true. If an errant slug cut down someone weaving in and out of his line of fire, he would have the death of an innocent passenger to add to his backbreaking bag of sorrows.

One clear shot was all he needed.

There it was!

Blam! Blam! A double tap.

Both .357 rounds plunged into the green flesh at the center of its torso. Spot-on where he was aiming, hopefully where its maggoty heart would be. Two kill shots got him a whole lot of nothing. He might as well have thrown two marshmallows at the behemoth. Pale green blood, almost neon green, spewed from the holes and splattered on the floor and on the back of the seat beside the animal.

"There's an old lady hemmed off," a man shouted behind him.

A tentacle lashed at her.

Quentin fired another round into the creature's chest. The animal didn't even stagger. It wasn't a surprise. But the bullet gave it and its tentacle something else to think about. He ran to the woman, picked her up, and delivered her into the massive arms of a short stump of a guy.

The last of the passengers blocking his view had fled, and he wasn't prepared for what he saw. The back of the main deck was a bloody battlefield of stray arms and legs, of twisted and broken bodies, of torn-apart or partially eaten people.

The big bastard was going to eat every bullet he had if that's what it took. He put a fourth round in it close to the spot where the third had landed. What was it going to take to kill the damn thing, a nuke? If he couldn't kill it, he could at least buy the last two passengers time to get to the stairs. His finger tightened on the trigger again.

Sizzling sounds floated up from the floor.

He looked down and cringed. His finger jumped off the trigger, and he all but slammed his weapon back in the holster.

There was no way he was going to fire another shot. If he could, he would take back every one he had already discharged.

Four green rivulets gushed from the open wounds in the animal's chest, dripped onto a seat, and made little sizzling sounds. The seat melted away like an ice cream cone at the mercy of a blowtorch. The cloth covering, the foam, the metal springs—all were empty voids now. A wisp of smoke rose from the armrest, danced in the air, and quickly disappeared. The armrest itself slowly dripped to the floor in a puddle of metallic soup.

A stream of blood ran down the monster's chest, down its muscular right leg, and dripped off its knee. *No! Stop! Stop!* The blood splattered on the floor and ate a hole the size of a basketball that probably ran through to the cargo hold below the cabin.

If he fired another shot at it, that one bullet could trigger a catastrophe, although it may already be too late. Who knew what smoldering mechanical failure lay beneath the floor—a now severed wire or some newly burned vital component or a dissolved bolt that held the 747 together, keeping it from crashing into the Atlantic. Quentin shuddered.

The animal lowered its eyeline to his, mean-mugging the shit out of him, and for a moment, he would have sworn it was trying to stare him down. In a flash, it dropped down on all fours and charged up the aisle, mouth agape.

Damn, that thing was fast. In his mind, he was already a dead man.

The animal had barely enough room to squeeze between the seats along the portside aisle. Its right flank smashed against a seat and knocked the armrest off, slowing the behemoth down enough to give him a slim chance to escape.

With a loud crack, a tentacle lashed up the aisle at him. He dove into the row of seats to his right. Only his right rib cage landed across an armrest, but fiery knives jabbed his entire midsection, and he couldn't inflate his lungs. A tentacle had a crushing grip around his abdomen and was steadily squeezing tighter. Using the butt of his gun, he hammered the section of the tentacle above his navel. The grip tightened. He raised the gun above his head with both hands, and when he slammed the butt down on the part of the tentacle draped over the armrest, it recoiled. Another bone-rattling roar filled the fuselage.

Above him, a massive tail with three long spikes on the tip appeared. He rolled onto the floor as it hammered the bottom of the seat. The spikes jabbed through and punctured the floor inches from where he lay.

Quentin leaped to his feet and dashed up the aisle toward the front of the plane. It grabbed for his waist again, and he swatted it away with all the strength he had in his left forearm. Or at least he tried. He felt a tug on his left side. Something made a tearing sound, and then the tentacle's grip ripped away. Where his left jacket pocket had been was a hole.

He whipped the gun back into his holster and careered up the aisle, leaving behind a cabin of slaughtered bodies, debris, and desolation. The back of the main deck had become a killing ground. Silent and deserted.

"Anyone in here?" He sliced through one set of curtains into the forward coach section and out of another into business class. "Anyone in here?" It appeared that everyone in forward and aft coach who could have escaped to the upper deck had. Anyone who had been forward of the stairs in business and first class would have been out of the reach of the bloodthirsty brute and should have escaped as well. *Should* have.

He had better check.

Another passenger might not be fully functional, worse than the man with the toupee who staggered out of the back of the cabin. He had seen his share of passengers who passed the time onboard by getting so sloshed they couldn't tell their own ass from an apple.

"Anyone in here?" he yelled, barreling through business class. He shot through the closed curtains into first class at the nose of the aircraft, still yelling. Still getting no answer. Both cabins looked as deserted as the back side of the moon, like the rest of the lower deck.

Sprinting two-thirds of the length of the main deck had left him a little winded. Now he had to run back half that distance to return to the stairs behind business class, and the monster could be waiting for him somewhere along the way.

When he made it back to business class, a cracking sound like a branch splintering off a tree came from behind the curtains in forward coach. He eased down and peeked under the curtains. Six claws from hell pointed at him, dark beige with black striations running from their base to the tips. Long and crooked. And judging from how strong they looked, they could split steel. A severed head hit the floor between the two feet. He sprang back up and nearly jumped out of his skin. The head was too bloody to tell if it was a man's or a woman's.

He silently backed away and vaulted up the stairs to the upper deck.

———◦◦◦———

Down on the main deck, the monster was not alone. Barely sticking out from under a seat close to the back, ten tiny fingers quivered.

PART II
SOMETHING BAD

CHAPTER 11

Quentin peeked back down at the main deck. He didn't see any sign of the animal or one of its tentacles. He took a deep breath and grabbed his head with both hands. He was lucky it wasn't rolling around on the floor next to the one downstairs. *God Almighty*. All of those dead people down there. Slaughtered and mutilated and beheaded and dismembered. And that … whatever it was. After seeing that beast, he didn't need any more coffee or anything else to keep him awake ever again.

His hands slid down to his neck, and the left one slid over a small, raised bump. A mosquito bite from the patio last night. No, a needle. A needle? Flashes came to the forefront of his consciousness, memories of pain from an injection in his neck, memories of hands digging through his pockets searching for … something. *What the hell?*

A man wearing a dark gray suit with gray around his temples broke through the cluster of passengers near the back of the upper deck cabin and pointed at him. "That Black man's got a gun! He's got a gun!"

With his hands still on his neck, Quentin looked down. The butt of his gun and part of his holster poked through the hole in his jacket. So what. The jig was up when he first pulled out his weapon. He dropped his hands. "My badge gets lonely without it. I'm a federal air marshal." He held his badge up to the man and then to the other passengers around him in the upper deck. It might calm them down to know someone onboard would stand between them and that big bastard downstairs.

"Well, blessed be me." The man stuck out his hand. "I'm Senator Thaddeus Rutherford Dunn. It's a mouthful, I know, but 'TR' gets the job done." He crowed like he was campaigning, and the double entendre sounded over-rehearsed and wildly inappropriate for their situation. He had a voice like the serrated edge of a knife and murky green eyes like swamp water. Only an asshole would glad-hand when the world around him was circling the drain, someone who didn't give a damn about the people who had just lost their lives or the traumatized people crying their eyes out around him. They were flying over the middle of the Atlantic Ocean thousands of miles from a single speck of dirt with a vicious beast onboard, and trying to buddy up to him wasn't going to help the senator one bit.

Quentin shook his hand just to get him out of his face.

With all the victims who hadn't survived, it was a godsend to see Sierra prying her way through the throng of passengers.

"How are the survivors?" Quentin asked.

"No serious injuries. Some minor ones, bruises, cuts, and scrapes. That's about it." She didn't have a scratch on her. But she still had that "oh shit" look on her face.

"Good. Clearly, there aren't enough seats for the influx of new passengers." The upper deck cabin had only twelve rows of seats with three seats on each side of the aisle and an exit row that bisected it in the middle. The front had six rows on both sides of the aisle whereas the back had six only on the starboard side. The portside had only five in the back. Where the sixth row would have been, the stairs took up the space. Quick math added up to … a shitty flight for some. "A good 25 percent of us will have to cop a spot wherever we can."

"Mr. Kane, there's something very important I need to t—"

"What's going on?" a woman wearing dark shades yelled from a window seat. "We heard loud roars. What was that?" Her voice sounded feeble and anxious even from a distance.

"That's Amarant," Sierra whispered. "A blind passenger who's traveling alone."

"Thank God she wasn't down on the main deck."

"There's nothing to worry about, ma'am," Dr. Speck said. "You're safe."

Kito scoffed. "Humph. That's the biggest lie since 'The earth is flat.' There's a—a—a beast down there that's killing everybody. If I hadn't got my mother out, she would have been one of them."

Amarant cocked an ear toward Kito. "Beast? What kind of beast?"

Kito flung dreadlocks out of a face that was the color of a Hershey Bar. "I don't know. I mean … I ain't never seen nothing like that in my life."

"Where did it come from?" Amarant sounded even more worried than before.

Quentin jumped in before Kito could champion any "it's the apocalypse" theories. "Most likely from one of the cargo holds below the main deck."

"A hole big enough for that thing to come through would have to tear up something," Kito said, eyes wild. "Cut some wires, cut a fuel line, damage something important. Shit, we're lucky if we're not already doomed to a watery grave."

I wish he'd shut the hell up.

But Kito had a point. A damn good point. Logically, any hole big enough for something that enormous to come through would have to be even bigger.

A quiet unease settled over the entire upper deck. A deadened hush. Out of the stillness, a tepid grumble arose.

"If it can come up from the cargo hold to the main deck, what's to stop it from coming up here?"

Quentin hadn't thought about that, but the animal didn't necessarily have to come into the upper deck to kill more of them. If it unfurled its longest two tentacles, it could reach up the stairs and into the back of the cabin. And they were strong enough to break a human in half. The only reason his internal organs weren't mush and his spine wasn't snapped was because an armrest got caught in the loop when the tentacle had coiled around his midsection. Even with the armrest preventing its grip from getting tighter, he would probably still be pissing blood for a week.

"Well, what if it does come up here?" Amarant asked.

A middle-aged man yelled, "They looking up my ass for explosives, but they okay with putting something like *that* on a plane?"

A Latino man wearing a camouflage baseball cap wiped his eyes. "Who thought that was a good idea?" He burst into wails. "My brother. My twin brother. Alejandro. Alejandroooo!"

"I'm really sorry, sir." Throughout the cabin, face after face looked like Quentin's had. Twice. "To everyone who lost someone, I know how you feel. Trust me when I say that. I *honestly* know how you feel."

"What is it?" the middle-aged man asked.

A cacophony of other voices shouted in languages Quentin couldn't begin to understand.

"Please." He raised a hand and quelled the shouting. "I know little more than you do about the animal, other than the fact that it's got one heck of a grip."

"Do something," TR demanded. "You've got the gun. Go back down there and kill it."

"No," Kito said. "I nearly lost my mother already. He could blow a hole in the skin of the plane, and we'll explode."

Quentin shook his head. "That's just in movies. Even if a round pierced the hull of the fuselage, it wouldn't cause the kind of catastrophic depressurization it would take for the plane to break up in midair. And, Senator, I poured four rounds into it. The little damage I did only made it bleed, and its green blood ate holes in the floor. That liquid is extremely corrosive. I don't know what the beast is. I don't know how it got onboard. I don't know how we're going to stop it. What I do know is that if we sever one of its major arteries, the blood could eat through the cargo hold clear through to the outside of the aircraft. A hole that big *could* cause a rapid decompression. The blood from that thing could kill everything and everyone on this plane."

"Marshal, if we can't allow it to bleed, how are we going to kill it?" Kito asked.

Quentin could probably steer the topic back on course if Kito would stop grabbing the wheel. "I'm still working on that. Until we can come up with a sound plan, it's better to leave it alone. While we're doing that, it wouldn't hurt to hope we can reach land before it does any more damage or any more killing."

The senator's eyes spewed venom at Quentin. "Nice fantasy. That's the best you can do? A 'no plan' plan? When I get back on the ground ... Don't think for one minute I'm going to forget about that." He walked by in a huff.

"Whatever tickles your nickel." Quentin wouldn't waste a perfectly good give-a-shit on that jackdaw in peacock's feathers. He was too busy trying to develop a plan that didn't start with Step 1: Get killed. The senator's words played in his mind. *When I get back on the ground.* If TR had been down on the main deck, he'd change that insta-quick to *if* I get back on the ground. Who was the one with the nice fantasy?

"Mr. Kane, I need to talk to you." Sierra's voice had too

much sunshine and blue skies in it for their dreary situation. "Can you come with me, sir?" Her dry smile grew bigger. "I really need to talk to you."

"Every time someone's called me 'Mr. Kane' lately, it was right before they gut-punched me with bad news. Call me Quentin."

He followed her the few steps to the galley at the back of the cabin, wondering what new calamity or horror she would unfold.

———————————————

Daniel leaned over to Dr. Speck and whispered, "Is that what Professor Ogladorff meant?"

The doc frowned. "What?"

"When he said that later, the megateratoid could be just as lethal dead as it is alive. Maybe even more so. Was it because its blood could eat through to the outside of the plane?"

"I didn't think to bring your wittle pacifier, so put your wittle thumb in your wittle mouth, and let me hear what the grown folks are saying."

———————————————

When Sierra closed the curtains inside the galley, her sugary demeanor disappeared. Her face looked like it had done ten years of hard labor since the flight started.

Quentin braced himself. "This can't be about the animal: that secret is out." Something else was wrong. Terribly wrong.

"What I was about to tell you downstairs—" She stepped closer. "It's the other air marshal."

"What about him?"

"I'm sorry, but he's dead."

"Oh God! How? He can't be. The animal couldn't have gotten to him. He was in the upper deck cabin." Reeling from shock, he bumped his arm against a blistering hot coffeepot above the counter. The searing pain was proof he wasn't dreaming.

She grabbed him by the other arm. "Mr. Kane ... Quentin, are you all right?"

He held up an arresting hand. "No, but I'll try to stay upright." After what he had seen with his own two eyes, all the death he had witnessed, nearly losing his own life, and now his best friend, he was light-years from all right.

Through the curtain a light babble drifted in from the passengers.

"What happened to him?" Quentin asked.

"I don't know, but ..."

"But what?"

"Captain Locke is dead too."

"How? What is going on around here?"

"Neither showed any sign of injury. They both had spots where their blood appeared to be pooling under the skin— extremely pale skin—as if their bodies were bleeding out from the inside. And they both had red eyes. I don't mean blood-shot. I mean their eyeballs looked like someone had replaced them with clear balls filled with bright red blood."

"Two healthy people don't just die with the same bizarre symptoms at thirty-seven thousand feet." He thought for a moment. "The doll. What was that slimy stuff on it?"

"Ah, you did see it. I was hoping you had a clue."

"Did Red touch the doll?"

"Red?"

"I'm sorry. Ray Kross. I called him 'Red Cross' because he was always coming to my rescue. He helped me when my world shattered and crumbled to the ground."

Quentin couldn't get anything over on him. Red could read him like a ... He thought back to when they were at the airport and chuckled. ... Like a newspaper. Red had to look at Dr. Speck and Daniel. But not at him. His friend *knew* him, knew his ritualistic drunk-a-thons, knew his customary two cups of coffee, knew that whenever he had a good bit of down-time, he drank too much. Knew his whole pathetic routine. Mystery solved.

"Quentin?"

"I'm sorry, what did you say?"

"I said yes. Your partner touched the doll. Monty did too."

"And now they're both dead. Did either of the other three pilots?"

"I don't think so. I know Eden didn't. She didn't even want to get close to it."

"Did you?"

"Yeah. Mariana touched it too, but her daughter didn't."

"It doesn't make sense. Unless … unless it was some type of airborne virus or bacteria. Do you feel sick?"

"No, not at all."

"It's probably not airborne then."

"But I made sure I didn't touch the icky part. It was covered in some type of slime."

"Where are their bodies?"

"Aaron and Thiago put Ray in the crew rest with Monty."

He cocked an ear toward the closed curtains. "Do they sound like they're getting louder to you?"

"I'm sorry. I'm going to have to stay more focused on them now that I'm the only flight attendant."

"The very first time I worked with Red, minutes after takeoff, I heard the portside engine spool down. The captain announced, 'We have a minor malfunction.' It wasn't until we were back inside the terminal that the passengers learned what I already knew: that the 'minor malfunction' had been total engine failure in one of the two engines and—something I didn't know—that the other engine was about to stall out on us as well."

She grabbed the interphone off the wall and called the cockpit.

He waited silently and found it odd that the passengers were too loud while the flight attendant was too quiet. "Sierra, what's wrong?"

She held the phone crushed against her ear with a look of terror in her eyes. "The flight deck."

He frowned. "Are the phones out?"

"No, they're perfectly fine. I think something is wrong with the pilots. No one's answering. At least Eden should have picked up."

"I'm sorry I … I tried to save her, but people kept running into the line of fire." Their flight was down to only two pilots, and if something had happened to them thousands of miles from land … *Oh God!* "Try it again." He stared into her widening eyes. *Please let her get a different outcome this time.*

A few seconds later, a tear ran down her cheek as her trembling hand stretched the phone toward its cradle. Suddenly, she slapped it back to her ear. He perked up, hoping she had heard one of the pilot's voices. She slapped a hand over her mouth, then fumbled blindly for the cradle, happened upon it, and hung up the phone.

Morbid theories about the pilots ran through his mind. For all he knew, they might all succumb to the strange illness before they crashed fabulously into the ocean. Or the creature might break into the upper deck and save them from the other two forms of death. Or its corrosive, green blood might compromise the integrity of the plane. They were totally fucked to hell and back, and he didn't have jack shit in his repertoire to solve any of their crises. A moment without another mountain dropping on him would give him time to decompress after his close encounter with the beast.

Wham!

He spun toward the sound. The cabin. The din was definitely getting louder in there, becoming more of a clamor.

Then the noise started to decrease at an alarming rate. *How big is* this *mountain going to be?*

Wham!

Then there was little sound at all.

Quentin ripped open the galley curtains and rushed into the cabin with Sierra on his heels. Most of the passengers, including the ones with seats, were on their feet and eyeballing something at the front of the cabin. They blocked Quentin's view of whatever was going on. They weren't running and screaming, so the animal hadn't gotten into the upper deck.

Wham! Wham! Wham! The closer they got, the louder the sound.

When they reached the front of the cabin, standing at the other end of the short hallway where it dead-ended at the cockpit door was a group of Neanderthals with TR Dunn leading the charge. "Again!" he ordered, and the men rammed the cockpit door with their shoulders.

"Get away from that door!" Quentin yelled. "That's a bulletproof, grenade-resistant door. You could break your shoulders, and it's still not going to open. Stay away from it. Do you understand me?"

The men grumbled under their breath and left. Not TR. The defiant asshole pounded on the door with his fist. "Hey, how long is it going to be before you guys land this thing?" Only silence answered. He raised his fist again, and Quentin caught his arm in midswing.

"Let go! Have you forgotten who I am? I'm *Senator* Thaddeus Rutherford Dunn."

"That doesn't have a damn thing to do with a damn thing."

The senator looked over at the biggest brute in the Neanderthal brigade. "Victor, get this guy off me."

Victor's arms and shoulders had spent some time in the gym; that or he had a job pushing eighteen-wheelers uphill. He turned back toward the front of the cabin.

Big mistake, buddy. Quentin locked gazes with him.

Victor stood down. Wise decision.

Quentin seized TR by the arm and relocated him back into the cabin. "If you touch that cockpit door again, I'll put my foot so far up your ass, people will think we're Siamese twins. Their job isn't to answer to you."

"They're not answering at all," the senator said, rubbing his arm. His voice was loud enough for half the upper deck to hear him and obviously not by accident. "That's the problem, Mr. Marshal. They can't. They're probably dead, and dead men can't fly planes. Why haven't they told us what's going on?"

A cacophony of worried voices rose around him.

"Tell us what's going on, Marshal, please."

"Yeah."

"I want to know too."

"Why won't the pilots talk to us?"

"Are we all going to die?"

My God. That's a child's voice.

Eyes bored into Sierra and him. Mainly him. The panic level soared. With the shouting and pointing, the stern faces before him resembled an angry mob.

He closed the gap between Sierra and himself and whispered, "If the last two pilots *are* dead, the last thing we want is for the passengers to have confirmation of it. They're on the verge of hysteria as it is. If they find out that the only people capable of landing this aircraft are dead, we're going to have a riot on our hands."

"The way they're looking, we could very well have one before then. Keep everyone back and I'll try the code."

Quentin stood sentry, hawk-eyeing the senator and his men in particular. If they were brazen enough to take one move toward the cockpit, they would regret it.

Sierra tugged on his arm. "I can't get the door open."

"What?"

"Sir, we need to do something. Fast."

"May I have your attention for just a moment, please?" Quentin said, raising his hands. "I know you're all frightened right now. But the only thing we can do to help the pilots is to stay calm and let them do their job. I'm sure there are more important things they need to do right now than talk to us. I would rather they communicate with air traffic controllers, or whoever they need to talk to right now, and talk to me later. So let's not get going over nothing."

"Nothing?" TR said. "Without pilots, our chance of surviving dips to a snowball's chance in hell. If *they're* dead, that means we're all going to die too."

The senator and his lackeys cleared out and gave Quentin a clear view. Dr. Speck and Daniel had wormed their way from the back of the cabin to a spot near the front of the aisle.

Quentin glanced down at Sierra. "I would love to hook that guy and his sidekick up to a polygraph machine. Preferably one equipped with a cattle prod."

"My foot!" a woman screamed. "I think it's broken."

"Dr. Ross," Sierra called out to an African American woman bandaging a teenage girl's head. "I have another one for you."

Dr. Ross snapped off her beige rubber gloves. "I'm just finishing up. I'll take a look at it now."

"I think I did break my shoulder." Victor rubbed it as he and the doctor walked past each other, but he wasn't injured enough to stop and let her take a look at it.

TR slapped him on the back. "Don't worry about it. We'll all be dead in a few minutes."

Quentin shook his head. *Two assholes trying to out asshole each other.*

The jet bounced abruptly, an unusually jarring dip with a giant aircraft like theirs. Someone could get hurt, especially the throng that was standing. There was no message from the cockpit about the turbulence, no ding warning them to get back in their seats, no seat-belt glyph illuminated in the overhead panel. There had to be trouble in the cockpit, and he wasn't the only one who had noticed. Desperation and panic showed on face after face. Quentin envied them; he was obligated not to show his. He and the purser were the only things holding the sanity of the upper deck together. If he lost it—and oh, how he had earned the right to go a little batshit—Sierra would have to solve their escalating problems alone.

The animal was still loose with nothing to stop it from coming into the upper deck; the source of the mysterious substance on the doll hadn't been identified and could be waiting anywhere to kill the rest of them; and God only knew what unimaginable hell lurked on the other side of the locked cockpit door. Oh yeah, there would be some batshit time in his future. If he had a future.

The jumbo jet bounced hard again. The third was the strongest yet.

"God help us!" a panicked woman's voice screamed from somewhere in the middle of the portside.

Sierra slapped a hand on the bulkhead wall and steadied herself. "For those of you with seats, buckle yourselves in!"

"We're going to have about ninety people taking turns at us soon," Quentin said above the steadily growing clamor. "Can you check the passenger manifest to see if anyone is a pilot?"

"I already did."

CHAPTER 12

"Mommy?" Rona whispered under a seat close to the back. A teeny-tiny whisper.

She was really, really, really, scared. "Mommy? Where are you?" She would know what to do.

People had been talking and laughing and snoring before the monster came. Now no one made any sounds at all. She lay flat on the floor and looked around. A whole bunch of big bags and briefcases and other stuff was on the floor, but she didn't see her mother's feet. *Any* feet. Everyone had run away and left her all by herself. Well, not *all* by herself. Something Bad was still there.

She should have run away too. All she had done was hide like a baby. Scaredy-cat.

Her mother had never left her all by herself this long before. Tears filled the corners of her eyes. *I'm not going to cry. I'm not going to cry.* She was a big girl, and big girls don't cry. Tears ran down her cheeks. *Well, I'm not going to cry* out loud *no matter what.* Something Bad would hear her and eat her.

She brushed the tears away and looked toward the back. She wasn't alone. Some people were lying on the floor. Grown adults were too big to sleep on the seats. Or maybe they were make-believing that they were asleeping so the monster wouldn't get them.

Two big, ugly, green heels stood near one of the men lying on the floor. Gross. She pinched her nose. The monster smelled a thousand hundred times worse than dog doodie.

A crunching sound came from the back where the big, ugly feet were. Then a sound like sticks breaking. Bright red blood splattered on the floor between the feet. Her mouth jumped open and a loud breath came out. She slapped a hand over her mouth. She couldn't make any more sounds. The two big feet turned toward her. *Uh-oh!* The three wide toes on each foot had long, nasty toenails that bent over the toes and clawed at the blue carpet. It was looking for what had made the sound. It was looking for her.

The yucky feet turned back around.

Real quiet and real slow, she crawled under the seat toward the front of the airplane. She had to get away from Something Bad before it found her. She didn't want to take a nap forever.

What if Something Bad ate my mommy? She started to cry again and made a scared, whimpering sound. She slapped her hands over her mouth again. The crunching sounds got louder, and she switched her hands to her ears. When she looked back, the feet hadn't moved.

Yes!

Her mother didn't go to the bathroom. Nope. She would have been back by now. She must have gone to the front of the airplane with all the other people. *Man oh man.* It was going to take a long, long time to get all the way up there, and Something Bad might see her or hear her. But when she got there, she would be safe like them.

Something was moving. Really quiet. It was coming from the back of the other aisle.

Oh shoot!

Something Bad was trying to trick her. She stayed very, very still, and it went by.

———————◆◆◆———————

"Did anyone else hear that?" Amarant asked.

Quentin frowned. "Hear what?" He had heard that when people don't have one of their senses, the others become stronger to compensate.

"I heard a noise. A soft, scrubbing sound. There it is again! It's coming up the stairs!"

Quentin primed his ears and then heard it too. The faint sound was barely detectable. "Quick. Move to the—"

The passengers near the stairs were already scurrying toward the front of the cabin.

He rushed to the back and looked around. *Come on, come on.* There had to be something that wouldn't make the creature bleed. The hot coffee! He dashed into the galley and ran back out wielding the same cursed coffeepot that had tried to cremate his arm. He crouched beside the partition next to the stairs and waited. For that big bastard, he needed every drop to burn like hell.

More scrubbing sounds came from the stairs. They were getting closer and faster.

He lunged around the partition to the landing, swung the coffeepot, then checked his swing. *Holy shit!* It wasn't the animal.

It was Eden.

She threw up her blood-stained hands at the sight of the coffeepot, lost her balance, and stumbled backward from the top of the stairs. A wet hand hooked the railing, then slipped off.

"No!" Moving at the speed of light, he leaped over to the top step and caught her arm. He wasn't about to let a living pilot plummet down the stairs, no, sir, and no way was he going to fail her again. He pulled her onto the landing. "I thought you were dead. You're hurt."

"No, no. I'm fine."

"Are you sure?" He could barely find any part of her white blouse and blue slacks that wasn't covered in blood. "You look like you just climbed out of a Stephen King novel."

"It's not my blood. The man in front of me tripped and was getting back up when that animal sank its claws into him. When his body fell, it knocked me down. The next thing I know, I'm waking up covered with blood and—"

"Something's wrong," Sierra said, bursting through the crush of passengers. "The cockpit's not answering."

Eden hurried up the aisle toward the cockpit. When the passengers saw her uniform with the three gold stripes on the shoulders, they cheered and clapped like she was Jesus Christ walking on water. At the front of the cabin, the three of them rushed into the short hallway with two lavatories on the right and the wall of the pilot's crew rest on the left.

Eden reached the cockpit door and paused unexpectedly. "It's broken."

"What's—" Quentin looked over and shook his head. Damn Neanderthals. Some of the guts of the cracked interphone fell to the floor.

Eden put the phone back in its cradle and punched a code into the keypad. Quentin listened intently. The sound of the door lock disengaging didn't come. About half a minute later, the three of them were still gazing at a locked cockpit door.

Hidden under the cheers and clapping was another sound. He blocked out the noise in the cabin and zeroed in on it. If the passengers knew what was going on, they would stop cheering and start praying. Obviously, Eden heard the sound too, and by the plagued look on her face ...

She *knew* what it was.

The stupid dog doodie monster was crunching and stinking.

Rona crawled under the seat in front of her next to the wall. The crunching sounds stopped, and big footsteps jarred the floor behind her. She looked back. *Oh no!* The feet were coming toward her. She froze. The footsteps passed by and stopped ahead of her.

Then it went quiet again.

Whap!

A hand with red fingernail polish hit the floor in the aisle next to her. Rona jumped and covered her mouth. *My mommy's hand! Oh, that's right.* Her mommy was wearing pink fingernail polish like her pink-and-white dress.

As the hand slid toward the back, Rona took off the other way and bumped her head on the bottom of the seat real hard. Stupid seat. A purse fell off the tray table, and a key ring fell out and made loud rattling noises. She hurried to the next row and peeked toward the back. The monster ran up the aisle and stopped right behind her. So close. Three long, crooked claws stabbed and stabbed the purse and tore it up bad.

Go away! Please, go away!

Aw, man! Her feet and hands were sticking out from under the seat. She balled up and squeezed her eyes shut. *Don't cry.* Tears ran down her face anyway, but she didn't make a sound.

The big, ugly feet went back to the back, and she crawled under some more seats toward the front.

A voice! A quiet voice somewhere in front of her. Someone else was hiding too. Maybe it was her mommy.

She's looking for me!

Rona took off. The quiet voice said something again, but it sounded funny. There was something wrong with it.

———◦∞◦———

As the passengers grew quieter, the sound grew clearer, more insistent, more nerve racking.

That's an alarm! Quentin's eyes flew to the cockpit door, where the sound blared from the other side.

Eden appeared to be deep in thought. Sierra stood with her back to the passengers. Her body trembled and her eyes glistened with unshed tears as if she knew what the alarm meant too. Okay, he was the only hayhead in the bunch. So what. An alarm of *any* kind wasn't a signal for the flight crew to shut down the engines and have high tea.

A stillness rippled through the upper deck. All eyes targeted the same bull's-eye: the cockpit door. Eden punched in the code again. Still nothing.

Quentin was a second away from tackling the door, bulletproof, grenade-resistant, steel-reinforced be damned.

In one stealthy motion, Sierra brushed her hair back and wiped away tears. "The pilots may have disabled the keypad after the group of passengers started pounding on the door and trying to break in."

Eden banged on the door. "It's Eden! Unlock the door!" Like the phone calls to the cockpit, her knock didn't get an answer. Just the blaring alarm.

A thunderous silence fell over the passengers. Eden entered the code again, and for the first time the beeps from the keypad were crystal clear. *Wait!* Those weren't beeps this time. It was a single, sustained note.

Ka-clank. The door! She did it! Eden had unlocked the cockpit door.

Raucous cheering and clapping filled the cabin as the passengers released an avalanche of pent-up emotions. Not Quentin. He braced himself.

TR and his group of miscreants rushed toward the short hallway. A slim man with a bloody left sleeve jumped in front of them. He stared them down, towering over them. It was the first time Quentin had ever seen him in person, but he wouldn't mistake him for anyone else, even without his gigantic guitar. Easily the tallest man he had ever seen in the flesh was probably a first-class passenger before the main deck fell to the great conqueror. The man was the seven-foot rock star Hercules, Mount Everest in a pair of jeans.

TR and his men cowered down, even Victor.

Well, look at that. Quentin smiled. How quickly the Neanderthal brigade became civilized. And without Hercules having to say a word.

TR leaned over. "Hey, what's that sound?"

"Oh my God!" Eden slapped a hand over her mouth. Her eyes widened. Her head shook back and forth. "No!" Muffled or not, her voice clearly trembled.

Quentin spun around, looked through the cockpit door, and couldn't speak at all.

CHAPTER 13

Quentin flew into the cockpit and bounded over to the captain's seat, then to the first officer's. Sierra's hail to the pilots was never going to be answered. Sitting beside the telephone were two dead men, not a single pulse between them.

Captain Wilcut's head lay cocked back over his left shoulder with his Adam's apple pointing toward the windshield. McGannahan was flopped over in the first officer's seat, his harness the only thing keeping him from crashing headfirst into the control yoke. Strange purple spots blotched their pale skin. Worst of all were their eyes, their dead, red eyes. Quentin had never seen eyes *that* red.

"What does that alarm mean? What's wrong?"

Eden pointed at the screen above the throttles between the two pilots' seats, where the words "PILOT RESPONSE" were displayed. "It's just the crew alertness warning. If the pilots don't interact with the systems every fifteen minutes, it sounds an alarm. It helps to keep us from falling asleep at the controls."

"So, whatever happened to them happened at least fifteen minutes ago."

"Between fifteen and twenty. At least for the last one alive. That was probably Thiago. See his finger by the flight deck door button? That's why the keypad wouldn't work at first.

Every time he reset that switch, he deactivated the keypad for another twenty minutes. When he was no longer able to do that, the locking mechanism automatically went back to its default position and the keypad was reenabled."

If Quentin knew where the damn alarm was, there would be one less bullet in his gun. "Did they touch the doll?"

"No. Neither one of them." She reached over McGannahan's seat toward a small, black square, the last button on the right in the row of buttons and knobs below the windshield.

Quentin grabbed her wrist in midair, then loosened a grip that was easily too tight. "I'm sorry. I-I … in desperation—"

"That's the Master Warning/Caution Reset switch. It turns off the alarm."

"I'm all for that, but it's important that the only person still alive on this airplane who can fly it *stays* alive."

She jerked her hand back with a look of sudden realization.

He couldn't take his eyes off her. "We have no concrete explanation why the other three pilots died, and we … until we can get a better understanding … I mean …" Why the hell wouldn't his mouth work? "One innocuous move could be cataclysmic." He pulled a ballpoint pen from the pocket inside his blazer.

"There's one over there by you." She pointed at a matching black square, the last on the left in front of Captain Wilcut.

He stretched his arm over the pilot's seat and pressed the tip of the pen against the switch. The "WARNING" light in the top half of the switch went off, and the siren stopped assaulting his ears. "Whew." He put the pen back into his pocket.

"I've seen those purple spots before, Marshal. The red eyes too."

"Where?"

"On the tarmac."

"You mean before we took off?"

"One of the men loading the cargo hold. Something had happened to him. When the paramedics wheeled him past me, he looked right at me and said something. Screamed it, actually. I couldn't quite understand what he said. In hindsight, I think he was trying to warn me."

"Do you need to do anything right now? I mean before I have a chance to make sure it's safe?"

"Put some speed on it. It's on autopilot, but I need to run a check on the systems."

He searched the cockpit, scanning the countless buttons, switches, and levers in the overhead panel.

"What are you looking for?"

"Window shopping, more or less. I think whatever was on that doll was toxic." Ah, so his mouth did work—as long as he wasn't looking at her.

"It was saliva. I saw it dripping from that animal's mouth before I got knocked down."

"That's some hellified spit."

"Crate. I get it now. That man on the tarmac *was* trying to warn me. He was trying to say 'crate.' The animal was being transported in a crate. I should have—"

"No. Don't start down that road. Trust me. It's pretty hard to get off."

"That man is probably dead by now."

"They have hospitals and medications and all kinds of ways to save people on the ground. You can't beat yourself up about it. No one could have figured anything out from those few clues. I was a detective, and I couldn't have figured it out."

"The animal was probably coming for us before we even took off."

Quentin searched the control panels in front of each pilot and the aisle stand between them. "If neither of them touched the doll, more of it is in here somewhere on something both of them touched." He zeroed in on the door to the flight crew rest. "There it is." A thin coating of the slimy gunk clung to the doorknob. "Aaron and Thiago must have touched it when they brought Ray in." He stepped back into the hallway and beckoned Sierra. "Can you bring me a trash bag, please?"

The purser returned and handed Eden a towel and him a thin, plastic bag that he placed over the pilots' crew rest door-knob and used it to open the door. Nothing could have pre-pared him for what he saw. A lump sprouted in his throat. Red was lying on the floor faceup with dark purple spots covering his face and hands. Mercifully, his eyes were closed.

Quentin dragged the two dead pilots into the flight crew rest with the others while the lump in his throat grew.

Red had two redheaded, green-eyed little boys who were going to have to navigate life without their father, and he was going to have to suffer the pain of losing yet another person close to him. His friend had been taken out without being given a chance. Blindsided. Seeing the end coming, not know-ing what was killing him, not being able to do a damn thing to stop it.

Eden pointed at a headset hanging on the hook above the pilot's seat. "Is that okay?"

He inspected every inch of it, then took it down and handed it to her. "Good to go." *Stop staring at her like a damn idiot.*

She donned it and adjusted the microphone. "Airland 1219 heavy. Airland Control." After a short pause, most likely for the controller to acknowledge the call, she continued. "Airland 1219 heavy, declaring emergency. We have numerous deceased onboard." She gasped and ripped off the headset. "They're all deceased," she said as if she just realized it. "I can't do this alone. This is my first flight since I got my 747 rating."

"You can. You just said it yourself. You got your 747 rating.

The FAA wouldn't have *certified* you to fly it if you weren't *qualified* to fly it."

Beep! Beep! Beep! Another incessant alarm lit up the cockpit. She dropped the bloody towel and took off.

"No. Stop," he said, reaching for her arm, but she deflected his hand and raced past him. Whatever the beeps indicated, it had to be something major.

She jumped into the captain's seat and changed the screen above the throttles to a diagram of something that was so foreign to him he couldn't tell which was the top and which was the bottom. He didn't know what the numbers on the screen meant either, but they oriented him like compass points on a map.

"What's going on?" he asked, his calm voice hiding the rising sense of doom. "What does that beeping sound mean?"

"We have a minor malfunction."

He blenched. Minor malfunction. The same haunting words he had heard on the ill-omened Memphis flight.

Same lie, different flight.

Hercules would have given anything *not* to see what blazed through every window. From his elevated vantage point above everyone's head, he had a clear view from the front of the cabin to the galley at the back.

La tormenta.

The Spanish had given it the perfect name. For him, the storm was a torment, especially one aspect of it. *Ka-pow.* He jumped. A bolt of lightning tore through the night sky. He leaned over the passengers in the front row on his right and slammed the shade down with a bang. When he pulled his hand away, the window's plastic grip was still in it.

Two boys sitting across the aisle on his left, who looked to be about eleven and twelve, burst out laughing.

The controlled breathing exercises his psychiatrist had taught him were not working. *Astraphobia is the seventh most common phobia in the world*, Dr. Phelps would often tell him as if that would make him feel less like a seven-foot lightning rod. Just as useless were the countless facts about lightning versus airplanes that he had memorized, evidence that he had nothing to worry about: the average commercial aircraft gets struck by lightning twice a year with no ill effect; the copper in the skin of the plane conducts electricity to the static wicks and from there, back out into the atmosphere, where it can do no harm.

"Static wicks?" The voice came from someone standing near his left elbow. There stood Senator TR Dunn with a charming smile that was obviously an implant.

"Uh … ye-yes," Hercules stammered, looking around sheepishly. No one else appeared to have caught him talking to himself. "Those objects that look like sticks, protruding from the trailing edges of the wings and the empennage. A relevant analogy would be lightning rods for airplanes."

TR looked down at the book that Hercules clutched. "What cha got there, dude?" He sounded like an out-of-touch elitist trying to relate to an inner-city youth.

"My name is not 'dude' or any other colloquial sobriquet you might attribute to the patois of today's pop culture. My stage name is Hercules. You may call me that if you prefer. Nonetheless, please don't insult me with diminutive language as if you feel it necessary to talk down to me. It shows that you have already prejudged me to be a man of lesser intelligence than yourself. I sincerely doubt that is the case."

The senator's mouth hung agape for a moment; then he reapplied his fake smile. "Hercules, do you know what the biggest problem is with transoceanic flights? No parking spaces. I've done it many times but never found it very comforting to fly thousands of miles with nothing below me except endless water. Oceans are just too big where the margin of error is so small." The senator's eyes widened abruptly. "Hercules. Well, blessed be me. You're that singer who almost died when you got struck by lightning on stage. Where was it?"

"Highbar Stadium in Florida, the lightning capital of the United States." Yet another useless bit of information.

Two years ago, his life had changed for the better and worse at the same time. Back then he couldn't pay people to buy his music, and his label had dropped him. He strapped on his custom Stratocaster and took the stage at an outdoor concert. No one had come to see the opening artist that sweltering July night, but the audience cheered and whistled after each of his first four songs, not bad for someone who was about to sing the last song in his foreseeable future. He launched into "Twinkling Hearts." He felt it and could tell the audience did too. A sea of cell phones aimed at the stage. By the time he hit the bridge, he was singing his most popular song like never before and was playing the strings off the Strat. If he was going out, he was going out with a—

Bang!

A bolt of lightning knocked him off the stage—though he didn't remember it—stopped his heart, and landed him in intensive care for a week. Audience members posted the videos online, gaining millions of hits and making *him* one. A year later, he had become famous, and the same album that had been languishing in bargain bins was certified double platinum.

Now, two years after he rode the lightning, some had started saying his name and "star" in the same sentence.

"Hey, Hercules," the oldest of the two boys yelled. When Hercules looked over at him, the boy jumped up, started playing air guitar and then started shaking like he was being struck by lightning. At the end of his routine, he collapsed back into his seat. Motionless. Tongue hanging out of the corner of his mouth. Both boys burst out laughing again.

Hercules shook his head and had to smile. "Little snots."

TR gestured with a manicured finger. "The book?"

Hercules held up the front of it so Mr. Intrusive could see it for himself.

"*A Better Understanding of the Old Testament*?" he read with the implied question: *What is a guy like you doing reading something like that*? "I guess if I'd been touched personally by the finger of God, I'd try to change my life too."

"I've been reading the Bible since I was four."

"A Bible-reading rock star. You're a walking oxymoron. Bet you have the pick of the ladies, though, right?" The much shorter TR tried to give him a buddy-buddy elbow bump but gave up in the middle and tucked his stubby elbow back down by his side.

"I *picked* just one and made her my wife."

"Where is she?" TR looked around. "I'd like to meet the lucky lady."

"She's dead."

"Oh no. Did the animal down there kill her?"

"No."

The senator paused, but Hercules didn't elaborate.

"So, why are you going to South Africa?"

"I'm participating in a concert to raise funds for the MAMA organization. Musicians Against the Mistreatment of Animals."

"I know what it stands for. I assumed you were more of the type to kill them and eat them raw right there on stage."

"It's okay to assume. It's *not* okay to assume you *know*."

"I'm sorry. I bet you get that all the time."

"No, actually I don't."

"Listen, Hercules, aren't you just a little concerned about how things are being handled around here?"

"I saw that coming way back at 'dude.' What I'm concerned

about, *more* than a little concerned about, is how things are being handled in the Senate lately." He leaned closer to the man's face. "Senator." Hercules lifted the tome to his face and pretended to read.

TR dropped the charm and meandered down the aisle, undoubtably in search of some other poor soul to recruit or vex.

"Mommy?" Rona whispered. *I hope the voice is Mommy's.* The voice ahead of her answered, but it sounded weird. She crawled toward it. Almost there.

Something hit the floor behind her. When she peeked under the seat, three big, crooked claws on three big, wide toes pointed straight at her. She slammed her eyes shut and didn't open them until she was looking toward the front again. She crept under another row of seats, but her way was blocked. *Oh man.* She was trapped.

A big, white paper shopping bag sat under the window seat, a black suitcase lay under the middle seat, and a shiny thing hung down from the back of the aisle seat. She remembered the name. A footrest.

She pushed the suitcase really hard, but it was too heavy to move even a little. As soon as her hand touched the shopping bag, it made a loud noise. She jerked her hand away and looked back. The ugly toes whirled around and pointed at her again. *Be still as a doll. Don't make a sound.* They slowly turned around and faced the back of the airplane again.

The aisle seat in front of her was the only one left, and Something Bad could see her if she crawled under it. She scooted over and pushed the footrest up. Real slow. Real quiet. When she was afraid, her daddy would tell her to muster up courage and march on with her bad self. She didn't know exactly what that meant. But she knew it meant she should be brave. She mustered up courage and took off, crawling really fast under the aisle seat. She got to the next row and hurried over to the seat next to the window. She did it! She looked through a crack between the shopping bag and the briefcase behind her. The monster was still turned the other way. *Yay!*

"Where are you?" The person should have heard her whisper. She was close enough. And she should have been able to see them, but there was no one under the seats but her, and the person wasn't saying anything anymore.

Something grabbed her by the back of her head. She screamed. It yanked her up between the seats and up on her knees.

"Noooo!" She pulled but couldn't get loose.

It was a man. He was lying across the seats, and he was moaning and moaning. "A-yu-da-may." He moaned some more, but he wouldn't let go of her hair. "Por fa-bor. A-yu-da-may!"

"Let me go!"

His eyes were open really wide and he looked scared, but he looked scary too. And crazy.

"Let me go!"

"Por fa-bor. A-yu-da-may."

"I'm *not* the May. Let me go!"

Rona screamed louder, then stopped. *Uh-oh!* Loud footsteps. They were running. "Something Bad is coming!" The yucky smell was stronger. She pulled at the man's fingers, but she didn't have enough muscles.

The monster was going to eat her!

She bit the man's arm as hard as she could. He let go, and then she flung herself under the seat in front of her and pulled her arms and legs in tight. Crunching sounds came from behind her, but she didn't turn around. *Be still as a doll. Don't make a sound.*

Then the noises stopped, and she couldn't tell where the monster was.

"Dr. Speck, I didn't know," Daniel said, glancing around. No one else in the exit row was within earshot. "I'm so sorry."

The doc furrowed his brow. "You didn't know what?"

"This is all my fault."

"Take the rocks out of your jaws and spit it out."

Daniel leaned his head against the right cabin wall next to the exit door. "I didn't know the mega-T's blood was green. I was looking for red blood in the cage."

Dr. Speck's face petrified right before his eyes. "I wish I could strap your ass to the front of my truck and crash into a tree."

"It was a spot about the size of a nickel on one of the tentacles. I didn't know it was blood. My field is mitochondrial DNA in humans, not recombinant DNA. We must have cut the megateratoid when we dropped the front of the cage. I have to tell them the truth." His sense of guilt was big and husky and no doubt could sing bass in the choir. He started toward the cockpit.

The doc yanked him back by the arm. "I remind you, this will be your third strike."

Daniel sighed and leaned against the wall again. He had made enough bad decisions for two lifetimes, and that wasn't even including the ones that landed him behind bars. Once he had gotten his shit together, he couldn't stand to look at himself in the mirror. Considering the bad decisions he had made recently, the jackass in the mirror apparently hadn't learned a damn thing since he got out.

"Daniel, stick with me and your career will be resurrected. The Granthom Research Group is the best-funded underground research group in the world. The biggest hogs at the trough. Wait till you see that sprawling facility, all that cutting-edge equipment."

"GRG is an abomination."

The doc continued undaunted. "Unlimited resources. Unlimited funding."

"Most of that came from byproducts of research that has been banned on planet Earth."

"So they wiggle through the cracks in a few international laws."

"A few? They're trying to develop a genocide virus that can target a specific race."

"They're also trying to develop ways to extend folks' lives."

"Before or after they give them the virus?"

"What if we could find a way to extend humans' ability to hibernate for more than a couple of hours? What if we could extend it? Who knows? Maybe for weeks or even months, like animals? Now, I'm not trying to throw stones, but think of all the drug addicts trying to kick. If they could hibernate past the excruciating withdrawal symptoms and wake up clean, they'd have a better chance of staying off the muckeration."

"That would backfire like hell. If it was that easy to get *off* drugs, there wouldn't be as much deterrent to getting *on* drugs."

"All right, then. How about this, Daniel? Think of all the people who suffer horrible accidents or long-term illnesses or debilitating diseases. They could be put into hibernation while their bodies heal. They come out the other side without having to go through all the pain and suffering."

"Again, Dr. Speck? Really? Like Rachel is going through; clearly that's what you're getting at. That doesn't change the fact that GRG wouldn't have a problem freezing untold numbers of humans to death while developing that procedure just to feather their own nests."

"If you think all the research being done in the world is above board and legal, then you have got to be some kind of newfangled fool. It's certainly nothing new. Look at Da Vinci.

What he did with dead bodies is still illegal to this day. So freaking what? His defiance led to a far better understanding of the human anatomy."

"Considering our current situation, my third strike looks like paradise." If his leg had another knee, he would kick his own ass for ever getting involved with the likes of Oggie and the doc in the first place.

"If you tell them that we are the cooks stirring this pot, our insides will instantly become our outsides."

"Like those people downstairs, Dr. Speck? Unlike them, we deserve it. We did this to them."

"Not by ourselves, we didn't. Something else had a hand in it."

"What do you mean?"

"A spot the size of a nickel? Come on. You may have nicked it, but you didn't cut off that tentacle. You saw it. There's more skin on a mosquito's pecker than there was holding that thing on. If you had done that, there would have been a lot more blood in that cage."

"Then what did happen?"

"The amount of blood from that cut tentacle could melt away enough of the cage for it to get free. We padded the cage with leather cushions to keep it from injuring itself during the trip. We did all we could."

"With this group's vast resources, why didn't they send a private plane for us?"

"Fuel capacity. Their private planes would have to fly to South America first and refuel. More miles. More time. More risks. And a different set of regulations. Anyway, none of that is worth the salt in piss right now. We need to focus on trying to fix this mess. We're the only ones who know that thing."

"We don't know shit, Doc. Oggie was the only one who really knew it. If he wanted to kill something that could have made him infinitely famous, what does that tell you?"

"Ah, pishposh. He always killed them, remember?"

"I would give you three guesses why, but you would only need one."

"Of course, there is the potential for danger when dealing with this type of research. We both accepted that. His risk tolerance was just lower than mine."

"We know now which one of you was right, don't we?"

"Are you blaming me for what happened to him?"

"No, but I think you should have taken his advice. I don't think it was just about risk. I think it was more than that. A dying man only has so many words. 'You must kill it' should have been all he needed to say."

"I was privy to all of his research data, Daniel."

"No matter how copious his notes, he knew something about the mega-T that we don't. Something he didn't have time to tell us before he died."

Minor malfunction. The words hung in the air like a dreadful odor, a powerful odor that Quentin could smell simply by thinking about it. He wasn't sure what the beeping sound meant but knew what it didn't mean. *Minor malfunction, my ass!* He leaned over the back of the vacant first officer's seat, his eyes racing across screens and gauges, wondering how anyone could learn how to operate all those gadgets. He might as well have been looking at the Dead Sea Scrolls. "What minor malfunction? When you say 'minor malfunction,' to me, that means we're about to crash land in the Atlantic."

Eden changed the display on the top screen between the two seats. "We may have a fuel leak."

"*That's* a minor malfunction? A blown light bulb is a minor malfunction. A fuel leak is a whole other nother."

"The computer can give this type of false reading. It's most likely nothing." A narrow strip of paper scrolled out below the words "DATA PRINTER" at the back of the aisle stand. She ripped the sheet off, then read it. "The fuel appears to be burning at a normal rate, as I expected. No fuel leak."

"Thank God." He looked down and realized that his hands were crushing the back of the seat. He let go and the color rushed back into his fingers.

A chime sounded. Eden checked the surveillance screen, then reached over to the aisle stand and unlocked the door.

Sierra popped her head in. "Get out here! Quick!"

He rushed to the door thinking the worst. If the animal had broken into the upper deck cabin, it would be game over.

<hr>

It wasn't adding up. Eden studied the paper clutched in her hand. The fuel seemed to be burning at a normal rate, but something was off. It had to be a false reading. What she needed was another pair of eyes from one of the more experienced 747 pilots. Either one of them. She would even take Thiago and his thousand and one questions.

Please let it be a false reading.

She had better throttle her ass up. If there was a discrepancy, it wouldn't find itself. A small part of her didn't want to figure it out, the same part that didn't want the air marshal anywhere near her at that time. The man wasn't lacking in the looks department, and sure, he had been there to keep her from falling apart, but now she counted it a blessing that he wasn't in the cockpit while she scrambled to figure out which of the data readouts were displaying false readings.

She pushed the fuel button on the Display Select Panel below the glareshield, and the fuel synoptic display splashed across the secondary EICAS again. She compared the current readings to the previous ones for the amount of fuel in each of the eight tanks and the total amount in all of the tanks combined. The current fuel-depletion rate was normal. *Well, once again that rules out a fuel leak.* One possibility eliminated, countless ones to go. It was definitely a job that required the undivided attention of a pilot who was not flying.

There was no problem with the fuel flow, with the position of the valves, or the pressure in the pumps. All four Pratt & Whitney engines were running within their normal ranges. She searched every screen. Every reading. Every printout. She hadn't found it yet, but there had to be a discrepancy somewhere and a hell of a big one.

She was glad for one more blessing: the air marshal couldn't read the displays.

CHAPTER 14

The passengers were in a fever, standing up and shouting. The leathernecks in the front of the cabin stared at something behind them. Quentin pressed through the throng. An acute outcry arose from the middle of the upper deck. Then screams.

"Somebody, do something!" a female voice yelled from the heart of the fray.

Quentin reached the clearing at the exit row. On the floor, Victor and another ruffian were a ball of entangled limbs and flying fists. Hercules bent down, and when he stood back up, he had one clamped in each fist.

"What is going on?" Quentin scowled at the rivals. "The two of you don't think we have enough trouble as it is?"

Victor yelled at the potbellied man in the ratty blue jeans and a light blue T-shirt that read: "Stop complaining. I only go fishing on days that end in 'Y.'"

"Let me go!" the potbellied man shouted.

Hercules, with his hellified wingspan, released the two men like a bomber releasing its payload. "Unfortunately, it's not just these two." The rock star sounded like he was struggling to control a desire to beat one of the men's asses with the other. "This cabin has turned into a powder keg." He jabbed a finger toward TR. "And he is the detonator."

Hercules was spot-on, and Quentin had to defuse the situation before it exploded. The senator didn't appear to be much of a danger himself, but he had the power to incite his lackeys.

TR pointed toward the cockpit with a hand that looked like it had never lifted anything heavier than his wallet. "That pilot needs to tell us what's really going on." His straight and proper gray suit; spotless, white dress shirt; and immaculate hair stood out against Victor and the other combatant with their wrinkled clothes, ruffled hair, and rose-colored bruises blossoming on their faces.

That appeared to be the norm. TR had commanded the Neanderthal brigade to try to break into the cockpit, but, as far as Quentin could tell, had only lifted his hand to knock on the door.

"We have rights!" TR continued his tirade. A grown-ass man with the voice of a boy's forever stuck in puberty. "I was sitting right next to a man when he died. I have a right to know what killed him. And we have a right to know what that animal is doing on this plane."

The more Quentin heard the senator's pitchy voice, the more he longed for earplugs. He stepped to within choking distance and jammed a set of handcuffs in the senator's face. "You have the right to wear these the rest of this flight. Would you like to exercise that right too?"

TR lowered his voice and took the acid coating off his words. "There's no way it got onto this plane without someone knowing something. How did it get past those dogs at the airport?"

Hercules fielded the question. "Those dogs are trained to alert, or signal, when encountering a *specific* smell, that smell and that smell only, whether it be drugs or explosives or cadavers or whatever. To train them, they have to first be introduced to that smell. How do you suppose those dogs could have been introduced to and subsequently been trained to detect the smell of that monster down there?"

TR gave Hercules the same venomous look he had given Quentin. A man with his middle finger in a metal splint and his elbow cupped in the good hand slid the finger over to the senator's snotlocker. TR looked down, rolled his eyes at the man, and walked away.

"Can I take a look at that?" Dr. Ross asked, pointing at the rock star's arm. Blood caked his left sleeve from bicep to elbow.

"I'm okay. It's nothing."

The pint-size woman beamed a low-watt smile and wagged a finger at the giant. "Don't make me come up there, young man."

"Yes, ma'am," he said in a playful, mousy little voice. He rolled up his sleeve with a hand as big as a dinner plate. A nasty, three-inch cut below his shoulder still trickled blood as Dr. Ross started working on it. Hercules looked up from his arm. "Marshal, is there anything I can do to help?"

"Keep an eye on things when I'm in the cockpit. If something happens, knock."

"Thank you, Doctor." Hercules examined his new bandage and then nodded his head over at TR, who was huddled up with his band of asshats, speechifying and gesturing about more asshattery, no doubt. "Does that include heads?"

"Hercules, as bad as I would like to get that guy out of my hair for a little while, better let me handle that."

"Spoilsport."

The senator had recruited a few new flunkeys. All big men. Not a one even close to being as tall as Hercules, whose only rival was down on the main deck, where, with any luck, it would stay. Or better yet, where it would fucking die.

At the edge of Quentin's peripheral vision, Dr. Speck and Daniel were laser-locked on him. When he walked over to the starboard exit door where they stood, Daniel averted his eyes, suddenly finding the floor captivating. Guilty. Quentin just didn't know of what. He let him stew in his own juices for a few more seconds while he turned his attention to the older man. "Dr. Speck, did you have anything to do with getting that beast onboard this aircraft?"

Dr. Speck's jaw lowered. Oh yeah, Quentin had put him on the ropes. He was probably wondering what else the air marshal knew if he already knew his name.

"No. I most certainly did not have anything to do with it." Dr. Speck sounded incensed.

Quentin wasn't buying his penny act. "Do you know anything about it? What it is, or where it came from?"

"Absolutely not."

"Somehow, I don't believe that. If you do, you could help save the rest of us. At least let us know what we're up against."

"I told you, I don't know anything about it."

"What about you, Daniel?"

"I don't know anything about it."

Quentin shook his head. Same shit, different asshole. He nodded toward Dr. Speck. "He's the one running this circus, isn't he?"

"I don't know anything." Daniel refused eye contact again while a trembling hand played with his jacket zipper. It was a tell, something he apparently resorted to whenever he was nervous and evidently didn't realize he was doing.

"You're lying. I can tell you know something. You're not talking to that dumb animal down there."

"I'm sorry. I don't." *Zip, zip, zip, zip. Zip, zip, zip, zip.*

The hell he didn't.

Daniel's trembling hands stole into the front pockets of his pants. Quentin had seen people in the grips of a seizure who didn't shake as badly. Whatever they were up to was likely new territory for them. Especially the sidekick. They were guilty of something, all right.

Dr. Speck held his silver briefcase against his chest like it was the last piece of bread on earth. That cherished briefcase again. Most of the passengers who had escaped from the lower deck cabin had come empty-handed. Not the gray wolf. Another wolf came to mind: the Big Bad Wolf. Suddenly, images of three men dressed in black popped into his consciousness. *Where the hell did those memories come from?* He felt the bump on his neck.

Something the senator had said shot to the forefront of Quentin's mind. He should have realized it sooner. It might already be too late.

He scissored through the passengers clustered in the exit row and tore ass up the aisle to Sierra. "Where did Ray die?"

She whirled around, her eyes widening with the sudden realization that they had a five-alarm fire on their hands. "F-follow me," she stammered. He tailed her to an aisle seat five rows from the front, one row behind Amarant. The purser stopped at the starboard aisle seat. "Right there."

The middle-aged man sitting in it looked up at them and then clutched the hand of the woman sitting in the middle seat. The elderly lady who had been the last to leave the rear-most cabin on the main deck sat next to the window.

"Can I get the three of you to step out into the aisle for a moment, please?" Quentin used his best sterilized voice. The man stepped into the aisle and extended a hand to both women. Quentin stepped aside as they moved into the aisle. His eyes landed on the last place where Red sat, where he most likely took his last breath.

"Is something wrong, sir?" the man asked.

"I'm sure everything's fine." Quentin bent down and scanned the section. He gave special attention to the places

Red had likely put his hands: the armrests, seat belt, buckle, and tray table. He kneeled down on the floor in the aisle and looked under the seats. There was no sign of the saliva's sticky venom. "I'm sorry to have bothered you. You can sit back down now."

As they settled back into their seats, he inspected their skin and observed their behavior. None of them had purple spots or exhibited any sign of illness. What a relief. He relished even a small victory after having his ass handed to him every time he turned around.

"Have we all been infected?" squawked an unmistakable voice that was to the ear what a sharp stick was to the eye. Quentin shook his head and turned around as the senator nudged apart two passengers standing in the aisle. "Tell us, Marshal. That's the seat where that guy died. What exactly were you looking for?"

What a jerk. As if the passengers needed another reason for their supercharged imaginations to conjure up all the plagues in the Bible. "Spit," Quentin answered. "What the other air marshal died of is *not* contagious. It's the saliva from the animal."

From behind him, Amarant said, "That man died in back of me, and now you're checking the seats? I'm afraid to move. I'm afraid to touch anything. How did the saliva get up here in the upper deck?"

"On that doll is my guess," TR butted in. "I saw it go into the cockpit, and then that other air marshal went in. When he came back out, he died. Other than that one time, he didn't move from that seat."

Kito asked, "What about the pilot?"

"Yeah, what about her?" TR asked. "Does she even know what she's doing?"

Kito shook his head. "Come on, man. You know damn well

she knows what she's doing. My mother drove a city bus and had to be twice as good as the men just to get half the credit. She trained the man who ended up being her supervisor."

"I wasn't being chauvinistic—"

"The hell you wasn't. You were being racist too. What I meant was, how badly is she hurt?"

"She's fine." Quentin said, steering the ship back into calm seas. "That wasn't her blood. Although she was exposed to the venom, she didn't come into contact with it. She is in control of the plane and has shown no sign of illness whatsoever."

A sudden urge to find out if that was still true overpowered him. The passengers might need him to stave off the creature if it broke into the upper deck, but the last pilot on the plane had to be protected at all costs. The urge intensified into fear that something dreadful was going on in the cockpit.

———————◆◆◆———————

One of Eden's screens gave a puzzling update. She was about to give up on finding a discrepancy when one found her. Not one any pilot would ever want. If it held up, Flight 1219 to Cape Town could turn into Flight 1219 to the bottom of the Atlantic Ocean.

She haphazardly rammed the tail of her newly donned, clean blouse into the waist of her clean pants and jumped back into the pilot's seat. On the secondary EICAS screen, the numbers below "STAB" had plummeted to "2.1." No doubt about it. The horizontal stabilizer tank was supposed to have a hell of a lot more than twenty-one hundred pounds. If the reading was correct, there were only three hundred gallons in the tail. Damn near empty. Three hundred gallons in a tank that held thirty-three hundred was like having a gallon in her Shelby. Goose bumps dappled her arms.

It couldn't be. Were the crossfeed and jettison systems off? She checked the overhead panel. Affirmative. If the fuel wasn't being transferred to another tank or being jettisoned from the aircraft, then the problem was likely a malfunctioning sensor in that tank. It had to be. Three thousand gallons of fuel don't just vanish.

The number on the screen returned to "22.6" thousand pounds. Unbelievable. Eden shook her head. Whoever said "numbers don't lie" had never worked in a cockpit. She slouched back in her seat, then sprang up. Her eyes flew back to the screen. She was puzzled. Why was the thirty-three hundred gallons of fuel still in the tank in the empennage at all?

Her fingers raced across a small calculator, and then she fixated on the results.

No, no, no! It can't be! It isn't possible.

A groundswell of cold reality rushed through her body and crashed against her bones like a rogue wave, washing away all doubt …

And all hope.

The numbers still made absolutely no sense, but there was no denying what that meant. Clearly, none of the current readouts were giving false readings.

CHAPTER 15

Quentin stepped down the two-inch lip into the cockpit and bounded over to the first officer's seat. "Did you figure out what the problem is with the fuel readings?" His eyes happened upon an unfastened button on Eden's blouse. On her freshly washed face was a nick about three quarters of an inch that ran across the nub of her cherubic little chin. He averted his gaze, settling on the neutral displays.

"Something's wrong, but it's not a fuel leak," she answered with what might have been a minute hint of tension in her voice. "How are the passengers?"

"Besides being scared to death, distraught, crazed, hostile, and homicidal, they're fine."

"When people feel their lives are in danger, their true selves emerge. You want to find out what kind of person someone really is, put his butt in a vise and squeeze." She glanced down, then fastened the wayward button.

"Any idea what the problem is or if there really is one at all?" he asked.

"I'm getting inconsistent readings for the fuel tank in the horizontal stabilizer. Without the fuel in that optional tank, a flight this long wouldn't be possible. What's confusing me is"— she paused like she was thinking—"why is that tank still full?"

"That's not a good thing?"

"The fuel in the CWT and that tank get used first. It should be empty by now. What reason would Aaron and Thiago have for transferring fuel to it?" She sounded like she was thinking out loud rather than talking to him. Something was definitely up.

"The CWT?"

"The center wing tank. It's a misnomer. That tank is located in the fuselage below the stairs and the forward coach cabin, not in the wings." There was definitely tension in her voice now. She attacked the buttons on the aisle stand, and her eyes jittered across one screen, then another.

She hasn't made eye contact with me since I came back into the cockpit.

"Is something wrong? Another minor malfunction?"

There was no answer and still no eye contact.

"I can see it on your face. I can hear it in your voice." Panic started swelling inside him, and he struggled to keep his voice from sounding like hers. "You're going to have to trust someone. If not me, who?"

"I don't know if you can handle this, but I know the passengers can't. We can't let them know until ... until it's time."

Whatever it was, it was damn sure no minor malfunction. "I won't. I promise."

"We're not going to make it to Africa. We don't have enough fuel."

"Are you sure?"

"I've checked every screen. Every reading. Every printout. There is absolutely no way we can make it. Not even close. Not even with the strongest tailwind in history."

"Oh God, Jesus Christ, all the angels in heaven."

"The only thing between us and Africa is eleven hundred miles of Atlantic Ocean without so much as a fistful of dirt to land on."

"Okay, so. We can just turn around and land in South America, right?"

She looked him in the eye for the first time. "From where we are in the South Atlantic, the nearest continent *is* Africa."

CHAPTER 16

It was so quiet. The monster hadn't made any crunching sounds behind Rona for a long time. It could have been right above, waiting for her to come from under the seats. If it was in the back, she was too far away to hear it. Maybe it was in the other aisle. Or up ahead somewhere waiting for her. She couldn't move. Scared little baby.

Oh yeah. When Something Bad was right behind her before, it smelled really, really stinky. If it was still close, she could smell it. She wasn't a baby. A baby couldn't figure stuff out.

She sniffed the air like she had seen her dog do. Something smelled like oranges. No yucky stuff.

She uncurled her arms and legs real slow and looked around. *Wow!* A thousand hundred seats. Some had bags and purses and briefcases under them. And one had a pair of grown adult shoes under it. The row of seats behind her was twisted and lay flat on the floor like a big, fat elephant had sat on it.

But no big, ugly feet anywhere. *Yes!*

She got up on her hands and knees again, and her right knee landed on something squishy. Half of an orange. *Eww!* She started crawling again, and it fell off.

A loud bang came from somewhere ahead of her. She

stopped. It sounded like a hugemongous pot hitting a hugemongous pan. A wall was up ahead with dark blue curtains covering the place where the noise had come from. *Uh-oh!* The monster. Or another grown adult who wanted to grab her by her hair.

CHAPTER 17

Eden changed the transponder squawk code to 7700. She grabbed the headset off the hook and snapped the microphone toward her mouth. "Airland 1219 heavy. Airland Control." She cleared the bugaboos out of her throat and swallowed hard. A crisis was not the time to let desperation overwhelm her.

"Airland Control. Airland 1219 heavy, go ahead," the Airland traffic controller responded with the clarity and tone of a male radio DJ.

"Airland 1219 heavy," Eden answered. "Declaring fuel emergency. Please advise on the nearest airfield."

"Airland 1219 heavy. It's still Wideawake Airfield on Ascension Island. Eight-three-zero nauts."

"Roger, Airland Traffic Control. Wideawake Airfield on Ascension. Eight-three-zero nauts." She banked the 747 hard to starboard, made a wide half-moon in the night sky, and headed back in the opposite direction. Through the glareshield, lightning slashed diagonally, then forked. Thunder rumbled and rolled across the sky.

She pulled out the Jeppesen Manual and flipped through the weighty spiral-bound manual. "Got it." The conditions on the approach plate for Wideawake Airfield were worse than she had thought. Pure hell.

"What is Ascension?" the air marshal asked from what had been her seat.

"Ascension is an island. Just a mountain peak, really. But there's an airfield on it." Her eyes darted to the fuel synoptic display again. "I know this sounds crazy, but the other pilots dumped fuel."

"TR said that Ray started behaving strangely. Like the hard drive in his brain was crashing. Maybe the same thing happened to the pilots before they died."

"Maybe." She thought for a moment. "Wait. The other pilots weren't losing their faculties, at least not at that point." She turned her attention back to her headset. "Airland 1219 heavy, Airland Control."

"Airland 1219 heavy, go ahead," the Airland traffic controller responded.

"Did you say *still?*"

"Affirmative. We first advised Airland 1219 that the nearest runway was Wideawake Airfield"—the man paused like he needed to check—"over two hours ago."

Suddenly, she couldn't seem to get enough air. "Roger, Airland Control." She ripped the headset off. "Shit!"

"What's wrong?" Quentin asked.

"They dumped the fuel on purpose."

His brown eyes narrowed beneath an intense frown. "What?"

"To get the landing weight down. They were planning to land. The venom must have taken effect before they could turn the aircraft back toward Ascension Island. The Combi was on autopilot and simply continued on its course to South Africa for two more hours."

He shook his head slowly. "Adding the two hours it's going to take us to get back puts us *four* hours beyond the point where they dumped the fuel."

"Worse than that." Eden took his emotional temperature. As usual, everything about him screamed "stable." Granite to the core. "I'm sorry to say that's only part of the problem, Marshal."

"There's more? I'm not sure I can handle any more."

"We're heading east now, against the jet stream, a powerful one that's doing its damnedest to push us backward."

CHAPTER 18

The smell was back. Rona pinched her nose. *Eww!* It was getting stronger. Something Bad must have gotten closer, sneaky monster. She lay flat on the floor and looked all around. She didn't see any big, ugly feet anywhere. No yucky, crooked toenails. *Whoa.* She was really, really close to the wall and curtains up ahead. *Yes!*

Bang!

She whipped her head toward the loud noise coming from somewhere on the other side of the curtains in front of her. "Mommy?" she whispered. A teeny-weeny whisper. Then she crawled out from under the final row of seats and finally reached the wall and the curtains she had seen all the other people's feet run through. *Man oh man.* She couldn't wait to see her mommy. She ripped the curtains open.

Oh no!

A big, dark green tail lifted a cart in the air and slammed it back down in the aisle in front of her. The tail was like something she had seen on TV once. She tried to remember the name her daddy had called the animal. Alley gator. Something Bad had a tail like an alley gator, except its tail was bigger and had sharp, scary-looking, spiky things sticking out of the top of it. The cart must have gotten stuck on some of the spiky things, and the monster was trying to get it off.

141

Rona slammed the curtains shut. If her dog was there, he would bite the monster's leg if it tried to eat her. There was another bang, but it sounded farther away. She eased open the curtains just a little, little bit. Something Bad was gone. She eased it open a little more. It wasn't anywhere.

Don't be a silly Millie. It couldn't have just disappeared.

———◦◦———

Quentin rushed down the upper deck aisle toward the loud banging rising up the stairs. As hard as he wished that the animal would keep its big ass down on the main deck until they landed, it was a miracle he hadn't suffered a groin pull. From the sound of things, that wish was going to be returned to sender—and sooner rather than later.

Sierra came flying out of the galley at the back of the cabin. They came within inches of having a two-car pileup at the seat-high partition that prevented inattentive people from tumbling ass over teakettle down the stairs.

The clangor sent the passengers into a rage. The decibel level of their voices neared the magnitude of a prison cafeteria melee.

"Everyone, please, be quiet!"

All but a few defiant voices obeyed his charge.

"Please. Every—"

A high-pitched screech interrupted him. Metal against metal this time. Louder than before but not so distant anymore. Even the rebellious passengers zipped it. He could feel their eyes boring holes into his skull as the cabin went silent. The clanging promptly went silent as well.

It seemed the noisemaker below was listening for signs of movement like he was.

"They may need help," Sierra said with a far more optimistic view than his, a more plausible one too. After all, if Eden could survive the slaughterhouse down on the main deck, there was a possibility, however small, that someone else could too, and if that person was staggering against the rails, they were probably in terrible condition.

Quentin hurried around the partition and looked down the stairs. He didn't spot anything. With hope feathering one shoulder and fear crushing the other, he started descending the stairs. When he was halfway, the creature stepped into view at the bottom. *Son of a bitch!* It had set him up. Tentacles writhed and cracked the air like whips. Fear grew claws and cut to the bone. He leaped back up the stairs double-quick, while below, the banging sounds started back up again, a jarring cacophony coming from the horror standing at the foot of the stairs—or was it? The animal wasn't moving.

Its tail flung into view, and attached to the tip, a beverage cart that looked like it had shaken hands with a tornado whipped back and forth through the air. It took out one of the metal posts supporting the handrail at the bottom step, then slammed against the top corner of the galley next to the stairs like a wrecking ball. The cart dislodged from tail spikes that resembled the ones on the tail of a stegosaurus.

The animal looked up at him, then dropped down on all fours and pounded a forepaw on the bottom step. It did the same with the other front paw on the second step. *Dumb animal, my ass!* The damn thing was testing the steps for surety.

"We can't let it come up here!" They had nowhere else to run. Quentin darted passed Sierra into the galley and shot back out, pushing a beverage cart. *Holy shit!* The behemoth was halfway up the stairs, with its tentacles coiled around the rails and banisters, using them to help pull itself along. It was making the same scuffing sounds on the carpet he'd heard when Eden came up the stairs.

The puke-worthy smell grew stronger. Given the choice between smelling the beast or a week-old dead body, he would have gladly headed off to the nearest graveyard with a shovel. The odor attacked his senses and made it a chore to concentrate.

One of the longest tentacles uncoiled and lashed up the stairs at him. He ducked behind the cart. The tentacle flashed by with a loud crack above his head. After another quick recoil, the tentacle sailed straight for his face. He ducked, and it smashed into the wall where his head had been. Damn if the animal wasn't fast. And pissed off. It was clearly trying to take his head off.

He peeked above the cart. Sierra was no longer standing at the back of the cabin. He couldn't blame her for that. When his sight line was high enough to see down the stairs, he cringed and knew why she had decamped.

"Oh hell!" He was looking right into the face of death.

The animal now had only four steps to go before breaching the survivors' only safe haven.

Quentin dug his feet into the floor and put his full might behind the cart, launching it off the top step. It slammed into the titan's face but might as well have been yet another marshmallow. A forepaw knocked it away.

He should have known. If four bullets to the torso hadn't stopped the beast, a beverage cart sure wouldn't.

The giant took another step up the stairs. Quentin had the time it would take the colossus to climb three steps to think of a way to stop it, and he had no clue.

The crown of its head poked into the upper deck. He ripped his Sig Sauer out of its holster and took aim. It was the best idea he could come up with—pitiful as it was—to pour more rounds into it and pray they worked this time, pray that its blood didn't eat catastrophic holes in the aircraft.

With the creature on the stairs and away from any exterior walls, there was a good chance that even if it bled out, the blood wouldn't reach the skin of the aircraft.

A good chance? Fair, at best.

144

As his finger wrapped around the trigger, a tentacle slashed at him again. He dipped behind the partition, and the tentacle recoiled. He jumped back up with his finger on the trigger.

The CWT!

The center wing fuel tank, or whatever the hell Eden called it, was somewhere below the stairs. If the corrosive blood ate a hole in that tank, the aircraft would explode. Now out of options, he holstered his weapon.

Below, the beast's left hind paw landed on Quentin's cart. It lost its balance and tumbled down the stairs while the cart ricocheted off the rails, then landed atop a giant belly that was slightly lighter green and smoother than the other hide. A forepaw pounded the cart flat, slammed it against the bottom step half a dozen times, and then hurled it away. Better the cart than him. He didn't want to be on the welcoming end of those kinds of blows. The cart banged against the floor somewhere beyond Quentin's purview. The creature hurled a loud, angry roar in the direction of the cart and took off in the same direction. For the moment, Quentin wasn't the focus of its anger.

They were still many hours away from land. If that hot-tempered, bloodthirsty animal broke into the upper deck, they wouldn't survive *one* more.

CHAPTER 19

The passengers must have seen the desperation on Quentin's face. The ones standing in the aisle slid out of the way as he sliced through them until he came to a man sitting on the floor facing the front.

"Excuse me." Quentin's directive was rather rough, but there was no time to exchange pleasantries.

As the man looked up, a tentacle punched up through the floor and wrapped around his neck. Screams lit up the upper deck cabin. Quentin leaped over the man's shoulder and pried at the cold, spongy flesh with his fingers, not knowing if he was risking his own life, but the young man turned blue. Quentin put the soles of his size 12s to work on the part of the appendage that was writhing on the floor, stomp after stomp. Finally, the man drank in a gulp of air as the grip loosened a bit, not enough to free him but hopefully enough for him to inflate his tanks. The tentacle tightened again.

Hercules broke through the passengers clustered behind the victim and didn't bother to try to pry him loose. He grabbed the tentacle where it was coming out of the floor and gave it a yank powerful enough to pull an oak tree up by the root.

Something slammed hard against the floor under Quentin's feet. That brought a quick smile to his face. As the tentacle slithered back down the hole, the pink rushed back into the man's face.

"Quick!" Quentin yelled to Sierra, who was trying to see past the passengers standing in the aisle. She had been cut off by a couple of wide bodies. "Get me some forks and anything else you have with pointy tips or sharp edges. And a trash bag to tie them together."

"Pass him this," a man's voice shouted.

"I still have mine too," a woman chimed in.

The passengers passed him forks, knives, pencils, a pair of tweezers, a metal fingernail file, a rattail comb, and what appeared to be a drawstring from someone's waistband. It wasn't a bad assortment for people who had to pass through TSA checkpoints. He bound the items together with the drawstring and plugged the mass into the fist-size hole with the business ends all pointing down.

Quentin took off running up the aisle again. Passengers parted like the Red Sea.

Ever since the creature set foot on the main deck, they had been working against a short clock. With two attempts to break into the upper deck in less than five minutes, it would shock him if they had enough time to kiss their asses goodbye.

———————◆◖———————

The second Eden let him in, the air marshal flew into the cockpit, sweaty and agitated. She could tell something had happened.

"Can we fly any faster?" he asked.

She shook her head. "The aircraft—"

"We're not going to make it. By the time we reach land, that thing will have broken into the upper deck." The words gushed out of his mouth.

She pointed at the top left number on the primary flight display in front of the control yoke. "We're flying at Mach point eight-five. The most efficient cruise speed. If we fly faster, we burn more fuel and have *no* chance of reaching Ascension Island."

"Then we have to think of some way to kill it or incapacitate it."

"The only thing I can come up with, I don't like at all. I don't think you will either, Marshal."

"So much hype. You sure you don't want to try your hand as a used-car salesperson? Go ahead. Hit me with it."

"If we depressurize the cabins, the animal will lose consciousness."

"Or die. If it breathes air, it's probably just as vulnerable as we are if it can't get any. I actually like that idea. A lot. Can you depressurize the main deck without depressurizing the upper deck?"

"I wish I could. It's all or nothing. Of course, that is a treacherous road we don't want to take until we absolutely have to. To depressurize the aircraft, I will have to open up the outflow valve and turn off the PACKs, the air packs. The PACKs also control the temperature, another drawback. And this one's a biggie. For every thousand feet of altitude, the temperature drops about four degrees."

"I'm not quite sure I understand the point."

"It's sixty-five below outside. The reason it's not sixty-five below in here is because pressurized air heats up. But that's what it will get to if those PACKs stay off long enough."

"So what we have is no real choice at all. Hobson's choice. Death versus death."

"If I have to choose between the creature killing the passengers or freezing them to death, I'll turn the PACKs back on. They'll have at least some chance of surviving. I may have to turn them back on for a few minutes anyway when the instrument panels frost over. Marshal, I'm going to shoot straight with you. Depressurizing the cabins comes with another grave risk."

"I get the feeling I don't want to hear this."

"The upper deck cabin was configured for no more than sixty-nine passengers. Not the ninety-two that are now crammed into it. So it has only sixty-nine oxygen masks. Plus the ones in the lavatories and the galley."

"So that's what? About eighteen? Eighteen people would die?"

Just the thought of it ate away at her soul and made her feel like a heartless psychopath. She certainly wouldn't be the one who would play God and choose which ones would live and which ones would die a horrible death. Tears blurred her vision. "Without oxygen masks, they wouldn't stand a chance."

———◦◦◦———

"Once the cabin is depressurized, it's going to get extremely cold." Sierra walked the upper deck aisle repeating the same announcement. "If you have any coats or extra clothing in your carry-ons, please put them on now."

"I have a light sweater," Amarant said. "Do you think that's enough?"

"If that is all you have, I will give you some blankets." If she had to alarm the passengers to protect them, so be it. They needed to understand that they would soon think they were standing on a sheet of ice in Antarctica. "I'm not talking 'sweater' cold. I'm talking 'put on everything in your suitcase' cold, and even put your feet inside the suitcase if you can."

Dr. Speck took off his jacket and wrapped it around Amarant.

Sierra drove home the dire consequences of disobeying the guidelines. "Once you put on your oxygen masks, don't take them off. Hypoxia can render you so mentally impaired, you could literally forget how to lift your arms to put them back on."

Gasps broadcasted throughout the cabin. In this case, that was good. They understood how serious the situation was.

"Don't worry," TR bellowed. "We'll all be frozen to death long before then."

It's coming!

The monster's head came around the corner at the other end of the aisle. Rona smooshed the curtains together, rushed back under the first row, and lay flat on her tummy. Quiet as Mona.

The monster's feet slammed down in the aisle nearby. They looked bigger than they were before. *Oh shoot!* Her shoes were sticking out. Something Bad was going to grab her by the legs like it did Mona. A giant mouth and nose came down and made sniffing sounds at her feet. She didn't move. *Go away!*

The stinky monster's head went back up, and its feet walked toward the back. When she couldn't smell it anymore, she turned back toward the curtains in the front and crawled as fast as she could. Her stupid shoelace was untied again and was dragging behind her.

Something Bad was back there messing stuff up, and she could finally crawl under the curtain up ahead to get to the front of the airplane where the other people went. She couldn't wait to see her mommy again. Her mommy would tie her shoe. Once she was safe from the monster, she could stop crawling like a little baby, and she wouldn't have to look at ugly feet anymore.

A voice on the speaker was saying stuff about the plane. Rona didn't understand it. It was that nice lady flylot who had let Rona sit in the flylot seat. She tried to remember her name. Miss Eden.

The flylot said, "I am about to depressurize the plane now. Do not be frightened."

But I'm already frightened.

"The oxygen masks will drop from the overhead compartment. You must put them on or you will die."

Rona's mouth flew open, and she whimpered. "Like Josh."

She hurried under the curtains into a whole other part of the airplane. "No! Mommy!" She looked around, and tears splashed on the back of her hand. The new cabin was as big as the old one.

When that nice lady had taken her to see the cockpit, Rona had passed by a whole bunch of people. There was no one now. No one but her.

———————— ⚙ ————————

Hercules's eyes were taking in the last sights they would ever see before being deprived of oxygen and darkening forever. As he sidestepped toward the back of the cabin, his eyes flitted from one face to another without taking up residence, each countenance a summation of grief, pity, and sadness he couldn't bear, each a confirmation that in minutes his would be one of eighteen dead bodies lying in the galley and spilling into the aisle at the rear of the cabin.

He never thought of his eleemosynary work or donations as a means to amass goodie points, but it seemed unjust to die on the way to perform at a MAMA charity concert to raise money to save animals from neglect and abuse.

The oxygen masks dropped from the overhead compartment above the passengers who occupied seats. None would be dropping for him or the other ill-fated men who had volunteered to sacrifice themselves for the sake of the others. A rush of anxiety came over him. The oxygen masks deploying signaled the official start of the countdown, the second from the last step before the air would become too thin to provide enough oxygen to sustain life.

The oxygen masks—that was where his eyes landed, watching the difference between life and death sway back and forth.

He paused while the young man blocking the aisle kissed a woman that Hercules assumed was his wife. What did he have to rush off to? An airborne version of the gas chamber? He waited silently and let the young couple have their last moment together.

"I love you," the woman cried, clutching the man's hand. When their hands slipped apart, she burst into tears. Hercules's heart twisted into a pretzel knot. He would never forget the moment his wife's hand slipped from his forever, never to be held again in this lifetime.

The young man plodded down the aisle. As Hercules followed, one of the oxygen masks brushed his left arm. Tantalizing. He remembered where the word had come from. He and Tantalus now shared a certain kinship. Zeus's son Tantalus had made the grave mistake of trying to deceive the gods and was damned to dwell in the underworld beneath a tree with fruit at his fingertips while standing in a pool of refreshing water. Whenever he reached for the fruit, the wind would blow the branches out of reach. Whenever he stooped to quench his thirst, the water would recede. With food at his fingertips and water at his feet, Tantalus was condemned to starve and thirst for all eternity. For Hercules, his tantalizing fruit was the oxygen masks.

He had nightmares about dancing at the bottom end of a bolt of lightning that was determined to finish what another one started, not about dying of apoxia.

The mental impairment that the flight attendant warned them of would be only one of the symptoms of hypoxia. In the end, although none of them would know anything about it at that point, their skin would turn a cyanotic blue and their blood pressure would tumble, followed by the worst symptom known to mankind—death.

The pilot's voice came over the PA. "Please put on your

oxygen masks at this time. As soon as the flight attendant has assured me that you have done so, I will start the depressurization procedures."

The passengers' hands reached up for the oxygen masks in quick succession.

That was it. The final step.

Hercules walked into the galley. Hushed sounds of despair greeted him. Some of the men leaned against the counter while others sat on the floor with their backs against the food carts. The man sitting in the right corner in front of him had his elbows resting on his bent knees and his head down, sobbing quietly. Another was on his knees praying with his hands pressed together, tears streaming down a face that was turned up toward the arched ceiling.

Hercules found a vacant spot barely inside the entrance, sat down on the floor, leaned his head back against the wall, and closed his eyes.

Tears stung Eden's eyes. "It's time."

The marshal unbuckled his harness and leaped out of the first officer's seat. "I can't. If anyone should sacrifice themselves, it should be me. I'm going to switch places with one of them." He turned toward the cockpit door.

"No, Marshal. I need you. The other passengers need you."

"Hercules can protect you just as well as I can."

"I'm sure he would do all he could, but you're trained to protect us. He's not."

"I'm sorry. I can't just sit here while they die. That's not who I am."

"I'm going to need you when … Just trust me. I'm going to need you."

"When what?"

"Just trust me."

He sat back down. "It would be a lot easier to do that if you leveled with me."

They donned their oxygen masks in silence, then she leered up at the overhead panel. The three identical white PACK control selectors were set in their "NORM" positions. She didn't give a flip about the "A" and "B" selections to the right of each "NORM," but the three to the left that read "OFF" would turn her into a mass murderer.

You can not *go through with this.*

A hand that functioned as if it belonged to someone else reached for the PACK 1 selector on the left. She turned the switch to "OFF," and a soft click reverberated through her fingers. Skipping over the PACK 2 switch in the middle, she turned the PACK 3 switch off. The click seemed to reverberate harder than the first one.

No matter how much she played up the positive or played down the negative, innocent people were about to die at her hand. She was no better than a Charles Manson or a Timothy McVeigh. This would be one secret the FAA *would* find out about, one that didn't depend on her willingness to self-disclose. *The proof, ladies and gentlemen of the jury, Exhibit A: eighteen dead bodies. Not an accident. A willful act. A turn of not one, not two, but three switches.*

Even if she could somehow escape a prison cell, the victims would haunt her the rest of her life. She could barely live with herself as it was.

Her fingers edged toward the PACK 2 switch in the middle. The execution switch. She gazed up at it as a rainstorm ran down her face and dripped off her jawbone. She wiped the tears away, knowing she could neither keep up with the deluge nor stop it.

Turn the switch and stop procrastinating. Sacrifice a few to save many. She could bomb the shit out of an entire fleet of enemy ships. Surely, she could do this. No. These weren't enemy combatants. They were innocent people who had been entrusted to her care. She jerked her hand away. The air marshal's face was wholly focused up at the sole switch in the "NORM" position, and she could see in his eyes that he was listening to the same sorrowful epicedium that she was.

She forced her hand back to the last switch, closed her eyes, and turned it to the left. Its click reverberated like a ringing church bell, her own private death knell.

Quentin forced his eyes away from the three switches but couldn't turn them to Eden. She might misread the agony that had to be visible in them as resentment or anger. Instead, he stared blankly through the windshield at the darkness and flashes of lightning engulfing the aircraft. He wondered how long the passengers in the galley who didn't have masks would have to live and whether the cabin pressure would drop instantly or trickle away.

Abruptly, Eden snapped open the buckle of her shoulder harness and yanked off her oxygen mask.

"No!" he screamed through his own mask. "What are you doing? You're going to die! You're the last pilot we have!"

She shot out of her seat and rushed to the back of the cockpit. *Wait!* She wasn't gasping for breath. His head whipped back to the overhead panel, and he smiled inside and out.

All three switches were back in their "NORM" positions.

He yanked off his mask and sprang out of his seat. She had already reached the cockpit door, but he could cover ground with a quickness. By the time her hand hit the doorknob, he was already clutching her around her waist. She opened the door. He pushed it shut.

He turned her around. Face to face. So close. "Wh-what are you doing?"

155

"Let me go."

"I know you have the final word. I'm just trying to protect you."

"No! I will not kill any of them. That's not an option. That's not who I am either. It is my sacred *duty* to get them back to their families safely, and it will be my honor to perform that duty. When my feet hit the ground, every one of their feet will hit the ground too. Period. Not one of them is going to die by my hand. I. Can. Not. Do it."

"I know you can't."

"I'm sorry. I don't care what anyone says. I—"

"Look at me, please," he interrupted. "I know."

Eden looked stunned, as if she had expected him to try to convince her to go through with it. And there was no doubt she had a passionate argument ready, but she wouldn't get one from him.

"Where were you planning to go?" he asked.

"I've figured out a way to kill that thing without killing any of the passengers."

"Whatever it is, you can't be the one to do it."

"The ones without oxygen masks can use portable oxygen bottles."

"How many do we have?"

"Twenty. I'm wasting time. I have to go." She opened the door again.

He pushed it shut with one hand, then realized the other was still holding her around her tiny waist. Reluctantly, he let go. "Eden, please. A minute ago, you were telling me how important I am to the passengers. You are far more important to them than I am. If something happens to you, those oxygen bottles will be useless. We'd have plenty of oxygen, sure … while we're plunging to our deaths. I'll go."

"You don't even know where they are."

He tapped one of his ears. "These work."

"No. I ..." She sighed. "You're right. I'm sorry. Most of them are under the outboard seats, just forward of each of the ten doors," she explained as if he were both hard of hearing and slow of wits. "We need every one of those oxygen bottles for this to work. But this plan has a terrible drawback."

"I get the feeling I really don't want to hear this."

"You don't, I'm afraid. Count."

Reality hit him like a bucket of ice water had splashed in his face and then had the bucket crown him a good one too. As carefully as she had explained it, he should have realized it, not that it would have changed his mind. "Ten doors. There are only two up here in the upper deck."

"Right. The aircraft has twelve passenger doors total if you include the two at the back of the main cabin. I left them out because on the Combi, there aren't any oxygen bottles there, and if there were, they would be covered up by freight."

He slowly nudged her away from the door and switched places with her, making that one less item to worry about. He still didn't trust her not to make a play for the door.

"Marshal, this is important."

"I assure you. I'm listening like my life depended on it."

"Of the twenty oxygen bottles, eighteen are down on the main deck."

He couldn't stay out of trouble for shit.

Quentin panned the upper deck cabin for a nod or a raised hand. Eighteen oxygen bottles were too much for one person to wrangle. His request for volunteers received a few mumbles and eyes that looked in every direction except in his. One trip back down to the main deck to face the animal was terrifying enough, but the idea of having to make multiple trips alone ... He got the shakes.

If someone had told him after the animal's first attack he would be bonkers enough to take his Black ass back downstairs into its lair, his only question would have been whether they had a prescription for the powerful drugs they had obviously taken.

He advanced down the aisle to the galley, where he might have better luck since they were probably jumping up and down about having their death sentences commuted.

The ones who could cover the most ground in the least amount of time would make the best recruits. Downstairs was a no-slowpoke zone. He had already witnessed the rock star's speed and agility, ace qualities if they had another close encounter with the animal. What he coveted most was the rock star's bravery. Anyone who didn't have all those qualities stood no chance against the animal.

The galley entrance was as far as he could go without stepping over sprawled legs and feet. Hercules stood up and cleared a path.

One man sprang up off his knees and rushed over. "I knew God would answer our prayers. I never lost faith."

For the second time, Quentin gave his pitch for—and warnings about—the mission. The first to volunteer was the one he wanted most: Hercules.

"I ran fourth leg on the relay team back in college," a man with brown hair said, who looked young enough to still be in college. "I'm Matt. I might not be quite as fast as I used to be, but I'm probably the fastest thing on two feet on this plane. My brother, Tyler, ain't no funeral procession either." He cast a thumb at the blond man standing next to him.

Quentin sized up their athletic build and knew just which part of the aircraft he would assign to the sprinters. Once he had the members of his team, the other men piled out of the galley and went back into the cabin.

Quentin laid a diagram of the aircraft on the countertop. He started by explaining the general layout of the main deck but spent most of his time focusing on the locations of the oxygen bottles as he and his crew of seven prepared to invade the warzone.

⚓

"Doc, you can't let them go back down there," Daniel whispered in front of the starboard exit door. "You have to stop them."

"How am I supposed to do that? No matter what I say, they're still going to try to get those oxygen bottles. Just keep your beak shut. When we come out the other side of all this, you'll have enough money to buy someone else's conscience if yours still bothers you."

"I don't care. I'll trade being a dead ass for being a broke ass any day of the week."

"If you're broke, how are you going to afford Dr. Minkowsky?"

If anyone could raise Rachel out of that wretched wheelchair, he would gladly saw off his own legs to pay for it. He couldn't argue the fact that she shouldn't have been talking on the phone and driving, but no one could do anything about that now. Oggie's friend in Germany had a high rate of success—and had a high fee to match—using what the medical field in the United States still considered experimental treatment. "Come on, Doc. You could at least try to help them."

"Nobody can help them." The doc lowered his voice and added, "The megateratoid has more tricks up its sleeve than an eight-armed magician."

Daniel stared blankly out of the window at the lightning. There had to be some way to help them. The storm was getting more intense, like his pangs of guilt. "We should have volunteered to go down there."

"And risk our lives for nothing like they're doing?"

"What do you mean, for nothing?"

"That pilot will never pull the plug. If she could, she would have done it already."

"I think she will. If the mega-T threatens to break into the upper deck with us, she'll depressurize this plane in a heartbeat. Whether she will or won't doesn't matter. We may not know much, but we know more about the megateratoid than anyone else here."

"It doesn't matter what we know. The mega-T is loose down there, and you can bet your lass's ass it's not the same animal it was the last time we saw it."

CHAPTER 20

"Matt and Tyler, you two get the four oxygen bottles in first class in front of the first two doors," Quentin said, pointing first at two cylinder shapes in front of the starboard door on the diagram of the 747, then to two more on the portside. "Your four oxygen bottles are at the front of the main deck cabin. You'll find them under the seats next to the walls." His finger slid to four more cylinders, two in front of each door near the stairs. "Sebastian and Hans, you two get the four at the second set of doors. Kinley and Gaston, get the four at the third pair. Hercules, you and I will have to lug the six from here." Quentin tapped the rearmost pair of doors in the passenger cabin. "Each of the other locations has two oxygen bottles. Ours has three."

Hercules pointed at the fifth pair of doors at the tail of the plane. Each had two cylinder shapes in front of them. "What about these?"

"The last two doors are in the freight section. The Combi cargoes freight on the main deck with the passengers. From the fourth pair of doors on back is all freight. The creature can't get back there." Quentin looked up from the diagram to gauge the reaction of the men to what he was about to say. "Which means at least one of us, if not all of us, will definitely have to face the creature. It has to be in one of our areas."

If any member of the Tough Luck Chucks chickened out, he would have to make more than one trip. They all stood firm. "I have to warn you. The mission could get even more complicated. If one of us gets cornered by the creature, we have to be prepared for this to turn into a rescue mission."

Quentin stepped to the lip of the landing and listened for telling sounds. Only a woman's hushed whimpers behind them interrupted the silence. "You guys ready?"

Hercules stepped into position behind him. "Well, my feet are moving."

"All right then. Let's go." Quentin took a deep breath and stepped down onto the first step, followed closely by his newfound seven-foot shadow.

The colossal, green death was too big to attack them from out of nowhere, but its tentacles weren't. A blinding-fast crack through the air, and it would be game over.

At the bottom, Quentin stepped into the exit row that ran between the stairs and the closet in front of him. The main deck looked like it had taken a direct hit from a Category 5 hurricane. Holes and dents pocked the walls. Drapes hung shredded from top to bottom like the hanging strips at a car wash. Possessions that used to be stowed in bins were trashed and strewn around. The only sound, the incessant monotone drone of the engines. Thank God.

A piece of the ceiling broke free and crashed to the floor in the portside aisle to the left of the stairs. Quentin jumped.

"That scared a year off my life," he whispered, easing his foot between shards of a broken coffee cup and a teaspoon without making a sound. "Be careful of the broken glass." Cups, napkins, silverware, and spilled coffee littered the floor from the bottom of the stairs to a cart that lay at the mouth of the aisle and was beaten to shit.

Another carefully placed step brought him clear of the litter and into the portside aisle, where he had a clear view toward the nose of the 747. There was no sign of the creature in business class. Matt and Tyler cleared the stairs last, side-stepped the cart, and tore ass up the aisle toward the nose.

Quentin could only shake his head. Young jackrabbits. Track stars, for damn sure. If any of the men had it easy, it was Sebastian and Hans. Their oxygen bottles were waiting for them as soon as they stepped off the stairs. Hans had already collected his portside bounty and was on his way back to the stairs. Lucky man. Quentin turned down the aisle toward the tail with Hercules trailing him.

Hercules pointed through the curtains of the galley to their left. "Look!" His voice sounded frazzled.

"What? I don't see anything."

"No, no! All the way over there!" The rock star pointed emphatically. "Not *this* galley. The one across the other aisle. The one against the starboard wall. Look under the curtains."

Quentin looked through the open blue curtains of one galley all the way through to the closed curtains of a second one. "What the—!"

A pair of pink leather sandals stuck out from beneath the closed curtains.

The two men crossed through the galley under the stairs. When they reached the one against the starboard wall, Quentin opened the curtains.

"My goodness," Hercules said.

Mariana's body lay on the floor with blood-red orbs giving Quentin the dead eye. As far as he could tell, her clothes didn't have a drop of blood on them, but purple spots speckled her face, limbs, and feet.

"This doesn't make sense," Quentin said.

"Why doesn't it?"

163

"She wasn't here when I first went up the stairs. She must have died later. But if Sierra is right, Ray and at least one of the pilots, if not all three, were already dead before I went up the stairs. At best, she was the third to die, but she was the first to touch the venom. If she was the first to touch it, why wasn't she the first to die?"

"That *is* a bit of a head-scratcher."

"Some of the venom may still be on her. It's best we don't touch her."

They crossed back through the galley to the portside aisle and turned toward the tail. As Quentin eased open the curtains and ventured a step into forward coach, his right shoe came down in something slushy. It wasn't something that *hadn't* been there before, like Mariana's body. It was something that *had* been there before but was now missing.

Blood soaked the carpet around his foot. He stepped out of the puddle and scrubbed his foot clean on an unsullied spot in the carpet. "There was a severed head here before," he whispered to Hercules.

He skirted the puddle, and they headed for the back of the passenger section where the creature first appeared.

CHAPTER 21

It's coming. Rona got even more scared. Footsteps were coming from the front of the airplane. They were different than before. Quieter. And walking really, really slow. *Something Bad is trying to sneak up on me.* She moved closer to the wall. The monster wouldn't see her under the seat.

The footsteps walked up to her row and stopped. She scootched back some more and didn't dare look. If she peeped from under the seat, the monster would see her. She covered her mouth and was so scared she forgot to breathe. When the footsteps went on down the aisle toward the back, she took a deep breath. Then she heard more footsteps but couldn't tell if they were coming toward her or going away. It sounded like both. The feet could be going away, and the arm thingies could be coming to get her like one of them did Mona.

It was a trick.

No. Now she heard whispers.

———◦◦◦———

Quentin reached the last curtain before the rearmost passenger cabin. His heart was a firing squad in his chest. Up to that point, the fuselage had shown no signs of movement. With the kind of luck Flight 1219 had been cursed with so far, he wouldn't have been surprised to see the beast standing right next to some of the portable oxygen bottles when it did appear. He silently eased the curtain open.

A loud clang came from behind him.

The clamor scared the curtain out of his hand and yet another year off his life. If the creature had been asleep, it damn sure wasn't now. Kinley and Gaston stood over an oxygen bottle that had no business rolling around in the middle of the aisle. Which one had dropped it, he didn't know. Both of them were staring at him with goofy "forgive me for I have sinned" grins. If they made only twice as much noise as necessary, it would be a vast improvement. As if he and Hercules didn't have enough to deal with. They had farther to go than all of the volunteers and had the toughest assignment too.

He opened the curtain and stepped into a deserted wasteland. A new revelation stopped him cold. It didn't look like the same cabin where he had come close to having the life squeezed out of him by the tentacle, even though he had a clear view all the way to the partition beyond the galley where the freight section started and close to where he thought Eden had died. He could see just as clearly all the way over to the starboard wall on his left. The cabin was definitely different. Baffling.

From the look on Hercules's face, the rock star was as bewildered as he was. No doubt, it was the first time Hercules had seen the cabin. He couldn't possibly comprehend the true magnitude of what they were viewing.

A faint, squishy sound registered only at the fringes of his awareness. Only when he looked down did he realize that he had moved and was now standing in a huge puddle of red blood. Hercules probably didn't know how quickly their situation would deteriorate if they looked down and saw that much green blood. All around them was blood. Splatters of it.

Pools of it. On the ceiling. The floor. The seats. The overhead compartments.

"No bodies," Quentin whispered. "They were scattered everywhere in here when I left."

Hercules looked over the top of Quentin's head like he wasn't even there. "What do you think happened to them?"

"Hell if I know. A pretty gruesome possibility popped into my mind, though."

"I bet it's the same one that popped into mine."

"God rest their souls. Every blessed one."

"Mariana's body didn't have a scratch on it. That, compounded with the fact that it's the only body remaining, is now even more of an enigma." He patted Quentin on the back and cut across the exit row over to the starboard aisle.

Quentin soldiered on toward the back. So far, there were no sounds, but the space up ahead was far from being an open area. The sleeping quarters and the galley behind it both had walls and spanned from one aisle to the other, more than enough room for the giant pain in the ass to hide. All six of their oxygen bottles were near the very end of the passenger section where it met the freight area. Six portable oxygen bottles. Six lives depending on them.

<hr/>

Cloaked worry quickly turned into buck-naked hysteria. Sierra peered down the stairs. By her estimation, all eight of the men should have returned to the upper deck by now, but only Sebastian and Hans had returned. The purser knew the 747 front, back, and center.

She paced back and forth between the landing and the cart lift across from the partition. The men didn't know the layout as well as she did, but the detailed diagram showed them exactly where to find the portable oxygen bottles. Something must have gone wrong.

167

Footsteps! She rushed over to the landing to see who they belonged to.

Kinley and Gaston bounded up the stairs like their tails were on fire.

She ducked out of the way. "Where are the others?"

"Herc and Q were heading into the tail last time we saw them," Gaston answered, panting.

"Did you see that … that thing?"

"No, thank the Lord."

"Then why were you running so fast?"

Kinley gave her an askance glance. "Just scared is all it boils down to."

"I see it as bravery. You can put your oxygen bottles in the galley with the others. Thank you so much, guys." She looked back down the stairs. Four safe, four to go.

An acute somberness came over the souls standing at the top of the stairs. They all stood looking down the steps in silence.

———◆◇◆———

The wait was killing her. Eden had to know what was going on. She picked up the interphone for the third time. This time she made the call. "Sierra, can you give me an update? Please tell me they are all back safe."

"I wish I could. Matt, Tyler, Hercules, and Quentin are still down there."

"I was hoping they would all be back by now."

"Wait. Someone's coming up the stairs now. Let me go take a look."

Please let it be all four of them, Eden prayed.

Sierra's voice came back on the phone. "It was Matt and Tyler. Six safe, two to go."

"Quentin and Hercules are still down there."

The question, Which of the eight men would have to face the creature? was now down to, Which two?

168

Quentin walked facing the rear, dreading each step more than the last. When he reached the door to the flight attendants' crew rest, the creature's stench came to life. It smelled like a dead, bloated whale steeped in skunk juice. How could anything alive smell that dead? He pinched his nose. A lot of good that did. It diverted the fetor into his mouth. His hands grew sweaty. The closer he got to the back, the stronger the stench. Every delusion he had that the creature could be anywhere except the tail vanished.

He stooped to retrieve his oxygen bottles. With any luck, Hercules had already done the same on the other side of the crew rest and was on the way back to the upper deck. There was little chance the creature could attack Hercules without Quentin hearing it through the crepe-paper walls of the crew rest and galley, although they blocked his view of the other aisle.

The oxygen bottles were exactly where Eden said they would be. He would have to pay her a visit and thank her for giving him great instructions, a lame excuse to behold her elegance and beauty. She was a shining beacon, and he had been living in a world of darkness for a long time. He retrieved the oxygen bottles and headed back up the aisle toward the nose.

A scuffling sound arose from somewhere in the other aisle.

Ah, shit. His stomach did a somersault.

Hercules!

Quentin rushed to the galley at the back. A couple of quick steps would take him through the shortcut to the other aisle. He slapped the curtains to one side without slowing down and charged into the galley with his adrenaline pumping. He took one step inside but couldn't take another. Momentum hurled him forward anyway, but there was nothing there.

Where the floor was supposed to be was a two-foot hole. The toes on his right foot teetered on the edge of it while his left foot dangled in the air. His foot had no place to land. Momentum thrust him toward the cargo hold below. Instincts had already kicked in, urging him to flail his arms out to regain balance. That was not an option. The oxygen bottles would fall down into the chasm for sure. Instead, he planted the foot that hung in the air against a food cart on his left and pushed backward. The one teetering on the edge rocked back on its heel, then his left foot touched down behind it.

The food cart slid sideways and tumbled down the hole with a muffled thump. *That's odd.* It should have made a loud clang. He peeked over the edge. The scant light shining down through the gloomy cavity landed on two blue flight attendant uniforms lying motionless on top of a pallet of shrink-wrapped boxes. Judging by her height, the woman on the bottom had to be Candice, although the body no longer had a head. In his detective days, he had seen enough dead bodies to gauge their height with few clues. Lauren lay diagonally on top of her crewmate with her neck draped over the edge of one of the boxes and her blonde head twisted at an angle that would have been impossible without a broken neck.

The question that had plagued him about how the creature had gotten into the passenger section of the plane had finally been answered, to some degree, but the answer led to yet another question, one more mind-boggling than the first. It didn't explain how that big bastard could have come up through such a small cavity. If the size of the hole tripled, it would still be too small.

He skirted around the hole and crossed through the galley into the starboard aisle, where the fetid stench once again engulfed him. He wished he was wearing an oxygen mask already. It smelled like someone had cracked the seal on a can of assholes in there. A bitter taste rose up from his stomach

170

into his mouth, a taste he was familiar with that came post-binge drinking and pre- projectile vomiting.

As soon as he stepped through the curtains into the starboard aisle, he realized something was wrong there too. Familiar. Yet bizarre.

A lavatory sat across from the galley's entrance slightly to the left, and the exit door was slightly to the right. Hercules's destination was the row of seats immediately to the left of the lavatory, but Quentin's gaze flew to the right, to the partition beyond the exit door where the cabin dead-ended at the back.

The tableau at the back of both aisles should have been mirror images of each other. He was sure they had been, but that had changed at some point after they had to abandon the main deck. The partitions were no longer even the same color. The one at the back of this aisle was no longer blue. Instead, it had a strange, multicolored mosaic. He had seen more than his share of the macabre but nothing like this. As far as he could tell, none of the wall's blue color was visible anymore. Against the partition was a wall of dead bodies, stockpiled from floor to ceiling like cordwood.

The beast stood in front of them with its tentacles coiled around the horizontal body of a dead man who was wearing gray dress pants and a light pink dress shirt. The creature wedged the body into place where the partition met the ceiling and then slathered the man with spit.

With a long, powerful whoosh, the beast blasted the man from head to toe with its breath. The spit hardened, turned white, and webbed the body into place.

Quentin froze. One of his oxygen bottles slipped out of his sweaty hands and crashed to the floor. As he snatched it up, the creature spun around. His heart sailed up the aisle, and he took off after it.

Crack! One of the tentacles snapped in the air behind him.

171

He tore into the forward coach with his arms wrapped tightly around his oxygen bottles. His sweaty hands had proven they couldn't be trusted. Hercules was hurrying up the aisle in front of him but not fast enough. Not fast enough for his liking and damn sure not fast enough to stay ahead of the creature now barreling up the aisle in turbo mode behind both of them.

If it caught them, it would be Quentin's ass the creature tasted first.

———◦———

"Go! Go! Go!" a voice bellowed behind Hercules. The voice could only be the air marshal's. Quentin streaked up the aisle, and behind him the dark green creature loped on all four feet.

The term *lusus naturae* popped into Hercules's mind. Running definitely had been the right thing to do when everyone in first class started screaming and yelling out expediencies. The animal had the stride of a bear.

"Run!" Quentin yelled.

As Hercules charged toward the front, an oxygen bottle slipped out of his arms and landed under the aisle seat to his left. He reached for it, and his hand tangled in the world's strongest and thickest spider web. As he freed his fingers, his right foot kicked the oxygen bottle across the center section all the way over to the seat sitting next to the other aisle. It clanked against its leg and came to rest there with the bottom of it sticking out from under the seat.

"Leave it!" Quentin urged. "Go! Go!"

———◦———

Voices! Rona was sure of it. *People* voices! She looked under the seat to the other side of the airplane where the voices were coming from. A pair of big feet were running up the aisle. Not Something Bad feet. *People* feet. Then another pair of people feet. *Yes!*

She jumped up between the seats. They had finally come
172

to save her. Then Something Bad ran up the aisle too. *Oh shoot!* She ducked back under the seat, and the people feet weren't there anymore. *Everybody's gone.* Tears ran down her cheeks. *They left me all by myself again.*

───────◆───────

That big son of a gun could move. They both could.

Quentin was running as fast as he could up the aisle, but Hercules was pulling away. A loud roar blasted his eardrums from a position closer than expected. He didn't have to look back to know that the green hulk was gaining ground.

He barreled through forward coach with the beast's pounding footsteps getting closer. Up ahead, Hercules ran through the drapes at the other end of the aisle without bothering to open them while the other giant grunted and snorted at Quentin's back.

Another loud crack of the creature's whip. This time, it was right next to Quentin's left ear.

He didn't have a faster gear. He would never make it to the stairs before the creature caught him. It was far faster than he was, but he had one advantage. He abandoned the starboard aisle and cut across the row of seats in the center. The beast couldn't fit its big carcass in the narrow space between the rows. He could barely fit himself even though he was sidestepping across the seats to the portside aisle.

What!

The creature was still dead on his ass.

───────◆───────

When Hercules reached the first row of the forward coach cabin, the air marshal wasn't behind him, nor was the green lusus. He started back down the aisle to check on him, then stopped. He had already lost one oxygen bottle. One life. He had to deliver the remaining two first.

He pressed forward up the aisle, crashing blindly through the curtains and zipping by the starboard galley where the dead

173

woman lay. All manner of pernicious detriments to Quentin's wellbeing popped into his head. When he reached the exit row, he hung a sharp left and flung himself up the stairs to the top landing. He stevedored his cargo into Tyler's arms, unable to shake the thought that it might be too late, given that the beast had already transformed the entire coach section into an abattoir.

———————

Two seats hit the overhead compartment inches from Quentin's head, then ricocheted off the seats in front of the row where they once sat, before the creature ripped them out of the floor. A claw yanked up a third seat and launched it toward the back of the cabin; a second claw ripped up another and flung it into the starboard aisle. The creature tore a clear path from one aisle to the other in less time than Quentin took to sidle the same distance. The beast didn't need a wide space: it could make one.

Quentin punched through the closed drapes at the front of forward coach. The colossus banged around behind him but had yet to poke its head through. He raced over to the stairs and jittered to a stop a couple of feet past them. He and his forward momentum were going to have to come to some type of agreement before it got him killed. Once he got back on the right track, he barreled up the stairs just as Hercules charged down them. Quentin was going to get crushed if he had a head-on collision with him.

Hercules bounded back up, skipping two and three steps at a time.

Talk about one giant leap for mankind. Quentin bounded up after him. When he reached the top, where Sierra and the other volunteers were waiting, his lungs were on fire.

Hercules scooped the payload out of Quentin's arms. "That creature must die, and I would be most happy to kill it."

"That's saying a lot, coming from you," Quentin said,

panting. The animal lover was well known for his global crusade to save the lives of animals.

"You two were lucky to get out of there without being added to the animal's menu," Matt said.

"That thing's a walking warzone." Quentin rubbed the back of his neck. "We could only get seventeen oxygen bottles. We're still one short."

"Ah, I'm sorry." Sierra's voice quavered slightly, clearly the foreshadowing of more bad news to come. "Actually three. Two people were in the lavatories when I counted. We are *three* short."

Hercules cast a pair of melancholy eyes down to the floor. "Two." He turned his back to the group and leaned his forehead against the wall. The wide-shouldered man was obviously fighting to keep from falling apart. The others regarded him with puzzled faces, but Quentin knew what he meant. The rock star was taking himself out of the equation, sacrificing himself so someone else could live.

A sudden look of realization swept over Matt. His eyes grew glassy. "One."

His brother Tyler was already smearing tears across his cheeks. "Your count was right the first time."

The passengers rubbernecked, no doubt wondering what was the reason for the upsurge in emotion. Less than a minute later, a finger tapped Quentin on the shoulder. Hercules shook his head and rolled his eyes but didn't say a word. There was no need. His expression alone spoke the person's name out loud.

"What is all this?" TR and his irritating voice pressed in closer. "You're having a secret meeting or something? I demand to know what's going on."

Hearing the senator's voice come out of nowhere was right up there with finding out the hard way that your dog had taken a dump inside your shoe. "Back off!" Quentin had one nerve left, and damn if TR wasn't using it to floss his teeth. "We have enough to deal with."

"If you don't tell me what's going on, I will see to it that you're fired."

Like Quentin gave fuck all about being fired at a time like that.

"Don't you know who I am? I'm Thaddeus Rutherford Dunn. US *senator* from the great state of—"

"Excuse me," Quentin cut in with a sweet voice that could spin cotton candy. "If I may interrupt, Senator. Has anyone called you a son of a bitch today?"

"What?" the pain in the ass asked with a look that appeared equally dumbfounded and offended.

"How about arrogant piece of shit? Because I don't like being the second one to do anything." Quentin's voice was now rough enough to scrub a cement block down to a smooth shine. "How about selfish bastard? Is that one taken?"

"You can't talk to me like—"

"When we get back on the ground, you can kiss my ass or go blind. Whatever tickles your nickel."

TR puffed up his chest, thrust a finger in Quentin's face, probably about to spout more invective.

Quentin cut him off before he could utter word one. "I want to point out that you're standing within point-blank range of my fist right now. *Senator.*"

"We've already had a lifetime supply of you," Hercules added. "You really are just what your initials indicate."

"Who are you supposed to be? You can't talk to me like I'm one of your little groupies. You don't scare me you big … freak of nature. I'm—"

Hercules grabbed him. "I know perfectly well who you are. So did my wife, God rest her soul." He lifted the senator off the floor, and now the two of them were eye to eye. "You're a wretch who makes backdoor deals to pass legislation to keep pharmaceutical companies in business that do little more than batten on the terminally ill. Here's something *you* should know. I really hate to harm dumb animals, but I'd make an exception with you." He planted the senator back down on the floor unharmed.

What a shame.

TR made a big show of straightening his clothes and brushing off dirt that didn't exist while shooting Hercules a scalding look. "Keep Paul Bunyan away from me."

Some of the steam that Quentin had built up slowly seeped out. "If you can fit in his pocket, you should have enough sense to keep yourself away from him. To piss off a guy that big, you'd have to be *felony* stupid. Maybe you should—"

Behind TR, Dr. Speck launched a finger in Daniel's face. From the look of it, he was spouting his own acid-coated words.

Daniel withered. He clearly wasn't the alpha male there.

"Kinley, come with me," Quentin said for no other reason than Kinley happened to be standing closest to him. They walked up the aisle to the exit row, where Dr. Speck stood with his back to them.

"I won't let you," Dr. Speck snapped.

"You won't let him do what?" Quentin asked.

Dr. Speck whirled around, his eyes flaring like two high-beam headlights. "We were having a business discussion. A little on the private side, if you know what I mean."

"Dr. Speck, you and Kinley are going to occupy the lavatories."

"But Daniel and I are together."

Yep. And that's the problem. Quentin read Dr. Speck as the kind of man who would cut a hard line. Daniel, on the other hand, seemed easier to crack if he could separate them. "It doesn't matter, Dr. Speck." Quentin kept his voice flat and hopefully disarming. "You will be in one lavatory, Kinley in the other."

Dr. Speck picked up his briefcase and slogged forward.

Sierra rushed up the aisle and caught up with him. "I need to stow your briefcase in the overhead compartment." She reached for it, and he jerked it away. "For safety. I'm afraid I'm going to have to insist."

"I'm a diabetic. My insulin kit's in here."

Shit! Quentin had an urge to wrestle it away from him anyway.

Dr. Speck cast a stern look back over his shoulder at Daniel and then walked on toward the front of the aircraft. Near the end of the aisle, he went into the first lavatory on the right, and Kinley went into the one next to it just shy of the cockpit door.

"That guy." Quentin gritted his teeth. "He saw it coming. Probably prepared for it. You had an excellent plan, Sierra. The idea of separating him from his briefcase didn't cross my mind at the time."

"Sorry it didn't work. I saw you eyeing it down on the main deck when I tried to stow it."

"I don't think he's any more diabetic than a stick of wood."

"Let me brighten your night with more bad news."

"I really wish you wouldn't."

"One of the oxygen bottles is empty."

Dr. Speck closed the lid on the silver toilet and sat down. The shithouse was smaller than a flea's asshole. He should have claimed he was claustrophobic too.

A thump arose from somewhere below him. He searched both sides of the stool but saw nothing except a wad of toilet paper some lazydinkus had chucked on the floor. Another thump startled him. A tearing sound quickly followed. He looked around, wondering if the air marshal was playing tricks on him—either the air marshal or the skirt. He stood up and flipped the toilet lid open. When he looked down into the bowl, something started to materialize. The more blue water that seeped out, the clearer the object became. It could have been a severed, black thumb.

Gradually, the muckadoo revealed its true color—green.

When the water level dropped below the top of it, it gave a tiny quiver.

"Shit fire over a barrel of gasoline!" He slammed the lid shut and reached for the door latch, but his fingers came up short. A tentacle stabbed up from the toilet bowl and knocked out his front teeth. Dr. Speck had known the mega-T would come for him sooner or later. The appendage slammed him against the wall and wrapped around his neck, choking him. As his knees slowly buckled, his fingers pulled and clawed at hide as tough as baked leather.

Another tentacle splashed out of the water. When it went back in, it took his head in with it. The back of his head slammed against the top of his shoulders while the tentacle that was clamped around his neck steadily pulled it down. At any second, his neck was going to snap. A wet, warm sensation emerged between his legs, accompanied by excruciating pain in his head, his face, and his neck.

Someone knocked on the door three times.

Help! he yelled only in his mind. He didn't have enough air in his lungs to speak.

Crack! Crunch! Crack!

They were the sounds of his own bones breaking and shattering.

"Hey. Are you all right in there?" Quentin didn't get a response. He pounded on the lavatory door again. Pangs of guilt radiated through him. The man must have been a diabetic after all.

That would explain the bumping around. He heard something hit the floor. And then dead silence. Dr. Speck could be lying unconscious in a diabetic coma, and it was all Quentin's fault. Not just unconscious. The man could be dead.

"Dr. Speck?"

The door latch! It was in the "Vacant" position. Quentin eased the door open. Lying on the floor was Dr. Speck, feet splayed out, head facedown and draped across the toilet. Blood cascaded from his face and pattered onto the blood-soddened floor beneath him. Dr. Speck hadn't died of diabetes, but that didn't make Quentin feel any less guilty. When he turned him over, he landed faceup with his shoulders straddling the threshold and his head sprawled in the hallway.

The blood wasn't gushing out of the doctor's face; he no longer had one.

No one else could see the body, especially in that horrifying state. Quentin wrestled him back into the lavatory and propped him up in a sitting position against the wall. As soon as he closed the door, Dr. Speck's body thudded against it.

Quentin banged on the other lavatory door. "Kinley!"

Kinley opened it, his face already screwed into a frown. "What was all that noise?"

"Get out of there. Now! You're in danger."

<hr>

"It was the m-meg ... ah ... the creature, wasn't it?" Daniel stammered, zipping and unzipping his jacket with blurring speed.

Quentin didn't know how much more of that *zip, zip, zip* shit he could stomach before he shot off one of Daniel's hands. The detective part of him saw something different in Daniel's eyes this time. Worry, sure. But he also seemed lost and dejected. Broken. "Are you guessing, or did you already know that?"

Zip, zip, zip. Zip, zip, zip.

180

Quentin was going to kill him. He wondered if Daniel realized how telling that nervous little habit of his was.

"Non sum qualis eram," Daniel finally said.

"What does that mean?" Kito asked. "I don't speak … whatever the hell that was."

"It's Latin," Hercules replied instead of Daniel. "It's an often-quoted phrase. It means 'I am not what I once was.' I've heard it used by people who were once at a better place in life but have fallen as well as by people who were once at a low place but have risen."

Daniel let go of the zipper. "In my case, both." There was something new in his eyes—remorse. "The creature was created by a man named Wilhelm Ogladorff, one of my graduate school professors and a surgeon who I wouldn't let cut my toenails."

Quentin raised his eyebrows. "That sounds a little extreme."

"A man who grew a third foot would find it difficult to buy shoes. That would be only one of innumerable possible body parts you might grow after letting Oggie have access to your body. He's like a modern-day Dr. Frankenstein. He's the real genius behind it all. Dr. Speck's glory-grabbing ass latched onto Oggie somewhere in the later stages of the research and brought his connections to the Granthom Research Group with him. That organization gave the project a big boost in funding and equipment. I came on later. The GRG is the one that arranged for a shipping company to transport the mega-T."

Kito scrunched up his face. "The what?"

"Oggie called it a megateratoid because it looks like a giant teratoid, a grotesquely deformed monster. The mega-T was made up of recombinant DNA from different creatures. Creatures built for survival. Adaptable to different environments. And smart."

Quentin shook his head. "Playing God. That's what you all were doing."

Daniel sighed. "You're right. During my last year of graduate school, I wrote a paper titled 'Mitochondrial DNA: The Eve Hypothesis.' It got published. It was lauded in the academic and science communities. If it had been an album, it would have gone double platinum. I was asked to give speeches all over the country. Everyone was throwing bank accounts at me. 'Come work here.' 'Come help us develop this.' 'We're on the edge of discovering that.' Howbeit, I ..." Pride gave way to grief again. "I started taking cocaine to put a little pep in my step. Got hooked. Got caught with it. Twice. Got some time in the cooker."

"Been there, done that," Kito chimed in.

Daniel cleared his throat. "I got clean, but I had fallen from grace. All I wanted was to resuscitate my career, not play God. No one would give me a chance except Speck and Oggie. I went from having people beating down my door to having doors slammed in my face. By the time I realized what they were doing, I couldn't quit. My sister needs every penny I can make."

"I don't feel like extending any olive branches right now," Quentin said. "You had a number of opportunities to save those peoples' lives. You even lied to me about it."

"I'm sorry. I should have told you the truth. Bad decisions are like viruses. They're contagious. One leads to another and another."

"Yeah, excuses are too. I've seen a lot from behind this badge ... had the worst imaginable nightmares about what could happen. Not one comes close to this. The FAA will have to rewrite the book after the mess you helped create."

Daniel started playing with his zipper again. "I'm afraid there is more you need to know about the mega-T." He gave Quentin a long, hard stare like he was studying him and then looked down at his gun.

Ah shit. This can't be good. If he's worried about me shooting him, it's going to be hella bad.

Daniel's eyes trailed a slow path from the gun back up to his face. "When it feeds, it gets bigger. That's why we didn't feed it. It had to fit in the cage we constructed."

Quentin all but had steam coming out of his nostrils. "So you all starved it, then loaded it on a plane with an ample food supply. That's just brilliant. If we couldn't handle it before, how are we supposed to handle it now?"

TR scoffed. "Aren't you going to handcuff him? Do your job for once."

"Fuck the handcuffs," Kito countered. "How many bullets you got left in that gun?"

⎯⎯⎯⎯⎯⎯⎯⎯⎯⎯

"Everything is going according to plan. Thank you all for cooperating. I'm about to depressurize the aircraft now."

That's the flylot's voice again. Rona crawled under another seat. *But I don't know what "depress your eyes" means.* She pulled her left knee forward and realized it was stuck. Her shoelace was caught on the thing at the bottom of the seat. She jerked her knee up, but it didn't work.

"I remind you this is a controlled process." The flylot had a nice voice like her mommy.

Rona finally yanked her shoelace free. The nice flylot kept talking about stuff that she didn't understand. Stuff about hypoxia, whatever that was, and oxygen debabation, or something like that. One of them probably had a fever because Miss Eden started talking about their temperature. It sounded like she was talking to someone named Faren Height, anyway.

I just want to find my mommy.

She peeked under the seat. *Yes!* She had made it halfway to the curtain in front of her, and there wasn't anything big enough to block her way. Then there *was* something big enough.

183

Two big, ugly feet were coming down the aisle. Coming right for her. She froze and watched every step the monster took. One of its toes hit something small and flat in the aisle and kicked it under a seat up ahead. It was too small to block her way. The stinky thing walked by and went on to the back. She didn't move. She just used her ears and nose. Its feet scrubbed against the floor, and it was getting farther and farther away.

Miss Eden said, "Before I do that, the oxygen masks will drop from the overhead compartment. You must put the masks on, or you will suffer hypoxia."

There was that stupid word again. Maybe the flylot would say what it meant.

"You will not be able to get enough oxygen, and in only a few minutes, you could die."

Rona's mouth flew open. No! She knew what "you could die" meant, and she didn't want to sleep forever and ever.

CHAPTER 22

Quentin slapped a hand down on the back of the first officer's seat. What he wouldn't give for it to be Daniel's face. "Five more men are going to die because of those two self-centered assholes."

"Let me get this straight." Eden counted on her fingers. "First, Hercules dropped one of the oxygen bottles. Then Sierra realized she had miscounted by two. That makes three. Then she discovered that one of the oxygen bottles was empty. At that point, we're four oxygen bottles short. Right?"

"So far, yes."

"Then we have to take away the oxygen masks in both lavatories, but one is offset—not to be callous—by one death. So we're down a net of five oxygen masks."

"Exactly. When we depressurize the plane, they're not going to be able to breathe. Daniel, on the other hand, I'm having trouble *not* choking the breath out of."

"If given the opportunity, you would have to beat me to it. The only reason I wouldn't say just toss him back down the stairs with the mega-T is because he might be able to figure out how to kill it."

"The lives that have been lost because of Daniel and Dr. Speck and the danger they have put the rest of us in … all of it … it's just too much. Five *honorable* men. Brave men. It's not right." He paced back and forth behind the jump seats, then stopped. "At what altitude will the air in the cabin be breathable?"

"A minimum of ten thousand feet, eight thousand recommended. But it's not that simple."

He stared at her for a moment. "I can't read you. You are a spinning cursor on a blank page."

"The engines burn less fuel at higher altitudes, where the air is colder. The higher we fly, the farther we fly. If we descend to ten thousand feet too soon, we're going down in the ocean. Guaranteed. The only way we have a chance of reaching Ascension Island is if we stay at this altitude as long as we can."

An idea took shape and rattled around inside his tin can. "All we have to do is make sure that the mega-T can't get to the five of them."

Her head snapped toward him. "No, Marshal! They could die!"

"If we don't do this, they *will* die."

CHAPTER 23

A deep growl echoed from nearby in the stygian hell, judging by the sound. The reverberating thunder didn't exactly help Quentin pinpoint where the mega-T was lurking.

Fear had sharpened his hearing to the point he could hear thread sliding through the eye of a needle, but he didn't hear any sounds at the bottom of the stairs, other than portents of doom echoing inside the hollow space in his head where good sense no longer resided. Good sense and his crackbrained scheme couldn't coexist in the same universe, let alone in the space between his ears.

The plan made as much sense as a screen door on a submarine. But Hercules, Matt, Tyler, Kinley, and Gaston hadn't balked at the idea of going back down to the main deck, where the overhead compartments would soon rain down an abundance of oxygen masks, albeit guarded by one mean sentry.

A peal of lightning lit up the cabin with a loud crack. The main deck cabin went black except for the scant white lights in the aisles and the red lights in the exit rows. Now they were blind as well as out of their minds. Five human forms grouped haphazardly in the exit row behind him. No light, no plan. It was blown up from the jump. The emergency lights doled out just enough light to get them killed, not enough for them to see the mega-T far enough in advance to escape it, not that their chances were much better with the light.

Come on, lights. Do your thing.

The old familiar stench shrouded him. From a whisper away came another deep growl followed by a different sound. He couldn't quite make it out. It sounded like a little kid, a young child whimpering at a distance somewhere in the darkness. He listened again. Whatever it was, it wasn't there anymore. No one could survive that long with the mega-T, especially not a little child.

The lights flickered and then sprang back to life. Right in front of him, at the corner where the exit row met the portside aisle, was the mega-T standing on all fours. Glaring. Reeking. Quentin gestured for the men behind him to back up. When they inched backward, the mega-T took a step toward them. The temperamental lights went out again. A bumbling sound arose behind him. The mega-T's head whipped toward the sound. Hercules had fallen or tripped and lay sprawled on the floor on his keister, swaddled in the red glow from the emergency lights in the floor. It was something out of a weird fantasy movie populated with giants and hideous monsters and lit with an ethereal, red motif.

The creature lowered its head and stepped toward him. Hercules slowly got up, and the mega-T's head rose in lock-step. Then it tilted up as the tall man soared above the green terror.

The lights popped back on. The beast looked Hercules up and down. Quentin couldn't tell if it was studying him, or if it was puzzled. The mega-T could have been perplexed by the rock star's height or by the whole lights-on-lights-off thing.

When the creature stood up on its hind legs, the rock star and the mega-T stood eye to eye. As the beast kept rising, Hercules had to tilt his head higher and higher, bested by five or six feet beneath the high ceiling at the bottom of the stairs. Now Hercules appeared to be the one who was mesmerized. Quentin was even more so.

Daniel had told the gospel truth that time. The creature was much bigger than it was the last time he had seen it.

Ka-pow! A fierce lightning flash lit up the cabin, and Hercules jumped halfway to Ascension Island.

"Stand still!" Quentin whispered to Hercules in particular and to all of them in general. The answers to two nagging questions had been right in front of him the whole time. "Remember Mariana."

The air marshal must not have known how difficult it was for Hercules to stand still when every bolt of lightning appeared to be closer and more powerful than the one that preceded it. The storm had picked up at a particularly inopportune time. At the next intense flash of lightning, he was either going to incur the wrath of the megateratoid or do something he hadn't been able to do since he had been struck by lightning: stand still.

Maybe he should have chosen a different stage name, one whose father didn't wield a mighty thunderbolt. Perhaps he had angered Zeus by using his son's name and had received a ten-billion-watt spanking for the faux pas.

Before he could manufacture a surge of courage, an angry bolt cracked loudly and sent a bright flash through the cabin. He jumped again. The mega-T's head whipped around, descending until Hercules was gazing straight into two coal orbs.

A tentacle lashed through the air and snapped shy of his face. A test. He didn't so much as blink, finding it so much easier to refrain from jumping at the tentacle than the lightning. The mega-T's head narrowed the gap between them until their heads were less than a foot apart, too close for him to blink and live to talk about it.

The sky waxed silent, long enough for him to reclaim a fragment of his wits, but the fermata surrendered to a loud crack and a blinding flash—bigger than any up to that point—that relit the cabin with a sudden explosion of daylight. Anxiety swelled inside him, a volcano on the verge of blowing its top. The breathing techniques Dr. Phelps had taught weren't working, and the creature showed no signs of hurrying to make an exit.

The heavy bombardment of lightning flashes bursting through the windows and the associated fusillade of pops and cracks were driving him nutzoid. If the mega-T didn't move or at least turn away soon, he would do a great deal more than just flinch, having sailed past panic already and was well on his way to hysteria.

The mega-T turned away, at last, and headed up the starboard aisle toward the front of the cabin.

Hercules was emotionally spent. He doubled over and rested his hands on his knees. The ordeal had only lasted a couple of minutes but seemed like hours.

"Remember Mariana?" Quentin repeated.

He stood back up. "As soon as you said it, I realized what you were trying to tell me."

"Thank God you did."

"What does 'Remember Mariana' mean?" Matt asked.

"If it thinks you're already dead, it won't try to kill you," Quentin explained . "That's why the mega-T didn't kill Eden and why Rona's mother didn't have a scratch on her."

"That was an insightful observation." Hercules exhaled a long, cathartic breath. "Timely as well."

"While we have the opportunity, we should do what we can to keep the mega-T from climbing back up those stairs or at least slow it down," the air marshal said.

Hercules had come to trust his intelligence. "Whatever it is, let's do it."

"And quick," Matt added.

Quentin waved four of them toward the rear of the cabin. "You guys hurry on to the back. If Hercules and I don't catch up ... Well, that will mean the mega-T is busy, and you guys have a little more time."

Hercules and Quentin wedged two beverage carts between the metal railings about midway up the stairs. Metal groaning and bending into submission kicked up quite a clatter. A loud roar emanated from the front of the plane, and they took off down the aisle.

———————◦◦◦◦———————

When Quentin and Hercules caught up to the other men at the back of the cabin, they were carrying bright yellow life jackets, armloads of blankets, and makeshift weapons they had pilfered on their way, a little petty thievery, *too* little in Quentin's opinion. They were still missing a couple of vital items.

"Hey, guys," he said. "I'll be right—"

Something shattered in the front of the cabin, followed by a deep grunt.

"It's too late. It's coming." Hercules's eyes pleaded with Quentin not to go.

"It's not that close. I still have time. Go. Get in." Quentin hurried them into the crew rest and sprinted back into the passenger area. The regular life jackets stowed under the seats were inappropriate for infants and stood a good chance of being inappropriate for giants. He pulled a handful out from under the last two rows and tried one on. It appeared to be identical to the ones the other four men had. They all did. Hercules needed a little more loot, and Quentin knew where the family hid the good jewelry.

When he returned to the crew rest, Hercules was sitting in the chair on the right side of the door with a phone hanging on his right. Gaston dropped into the one on the left, and the others camped out on the bunks. Quentin handed Hercules a fire extinguisher and a crash axe.

"I guess you didn't have any luck finding a bulldozer?" Hercules took the items with a grin. Looked like he was back in fine fettle.

"Well, the senator did call you Paul Bunyan. Now you have your axe. Use it only as a last resort. Try to cut off a tentacle or claw. Something that won't bleed too much."

The five of them had gone through hell. The way things were shaping up, those troubles were only a down payment on much worse to come. It was a good thing they still had their sense of humor. He took off the life jacket and handed it to Hercules.

"No, I can't take your life jacket."

"This one's yours. I was just warming it up for you. I've got to get a load of them from down here anyway for the passengers in the upper deck who don't have them."

"A man who literally gives you the shirt off his back." Hercules took it and loosened the straps, then laid it on the floor next to his feet, seemingly satisfied with the size. "Quentin, I can tell you're apprehensive about leaving us. We'll be fine. It's our turn to worry about you now."

Quentin couldn't stop thinking about Eden's warning that the men could die. Being down on the first deck with the mega-T sure wasn't ideal, but at least the men had a chance. The flight attendants' crew rest would provide them with oxygen masks and keep them safe from the mega-T—if he was right. If it turned out Eden was right …

God help them.

———◆———

Quentin had snuck all the way up the portside aisle to the last set of drapes between him and the stairs when the stench enveloped him like an evil fog. The megateratoid had to be close. He listened, but all was hushed. Not even a peep. Yet the stench wasn't waxing or waning.

It had to be standing still. Waiting for him. Probably in another trap. *Where are you, you smart son of a bitch?*

As close as he was to the stairs, he could dart over to the starboard aisle and race for them from there if the mega-T was in his aisle.

He slid the portside drapes open. Slow and easy. A big, black eye stared back at him from a foot away. He recoiled. Just as the curtains flapped shut, claws ripped them to the floor. The mega-T poked its head through the opening. It was too late to run to the other aisle.

He flattened his body against the portside bulkhead and did his best impersonation of a corpse. More of the giant head crept through the portal until Quentin was looking at the back of its green pate. The huge noggin turned left toward the other aisle, then pointed straight ahead. Quentin plotted an escape route. Cut off from the other side of the cabin by the mega-T on his left. Hemmed in by the portside wall on his right. Blocked by the bulkhead wall behind him. Fenced in by the row of seats in front of him. There *was* no escape route.

The behemoth swung its head toward him, its right eye scanning the row of seats in front of him. Its odor was a living thing, attacking him in a cruel and vicious assault. As the mega-T lumbered through the doorway, its hide grated against the frame next to him and made a long, scraping sound like a knife scraping scales off a fish. It walked on down the aisle.

Keep going. Keep going.

He inched toward the doorway as the mega-T continued down the aisle. Suddenly, it stopped. Its head whipped around. Both eyes pointed back up the aisle at him. His chance to *get* away may have *gotten* away. The behemoth turned around, smashing two of the aisle seats in the center section with its oversize body, then rushed back up the aisle toward him.

Quentin played dead. The mega-T only increased its speed, then lowered its head and charged like a bull, leaving a swath of flattened and uprooted aisle seats in its wake.

Oh shit! It's not working!

The stampeding creature closed to within a few feet of him. Quentin had to decide quick whether to stand still or run. It wasn't slowing down or deviating off course one bit.

He vaulted to his left.

The mega-T's head slammed into the bulkhead and buckled it. He jumped over the fallen curtains. *Wham!* The spiked tail pummeled the doorframe. He hotfooted it past the two lavatories on his left, then vaulted up the stairs on his right.

Something Bad had been so close, and it had been making so much noise like it was trying to tear everything up, but now it was quiet again. Rona uncovered her eyes and pulled the collar of her dress up and wiped the tears from her face. *Whoa!* A whole bunch of seats were messed up bad. The monster was still making noises, but not scary ones like before.

Oh, shoot!

Footsteps! They were coming down the aisle toward her. She moved closer to the wall under the window seat and listened. Something Bad walked by. She covered her nose and mouth with her hand until the smell was gone. Then she crawled under the seats some more. The curtains in front of her were really, really, really close but they were lying on the floor now.

A click sounded above her. *Oh no! Something Bad is back.*

It wasn't the monster. The oxygen masks had dropped down from the ceiling. Miss Eden had said that they must put them on or they would die. A piece of someone's blonde hair was caught on the air conditioner button above her and whipped around in the air coming out. She stretched her hand up at one of the masks but couldn't reach it without getting up on one of the seats. *No. Something Bad will see me.* She jerked her hand down. *Be brave, with your bad self.*

She got up on her knees and stretched and stretched. Her hand got a little closer. It wasn't working. She pushed herself higher with her foot, and it landed on something that started playing loud music. She ducked back under the seat. Her foot had landed on the thing that Something Bad had kicked under the seat earlier. It was a cell phone, and it wouldn't stop playing music.

Uh-oh!

The monster's feet started running up the aisle.

Somebody help! Rona screamed in her head. *The monster's gonna eat me!*

She grabbed the phone and touched all the buttons on the screen, but it wouldn't stop. Stupid, stupid, stupid phone. It was too late.

———◗◖———

Hercules and his team settled under the deployed oxygen masks inside the flight attendants' crew rest. Unlike Tantalus, he now held his tantalizing fruit firmly in his grip, a feat that seemed impossible a short time ago.

"This wasn't a half-bad idea," Gaston whispered. "I can't believe how quiet it is. Herc, does this mean it's time to put on our life jackets?"

"If it makes you feel more comfortable, go ahead," Hercules whispered back, then quietly set his fire extinguisher on the floor. "Is everyone ready? The pilot is going to give us the word any minute now. When she does, put your oxygen masks on without hesitation."

———◗◖———

The phone slipped out of Rona's hand. Instead of picking it up, she slapped it two rows back. The monster beat up the seats there, then ripped them apart. Big, yellow teeth slammed down on the phone. The music stopped.

She stayed still until the monster's feet turned the other way. Then she poked her head out from under the seat.

She screamed.

A long, skinny, arm-looking thing hung above her head and wiggled around like a snake. She jumped up and ran up the aisle screaming.

When she looked back, she saw the whole monster for the first time. She screamed really loud and really long until she had to breathe again. Something Bad's mouth was big enough to eat her whole.

"Mommy! Mommy! Make it stop chasing me!"

The skinny, arm-looking thing grabbed her left foot and made her fall on her stomach. She yanked her foot away, but it didn't work. She kicked and kicked the skinny arm with her other foot. It started to drag her back toward the monster.

"Mommy! Help me!"

This time she yanked her left foot as hard as she could, and her shoe slid off a little. She yanked again, and the shoe flew off. The skinny arm jerked away with the shoe.

Rona jumped back up and ran toward the front. The footsteps behind her were getting closer. She looked back, and when she turned back around, she stopped. She had nowhere to go.

The skinny arm was waiting for her. It had sneaked under the seats and come out ahead of her in front of the curtains lying on the floor. The monster's hugemongous head was right above her. Tears ran down her face. She backed away from the monster, but that meant she was going toward the skinny arm, and the skinny arm was keeping her from going where the grown adults all went.

"Help." The word was tiny and barely came out of her mouth.

Something Bad opened its giant mouth, and yucky spit ran out. Its head jerked up, then came down fast. She screamed and spun around to face the skinny arm.

A big, black shoe heel stomped it down to the floor and smooshed it.

———◦———

Quentin ground the tentacle into the floor with the heel of his shoe. The mega-T roared in what he hoped was excruciating pain, a magnificent sound that sent ripples of pleasure through him while the feel of the tentacle writhing and squirming beneath his foot filled him with sheer bliss. When he stooped down to scoop Rona up, the little girl lunged into his arms, squirming and clinging as if she wanted to crawl inside the skin on his chest for protection.

She pointed back at the mega-T and shrieked, "Something Bad!" Her little knees and feet bounced impatiently. She wasn't the only one who wanted to get the hell out of there. Behind them, the tentacle uncoiled and rose off the floor like a king cobra. In front of them, the mega-T bared its teeth. Quentin and Rona were trapped.

———◦———

"Where's the air marshal?" Eden asked, handing Sierra her empty coffee cup and saucer.

The purser gave Eden a sly smile. "I thought he was in here … with you."

"What do you mean by that? That little tone there at the end."

"I think he's interested. The man can't stay out of this cockpit, and as good-looking as he is, why would you want him to?"

Eden waved her hands around as if to ask: *Do you see him anywhere?*

"He's gotten those five passengers tucked away in the crew rest."

"Then that settles it. We need to hurry. I have to start the depressurization process pronto. For their sake. Before that beast figures out it's got company. I need an all-clear as soon as you can."

———◦◦———

Sierra whisked through the upper deck cabin. The passengers were wearing every stitch of clothing obtained from what turned out to be a woefully dismal number of carry-on bags and every blanket she could scrounge up.

"Put on your oxygen masks now, please." She checked each mask, including the portable ones. They were all systems go.

———◦◦———

Eden bundled up in her thick winter coat. When Sierra gave her the all-clear, the purser didn't have to tell her that the update was only for the upper deck. Neither one of them had put eyeballs on the six men downstairs. It would have been good to know that they were all set too. Better to know that they were still alive. If they were, the calvary was on the way.

She put on her oxygen mask and reached up to the three PACK switches. Unlike the first time, she didn't hesitate.

PACK 1: OFF.

PACK 3: OFF.

PACK 2: OFF.

After all the mega-T had put them through, the thought of it suffocating to death brought a smile to her face.

CHAPTER 24

A lock of blonde hair that had been caught in the gasper above one of the window seats slowly wended to a stop. The whoosh of air coming through it fell silent.

Quentin looked all around. There had to be some way to escape, some way to gain an advantage over the creature. Clutched in one of the undulating tentacles, his left jacket pocket waved slightly, barely visible in the coils.

A cup of coffee sitting on a tray table in the aisle seat to his left caught his eye. The lock of hair had been a warning that time was up. The cup's warning; get the hell out.

"Eden! No!"

Rona whimpered, about to burst out crying. Tears coated her eyes and turned them into glassy little balls that gazed up into his.

"I'm sorry. I didn't mean to scare you. It's okay, sweetheart." Steam floated out of a cup where there had been none before the airflow stopped. The main deck cabin had been abandoned hours ago. There was no way the cup of coffee was still hot. Yet the steam mushroomed into a small cloud, grew bigger, and rose higher. He remembered enough from his college chemistry classes and one vacation to know it was too late. He and Rona couldn't go anywhere if they wanted to.

He grabbed an oxygen mask dangling on his right and cupped it over her face. "Here, dear. Hold this to your nose and mouth and breathe through it. Put both hands on it and hold it tight."

"So I won't sleep forever?"

"Don't worry. I'm not going to let that happen." He seized another mask and snatched a few glorious breaths. The mega-T blocked them one way, the tentacle another, and with the cabin depressurizing, they couldn't move farther than the length of the tethers on their oxygen masks. They were in a three-way death trap.

The mega-T started to shake its head. Hopefully, it felt the effects of oxygen deprivation. *Die, you big, green bastard.* Their oxygen masks suddenly ripped away, and they were sliding on the floor feetfirst, winched to a green tow truck. Pain shot up his left ankle. His toes started tingling. The tentacle had a bone-crushing grip around his ankle, cutting off the circulation to his foot. It pulled them toward waiting, big yellow teeth. It pulled *him*. Rona was just a passenger in his arms. He could let her go. Hell no. If she wasn't in his arms, she would be a much easier target.

With his free hand, he clamped onto the leg of a seat as he slid by and clung to the cold metal with a death grip. The strain from the tentacle loosened his grip. The leg quickly slid down his palm to his fingers. They would rip off before he willingly let go. He groaned as the leg slid down to his fingertips, then slipped off. They flew down the aisle again.

There! Two seats away.

But it was on the left. In a flash, he shifted Rona into his right arm, stretched the fingertips on his left toward the portable oxygen bottle that Hercules had dropped. He slid closer … closer … He missed. *Damn it!* His fingers clamped onto the leg of the next seat. But there was no strain this time, and the tentacle's grip loosened. The reason was patent: he and Rona had reached their destination.

"You can't have her!"

The creature stood above them on its hind legs, stooped over to fit beneath the low ceiling. Spit dangled from its bottom lip like stubborn streamers, stretching thinner and longer, growing closer to his face. To avoid the stream of spit he judged most likely to succeed, Quentin moved to his left. So did the giant head above him, mimicking him. The rope of spittle directly above him swayed left, right. It snapped loose, freefalling straight for them.

He rolled over, covered Rona's body with his, and cringed. The spit would hit him in the back of the head for sure, judging by its trajectory. As short as his hair was, he should have felt an impact. He lifted his head. The puddle of death had missed his ear by an inch.

When he rolled back faceup, he felt a heavy thud against his sternum. The little girl's curly head lay still against his chest. "Rona!" He shook her. "Baby, wake up!"

She raised her head a couple of inches, then it collapsed against his chest again. There was still life in her. There was still hope.

He couldn't save his own little girl, but no way in hell was he going to let the predator or oxygen deprivation take this one. With every ounce of strength he had, he lunged for the oxygen bottle and snagged it on the first try. He slammed it down on the tentacle with force that would not be denied. The tentacle uncoiled from around his ankle. He cupped the oxygen mask onto Rona's face and opened the valve, ignoring the million little pins and needles that pricked him every-where. He wouldn't be any good to Rona if he went down for the count. He jumped up with her in his arms and got a hit of oxygen from a dangling mask. All of the squirming around and little knees jabbing him in the stomach and ribs couldn't have made him happier. "Good girl."

The mega-T staggered and then lifted one of its feet.

Oh God! It's going to charge. He primed his lungs with air. The only way to survive its charge was to be somewhere else.

The beast lowered its foot back down to its original spot. Swayed. As soon as it steadied itself, it lunged hell-bent toward them. Quentin dropped his mask and bolted toward the front of the aircraft, heart pounding his rib cage, toes tingling like a bastard. After only a few steps he was as winded as he would have been if he had run a marathon. The cabin swam in and out of focus.

"I'm cold," Rona said through her mask.

If he didn't get oxygen, Rona and her portable oxygen bottle would slip out of his arm. Without it, the little girl would experience the same effects he was. Her little developing brain and body didn't stand a chance.

His knees buckled. He found the back of an aisle seat for support. God only knew how. His thoughts were breaking up like spotty cell phone reception. A mask. He groped for it. The next thing he knew, it was in his hand. Somehow. He recognized the feel of it. He slapped it over his mouth and nose and fed his hungry lungs.

The mega-T was no longer charging. Dazed, it took a drunken step toward them.

———◦———

A rime of frost coated the windows, the glareshield, and the instruments. Eden wiped them off with a paper towel. She needed to turn the packs back on and thaw the instruments. If the mega-T was dead, she could turn them back on permanently. By now, they could be freezing their butts off for nothing. The mega-T might already be dead for all she knew. Or it might have some built-in mechanism to survive in extreme conditions like the organisms that astronauts found living in the harsh environment of space, clinging to the outside of the International Space Station.

Without knowing the exact status of the men or the mega-T, the prudent thing to do was to keep the air packs off for as long as she could without endangering the passengers. She wiped off the secondary EICAS screen and studied it for a moment. *That can't be right.* There had to be a bad sensor somewhere, or it was the product of another questionable decision the other pilots made before they died.

Quentin checked Rona's oxygen mask. She was ready for their big move. He wondered if he ever would be. He cautiously watched the mega-T as it teetered to its left. *This might work after all.*

All eight of its tentacles uncoiled and shot straight out from the sides of its body. The four on the left fanned out to the left. The four on the right, to the right. A grotesque peacock with eight long, skinny plumes. They punched through overhead compartments and looped around the seat backs on both sides of the aisle, mooring itself to the aircraft.

His first impulse was to take off running and get the child and himself away from the beast and whatever it decided to do next with those tentacles and what it would do to overcome the next useless hurdle they put in its way, but he was tethered to the oxygen mask and had always held a fondness for breathing. He could hopscotch from one dangling oxygen mask to another until he reached the area near the stairs. From there to the upper deck cabin was a barren wasteland with not a single mask.

Without warning, a ten-foot section of an overhead compartment dislodged from the ceiling. One end dropped down and wedged diagonally across the aisle between two rows of seats. It separated the stranded pair from the mega-T, although he could still see the giant's head and torso above the mauled chunk. The beast gave it a long look, the same look it had given the stairs when it studied them earlier. Based on its track record, the two of them shouldn't stick around for it to figure things out.

Parting company with the oxygen mask was harder than he thought. His strategy to reach the stairs wasn't perfect but doable. If he started to feel the effects of hypoxia between where he stood and the curtain, he would grab one of the dozen oxygen masks hanging next to the aisle. More than enough. Maybe he shouldn't wait for hypoxia to set in. Too risky with the little girl's life on the line. Maybe he should stop at each oxygen mask whether he felt he needed it or not. That would get him to the curtain, but beyond that—

Fuck it.

He dropped the oxygen mask and hauled ass up the aisle. If he planned until doomsday, he would never be confident enough to let go of the oxygen mask. Stripped down and exposed for what it really was, it was nothing more than bare-assed fear. He trampled the curtains at the front of the cabin. He would never make it all the way up to the top of the stairs without another oxygen mask. His feet weren't just tingling now; they were going numb. Soon they would punch the clock and call it a day along with the rest of him.

He stepped into the galley, seized an oxygen mask, and gulped a few deep breaths. On the counter next to him, an open can of Coke, a carton of milk, and a cup of what looked like apple juice all emitted nearly twice as much steam as the coffee cup had. So were the three coffeepots in the dispensers above them. He touched one. *Just like I thought.* The one upstairs had nearly sautéed his arm. This one was room temperature. In addition to that, the coffee makers were all in the "Off" position.

Rona leaned into the aisle and pointed to the back of the cabin. "Look!" Her eyes stretched wide. A sound like rubber or thick leather stretching to its limit wafted into the galley.

He stepped back into the aisle. Instantly thunderstruck. His mask drifted away from his nose and mouth. "What the f—?" he said, sliding his mask back on. What he could see of the mega-T behind the dislodged chunk of overhead compartment shook violently. There was no connection between that and the strange noise he had heard, and if he wasn't mistaken, it was growing louder.

The beast disappeared behind the hanging overhead compartment.

Whatever it was up to, it couldn't be good. He didn't plan to stick around to see what that was. In his hand was the last mask he would get his hands on before reaching the upper deck cabin. Letting go of it was going to be torture. He took a few breaths and cherished the oxygen-rich air. Cracking and tearing sounds came from the overhead compartment, then the top bin door blasted open. Carry-on suitcases, duffel bags, and briefcases spilled out onto the floor. A giant, green head poked through the opening.

The cracking and tearing sounds stopped. The weird stretching and straining sounds sprang back to life. Certainly not the kind of sounds that would calm his ever-increasing heartbeat. The head protruded more on an absurd neck that was undoubtedly longer and skinnier than it had been. An elongated shoulder and contorted torso followed.

No way! Hypoxia must have scrambled his brain.

The beast's body was shape-shifting and doing it with speed. The two front feet and the upper half of its body had already squeezed through the hole. A few seconds later, the two hind feet hit the floor in front of the bin. Its body reeled from side to side. Its hind legs buckled. The giant head dropped down, then jolted back up like a stoner going in and out of consciousness. If the beast was an affront to the sighted before, that was nothing compared to what it looked like now with its stretched, twisted body, resembling a deformed, humpbacked alligator with scoliosis.

That's it. That's how it could fit its huge body into the small hole in the galley floor. Shape-shifting.

It locked its black eyes onto his and shook violently again. Its spine straightened, and the hump flattened. The mega-T was reforming to its original shape—or what he thought of as its original shape. What little he thought he knew about the beast had turned out to be fictitious.

He wasn't sure about anything anymore, other than the fact that he needed to get the child and himself the hell out of there. And hella fast.

The shape-shifting was his scared-straight event. Rather than stay and find out what other tricks the mega-T had lined up for them, he would take his chances with hypoxia.

Quentin dropped his oxygen mask, cupped the back of Rona's head, and bounded up the steps. Trying to navigate around the two beverage carts that he and Hercules had wedged along the steps slowed him down. When he climbed over the first one, his foot sank into one of the folds of metal put there by a powerful stomp from a giant paw, a minor hitch that he overcame instantly. The last cart slipped out from under him. He banged his knee against one of its hard corners. His free hand clamped onto the railing and pulled himself upright, but his knees became wet noodles. The carts and the steps started to swim in and out of focus.

There was a pretty little girl in his arms. "Kellva?"

His feet kept going in what seemed to be an upward direction. The world became a disoriented milieu. Up was down. Down was sideways. Everything spun. Then the plane went out of focus and turned into a blurry, swirling mishmash of shapes and colors. When his back crashed against the floor on top of something hard and pointy, he found out which way down was. And then his world went black.

CHAPTER 25

A dancing rope. An arch. Echoes.

Quentin's world crept back into focus, though he couldn't make out the minute details of anything in it. Everything blended together in a wash of pied patterns and shapeless figures.

The little girl's face appeared again. "Kellva?" He tried to reach for her, but his arm was a bag of bricks. That triggered another memory. His arms had felt the same way yesterday on his patio for some reason. Something had happened, and based on the bits and pieces he could remember, he was starting to think it had nothing to do with alcohol.

He wrestled one arm off the floor and extended it in the little girl's general direction. "You're not blue anymore." His own voice sounded foreign and distant. Was he in heaven? Was that what his daughter looked like in heaven?

Something covered his face. Beyond that, a thin, curly rope swung back and forth above him.

The arch was a ceiling. *Ahhh*. A narrow, arched ceiling, a distinctive feature of the upper deck. That's where he was. The ceiling down on the main deck was much wider and flatter. The distance he was from the ceiling was a clear indication that he was lying on the floor. Definitely not a surprise.

Faces from a collection of passengers peered down at him like mourners in a funeral home viewing a body. A woman's voice echoed from a place not too far away with words that floated into his consciousness: "Pressurize ... little girl ... Mr. Kane ..."

More of his mental faculties returned. His vision gradually cleared. The curly rope turned out to be a coiling telephone cord, and the thing on his face was an oxygen mask. He had no idea how long he had been out, but it was at least long enough for his breathing to return to normal.

A loud crash bubbled up from below. One of the carts, by the sound. Then came a deep *whump, whump* at the bottom of the stairs. He smiled a little under his mask. That had to be the sound of the colossus falling. He wasn't half as pleased with the banging and scrabbling sounds that followed. A roar thundered up from the main deck that abruptly cut off in the middle, replaced by a low grunt, which was followed by a single *whump*, eminently deeper and louder than its predecessors. Only one thing onboard could make a sound like that— the heavy giant crashing down hard. Delightful.

His smile grew bigger as he listened for another report from below. There was complete silence.

"Mr. Kane," a different voice said, not as far away as the first. The annoying echo was less noticeable. The little girl's big questioning eyes stared at him. Rona. Not Kellva.

"Mr. Kane." Same voice, no echo at all this time. It was obviously coming from somewhere above him. His eyes followed the oxygen mask to the hand holding it, up to the arm, up to the face leaning over him. "You had us all concerned there for a moment," Dr. Ross said.

He flashed a thumbs-up to let her know he was okay. "You're a doctor. The strongest thing you got is oxygen?"

She chuckled. "Do you know where you are?"

"Disneyland. And I want to get off this ride."

She placed two fingers on his wrist and looked down at her watch. "Your pulse is back to normal."

"Can I have my shoe back now, please?" Sierra asked. It was the same voice he heard when he first regained consciousness.

"Your shoe?"

The purser smiled and pointed at the floor. He rolled to one side and pulled the navy-blue leather pump from underneath his back. Somehow, he had made it to the upper deck before he passed out.

"You crash-landed on my foot when I was trying to catch you. Sorry I missed."

"When you feel you're ready, you can take off your oxygen mask," Dr. Ross said. "The pilot has temporarily re-pressurized the cabin."

He ripped it off and stood up on those noodle knees.

"Slow it down, Mr. Kane." Dr. Ross held one of his arms as if she expected him to topple over.

He wouldn't bet against it. "Every time you call me Mr. Kane, I think it's going to come with some dire prognosis. 'Twenty-two minutes before your intestines come flying out of your belly button, Mr. Kane.' Call me Quentin."

"I'll call you anything you want after what you did. That little girl probably had only seconds to spare."

He had given up trying to untie the Gordian knot that had become his life after he failed to save his wife and daughter, but he had saved Rona. Maybe his life had meaning after all.

"How is she? Did you examine her?"

"She's fine. She still had on her oxygen mask when the flight attendant pulled her out of your arms."

The little girl looked up at him. "I held on really, really tight just like you told me because I didn't want to sleep forever."

Quentin rubbed her head. "You're a brave little girl. And smart too."

"How do *you* feel?" Dr. Ross asked.

"Like I just fell off a cliff and I'm waiting for my butt to hit the ground."

He looked back down the stairs. The creature lay collapsed with one of the beverage carts atop its chest. "The pilot can keep the aircraft pressurized. It's dead."

Daniel looked at him with an expression of surprise and something else. Doubt. He stepped away from the passengers huddled around and looked down the stairs for himself.

"It couldn't get oxygen, collapsed, and died," Quentin assured him. His legs were feeling as strong and sure as they normally did—as strong and sure as they did when his blood cells weren't marinating in Jim Beam.

He picked Rona up and toddled toward the front of the cabin. About a quarter of the way to the cockpit, a man got up and threw an inviting hand at his seat.

"No, Kellva—Rona—She—I have to keep an eye on her."

———————◆◆◆———————

Eden quickly changed the display on the secondary EICAS screen, then unlocked the door. Quentin came in carrying Rona in one arm.

"I'm so sorry, Marshal. I thought you stayed in the crew rest with the other men."

"Thank heavens I didn't. Look at the pretty little girl I found."

Rona looked tired. Other than that, she didn't look any different than she had during her first visit to the cockpit.

Eden smiled at her. "Hi, sweetie."

"I remember you. You're that nice flylot. I remember your voice."

"Hey, where's your other shoe?"

"The stupid dog doodie monster pulled it off."

The air marshal put Rona down in the jump seat behind Eden. "The pilot is going to be doing a lot of things that might seem a little scary, but she knows what she's doing. She's a professional."

Rona yawned. "Okay."

He stood back up. "I remembered the Mile High City."

"Denver?" Eden wasn't sure what Denver had to do with their predicament and wondered if the air marshal had ransomed a few brain cells in exchange for his life.

"When I was there, I learned that water doesn't necessarily boil at 212 degrees Fahrenheit. It boils at around 200 degrees there."

"Two hundred and one if you wanted to be a stickler about it."

"When I saw a cup of coffee start to steam, I knew you were depressurizing the aircraft. Where air pressure is lower, water boils at lower temperatures."

"So that's where you were going with that whole 'Denver' thing. It makes sense now. If you reduce the atmospheric pressure low enough, you can get water to boil at its normal *freezing* temperature. Even though it would be boiling, it would still be freezing cold to the touch."

Sierra was right. He is attractive. She was also right that he couldn't seem to stay out of the cockpit, and Eden sure had no intentions of kicking him out.

She reached up to her left between the glareshield and the side window and pulled a pencil out of one of the three pencil holders. Instantly, she felt some slime. *No, no, no. Please, no!* It was a simple act that she lamented immediately. She stuffed it back into its hole, but it was too late. The agony of what she knew was to come was unbearable. She wanted to scream. With Rona and Quentin in the cockpit, she wouldn't dare. That made it even more agonizing.

She had to look. She had to see it with her own eyes, or she wouldn't accept it. But she couldn't let him see her do it. She rubbed her fingers together, then pulled them apart slightly. They were sticky and viscous. When she finally looked down, she had confirmation that she had been done in by a damn pencil.

Oh God. The same slimy gunk she had seen dripping from the mega-T's mouth was on her hand.

Quentin was looking over at it.

He saw it!

He was going to think it was his fault, think that maybe he hadn't done a good job inspecting the cockpit. The poor man had gone through enough on the flight already. There was no need to tack on a guilt trip.

"I'm s-sorry," he stammered. "I didn't mean to stare. I was checking to see if there was a wedding ring on your finger."

His irenic eyes met hers.

She manufactured a smile, something she was becoming a pro at. "It's vacant." *Oh yeah, he's interested.* Just her luck. Finally, a guy who checked all the boxes, and it looked like they would never even get a chance to hold hands. He was self-less. Protective. Brave. The way he looked after Rona ... loving and kind. The way he swooped in like the calvary and saved her ... Wow! Her heart fluttered. If the flight's bleak outlook somehow changed and she survived, she would definitely go out with him. Who knew? The next chapter in her life might have had his name written at the top of every page.

Rona leaned forward. "Did Mommy go to South Acafa to see Daddy without me?"

Instantly, Eden knew. If the child's mother had been in the upper deck, the two would have been reunited. Her eyes silently pleaded for a rebuttal. The air marshal slipped behind the girl's seat, looked at Eden remorsefully, and shook his head.

For a moment, she forgot her own woeful plight and thought about all the struggles the little girl had gone through and all the agony she would go through when she found out her mother was dead.

He stooped down to Rona's eye level and spoke in a calming voice. "No, honey. Your mother did not go to South Africa without you. And don't you worry. You're going to see your daddy real soon."

Rona yawned, then started shaking her head, stuck in a "no" gesture.

He rubbed her head sweetly. "What are you doing?"

She squinted up at him from underneath eyelids that looked heavy but still put up a fight. "I'm trying to stay awake."

"You've had a busy day," he said. "You should take a nap."

"I want my mommy."

Eden didn't think the little tyke had another five minutes left in those eyes. Hopefully, she had more than that in her own.

Quentin buckled Rona's harness and kissed her head like a loving father.

Her head flopped down a few times, then jerked back up. It was a futile fight to stay awake. "I'm really tired." By then her eyes were merely tiny slits. "If I go to sleep, until my mommy gets here, will you make sure I wake up? So I don't sleep forever?"

"I promise," he said. When her curly little head drooped forward, he gently cupped it in his hands and leaned her back against the seat. Her chin came to rest on her shoulder.

The little angel was sleeping peacefully. For Eden, peace was now make-believe, a fantasy to be found only in the pages after "Once upon a time." But there didn't appear to be any "lived happily ever after" in her future.

Quentin quietly eased into the first officer's seat. "I struggle to go to sleep. She struggles to stay awake."

Eden stole a glance down at her hand. "You're … ah …" The gunk was drying and turning white. "You're good with kids." She fanned her fingers out and felt resistance as if they were trying to pull themselves in the opposite direction. When she relaxed them, they snapped together. She had to get that crap off her hand before it fused her fingers together. "You must have some of your own."

"My wife and I had a little girl. She died thirty-one days, three hours, and thirty-three minutes after she was born. She would have been about the same age as Rona."

"I'm really sorry to hear that."

"Kellva was born two months premature with congenital heart disease. Her tiny body was blue due to insufficient oxygen. I fell so far into a bottomless pit of grief I didn't realize I was losing Tracie too. Until it was too late."

The air marshal was laying his soul bare. For her to no longer be able to pay attention to him, she had to have icicles dangling from her wretched heart.

"She took an overdose. Two years ago. She never got over Kellva's death. Red Cross saw me through that."

Eden pulled herself together long enough to hammer out a few words. "Sounds like—a-a good man."

"Good friend too. I planned to turn in my badge a few times, but he talked me out of it. He said he needed my expertise. No way. *He* was the guru. He wanted to help me. To keep me on this side of sanity."

Marshal the proper words into formation and cast them out of your mouth. "I'm really sorry for all your losses. There's nothing you can do about the ones you've lost. I hope you find solace in knowing that many of those passengers back there are alive because of you. And the one sitting right behind me."

"That sounds like something Red would say."

"I could have used a Red Cross in my life a few times.

Especially when I was in the navy on the USS *Abraham Lincoln*. I had just—" She stopped abruptly. The mega-T's venom must have made her forget how dangerous the subject was, especially with someone as discerning as the air marshal.

Changing the subject, and fully aware that the perceptive marshal had to know she was doing it, she said, "I started flying when I was fifteen. My parents gave me flying lessons as a graduation present."

"Graduation? From high school? At fifteen? When I was fifteen, my parents would only trust me with the car from the garage to the end of the driveway. And you were flying planes?" He chuckled and shook his head.

"Just little puddle hoppers."

"I'm in the company of *two* smart ladies." He glanced back at Rona. "God. How could she have survived down there? She truly is a remarkable little girl. And a very lucky one."

While he was looking back at Rona, Eden wiped her hand on the paper towel she had used to wipe the frost off the equipment. The gunk was much harder to wipe off than she expected. It was nearly dry and stretched between her hand and the paper towel like a handful of miniature, white rubber bands. She snapped the last of it from her pinky. "Do you think there could be any more survivors down there? I mean, other than the men in the crew rest?"

"This little girl just proved anything is possible. Still, I think she was the last one. I hope she didn't see her mother in the condition she was there at the end."

"Condition?"

He leaned over and lowered his voice. "Sierra told me her mother couldn't remember where she last saw her daughter and described her in great detail as if Sierra had never met her. This was *after* she had brought Rona to visit the cockpit. *After* she had returned the little girl to her."

"What about Ray?"

"He asked Sierra for some aspirin but didn't take them when she first offered them to him. She said he just sat there, staring off into nowheresville until she shook the bottle at him."

Eden wondered how bad her "condition" would get.

When she looked over at him, his eyes were focused on the paper towel in her hand. She thoroughly cleaned the spotless glareshield. He seemed to have bought the ruse, though she couldn't be sure. Someone who was trained to read people could simply be allowing her some buffer room between a lie and the truth.

A sharp pain shot through her head. "How are the passengers? Why don't you go check on them?"

"Are you sure you two are going to be all right?"

Her forehead started to throb. "We'll be fine. They need you more out there."

"I don't know. You look like you're about to collapse," he protested, standing up. "Do you need me to get you anything? Boiling coffee? Steaming water? Simmering apple juice? Whatever tickles your nickel."

She offered a fractured smile. "No, I think I can live without *any* of that."

As soon as the door closed behind him, she changed the lower EICAS screen back and read the updates. Her hand flew to her mouth. Tears filled her eyes. She looked back at Rona. Hopefully she was dreaming about a world where her mother was still alive, a world devoid of monsters or dangers of any kind. Eden stroked her little cheek and sobbed, "I'm sorry."

CHAPTER 26

A question had been needling Quentin since the portable oxygen bottles mission, and it couldn't wait any longer. There was only one person on the flight who might have an answer.

"There she is." Sierra pointed toward the middle of the cabin. "She's in high demand around here, so she's a little hard to catch up to."

He made his way to the last row in front of the portside exit door, where the doctor was attending to his favorite person on the flight.

"Dr. Ross, can I speak to you for a moment?" he asked.

"Your pulse is fine, Senator. You likely had a panic attack," Dr. Ross said, standing up.

"You again," TR grumbled at Quentin. "You were rude to me, and I'm offended at how you—"

"Get to stepping." Quentin didn't give a hairy fart about his fucking feelings. "If you didn't like what I said before, your ears are going to catch fire at what comes out of my mouth next."

The senator took only twice as much time as necessary to haul his carcass away.

"Of course, Marshal. For as long as you need," Dr. Ross said.

Quentin led Sierra and Dr. Ross to the exit door, putting distance between them and any uninvited ears. A fair number of passengers in the front half of the cabin turned around, and all of the ones in the back appeared to be staring at the three of them. With the doctor in the mix, of course the passengers were going to think something was wrong.

Dr. Ross gave him a quick eyeball MRI. "Are you all right, Marshal?"

"I'm fine. I didn't mean to alarm you. I just have a question that I was hoping you might be able to answer."

"Sure. I'll do anything I can to help."

"Well, a passenger down on the main deck, Mariana, looks like she was the last to die even though she was the first to touch the toxin. Could there be any medical explanation for that?"

"There could be a number of reasons, along with countless variables that should be considered. In general, in the absence of autopsies or even a thorough examination of the bodies, I would guess that either something slowed her circulatory system down *or* something sped up the others' or a combination of both. Many prescription as well as over-the-counter medications can cause vasodilation and vasoconstriction, the widening or narrowing of blood vessels. When blood vessels dilate, blood flow increases. When they constrict, blood flow decreases."

"What are some of those variables, especially any that might be present on this flight?"

"Certain medications can have a profound effect on the circulatory system, sending it in either direction, depending on the medication. An underlying medical condition could certainly have an effect on it. Certain foods. Many supplements. Since we don't know any of these things, we have to assume they were factors."

219

"Things we have no way of figuring out."

"Well, I could put on a pair of gloves and examine the bodies."

"No way, doctor. Too risky. We don't know if gloves provide enough of a barrier."

"Well, some other things we should consider are substances as simple as caffeine, which will speed it up, and aspirin, which will dilate the blood vessels, causing the venom to course through the system faster as well."

Sierra placed a hand over her heart. "Oh my. Mariana asked me to bring her some aspirin, but I forgot. I gave Ray both."

Quentin said, "That's one thing Red and I shared. Each one of us could drink our weight in coffee."

———◆———

Eden picked up Monty's aspirin bottle from the worktable. Her headache had spread and intensified. White flashes of light zipped across her vision like miniature lightning bolts, and her heart rate was at full throttle, afterburners and all.

Her hand pressed down on the bottle's cap, but before she twisted it off, she regarded her left hand. Oddly, she didn't feel any pain or residual effects of the mega-T's saliva. She lifted her hand off the cap and spread her fingers. They separated with ease. She opened the bottle and shook two aspirin into her palm. No, sir. Not with her toe-curling headache. Two were not going to cut it. She added a third. *Nah.* The bottle wasn't going anywhere. If two didn't work, she could always take more. She dropped one back into the bottle, tossed back the other two, and downed them with a cup of coffee.

She started to get up. Her black kit bag was on the other side of the cockpit. Screw that. Monty's was right next to her, and those things were no joke. Each one was a portable library. And heavy. She rummaged through his and pulled out a pen, a notepad, and a calculator. Forget the pencil. It should be walled off from the rest of the world, shoved into a bottomless pit, and nuked to hell. There was a pretty good chance everything in the captain's kit bag was devoid of the mega-T's saliva. If not, tough turkey. She wasn't going to waste time or energy to get hers. God only knew how much of either she had left.

As long as the highly advanced aircraft received correct data, it was far better and faster at making calculations than she would ever be. Her math skills were A+, but the systems in the Combi were a computer farm. Throw in a bad sensor here and a malfunction there and kerflooey.

Trust but verify. She did a series of calculations and scribbled the results on sheet after sheet. One after the other, she ripped the sheets from the pad and kept them in order, then picked up the interphone. Sierra answered much quicker than she had anticipated, given she was the sole flight attendant with ninety plus passengers. "Can you bring me another cup of coffee, please? Strong as possible. If you can stand a spoon up in it, it's perfect."

Looking from one sheet to another, she sighed long and hard. The buzzer barely registered over her escalating headache. She hit the "FLT DECK DOOR" button on the aisle stand and hid the sheets under her thigh before the door opened.

She took the coffee cup over her right shoulder awkwardly with her right hand. "Thanks. It's good and hot. Just the way I like it."

"You're welcome." The voice clearly wasn't Sierra's.

Eden spun around. It was the air marshal. She wasn't expecting him and certainly wasn't prepared for him. She could feel him watching and analyzing even when his back was turned. She changed the lower EICAS and busied herself in a flurry of equipment tweakings.

Quentin wasn't buying it. Something was off about Eden.

She was fidgety, a little frazzled, and she looked worn out. Surprising her had knocked down her firewall and turned that spinning cursor and blank page into a database. It might take a little time to read, but he'd get there. "Eden, are you okay? Do you need me to do anything?"

"No, everything is fine in here." She shot a thumb over her shoulder. "They need you out there."

"Protecting you takes priority, right up there with inhaling and exhaling. You know that, whether it's against some crazed passenger, or that creature if it tries to get to you, or against anything else that can interfere with you flying this aircraft."

She kneaded her temples. "I'm sure I'll be fine, Marshal. Nothing is going to happen in here."

The old "kneading the temples to alleviate stress" technique. Boy, was he familiar with that one. "I can't take that chance, and neither can the passengers. Three out of four of our pilots are dead. You're our last hope."

"I-I," she stammered, sighed, and dropped her head. He sensed a shift in her, a weakening of sorts. Her hand fumbled with a button below the windshield that she couldn't possibly see with her head down. "I know. I get it," she said after a long silence. She looked back at the sleeping child, then swallowed a large gulp of coffee.

Something about the way she looked at Rona made him ask one more question before backing off. "Are you sure you're okay, no symptoms or anything?"

When she set the cup down, she placed it on the edge of the worktable. It teetered. She caught it, but some of the hot coffee splashed on her thigh. "I'm fine! I'm safe! I'm behind a reinforced door, for Christ's sake. They're going to need you more out there when we run out of fu—"

She stopped. But it was too late. A look of deep despair swept over her. She exhaled a long, tormented sigh and fell mute.

The silent, dead air seemed to crush him. He was stricken dumb as well. His senses heightened. The stars outside the windows looked brighter. The on-again, off-again rain hitting the windshield now sounded like gunfire on a battlefield. Finally, he found his voice again. "'When.' You didn't say '*if*.' You said '*when*.'"

She sat silently, staring out the windshield for a moment, then said, "It's no longer an *if*. It's a *when*."

Quentin stumbled on legs that were incapable of supporting his weight all of a sudden. The first officer's seat happened to catch him when he fell. "And a ... *Where?*"

"If only I had gotten back into the cockpit sooner," she said in an obvious attempt to evade the question.

"Could you shut down one or two of the engines to conserve fuel?"

"Feathering the engines would only conserve a little fuel. The risks far outweigh the benefits."

"So, you're saying we are definitely going to run out of fuel?"

"I'm 100 percent sure."

"Things were bad enough when we only had the megateratoid and its venom to worry about. Why didn't you say something earlier? I'm sure your instruments didn't *just* tell you that."

"I was about to when we were talking about the other pilots dumping fuel. Then you said that you weren't sure you could handle any more bad news. So I just told you about the jet stream. I was afraid you would fall apart if you knew we were running out of fuel. And I was afraid that if you fell apart, so would I. I need you."

Damn. While he was trying to read her, she was doing the same to him. "No." He shook his head. "No, you don't. I don't even know how to turn on the windshield wipers on this thing."

"You said Ray was the one who kept you on this side of sanity. You've been doing that for me. On top of that, you are the biggest help I have on this plane. The biggest asset those passengers have."

"Don't worry. I'm not going to go all loopy on you. Now tell me. Where?"

"The engines won't all flame out at once."

"I can handle it. I'm not Rona. No need to water it down. Where will we run out of fuel?"

She fiddled aimlessly with the controls.

"I can handle it. I promise."

She still didn't answer.

He reached over to the aisle stand and cupped a hand over the back of hers. "What about Ascension Island? Are we going to run out of fuel before we reach it?"

"We're going to run out of fuel over the ocean."

The sober truth settled over him. "A dead-stick landing. Over the ocean."

"I've recalculated everything, hoping the computer made an error somewhere. *Anywhere.* We're going to run out of fuel one hundred and ten miles shy of the island." Her voice quavered. "Maybe more than that if we hit turbulence."

All the air sucked out of the cockpit. Quentin's heart jumped into his throat. "Oh God! Our situation just turned from shit to shit on fire."

CHAPTER 27

The full moon, in its unhurried elegance, glinted off the sedate ocean's onyx surface, while the twinkling diamonds of the night put on a light show in a crystal-clear sky, nary a cloud in this picture of paradise, and it was all a lie, a grotesque fabrication of what lay directly ahead.

Eden had seen the weather report, and the Combi was heading straight into a storm that "Superman in the cockpit" wouldn't want to tangle with. It made the one that delayed their flight look like a lawn sprinkler. *This* storm wasn't supposed to be a factor. They were supposed to vector around it. She was about to get her ass chewed, for sure, and she couldn't vector around that either.

Her head felt like it would crack open and give a whole new meaning to the phrase "splitting headache." She took two more aspirin and washed them down with more coffee, then checked the fuel synoptic display again. The more the numbers dropped, the more her anxiety grew. Flight 1219 was flying toward all unholy hell, and with that kind of turbulence, the Combi would consume fuel even faster. Guaranteed. Storms showed up in red, and her screen looked like it was bleeding.

——————◆◆——————

Quentin closed the cockpit door behind him and stepped into the hallway, where Daniel stood waiting for him.

"Okay, Daniel. What did you want to see me about?"

"I remembered something important about the megatera-toid. When the cabins were depressurized, they got cold."

"Right. I'm waiting for the punch line."

"Well, the doctors said that the mega-T has the ability to go into a form of hibernation. The one common factor they kept talking about was cold temperatures. I hate to say it, but I don't think it's dead. I believe Dr. Speck knew all along that it wouldn't die. Before you all went downstairs to get the other oxygen bottles, he said that you were risking your lives for nothing. I asked him what he meant, and he changed his story. Now I realize what he meant."

"No. I saw it."

"Yeah, you did. Now ask yourself what all did you see."

Quentin had seen more than he cared to remember. "I don't have time to play guessing games, Daniel."

"I bet you saw something different about it every time you saw it, didn't you?"

"Damn. I sure did. Not just bigger. It was smarter too. And physically different. How can it do that in such a short amount of time?"

"Only Dr. Ogladorff could explain that, and he didn't part with too many of his secrets. The mega-T changes on the inside too. It's highly adaptive. It has abilities I doubt Dr. Ogladorff knew about, and he knew more about it than anyone."

"Now I see why you wouldn't let him cut your toenails. Hell, I wouldn't either."

"Think about it. Do you think it would die so easily? It didn't die, Marshal. It simply went into a state of torpidity."

"What is that?"

"It's a little bit like hibernation with a much shorter wake-up call. Decreased activity equals decreased oxygen requirement. I pray to God I'm wrong, but I'm convinced it's going to wake up again. Maybe even before we land."

CHAPTER 28

The main deck had been silent until then. Hercules was sure of that. The distant sound of metal grinding against metal changed that, although no distance could ever be great enough when the only remaining resident on the other side of the walls was a bloodthirsty creature with a fondness for human flesh. Judging by the expressions on the other men's faces, they had heard it too.

He and Quentin had created a sound like that when they scraped the beverage carts against the rails along the stairs. He guessed that was what happened this time as well. It sounded like at least one of the carts tumbled down the stairs and crashed against the floor. Metal screeched. Having to rely on one sense left a lot of room for imagination, but it wasn't much of a stretch to envision the cart flattening.

A long, loud scraping sound like the blade of a sword dragging across a sheet of ice arose from the other side of the crew rest's forward wall. If he needed any further confirmation that the beast was near, he found it on the faces of the other four members of the exiled team. They looked like they had been jolted awake from the same nightmare.

Matt quietly moved from the forward wall to the bottom bunk beside his brother in front of Hercules. Gaston poked a hand out from under the blanket draped around his shoulders and pointed a quivering finger at the wall. Hercules nodded, confirming that he had heard the noise as well. Tyler scrunched up one corner of his blanket and crushed it against his mouth and nose.

Battling the megateratoid was a Sisyphean task. As soon as he thought it was gone, it came right back.

All of them stared at the forward wall as if it were transparent. Surprisingly, a low, bestial growl reverberated from the one behind Hercules, the scariest of them all because it was the closest. Every head whipped around. The vibration hit him in waves.

"It's back!" Hercules mouthed. So was the smell. The mega-T made sniffing sounds. Only a thin shell of a wall separated Hercules's back from the animal's muzzle. He didn't move. A twitch could get him killed.

The mega-T slammed against the wall. Hercules's head snapped back as if he had been rear-ended, the hard jolt nearly knocking him out of his seat. Gaston stood up. Hercules wanted to get off the wall just as much as he did but resisted the temptation. He held up an arresting hand, and Gaston eased back down in his seat. The mega-T slammed against the wall again, though not quite as hard.

"It's testing the wall," Hercules mouthed.

From the lower bunk on Hercules's right, Kinley's eyes zeroed in on something between them. "Heaven help us," he mouthed. The two brothers were fixated on it too. Hercules was about to follow Kinley's gaze when something hit the toe of his right shoe and bounced on the floor. When he looked down at it, he knew why the other men were riveted. It was a screw, and others in the metal corner joint had jostled free during the creature's assault and battery on the wall and now lay on the floor as well. The ones that held on had only won a

Pyrrhic victory. A crack about two feet long and as crooked as a lightning bolt had formed in the corner.

With the next hard blow, the two walls would split apart.

Another of what Hercules judged to be half-hearted attempts bumped against the wall behind him. Then silence. The beast appeared to have lost interest in the crew rest. The rock star was never so thankful to not be the center of attention.

When he heard more distant noises, he crept over to the fissure and assessed the damage. The crack had widened into a crevasse. The aisle, the seats across the aisle, and the portside wall were clearly visible through it. The corner spit out two more screws, and the crack ripped from the floor to the ceiling.

Sierra closed the curtain behind her in the upper deck galley and collapsed against the counter, physically and emotionally exhausted. She was tired of masking how terrified she was, and her spirit was breaking under the crushing weight of nursing everyone else's fears and needs while her own went unattended and even unacknowledged. In the privacy of the galley, the deluge that streamed from her eyes could have floated Noah's Ark.

She spared herself a few more minutes, then stuffed a cork in her feelings. The passengers in the upper deck kept her hopping, but they were safe. She couldn't say that for sure about the heroes down on the main deck.

Her voice had recovered enough to fake it. Whenever she cried, she sounded like a feeble old woman. Passengers in their dire predicament didn't need to hear how troubled she was. She cleared her throat and picked up the galley phone.

The curtains suddenly flung open.

She swept away the tears with the heels of her hands. "I'm glad you didn't see the blubbering mess I was a minute ago." A stubborn whimper still hid in her throat.

The air marshal slapped the curtains back together. "I'm sorry. I didn't know you were in here. Are you all right?"

"I needed a moment."

"You've certainly earned it."

She took a deep breath. "Amazing what a good cry will do. I have to check on the passengers." She picked up the phone again and made the call.

———◆———

Quentin didn't want to tell the purser how to do her job, but she didn't need to use the phone. All she had to do was step outside the curtains to check on the passengers. It suddenly hit him. She *couldn't* call them. As far as he knew, there wasn't a phone in the upper deck cabin.

"Oh shit!" He swept the phone out of her hand and hit the "R" button.

"Why did you hang up?"

"If that phone rings, it'll be like ringing a dinner bell."

She gasped. "That means … it's not dead?"

"No. Just powered down to wait out the storm."

"Oh my God! I could have killed them."

He rammed the phone back into its cradle as if it had become the enemy.

"I wasn't thinking."

"Crisis averted," he said in his fake Mr. Calm, Cool, and Collected tone.

"I'd better go check on the other passengers." She finger-combed her hair, smoothed out her uniform, and left the galley.

He unlatched one of the beverage carts and rolled it out from under the counter. In the third drawer, he found his old friends: Jack and Jim and Johnnie.

Someone should write a song.

He pulled out a few of the mini bottles of alcohol, and they pulled at him, still as enticing as ever, but he pushed back.

He still felt the void left behind after his wife and daughter died, but he sensed it was closing a little.

Kellva's death had been expected, but Tracie's had blind-sided him.

He had cannonballed home on a flight from London with a tire iron in his gut that was twisting and turning and telling him something had to be wrong for Tracie not to return his six international calls with six increasingly concerned voicemail messages.

He had burst into the foyer calling her name. "Tracie!" The blaring news on TV would have drowned out her reply. He darted into the family room, grabbed the remote, and turned off the TV. "Traceee!" The tire iron in his gut spun on its axis.

From the doorway of the dining room, he saw her slumped over with her head on the dining room table, an empty bottle of sleeping pills on the floor beside her chair, and a "Sorry to leave you, but I must go" letter on the table. Her long, black hair covered a face that could have been dead not long after he last talked to her on the phone a day and a half earlier.

Now, for the first time since Tracie died, he had more reasons *not* to drink than he had *to* drink. He was now a godfather to Red's two sons, he had promised Rona that he would take her to her father, the passengers depended on him to keep the mega-T out of the upper deck, Eden had said he was the only one left to help her, not to mention Eden herself, still only a possibility, but ... wow! He would lose any chance he had of keeping them out of the "Mission Failed" column if he got into the teeter-totter water.

Today, his life had a purpose. Tomorrow ... well, he would figure that out then.

"Goodbye, Jack." He put the bottle of Jack Daniel's into the drawer. "Nice knowing you, Jim." He wedged the Jim

Beam bottle into a vacant spot. "Ahhh, Johnnie, the stories we could tell." He dropped the bottle of scotch into the drawer. After eulogizing them, he stared down at all the little bottles in the mass grave of old chums. His moment of weakness, like Sierra's, had passed.

Too many people had died. If he was the only thing standing between the creature and the survivors, then that was exactly where he would be. Sober and ready to kick some ass.

CHAPTER 29

"Airland 1219 heavy. Wideawake Tower," Eden said into her headset microphone. There was still nothing. Not a peep from Ascension Island, only cold, dead air every time she radioed. "Something is wrong. Wideawake Tower should have responded. I hope the storm didn't knock out their equipment."

Quentin took off the first officer's headset and hung it around his neck. "Do you think you can land without their help?"

"It certainly wouldn't be the best of circumstances. I have the Jeppesen chart. Airland control gave me some information. I have the runway numbers. That alone gives me the runways' general compass headings, just add zero. Runway Thirteen has a heading around 130 degrees, a southeast heading. Runway Thirty-one, somewhere around 310, a northwest heading. Yadda, yadda, yadda. If that was all pilots needed, air traffic controllers would be redundant."

"Well, two runways, two options. There is that."

"No, there's only one. It has takeoffs and landings from both ends. Each end has a different runway number to correspond to its heading."

"Airland 1219 heavy. Wideawake Tower."

The silence seemed palpable. She resisted the temptation

to rip her headset off and give it a good chuck against the wall. She looked heavenward. "It's like someone up there said, 'Let's throw in a fuel crisis and a storm of the century because Eden Stone doesn't have enough to deal with. Now let's make her fly alone. And take away the air traffic controller while we're at it.'"

And because she won't face her past, let's hit her with a deadly illness. Quentin didn't need to hear that part.

"Isn't that ironic?" the air marshal said. "An airfield named Wideawake, and they're all asleep."

If he was trying to lighten the mood, it would take a hell of a lot more than that. With all the fear, frustration, tension, and anxiety … *Good luck with that, Marshal.* She rewarded his efforts with a half-assed smile. It was the best she could do. "It's named after the birds, the sooty terns. They're nicknamed the wideawake birds because they sound like they're saying, 'Wideawake, wideawake, wideawake.'"

She rubbed her thumb and index finger together on her left hand and felt something strange. A small wheal protruded from her thumb. Tough turkey. *Go to the back of the line, buddy.* She pawed at her temple. Generic aspirin. What a joke.

Her heartbeat throttled up. The instrument panels started coming toward her, then retreating in rhythmic waves. She blinked a few times and squinted, but nothing cleared her vision.

Please. Not yet. Not this quickly.

She was deteriorating far faster than expected and wouldn't be able to keep her illness hidden for very long. Now the secrets were sprouting new secrets.

Secrets—the story of my life.

Repositioning the headset microphone closer to her mouth, she cleared her throat. "Airland 1219 heavy. Wideawake Tower."

"Wideawake Tower. Receiving Airland 1219 heavy. Go ahead," the voice of a man with a French accent crackled in her headset.

Quentin slapped his headset back on his head and did a fist pump.

"Airland 1219 heavy. We are critically low in fuel."

"Airland 1219 heavy, what is your current heading?" he said.

"Current heading is three-one-one."

"Flight 1219 heavy, change heading to three-two-five."

"Roger, Wideawake Tower. Changing heading to three-two-five. Confirm runway length."

"Ten thousand feet. Asphalt. You got the ocean at both ends of the runway, Airland 1219, so there's no room for error."

The breath rushed out of her lungs as if a horse had kicked her in the sternum. Her chest tightened. *There's no room for error*, her mind replayed, detached from hands that zipped around the controls on their own version of autopilot. His words triggered a dormant memory she had kept buried beneath her mind's crust deep inside its magma chamber. The scare she had with the rusty orange pickup truck and the lake had opened a fissure. His words had blasted open a crater. The hot, molten memory that had been waiting beneath the surface all those years, expanding and gaining energy, erupted into her consciousness.

———◦———

"There's no room for error on an aircraft carrier," Riptide had said in the ready room during many of his preflight briefings onboard the *Abraham Lincoln*. It was his favorite adage, declared so many times that Eden thought he should have it printed on a T-shirt. "There's no room for error where the difference between life and death can be measured in inches."

If the tales on the *Abraham Lincoln* could be believed, Billy

Tyler Crudup had gained the moniker "Riptide" early in his navy career when he was stationed in Hawaii.

One Friday night, he and a few of his buddies went out for a few drinks at a bar and met a group of University of Southern California marine biology students. Bailey, a slender beauty with raven tresses, caught his eye. In an attempt to impress her, he decided to show off his swimming prowess by going for a lengthy swim at breakneck speed. But the waters off Maui's coast decided to complicate things. He got caught in a riptide that pulled him under repeatedly, turning a nice dip to impress a girl into a fight for his life.

Years later on the *Abe*, Riptide stood at the front of the ready room, priming Eden and her fellow navy pilots before a training mission. "There's no room for error on an aircraft carrier. One lapse in judgment and you come up shy of the deck or you overshoot the deck. If you come in too low, you crash into the ocean. If you come in too high, you crash into the ocean." His unorthodox pep talks had a 100 percent success rate, and Eden certainly didn't want to be the first pilot he lost.

Later, on the flight deck of the *Abe*, the shooter in his usual yellow jersey and matching float coat signaled Eden to throttle up to full power. She checked the F/A-18's engine and controls, then saluted the shooter to let him know the aircraft was ready. He did some final checks of his own, then signaled the catapult operator to fire one of the *Abe's* four high-powered steam catapults. Two seconds after the Fat Cat fired, Eden and her thirty-three-ton aircraft had launched from a standstill to 165 miles an hour. Taking a cat shot off an aircraft carrier was like a gnat hitching a ride on a bullet. The force of four Gs crushed her against the back of her seat. Wham, bam, thank you, ma'am. That was it. She was airborne.

The belly of her aircraft could almost touch the ocean before she throttled up and it soared into the beaming, blue sky fifty thousand feet above the Pacific Ocean. The tranquil, blue surface below sparkled like the Hope Diamond whenever the sun glinted ever so lovely off a particularly vibrant wave. Up ahead in the distance, the ocean kissed the sky. She marveled at the curvature of the earth, her eyes drinking in the panoramic view from left to right.

When she approached the speed of sound, a giant, white vapor cone formed around the tail of the Super Hornet as it shot horizontally through the moist air. The cone looked like a spooky ghost lying on its side, eating her aircraft tailfirst. But it was no more than a cloud of condensed water. The narrow part of the cone fit snugly around the body of the aircraft. By the time the cone reached the tail, it had flared so big that two Super Hornets could fit inside it, wingtip to wingtip.

Not every day a girl gets to make her own weather. She allowed herself a proud smile. As the Super Hornet's speed increased, the vapor cone moved farther toward the tail, and when she burst through the sound barrier, it disappeared altogether. Her own private weather phenomenon had lasted all of seven seconds.

On her return, night had fallen. Suddenly, she heard a loud, piercing bang that certainly wasn't the F/A-18 breaking the sound barrier. An explosion jolted her inside the tiny bubble cockpit. Smoke billowed from one of the two engines, and she could feel the Super Hornet die in midair. Before she realized it, she was looking up at the ocean.

She rolled the aircraft right side up and pointed it straight for the USS *Abraham Lincoln.* "Whoo!" she sighed when she saw how far away it was. The deck of the floating airport didn't seem to be coming up fast enough for the crippled plane to reach it.

The landing signal officer confirmed her calculation. "Pull up!" he beseeched over the radio. "You're coming in too low! Pull up!"

She was already trying to do precisely that. The problem was that the crippled jet wouldn't respond. She struggled to regain altitude, yet the starboard wing dipped toward the ocean. She wrestled it back up, but her efforts sent the opposite wing toward the beckoning waves. "Come on!" she yelled. "You can do this. Trust your training."

Training or not, and despite how hard she grappled with the aircraft, the Super Hornet steadily lost altitude, dropping closer and closer to the briny.

The aircraft shaved the ocean's surface. She wrestled it up somehow. If she couldn't control the F/A-18 any better than that, it wouldn't be wise to take a chance on landing on the flight deck of the *Abe*, where scores of her fellow sailors performed the meticulously choreographed dance of launching and landing aircraft; where other aircraft filled with fuel prepared to take off; where others were returning from their own sorties; and where highly explosive ordnances were being loaded onto still other aircraft.

She was about to point the unruly aircraft away from the flattop and ditch it in the sea when it leveled out. Deciding on a new course, she angled it toward the fantail of the ship and searched for the meatball, an optical illusion emanating from the portside of the ship that would guide her down the slope to land at an airport that was heaving, pitching, and running away from her. The meatball got its name from its bright amber color, part of the ingenious Fresnel Lens Optical Landing System, primarily lights arranged in the shape of a cross. Twelve vertical lights ran down between twenty horizontal green lights; ten on the left arm of the cross, ten on the right. The other lights were wave-off lights that would flash red if the LSO wanted her to scrap the landing attempt, go around, and try it again.

The meatball represented her aircraft and moved up or

down and changed color depending on the Super Hornet's position relative to the deck. Ideally, she would see a bright amber image in the middle of the horizontal green line. If she saw that alignment, she would be coming in on a perfect glide slope for her wheels to touch down on the ship's flight deck. If she came in at an angle that was too steep, the meatball would be above the horizontal line of green lights and would be a lighter color. If she came in at an angle that was too shallow, it would be below the green lights and darker.

The most dreaded color was red. For a pilot attempting to land on a flattop, it was the color of death, a dire warning that the pilot was coming in extremely low and was in supreme danger of a ramp strike.

A mile and a half out, the ball blossomed into view but wasn't the bright amber color she hoped for. Nor was it positioned between the green horizontal lights. It was below them and a fierce red.

If she didn't pull the aircraft up, she would become bug splat on the ass end of the *Abe*.

The aircraft, though smoking and clanking and making a weird jittering sound, responded well to her commands. The ball rose, turned a bright amber, and positioned itself bang in the middle between the green arms of the cross to form a perfect horizontal line.

"I have the ball," she reported to the LSO over the radio. He confirmed her altitude, airspeed, and angle of approach, all perfectly within the strict limits for landing on the *Abe*.

If she hadn't been familiar with the lens system, she would have bet a year's salary that only one of the twelve vertical lights were illuminated. All twelve of them were on and angled to produce a single image depending on her glide slope.

Trust your training, she drilled herself. She would have to; she was fast approaching a procedure that ran in the opposite direction of any human's common sense, and if she wasn't diligent, her nerves would tell her training to plot a course straight to hell.

A hail of memories from her training exercises and previous traps volleyed through her mind at the speed of light. Four arresting wires lay across the deck of the ship fifty feet apart. If her landing went according to plan, the tailhook on her Super Hornet would snag one of the wires, and it would stop the aircraft going full throttle in a brain-warping two seconds. If it went wrong, the "oh shit" gauge would swing into the red area, and the LSO would say a word no navy pilot wanted to hear, some even feared—bolter.

It wasn't a good idea to aim for the first wire. It was too close to the stern, and she could crash into the back of the floating city. The third wire was the safest and the one she aimed for. She constantly monitored the Super Hornet for the first sign that it was returning to its difficult ways, but it cut a smooth path all the way down the glide slope to the deck.

As soon as she slammed down, she throttled up to full power, which ran counterintuitive to someone who was desperately trying to come to a full stop before running out of real estate and ending up in the ocean. The life-saving maneuver was drilled into all pilots landing on the deck of an aircraft carrier except those in helicopters and hovercraft like the Harrier. In the event she missed all four of the arresting wires, she would have enough speed to race down the waist of the ship and become airborne again. If not, she would crash into the ocean.

There's no room for error, Riptide's voice warned her again. *Missed it!*

The Super Hornet hurtled down the flight deck at 150 miles an hour. She had missed the third arresting wire and had to snag the fourth one or she would have to bolter. If she had to circle around and attempt a second landing, there was no way the smoking, clanking, jittering aircraft would still be in one piece. Not a chance in France.

She felt a slight reduction in the forward momentum of her aircraft. The hook attached to the tail of her aircraft had snagged the last arresting wire.

In a split second, the "Oh Shit" gauge swung back into the red area. Sheer panic filled her.

The aircraft wasn't slowing down fast enough. In fact, it was speeding up again because she had yet to throttle down. *Something is wrong.*

"Damn it!"

She knew exactly what had happened: the arresting wire had snapped in two.

Now she raced down the deck headed straight for the ocean, oddly going both too fast *and* too slow. Although she was throttled up to full power, the arresting wire had slowed her down to the point she was going too *slow* to regain enough speed to take off again and too *fast* to have any hope of stopping before she ran out of deck.

It was clear she was going into the Pacific Ocean. The only thing that wasn't clear was whether she would be alive or dead when they pulled her out.

The sound of her tires rolling down the deck came to an abrupt halt. Simultaneously, she felt them sail off the edge of the deck beneath her. For a second or two, the aircraft was airborne; then it took a nosedive toward the deep blue drink.

Fire and thick, black smoke billowed up from behind her.

She reached down between her knees and found the ejection seat handle. As her fingers pulled the yellow-and-black loop, the plane exploded. The canopy blasted away above her. A microsecond later, she shot into the sky as if she had blasted off from one of the launch pads at Cape Canaveral.

Fiery pieces of what was once her F/A-18 blasted into the sky and splashed down in the ocean, but one of the pieces defied gravity. Eden's parachute had deployed and her seat had separated. She floated down to the ocean, slow and peaceful, no longer confined to the world or encumbered by its problems, the complete opposite of what the previous few seconds had been. All of the harrowing sequence had taken place within a few seconds.

Floating quietly and serenely in the sky was a welcome respite. There wasn't a sound until she hit the water. Before long, she heard the *whoop*, *whoop*, *whoop* of helicopter blades.

The ash-gray Seahawk hovered above her while a rescue swimmer fast-roped down to the surface and plucked her from the briny.

When she got back on the *Abe*, she expected a sunnier reception than the somber mood of everyone in the ship's hospital. She had escaped almost certain death after all. Even the nurse who examined her seemed gloomy, which was odd for Lieutenant Commander Jess Velencort, a man who was always as bubbly as a truckload of champagne on a bumpy road and always had a joke or a riddle in the chamber.

"You're going to be sore for a few days," he said in a tone as sterile as the gauze he used to dress the cut on her shoulder while she sat on the examining table. "If your back gets any worse, we can give you naproxen, and if that doesn't work, we can try Skelaxin."

The same man had treated her a month earlier when she sprained her ankle climbing out of her rack. "If the pain gets any worse, we can cut off your foot," he had teased while wrapping her ankle. "The other one too, because I wouldn't want you to go home with a limp."

She had chuckled and shook her head.

That was a completely different person from the one taking

care of her latest ills. Something was going on, something other than her going for an unplanned swim or making an unauthorized $65 million deposit into the sea. Maybe their six-month deployment had been extended.

Velencort pressed into the back of her neck with his thumbs. "Is that tender?"

"What's wrong?" she blurted out and had to resist the urge to pull his hands away.

"I'm sorry. I'm not supposed to discuss it."

"Discuss what? And why not?" She was more worried now. "Look, I know that aircraft costs a lot of money, but I did everything I was trained to do."

"It's not the plane. It's Topperman."

"The shooter? You have to tell me now. You can't just leave me drowning in my own thoughts."

He held her hand consolingly. "It wasn't your fault."

It was then that she knew.

She didn't know the *how*, but she knew the *what*. It could have been a piece of the Super Hornet hitting Jonas Topperman when it exploded. Or a wing could have hit him as her aircraft raced down the flight deck. Or the engine blast could have blown him overboard. He was wearing his float coat to keep him from sinking down into the abyss, yes, but that wouldn't protect him from a broken neck or severed artery or disembowelment.

She realized that Velencort was no longer holding her hand. He was checking her pulse.

"I'm fine. Please. Just tell me what happened."

His Adam's apple bobbed up and down. He cleared his throat. It appeared he was still deciding whether or not to tell her. "When the arresting wire broke," he finally said, "one end of it snapped back and … and decapitated him."

Eden gasped. The next thing she knew, she was lying on

the examining table, not sure if she had simply collapsed back-ward or if Velencort had helped her.

She didn't see it his way: her plane, her fault.

———◦◦◦———

She felt the same way now. Her plane, her fault. The tragic accident aboard the *Abraham Lincoln* had made international news. From the way things looked, Eden was perched on the precipice of doing it again.

"Are you okay?" the air marshal asked.

"Just mentally rechecking my calculations," she fibbed, wondering how long he had been talking to her.

Topperman's yellow jersey fluttered in her mind, a caution flag. She had retired from the navy rather than risk killing another innocent soul. Not the smartest plan, now that she thought about it. She had traded payloads for people. Ninety-five souls, not including her own. Ninety-five potential Toppermans.

Her eyes skated past the glareshield. *That's unreal!* They were supposed to be thousands of miles away from that thing.

———◦◦◦———

Quentin glanced back at Rona. The little one must have been extremely tired to sleep through all the hullabaloo in the cockpit. She was still out and hadn't stirred since she first dozed off.

"Good God. Look at that." Eden pointed through the windshield. Her face turned into a statue with wide, frozen eyes and an unhinged jaw.

He turned to see what she was pointing at. "What the hell?" He already knew the answer but didn't trust his eyes. "Pull over and let me out. I'll walk the rest of the way. I've never seen anything like that."

"Neither have I. Not even when I was in the navy."

His eyes widened, trying to comprehend the full scope and magnitude of the giant looming up ahead. "Th-that can't be good." Far off in the distance, a white cloud towered over all the ones around it. The top of it flattened out into the shape of an anvil. "If Hercules stood on the top of that thing, he could touch the moon."

"Hugemongous!" A small voice came from behind Eden's seat.

He smiled. "Look who's awake."

Rona yawned. Her eyes drifted shut, then sprang open again.

"Just barely," Eden said, redirecting her attention back to the concern outside the windshield.

"I want my mommy," Rona said.

The windshield lit up with blue lightning bolts that danced and flickered.

"Jesus!" Quentin shook his head. "Blue lightning?"

"Saint Elmo's fire. That's all it is, Marshal. Static electricity."

Rona pointed a scolding finger at the windshield. "Stop that, Elmo."

"I'm with her," he added.

Eden squinted. "I don't mind Saint Elmo's fire as much as what it foretells. It's a sign that a violent storm is approaching."

As soon as the static electricity stopped, lightning emblazoned the sky dead ahead. Thunder shook the heavens.

"That certainly wasn't static electricity," he said.

"No. That'll part your hair quite nicely."

Rona leaned toward him. "It's okay. She's a ... she's a *professonal*. Remember?"

"You're right, Rona. She certainly is."

Rona leaned back in her seat, where another yawn awaited her.

"It's topping off at sixty thousand feet. That's rare." Eden hadn't once taken her eyes off the cloud.

"I've seen my share of rarities today. Enough to last a lifetime. So thank you very much, but you can keep that one."

"I wish I could," Eden said.

Behind her, Rona yawned loudly, and her head slowly flopped down on her chest. The little girl was asleep again.

"No. No," he said. "Don't tell me we're going to have to fly through that—that *thing* that bubbled up from the pit of hell."

"Worse."

His mouth flew open. "Worse? Oh God."

She continued to gaze out of the windshield with that wide-eyed, frozen stare. She leaned forward in her seat and exhaled a quick sigh.

It reminded him of the way he looked and sounded—before drinking became his favorite hobby—when he peered up to the top of a challenging rock face he was about to climb.

She rubbed the back of her neck. "Somewhere in that giant cumulonimbus is Ascension Island."

A sour taste rose to the back of his throat. He was suddenly in need of an antacid. "The moment we boarded this airplane, we opened a bag of nightmares."

"It doesn't look like we'll be able to close it anytime soon."

A loud beeping alarm sounded in the cockpit. Quentin didn't need to be a pilot to know that wasn't good. The little girl's head was still canted down on her right shoulder.

On the screen above the throttles was a message displayed in Amber: "ENGINE 4 FAIL."

Eden hit the Master Warning/Caution Reset switch and silenced it. "We've got flameout in the number four engine."

Inside him, panic was on the rampage. Quentin stripped every hint of it from his voice. "We're that close? I hoped we would have more time."

"That's the second time today someone's articulated what I was thinking. First Monty and the doll, now you and the engine."

"Okay, what now?"

"The three remaining engines automatically assume all the electrical load." She paused, squinted slightly, and frowned like she was concentrating. "She's trying to go right on me now. I've got a power imbalance. Two engines on the left and one on the right. That makes it a bit harder to keep her going straight."

She reached up to the overhead panel. There had to be another two or three hundred buttons and switches and dials above their heads. No wonder it took years to become a pilot. He had to take a class to understand how to work a fraction of the features on his phone. He gained a renewed respect and admiration for pilots, especially the one next to him who had to go it alone.

Above them, her hand twisted a dial.

Oh God! Purple!

It was his fault. He didn't know how or where, but he had missed something.

Her head snapped over to him. "What?"

His eyes stayed on her hand and guided her gaze to it. Her thumb and index finger were spread apart slightly, paused in a ready position to receive their next command. She spread her fingers apart, then turned her hand so that the outside of her thumb faced her. Below the bottom knuckle was a purple spot. She turned back to him at the pace of a glacier.

This time, he met her gaze. Her eyes were cherry red.

He took her hand gently between both of his. Neither said a word for a long moment. Then he broke the silence. "It's not going to happen. I won't let it. I will not add one more thing to my backbreaking bag of sorrows."

"There's nothing you can do."

"How else am I going to take you to my favorite sushi restaurant?"

CHAPTER 30

In Wideawake tower above the airfield on Ascension Island, Winston Françoise Le Blanc willed Flight 1219 to stay airborne. His throat tightened as he checked the radar screen. The little box with "AL 1219 37,000 FT" inside it was still there, proof, at least for the moment, that the pilot and her passengers still had a chance, however small, of surviving. A pilot flying an aircraft that big, solo, had a monumental task.

Thinking about how utterly destructive a brutal impact with the sea was on the human body, images of mangled, dismembered, and twisted bodies zipped through his mind. He finished off his warm Diet Coke and tossed the bottle into the wastepaper basket under his desk.

In the western noir sky, lightning zigged, forked, then zagged. A deep thunderclap shook the island. The tropical desert climate didn't impart much rain upon the volcanic island. On the rare occasion when Ascension did get a storm, each drencher spent a few days being a constant aggravation and a royal imposition, always making a mess of things and leaving it behind for others to tidy up.

Le Blanc looked out at the torment outside the window. Beauty was found on the island only when he closed his eyes or when night fell. Even on sunny spring mornings with postcard-blue skies above that stretched all the way to God's front door, the barren landscape wasn't much to wake up to, with its crater-pocked lava fields and boasting what had been named the worst golf course in the world, a raw sewage-colored boil on the island's ass that grew even worse when the greens—actually browns, for the most part—deteriorated into an outbreak of carbuncles oozing chunks of rocks and volcanic ash.

Somehow in all of that, enough decent land had been found to build Wideawake Airfield on the southwestern edge of the little landmass isolated in the middle of the South Atlantic Ocean between the horn of South America and Africa. The airfield was now sloshy and muddy, the asphalt on the airstrip now slick and rain-washed. Nonetheless, if he were stuck out in the middle of the Atlantic in an aircraft that was in danger of crashing in the ocean, he was sure he would see the island as the most beautiful piece of land on earth.

If the pilot made it to Ascension, she and her passengers would have to land in the blinding storm that had taken control of the island, all thirty-five square miles of it. Rain pounded the runway. Wind whipped across the wasteland. Cloudlings caught his eye whenever the wind blew the wispy vapor near the lights. Rain gusts whipped this way, then that.

Thunder and lightning, at times, seemed powerful enough to hammer the little pinhead island back down into the ocean. The windswept fog chased the night sky down to three hundred feet above the spayed and neutered landscape.

At some point, he had started to scratch the back of his forearm absentmindedly. He frequently caught himself engaged in the annoying habit whenever he felt stressed. He forced his hands to settle on the desktop. A second later he started scratching it again.

A fuel emergency on a heavy, compounded with the fact that the pilot was going to have to fly into *this* storm. Solo … *Oh, mon dieu!*

CHAPTER 31

Quentin bolted out of the cockpit. Daniel sat with his back to the cockpit door, blocking the other end of the hallway, but slid over to let Quentin pass. He didn't. Instead, he yanked Daniel up by the back of his jacket and pinned him against the bulkhead wall.

"It's the pilot, Daniel. You're going to tell me how to save her."

"Oh God."

"Tell me what I need to do!"

"I don't know. I don't. I'm sorry."

"Do you understand what's going to happen if she dies?"

A synchronized gasp rippled through the passengers in the front of the cabin.

"I do. I don't know how to save her. Honest to God. I wish I did." Daniel's wet eyes were pleading into his, wide and unflinching. Unblinking.

Through his grasp, Quentin could feel a tremble gathering momentum inside the man. He was telling the truth. For once, Quentin wished he wasn't. "Then *think*. There has to be a way to save her. To save *us*, Daniel."

Daniel looked over at the passengers sheepishly. His body went slack as if he had slid out of his own skin, leaving the air marshal to keep the remnant upright.

"I'm sorr—"

Quentin's fist was already in midair before he realized it. It slammed into the wall beside Daniel's right ear. "Yeah, yeah, yeah. I know. You're sorry. You said that already. What good is that going to do her now? Huh? Sorry and a million bucks won't do her a damn bit of good. Or us." He let go before another fist went flying, not sure he could abort the mission the next time. He grabbed his head and paced in a tight circle in the confines of the narrow hallway. The passengers were probably watching. Of course they should be concerned. But figuring out how to save Eden's life and theirs had become his raison d'être.

He yanked open the first overhead bin on his left, then its aisle mate on the right. He ransacked them with no idea what he was looking for. Sure, the chances of him saving Eden were miniscule. Sure, the venom had a 100 percent fatality rate. So fucking what. Still not enough for him to give up on her.

There had to be something. *Think.* He yanked opened the next set of bins. Searching feverishly, he tossed backpacks and duffel bags on the floor, then moved on to the next set. *Think medicine.* He didn't even know what it was he was trying to cure.

His mind was adrift on a sea of thoughts before landing on what might be solid ground. The bag in his hand slid from his fingers. Before it hit the floor, he shot toward the middle of the cabin.

Sierra met him near the exit row. "If you're looking for something, maybe I can help."

"It's Eden."

"She slapped a hand on her chest and gasped. "I had a feeling it was just a matter of time."

He looked past her. Near the back, Dr. Ross sat across the aisle from a teenage girl with jet-black hair, tattoos on her neck, and a narrow chain that ran from a piercing in her right nostril down to another piercing above the corner of her upper lip. The doctor finished wrapping a bandage around the teen-ager's ankle and looked up as he was about to call out to her. She rushed to meet them in the exit row.

"Doctor, Eden doesn't have long."

"I knew that the second I saw you. Your eyes could write a book."

"Can you think of anything we can do?"

"I was afraid it would come to this. I have been trying to come up with a solution in the event it did. I'm sorry to say I haven't come up with anything."

He rubbed a forearm across his forehead, realizing for the first time that he was sweating. "If you can't, I don't know what else to do."

"We need to keep her as calm as we can. I know that's going to be difficult under the circumstances."

More than you know.

"Marshal, I need to check her vitals."

The two of them walked up the aisle amid stifled whimpers from some of the passengers.

"For God sakes!" TR shouted as they passed him. "Just tell us what's going on!"

When they reached the front of the aisle, they passed through a huddle of two women and three men who were holding hands and praying.

He didn't want to disturb them. They could use all the prayers they could get. As it turned out, they didn't have to. The group stood up and made an archway above them with their fingers still interlaced. He and Dr. Ross ducked down and walked under it. The group never stopped praying.

"Give them counsel, Lord," one of the women said.

A hand slapped him on his shoulder, and he felt something

hard. He looked back. The hand belonged to the man with his middle finger in a splint. Then the group huddled back up behind them. Their prayers grew louder and more fervent.

Eden unlocked the door, and Quentin let Dr. Ross enter first. "Watch your step," he said as she stepped down the two-inch lip into the cockpit.

"This is Dr. Ross. She needs to—"

"There's no need. Besides, I need to keep my mind on flying this aircraft."

"I'm not here to upset you. In fact, that's what you need to avoid if possible," Dr. Ross said. "I would like to take your vitals, get a better idea of what's going on, and see if there's something I can do to slow down the progression."

Eden shook her head slowly and opened her mouth to say something.

"You never know," Quentin urged.

Eden cast a thumb over her shoulder at the pilots' rest quarters. "But the others—"

"The others didn't have any medical attention. Give Dr. Ross a chance. Please."

She fiddled with buttons and levers. "We're wasting time."

"Exactly." There was no way in hell he was giving up.

Dr. Ross moved closer, just behind Rona's seat. "It'll only take a couple of minutes. I won't poke you or prod you. I promise."

"I guess. As long as it doesn't take too long."

Quentin stepped out of the cockpit to give them some privacy. He leaned against the outside of the cockpit door. The cool of its metal seeped in through his back and sharpened his focus. Closing his eyes, he let the chill propagate through him. Within the silence of that brief moment, a bright memory flickered. His eyes sprang open and targeted the second lavatory door on his left. He raced toward it and shoved the door open. By some miracle, it didn't rip from its hinges. Dr. Speck's body fell against the small vanity. He confiscated the silver briefcase lying across the sink and closed the door.

Quentin laid the briefcase on the floor in the hallway and tested both clasps. Locked and locked. With their luck, of course they were locked. He snatched it up and tore a path down the aisle.

Quentin found Daniel standing beside the portside exit door, gazing out of the window with a distant look in his eyes. As soon as he got within reach, the briefcase popped Daniel in the chest, less intentionally, more due to Quentin's momentum and excitement about the possibilities. But he wouldn't waste a perfectly good give-a-shit on Daniel's ass either. During the entire flight, Dr. Speck had been protecting his briefcase. It was time for Quentin to find out why.

"What's the combination, Daniel?"

"I don't know. I … I saw it for the first time this morning."

"You don't give the impression that you know a lot about any of this."

"Oggie and the doc brought me on board just two years ago, and they only parceled out information I needed to do my job. They didn't want me to know everything. Every time I asked them to divulge more information, the doc would say it was like the atomic bomb: once the know-how to make it is out there, you can never get it back."

"Enough of that. What's in it?"

"Data about how Oggie created the mega-T, I suppose. Speck would have needed that when he got to South Africa. I guess that's why he didn't want anyone touching it."

"Help me find something to open it."

"I have a pocketknife in my suitcase, but that's stowed."

Quentin tore into the overhead bins again, ripping through their contents, trying to remember if he had seen anything narrow and hard and strong when he was searching them earlier. "Excuse me. Does anyone have anything we can use to jimmy open the locks on this briefcase?"

He heard a lot of grumbles but nothing else.

One of them might have something. He just didn't know it. Quentin ran back to the front of the cabin, jumping over the backpacks and duffel bags he had tossed into the aisle. "Sir, can I please have that?" He pointed at the metal brace on a passenger's finger. "That just might work."

The man with the injured middle finger didn't waste time answering. He lit into the bandage, first using his teeth and got a rip started, wincing but still tearing at it with zeal. With a little less than half of it left, the man yanked the brace out with one long wince and handed it over, eyes sparkling with hope.

Quentin kneeled and jabbed the brace into the seam between the top and bottom of the briefcase. The metal was too thick to squeeze into the thin slit, far too thick. He pried one shoe off with the toe of the other and lined up the edge of the brace with the seam between the clasp and the combination plate. Using his shoe for a hammer, he drove the heel against the top end of the brace. No luck. The shoe bent near the ball of the sole. He gripped it closer to the heel and drove it down with twice as much force as he had the first time.

Cla-clink. The spring-loaded clasp flew open. But the brace was bent and didn't look like it had enough strength left in it for the other clasp.

After one whack on the second clasp, the brace looked like a backward letter "C." Eden didn't have time for him to go rifling through the overhead bins to find a replacement. The seam on the side where the clasp was open was wide enough that the metal shiv just might fit. He wedged it into the seam and forced it through until the apex of the bend was in the seam. He pressed his knee down on the top of the briefcase and pulled the brace up. Voilà! It straightened out and roughly resembled its former self.

He placed the brace between the second clasp and the combination plate again and gave it a good whack. The clasp sprang open. Good thing it did. The brace now looked like the letter "S" and had little chance of withstanding another blow.

He yanked open the briefcase with no clue what he was looking for.

A thick, black three-ring binder lay in the bottom. He picked it up and fanned through a few pages before flipping back to the first sheet. Handwritten notes in black ink on blue-lined paper centered on formulas and chemical compounds. He could identify some of the symbols from the chemistry classes he had back in college, back when dinosaurs still roamed the earth.

He dropped the binder back into its spot and pulled out a small, denim-covered case with a black zipper on one end and a pouch on the outside. It looked soft and light, but it was heavy, and underneath the soft fabric, the case was unyielding to the pressure he applied with his fingers. He yanked the zipper open.

Come on, come on. Give me something to save her.

A white pack the size of his hand felt cold and squishy. When he pressed his fingers together around it, the contents shifted. It was a cooling gel pack. Two identical little white boxes lay in front of it. He pulled one into the light and read its label. "Insulin. Dr. Speck was telling the truth." He opened both boxes and pulled out the vials. On each label, below the name of the pharmaceutical company was the word "insulin."

A flap with Velcro attached sealed whatever hidden treasures that lay inside the pouch. He ripped it open and pulled out a black, felt bag with a drawstring closure. He loosened the string and let the contents slide out into the briefcase at an angle to keep from damaging them in case they proved beneficial. Packets of alcohol swabs and a pack of syringes with a small hole in the top slid out.

Okay, Dr. Speck. You've proven your point. What else do you have in here?

He rifled through the compartments of the attaché case and found a handful of flash drives, two external hard drives, and a loose stack of notes concerning research on the mega-T, some written on yellow sticky notes, some on white paper torn from some small notebook with rings at the top, and some on other colors of paper.

"A waste of time. *Valuable* time." He slammed the briefcase against the floor, jostling its contents.

Dr. Ross rushed out of the cockpit. All it took was one look at her, and Quentin knew the news was going to be bad.

When she stooped down, her knees crackled like a handful of dry twigs breaking. "Minutes," she whispered. "That's all she has."

Damn! He looked down. "What's that?" He pulled the briefcase back over to him. The binder lay sprawled open. Some of the pages on the top lay in a jumble of ruin. He flipped them to the left side of the binder. Through the center of the pages on the right, he could barely make out a dark area. Possibly a faint watermark. He flipped more of the pages to the left. *That's no watermark.*

A black rectangle about the size of a hardcover novel gradually took shape beneath the pages. With one more page to go, he realized what he was looking at. He looked up at Daniel, who had anticipation in his eyes. Until then, he didn't realize that Daniel had come to the front of the cabin or that he himself had drawn an audience.

Quentin flipped the final page over to the left. A space had been hollowed out of all but the last few pages. Hidden inside that hollow was a rectangular, black case.

CHAPTER 32

It's not real. It's not real. It's not real.

The cockpit was a cluster of shifting buttons, switches, and dials. The two screens behind Eden's control yoke slid to the right and crashed into the standby attitude indicator, the standby airspeed indicator, and the standby altimeter in the center panel. The screens in front of the first officer's seat pulsated with the rhythm of a steady heartbeat.

What was the venom made of, extra-strength LSD? The mega-T's saliva was toxic, hallucinogenic. Eden didn't want to know what else.

Trust your training. Bullshit. That adage had served her well in the past, but it stood a good chance of getting her killed in a world of upside-down rainbows. She wasn't about to put trust in her training or herself or anything she did when she couldn't tell what was real and what was mental hocus-pocus.

Once she made sense of dancing buttons and floating switches, she was going to try her hand at stacking raindrops on the tip of a needle.

The portside outboard engine spooled down.

Flameout!

The primary engine display drifted in and out of focus, but the message—"ENGINE 1 FAIL"—was clear. The same would happen to the two inboard engines soon. Outside in the cold night air, they would be roaring with 63,000 pounds of thrust one minute, pumping out searing heat, creating faint orange glows, making heat shimmers. The next, they would sputter. Their roars would wane to kitten purrs, and their orange glows would dwindle. At the end, they would spool down, then stop. The heat shimmers would vanish, and their orange glows would grow black.

She was already in some phase of her own engine flameout. She just didn't know which one. She and the Combi were in a race to the bottom.

Her eyes burned. Each heartbeat felt like captured thunder. Protocol for running on two engines mandated that she turn off some of the systems to keep the total electrical load down to 100 kilowatts or less. Trying to figure out the right buttons and switches to make that happen was tricky when they wouldn't stay still. Words on the checklist melted and blended together.

The tip of her tongue started to itch. She scratched it against the edges of her upper front teeth as she glanced around, not looking at anything in particular.

They had witnessed the effects of the early stages of the disease in Monty, Ray, and Mariana. Not much else. Monty had more hours in the cockpit of a Combi than anyone else onboard, and the illness had such a profound effect on him, he couldn't tell the difference between the cockpit door and the flight crew rest door. And Mariana ... that was pitiful. She forgot a heck of a lot apparently.

All three died. All three left empty, fill-in-the-blank areas between the early onset of the illness and their deaths. She had a ton of questions about what had happened to them during the gap, whether their deaths were agonizing, how long it took for them to die.

Sierra may have been right about Mariana's memory loss,

but she wasn't right at all about Ray being jumpy or distrait before he died. If his headache was anything like hers, there was no way he forgot about the aspirin. No, sir. There was another, more profound reason he hadn't taken the bottle of aspirin, and from personal experience, she now knew why: he couldn't see it.

———◆◇◆———

Quentin lifted the heavy, black case out of the hollowed-out pages in the notebook. "Please be unlocked," he said to the two chrome hinges on the front of the two-inch-thick case.

Something rattled inside, and he could feel it rolling around. Barely detectable. Another memory popped into his mind about feeling the same sensation when he held some-thing like it yesterday— a wooden box—and something had rattled inside it too. He turned the case around. No lock! Only a simple, chrome clasp, and he didn't waste any time opening it. Soft, black suede lined the interior. Two hypodermic needles filled with a yellowish liquid and a third filled with a clear liquid rolled to the bottom front corner of the case. He picked up the clear needle in one hand and one of the yellowish ones in the other.

Daniel pointed to the yellowish one. "That one looks like probetalamisol. A tranquilizer. I don't know what the other one is."

Quentin's memory came flooding back. One of the three men dressed in black had injected him yesterday on his patio. He remembered everything: the fake cruiser, the conversation he had with the woman in it, the van, the shit the three men had done to him on his patio. "Daniel, you said your sister needed every penny you could make. Why?"

"For her medical treatment. She's in a wheelchair, and her insurance company is a steaming piece of shit sitting on top of a pile of maggots."

Quentin's head was spinning. Everything came together. Daniel's sister had wanted him to keep the animal off the plane, and the three men had made sure he didn't succeed. He rubbed his hand on the bump on his neck while Daniel's warning played in his head. *A man who grew a third foot would find it difficult to buy shoes.* What the hell had they injected into his body? He placed both needles back into the case and poked his hand between two of the folder dividers in the top of the briefcase. It brushed against something that rattled. He fished it out. A king-size Milky Way bar. "Diabetic, my ass!"

"I've never seen him take an insulin shot," Daniel volunteered.

Quentin picked up one of the insulin bottles and the pack of syringes. "Then what is he doing with these?" He squinted at the items. "That's odd." He zeroed in on the insulin bottle. Barely visible, a tiny piece of what appeared to be the bottom edge of another label peeked out from behind the insulin label.

He peeled back the top label. One word printed in black ink on a plain, white label revealed itself:

"Probetalamisol."

He frowned up at Daniel. "The tranquilizer?"

"I didn't know he brought any."

"He must have had doubts that the creature would stay asleep during the entire flight." Quentin pulled back the label on the other bottle. Again, one word revealed itself. "Zexo-mili-tram-i-o-late." He butchered the pronunciation. "What's this one?"

Daniel took the bottle and examined it. "I've never heard of that before. Their field of science is vastly different from mine."

"Dr. Speck had three syringes filled and ready to go, Daniel. Why? And why is there only one of this one?" Quentin produced the clear syringe and pondered it. "I know why. This was *his* flotation device."

———◦———

Eden held her left hand up in front of her face. The purple spot had grown from the size of a grape seed to a walnut. She removed it from her view, leaving the glareshield. The giant cumulonimbus in front of the nose of the aircraft loomed ever closer, a white tower in the night sky rooted on earth, along with the smaller clouds around it, but soared to the heavens alone.

Fireworks were going off inside her skull, bombarding everything from her neck up. She kept her head still and let her eyes do most of the work. The little trick didn't work. Nothing worked. And her eyes ... Darkness closed in from her peripherals. The way things were unfolding, her vision would be the first thing to go. Handling the aircraft alone was hell *with* sight. But blind. And with no fuel. All three combined ... There couldn't be a word in the dictionary to explain how difficult that was going to be. If there was, it was the word "impossible."

Sierra had been wrong. Dead wrong. Ray wasn't jumpy or mentally detached. He couldn't see her standing beside him or the bottle of aspirin. By then, he had probably lost his peripheral vision too. He must have gone through hell, suffering in silence so he wouldn't worry the passengers and crew.

I know what you went through, Ray. In a distorted, twin-souls sense of déjà vu, Eden was reliving his final moments. Suffering in silence. In her case, if the passengers knew, they would have one colossal, mass panic attack.

Everything seemed distant. As she grew more detached from the world, the strand that connected her to consciousness grew thinner. Her eyes beetled from screen to screen and from switch to switch. Seeing them became more difficult as dark pilfered away more of her peripheral vision.

The alarm blared again.

She hit the Master Warning/Caution Reset switch, then squinted at the screen above the throttles. "ENGINE 3 FAIL."

They had only one engine left. And a precious few pounds of fuel. She brought up the fuel synoptic display.

Main #1 tank "0.0."

Main #2 tank "1.9."

Main #3 tank "0.0."

Main #4 tank "0.0."

Stabilizer Tank "0.0."

Center Wing Tank "0.0."

Only the Main #2 tank held any hope, though very little of that. That was all that fed the portside inboard engine, 1,900 pounds of fuel, 277 measly gallons to get an aircraft *that* size to land. Impossible. At the rate the last engine was burning fuel, the tank would be empty in sixteen minutes, less than that if they encountered turbulence.

Her eyes shot to the towering cloud up ahead. Darkness closed in from all sides.

She could do calculations until the Four Horsemen of the Apocalypse came riding over the horizon, but the outcome would never change. The Combi wasn't a sipper. It was a guzzler, and it would run out of fuel above the cold, tumultuous waters of the South Atlantic Ocean.

The words on the checklist were harder to read than before. One rose off the paper and jabbed at her like a shard of glass in a 3D movie. "One engine … electrical load must be reduced to … 50 kilowatts … or less."

Her world was one of churning buttons. A trembling hand, most likely her own, finally settled on a switch and then pressed it. It felt strange. Wrong. She flipped it instead. That worked. She turned off more systems while the strange illness stole more of her memory. Darkness encircled everything except a small bit of her world, shrinking slowly and steadily like the closing aperture in a camera. And then it closed.

There was nothing left of her world, only blackness. Emptiness.

Her fingers raced over the buttons on the aft aisle stand between the two pilots' seats, groping, trying not to disturb any of them while she tried to remember which one was which. Square ones, round ones, flat ones, tall ones. What had been familiar before was now the world's most difficult shell game, where some function lay hidden beneath *each* button. For many of them, she could no longer remember what that function was.

Her hand touched something short with a grooved head. *A screw.* She never realized how many different textures the different buttons had. Grooves and ridges and indentations.

Rona whimpered, then mumbled in her sleep. "Something bad."

Eden's hand skated over the top of a button about the size of a hockey puck with indentations for easy gripping. The rudder trim selector. Good. She was close. There were still some synapses snapping inside her skull.

Across a small ridge at the back of the aisle stand, her hand found the interphone and lifted it from its cradle in fingers that felt weak and unsure. To them, the phone was a kettlebell. It slipped from her hand. Her head flopped forward on a neck that was too weak to hold it up. Her body slouched forward. The harness was the only thing that held her up.

The strand that connected her to consciousness broke, and darkness wasn't just around her. She tumbled down inside it. She was consumed by it. And then she felt nothing at all.

CHAPTER 33

Quentin jumped up from the briefcase with the syringe filled with the clear liquid clenched in his fist. Out of nowhere, a tentacle punched up through the floor and wrapped around his leg. He tumbled to the floor, punching and kicking as the tentacle dragged him toward the hole. He was going to save Eden if he had to rip off his leg.

He screamed and tried to yank his leg free, but the tentacle pulled his leg into the hole. With a powerful lunge, he grabbed one of the syringes filled with the tranquilizer, uncapped it with his teeth, and plunged it into the tentacle. When he pulled it out, the metal tip was gone. It had been eaten away. The grip on his leg loosened. From what he had learned down on the main deck, the mega-T wasn't going to release his leg that easily.

"Let go, you big sonavu—" He weighed 185 pounds, and 184.99 pounds of that were completely pissed off. He put every ounce of it into a yank that was either going to tear his leg off or set it free. His leg flew up out of the hole with a limp tentacle loosely coiled around it. It slithered back down the hole. A loud *ka-thunk* rose up from below. *That's not just a tentacle*. The mega-T had hit the floor in the cabin below.

Daniel grabbed him by the arm and helped him up.

265

Quentin glowered at him. "You wait until now to help me?"

Daniel exhaled in a robust sigh like he had been holding his breath. "It's out."

Quentin took Dr. Ross by the arm. "I need you to come with me. Hurry! And grab that first aid kit."

"Eden!" Quentin yelled, running into the cockpit.

Her head was bent forward in her seat, slumped over, reminiscent of the way he had found his wife two years ago. Life had painted the same portrait again on a different canvas.

Dr. Ross sterilized an area of Eden's upper arm and injected her with zexomilitramiolate.

"Eden! Wake up!" He leaned the pilot back as he had done Tracie, and she was motionless. Like Tracie. No. Eden was still warm! That old bastard of a tire iron returned and spun in his gut. "Eden! Eden!" Neither Eden nor Rona stirred.

Eden's eyes fluttered, then crawled open. "Quentin." Her voice was low and feeble.

His name rolling off her lips was the sweetest sound he had heard in a long time, perfume for the ears. "I think that's the first time you called me anything other than 'Marshal.'" Her lips … *Oh! My! God!* Her luscious lips. Inches from his. Pouty and inviting. A perfect cupid's bow. Pulling away was torture.

She moaned softly and pulled herself upright. "Rona." She spun her seat around. The little girl's soft snoring sounded like an angel's whisper wrapped in velvet.

Eden's eyes zipped around the cockpit, and for some reason, she smiled. Yet when she leaned closer to the windshield, that smile vanished. He couldn't say the same for the spinning tire iron. But it had slowed down a bit.

In the middle of the windshield, the giant cloud was closer than it was the last time he saw it. He leaned closer and tilted his head higher to see the top of it. It seemed everything was gigantic around there. He couldn't dislodge his eyes from it. Its height, its width … both were mesmerizing. It dominated the sky. The other clouds were big, but they were Lilliputians compared to the Brobdingnagian hell-cloud.

The 747 pierced a smaller cloud, and the world vanished as the grayish-white cloud swallowed them whole. The good part about it was that he could no longer see the hell-cloud, although the smaller one displayed its own ill temper with its grumbling and stabbing the sky with jagged, white-hot daggers. When they came out of the other side, the angry cloud loomed right in front of them. A swarm of intense lightning bolts exploded rapid-fire from within its soaring, white column, the most convincing "Do Not Enter" sign Quentin had ever seen. And they were rushing straight for it.

"Try not to look at them." Eden averted her eyes. "They will temporarily blind you."

"Too late. I think they may have already fried my retinas." He wasn't particularly fond of the view anyway.

The nose of the aircraft plowed into the cloud. The world disappeared. Darkness compounded upon darkness. Even the moonlight was afraid to enter this beast. Booming thunder breathed life into it. The aircraft suddenly shuddered at the mercy of vicious turbulence.

Eden appeared to be on the mend, her backbone straight and true, eyes sharp, punching buttons with an assurance that she didn't have earlier. He couldn't help but smile, even if it was fleeting.

"Your vitals are all good," Dr. Ross said, removing her stethoscope.

"Thank you. If I need you, I know where to find you. It would be a good idea for you to return to your seat. Things are about to get rough."

"Marshal, can you stay with her? To be on the safe side, she probably shouldn't be left alone for a while."

"My pleasure."

Dr. Ross gathered her supplies, and Quentin ushered her past the trip hazard and out of the cockpit. He returned to the first officer's seat and strapped himself in.

Another explosion of lightning bolts from deep inside the cloud cast eerie, dancing shadows of the 747 on the opposite side of the aircraft through his window. Then the aircraft was gone again. So was the rest of the world, leaving only darkness. What the 747 needed was a good set of headlights. Cloud-busters. It was now just them and the bowels of the hell-cloud.

––––––––––⊰⊱––––––––––

Sierra clamped her hand on the back of the aisle seat and braced herself against the increasing turbulence. Other than the lightning blasting in through the windows, the aircraft sailed through darkness. "Here you go, ma'am," she said, handing Amarant a box of tissues. "Right in front of you."

Amarant felt around and found the box. "Thank you." She pulled out a handful as a tear hovered at the bottom of her dark shades, then trickled down her face.

The cabin lights flickered. A violent pocket of turbulence ripped Sierra's hand from the seat back and slammed her down on her rear end. The box of tissues crash-landed on the floor in front of her.

"Are you all right?" Amarant asked.

"I'm fine. I landed on my … my cushion," Sierra answered with a smile in her voice. She got back up and wobbled back to the galley, steadying herself with the assistance of every seat back next to the aisle.

When she reached the galley, the levee broke. Tears poured down her cheeks in buckets. The air marshal was right. She had earned a little break. She collapsed on the floor in the corner between two parked carts. If there was only some way to find out how the passengers down on the main deck were doing.

It wasn't safe on the floor, where there was no seat belt to keep her from flying around during the landing … or the ditch. No life jacket.

The lights went out. It was happening already. It took a good five seconds for them to come back on. They were fortunate to have them at all. Before long, they would go out and stay out. The hard realization set in. She dried her face and popped back up on her feet. This was no time to sit around moping. She had to prepare the passengers for a water ditch while they could see how to do it.

<hr />

"That's a lot of red," Quentin remarked, looking at one of the screens.

"No kidding." Eden jabbed buttons in a blur. "If that thing had a neck, I'd choke it."

What Quentin knew about flying a plane could fit in a thimble with room to spare, but he did know that storms on the weather screen were depicted in red. Even his aviation-illiterate ass didn't need a screen in this case. All he needed was a good pair of peepers and clean windows.

They hit another pocket of turbulence. His teeth clacked together as he bounced an inch out of his seat. Everything was trying to kill them. Lightning cracked through all of the cockpit windows. Thunder shook the giant 747, sending a palpable vibration through the aircraft's bones.

Those old, familiar twin furrows between Eden's eyebrows returned. "That was just the storm's way of touching gloves. Now it's about to come out fighting."

"Hey. Your eyes are looking better. They're back to pink now."

"I don't think I want to know what they looked like before."

Beautiful. Quentin had to tie his tongue in a knot to keep from saying it.

"I sure hope Wideawake's primary radar is in tip-top condition," she said. "Once the engines all flame out, the secondary radar couldn't pick us up even if we were parked on the roof of the tower."

"What's the difference?"

"The secondary radar tracks us simply by picking up our transponder signal. It's more accurate, but without engines, we won't be able to transmit a transponder signal. When we're down to standby power, we'll have only enough juice to run some of the most critical systems."

"Will it power at least one of the engines? I don't think we can get more critical than that."

"I wish. The battery won't power a single one of those babies back up. Not for one second. And the transponder sure didn't make the list. The primary radar doesn't get as much use anymore. It doesn't need a transponder signal. It bounces signals off the aircraft and gathers data when the signal returns. Without engines, if he can't pick us up on primary radar, he won't be able to pick us up at all."

Whack. Something hit the windshield on her side. *Whack.* The impact was in front of him this time.

Hailstones.

Frozen baseballs rained from the sky, attacking the windshield. They went from one to a smattering and then to hundreds insta-quick. It looked like they were in a snowball fight with God himself, and they were getting their asses handed to them. It wouldn't have surprised Quentin if the windshield cracked. He squinted. "I can't see anything."

"I can't see anything too," Rona said. With her big, terrified eyes, a crying spell wouldn't be far behind. "Mister, did Something Bad eat my mommy?"

"No, it didn't, sweetheart. I saw your mommy."

A smile as broad as daylight blossomed on her face. "You did?"

"I sure did. Do you know what she was doing when I saw her?" He asked only to buy time to think of something that wasn't a lie. The second hottest place in hell had to be reserved for people who lie to kids. The VIP section of hell most certainly was reserved for the ones who hurt them.

"What?"

"She was lying down."

He hunched his shoulders and gave Eden an "I didn't know what else to say" gesture.

"My mommy likes taking naps. I don't."

Without lying to her, he had pacified her a bit. The child shouldn't learn about her mother until her father was there to soothe her. Any other way would be cruel and inhumane.

"Heeey!" Rona said with a proud smile. "I always wake up by myself!" She rocked her feet back and forth as if she didn't have a care in the world. The smothering clouds lit up, followed by a monstrous rumble. Her feet stopped rocking. Her eyes gleamed with tears.

"Don't worry," he said. "It's just thunder. Thunder can't hurt you, baby."

"You promise?"

"I promise."

Maybe it wasn't a good idea to bring Rona into the cockpit after all.

Rona leaned forward. "You promise too?"

Eden rocked Rona's socked foot playfully. "I promise. Everything's going to be all right. I'm a professional, remember?"

Rona wiped her eyes and leaned back in her seat. "I'm going to be a flylot when I grow up. Just like you."

Rona's words seemed to spark a new resolve in Eden, and

he had a good idea why. If she couldn't save them, the little girl wouldn't have a chance to grow up.

Eden checked her systems and snapped into hyperdrive. Fingers flew over buttons, then ripped a small sheet of paper from the printer at the back of the aisle stand. She grabbed a thick notebook, a manual by the looks of it. It was as if a new person was sitting in the pilot's seat.

"Eww." Rona pinched her nose.

"What's wrong, Rona?" His voice was a gentle wind rustling up fallen leaves and phony as hell, given the whirling, fiery tire iron in the pit of his gut. Hopefully it didn't count as a lie.

"I smell Something Bad."

Eden nodded toward the dead men in the crew rest. "I've never been around people like them before. Do you think it's too soon for that?"

"It's here!" He ripped open his harness and shot out of his seat. "That's what she calls the creature. 'Something bad.' It's here!"

Rona pulled her feet up and wrapped her arms around her legs.

His eyes darted around the cockpit. Where was that relentless son of a bitch? His nose hadn't spent as much time with the mega-T as the little girl's. She was a bloodhound at picking up its scent. He sniffed the air and followed the scent over to the captain's chair.

A tentacle punched up through the cockpit floor and lassoed Eden's left ankle. Rona screamed, a high-pitched, ear-piercing scream.

Eden yelled, "The harder I try to pull my leg free, the tighter it grips."

"That's the mega-T's modus operandi." Quentin grabbed the fire extinguisher from the portside wall, about to hammer it down on the appendage with enough force to crack a cinderblock.

"Careful!" Eden yelled. "Don't break its skin. The electronics bay is down there, the brain center of this entire aircraft."

The butt end of the makeshift weapon hammered the tentacle with about a third as much force as his fight-or-flight impulse wanted. The crawler slithered back down the hole. He drew back the fire extinguisher. *There's more where that came from, buddy.* If it returned, he had a more discouraging blow waiting for it.

"Is it gone?" Rona sat straight up in her seat, frozen with fear, her gaping eyes fixed on him.

He stooped down with the fire extinguisher clenched tightly in one hand. Oh, how he wanted to scoop her into his arm and give her a big old bear hug. Neither time nor her harness permitted that. He settled for giving her a pat on the head. "It's all right. It's gone."

She gradually scooted back and relaxed her head against the back of the seat.

He returned the fire extinguisher to its home and sat back down, but his thoughts wouldn't leave the hole in the floor. His mind raced, trying to figure out what had lured the creature so far forward in the aircraft. It clicked. Some sorry excuse of a detective he turned out to be. He shouldn't have taken this long to figure it out. "This was a mistake! I should never have come in here!"

Eden frowned over at him. "What? Why?"

"I didn't just overlook it *this* time. I overlooked it *every* time."

"Quentin, you're not making any sense."

"During the first encounter I had with the mega-T, I shot it. Now it's tracking me. Everywhere I go, it punches through the floor or attacks."

"Nonsense. Of all the people on this aircraft, why you?"

"Revenge."

"How could it be tracking you?"

"It must have one hell of a sense of smell. I'm putting you both in danger. I've got to get out of here." He unbuckled his harness.

"No! What if it comes back? I can't fly and fight for my life at the same time."

He groaned, then grappled with the ends of the buckle. "Shit!" he shouted and launched out of his seat. "Hercules!"

"What—what's wrong with him?"

"My life jacket! I gave him my life jacket."

CHAPTER 34

Hercules sniffed around. The smell was barely perceivable. It certainly wasn't coming from anyone inside the flight attendants' crew rest.

The room's previous occupants had made a complete hash of the bottom bunk to his left and the top one in front of him. The pleasant bouquet of a woman's perfume was most likely emanating from somewhere amid the rumpled blankets and sheets. After giving an approving smile, he looked around to see if another member of the team had received a contradictory report. The faces that had been screwed into frowns and grimaces and gawping eyes were now beaming with hope.

A loud thud, though distant, sucked the hope out of them in an instant. Their eyes squinted as if they were listening with them.

He didn't know if modern neurologists were right in their belief that humans have far more than five senses—somewhere between nine and twenty-one, depending on whose book he happened to be reading—but he did know one thing: however many he had, all of them were focused on that sound.

Until he heard a much closer one.

"Get ready," he whispered. "It's com—No. It's already here." He pulled the front of the life jacket up and covered his mouth and nose with it. He listened for even the slightest sound to punch through the silence engulfing the compact room.

Wild eyes darted from wall to wall until a loud thud came from the other side of the forward wall. Every pair of eyes in the room snapped toward the noise. A sonorous wham and a metallic clang quickly followed. The megateratoid couldn't be more than a foot away.

Their improvised weapons snapped to the ready, sending out little *click-clack* sounds of their own. He trained his fire extinguisher on the spot where he had heard the noise. On his left, Gaston raised a broken armrest. Kinley, sitting on Hercules's right, reached down next to his foot and picked up a bent, metal post that was once attached to the stairs. He drew it back over his right shoulder like a Major League hitter. In the backswing, he came within a couple of inches of cracking Tyler's head open, missing only because Tyler was quick enough to duck. Matt and Tyler each wielded half of a set of someone's abandoned, metal crutches.

Hercules pointed the nozzle of the fire extinguisher at a bright rustling sound and tracked it from the door on the portside wall to the forward wall—where he could hear the beast bumbling over seats. To the starboard wall—where the aisle provided the beast with a much quieter pathway. To the aft wall—where the creature made quite a bit of clanging noise in the galley. And back to where it started. The animal completely circled them and ended up back in the portside aisle. There, without any warning, it stopped, and so did his nozzle.

It was studying them or the crew rest or both. Analyzing. Perhaps strategizing.

Hercules reversed his nozzle and trailed the rustling sound back to the corner and stopped right where he was standing. Seconds later came the sound of strong, hard teeth biting. The other weapons joined the fire extinguisher trained on the floor in the corner.

Then the noises came to a harsh and brutal cessation. They all jumped up.

He swung the nozzle in all directions. He couldn't pick up the sound, not even a hint to help him pinpoint the beast's situs. Every weapon in the room swung around in a different direction, shifting one way, then another.

"Where is it?" Matt mouthed.

Hercules shrugged in a "beats me" gesture.

The lusus slammed against the wall next to the starboard aisle behind Matt and Tyler. The brothers whirled around. Their crutches crossed swords with a *clack*.

That did it. The walls were about as thick as a cracker. If they could hear the hushed rustling sounds, the creature could certainly hear the loud clack. Hercules stood still, listening to the silence, waiting for the creature to claw the wall behind the brothers, bite a hole in it, slam into it—something. But the ensuing silence frightened him even more.

After a couple of minutes, the creature gave a disinterested snort.

No, no, no. It heard the noise. I know *it did.* Yet the animal made no attempt to attack. Whatever its reason, it couldn't be good. His palms grew damp from a cold sweat, creating a slippery grip on the fire extinguisher. He removed his hands one at a time and wiped his palms on his jeans. *What are you up to, lusus?*

Tyler lowered his crutch, and a smile crept into Kinley's eyes. Hercules shook his head with a scolding frown and raised his palm toward the ceiling, signaling for Tyler to ready his weapon. Then he closed his hand in a tight fist.

What had been beads of nervous sweat now drizzled down Hercules's forehead. The life jacket made it that much hotter, but he didn't dare part with it.

If the mega-T wanted them to give up, he wasn't going to fall for the legerdemain or let any one of the others do it either. The terrible smell of dead things rushed back into the sleeping quarters with the force of a wrecking ball. Yet there wasn't so much as a soft rustle. How could something that big move so quickly without making a sound? His grip on the fire extinguisher tightened. At the same time, the other weapons whipped around, and the men shifted into fighting stances.

Suddenly, a massive head punched through the portside door, taking out great chunks of the wall on each side as well. It completely blocked their only escape. The trapped men stood still as corpses. A slimy snout pushed in, sniffed left toward Kinley, then right toward the other three men. It settled on Hercules in front of the starboard bunks and pushed in to within inches of his face. He stopped breathing. The lusus growled, but Hercules didn't even blink. The snout dropped to his chest and sniffed.

In a flash, the giant head recoiled, then charged at him teeth first.

It's not stopping! Hercules dove to the floor in front of the bottom bunk on the forward wall as the massive head zipped by, smashed into the bunks, and punched a giant hole through the starboard wall.

He jumped up and swung the fire extinguisher, delivering a crushing blow to the back of the creature's neck. A grave mistake. The creature sent out a deafening roar that made his teeth vibrate.

Through the ringing in his ears, he heard a creaking sound above. The seam between the aft wall and the curved ceiling had separated. "We've got to get out of here!"

But the lusus had corked off the only two breaches in the walls. The creature tried to pull its head back through the hole, but it wedged in farther. It thrashed around, smashing away more of the wall and the bunks attached until the last few resolute pieces collapsed into the aisle. The entire wall on the starboard side was gone. The mega-T slung a piece of bent, twisted bunk from its craggy, green face. Hercules grimaced. It was clear where the missile would land. It wasn't clear if it would cause catastrophic damage and trigger a rapid decompression. It smashed against the exterior wall above the starboard seats. He expected at least one of the windows to break, but they held.

Something hit the floor and shattered in the galley on the other side of the aft wall. Then the portside wall ripped away from the ceiling, twisted, and finally fell into the crew rest. The men scrambled into the remaining bunks and took cover.

For the first time since they had entered the flight attendants' crew rest, he saw the entire mega-T. The visage froze him in place. He was mesmerized by how different it looked. It was considerably bigger, yet that wasn't the most terrifying change. It appeared to have done just that—changed. Most of its body had stretched somehow and rested atop the portside seats. Its neck had elongated. Its tentacles hung from new holes in the battered overhead compartments. Not only were the beast's feet not on the floor, it didn't seem to have any. It was readily apparent how the mega-T had snuck up on them.

The mega-T started to shake violently. A sound like stiff leather being strained and pulled made it past the ringing sounds in his ears. Tentacles snapped free from the overhead compartments. A foot hit the floor. Then another. More tentacles snapped free and whipped through the cabin. The beast's neck shrank, and its body compacted.

When the forward wall gave way and fell outward on top of the battered cabin seats, he was finally able to tear his eyes away but found the other men were gawking at the lusus as well. "Go! Before it finishes reshaping!" He quickly found out it didn't need to finish.

Matt led the stampede up the aisle with his brother Tyler right on his heels. Hercules was surprised to see Kinley keeping up with Tyler. Gaston, no slowpoke himself, was running up Kinley's tailpipe.

Heavy footsteps pounded the floor behind Hercules at the back of the pack. They were speeding up and closing in but had an odd cadence. They sounded amiss: *boom plop*, *boom plop*, *boom plop*. He took a quick look back. One thick front leg and one slim one charged up the aisle after him. Each had a comparably sized paw. What he could see of the creature's hind parts didn't look fully cooked either.

He crashed into Gaston's back and spun back around. From what he could glean, Matt must have stopped without warning, and the rest of them slammed into each other.

"Let's go!" Hercules urged. Matt had been running with his borrowed crutch—for whatever reason—and had gotten it lodged horizontally across the aisle between himself and the back of two aisle seats.

"Back off a second and give him room," Hercules instructed.

While the train remained stalled on the tracks, behind him, the lusus lowered its head to the floor and opened its maw like a runaway bulldozer.

CHAPTER 35

Whimpers and cries of panic rippled through the cabin.

"Please prepare for a water landing." Eden's voice sounded strong and healthy over the PA. "The flight attendant will instruct you on putting on your life jackets."

Sierra had already prepared for this announcement and was waiting for the pilot to give her the go-ahead. "Please do not inflate them inside the aircraft," she said as she walked from the back of the cabin to the front. Sodden faces and frightened eyes rose when she passed. "Wait until you are in the water. Otherwise, you will float to the ceiling, not be able to get out, and drown."

TR followed her up the aisle like a prowler, and behind him was Victor, the senator's new guard dog or lapdog. Sierra couldn't make up her mind which.

"It's just been one thing after another on this flight," TR griped as much to her as to Victor while she helped a little boy put on his life jacket. "Lady Luck must be on the rag. What the hell's the point of putting on a life jacket? A water ditch in the Atlantic is likely to kill us all anyway."

The little boy looked up at TR. His teeth bit his lip in an obvious attempt to keep from crying.

"Who knows?" TR added, disregarding the child. "We all

might be dead even before then. That creature is going to break into the upper deck with us at any minute. Who's going to stop it? That air marshal? Ha, ha! For all we know"—he jabbed a finger in the direction of the cockpit door—"that pilot might die before any of this and take us all with her."

Sierra wanted to slap his lips off. "That's enough. Do you think that's helping?"

The senator's eyes shrank down to thin slits. His monkey's butthole of a mouth drew into a shriveled circle.

"Stop scaring the other passengers and stop following me, or I will get the air marshal."

"I doubt if I'm his priority right now."

"Would you like to spend the rest of this flight in handcuffs?"

He smirked, looked at his guard dog-lapdog combo package standing behind him, and then looked back at her.

"Would you?" she asked Victor.

Victor skulked toward the back of the cabin, leaving TR standing there with his eyes running after the beefy man.

"Well, what's it going to be, Senator?"

He trudged after Victor while she progressed up the aisle, checking each passenger. She stopped and helped an elderly lady with gnarled fingers who was having trouble with her life jacket.

"Thank you. You're such a kind, sweet lady." The woman patted Sierra's wrist with a soft, smooth hand.

"I'm here to help. Anything you need, ma'am, just let me know."

The cabin lights flickered, returned to normal, taunting the survivors with hope that they would behave, and then flickered again. Tension clamped both hands around her neck. A deep stillness gripped the upper deck cabin, a deathly silence as if the plane was gasping its last breath.

She had been a flight attendant long enough to know that with a fuel-starved engine, the flickering lights signaled the beginning of the end.

***

The aircraft tunneled through the cloud that seemed to have swallowed the world. It was mad as hell and wasn't pulling any punches. It pressed up against the windshield and the side windows so closely Quentin had no visibility at all. The cloud was filled to near bursting with lightning, thunder, and hail. The hail came to a brusque stop and yielded to the rain.

A sight through the windshield filled him with anticipation. He leaned forward and looked down past the bottom edge of the windshield. The nose of the aircraft sprang into view. A few seconds earlier, he couldn't see beyond the windshield. He would take any positive sign. The rain and bitter cold at that altitude had gilded the surface of the big nose with a shiny shell coating. The nose disappeared from view again when the aircraft bored through another dense section of the cloud. Slowly it started to thin out a bit. A hole opened up to the left. *That's the sky. That's open sky!* The hole wasn't that big, but man, was it promising. Through it, stars beckoned them.

The 747 tore into the open sky, and the world opened up all around. Quentin had never been so happy to see the sky in his life.

The full moon found them immediately. It seemed brighter than he had ever seen it. It could pass for a distant cousin to the sun and made the ice-encrusted blue nose of the 747 glisten like a sapphire.

The full moon. What a beautiful sight. The crowning jewel in the nocturnal heavens gleamed all the way down to the ocean's surface where black water sopped up its light. His gaze swept the endless, ebony ocean. But he couldn't spot so much as a speck of dry land. They were merely an insignificant dot above the gigantic, unending ocean. "Where's Ascension Island?"

"It's just a tiny microbe." Eden was obviously avoiding the question.

I guess we're back to that again. He didn't push. He didn't need to. Her avoiding the question was all the answer he needed.

There was no island there. They were not close enough.

And if he had any doubt, he could see it in her eyes. She was about to go into that long, dark tunnel in the mind where no light shined.

———◆◆———

Eden fixated on the fuel synoptic screen. The final few scroungings of fuel ticked down in the Main #2 tank. Once the Combi scavenged every drop of fuel possible, neither of the four engines would start back up again. There would be no midair refueling like her Super Hornet or the president's Air Force One. Her Combi wasn't equipped with a midair refueling system. No highly classified aircraft would attempt a rescue. If they survived, and chances of that happening weren't in their favor, they would have to do it on their own, using their own resources, their own knowledge, their own training, and their own abilities.

"0.4," the screen read.

She felt helpless and inept, two old foes of hers. Her mind raced, preparing for the inevitable while trying to find a way to avoid it. She ran through a mental checklist to make sure she had done all she could and to make sure she hadn't overlooked a single thing that might save her passengers, save Rona.

"0.3."

The innocent little girl deserved a chance to grow up. A chance to be a flylot or anything else she wanted to be. Eden had promised her everything was going to be all right.

"0.2."

Pull it together. Stay focused. Follow the procedures. Concentrate on the protocol. Trust my training. Focus on doing what's within my control, nothing else. Not on the fact that I must land an aircraft that normally takes two pilots splitting up a mountain of work to get back on the ground safely.

"0.1."

The checklist. She had to read it again. To be ready. When the last engine spooled down was not the time to *get* ready. She had to *be* ready. She fixed her eyes on the primary engine display, waiting for something she wished she would somehow never see, never hear. For that wish to be granted, she and her passengers would need a miracle that came with another miracle strapped to its back.

"0.0."

Oh God!

Her world spun. The image of the zeroes lodged in her brain. Then her mind went blank. For a second, there was no training, no checklist. Nothing. Just her thinking about their empty tanks and how screwed they were.

All of them. Every last one of them. Empty.

"ENGINE 2 FAIL" splashed across the screen, accompanied by the dreaded, beeping alarm. Eden blinked away the sting of tears and peered through the glareshield.

With land nowhere in sight, the last living engine had given up the ghost.

PART III

A HOLE IN THE
BOTTOM OF THE SKY

CHAPTER 36

After Eden hit the Master Warning/Caution Reset switch and silenced the plangent warning, Quentin heard the most terrifying sound he had ever encountered—silence. Ear-splitting silence. Cold and pitiless. The sound of nothingness. A silent cockpit. A silent passenger cabin behind them. It was as if someone had hit the mute button on the world.

Aviate, navigate, communicate. Even he knew how pilots prioritized their duties, so it didn't surprise him that Eden didn't hop on the radio first thing and give an update of their dire state. Instead, she was turning off more of the systems. The high-tech cockpit was now a flickering candle. The aisle stand, the pilot's displays, and both upper and lower screens between them were illuminated, but his displays were already dark before she started the latest round of reducing power usage.

He gazed absentmindedly at the dead, black screens in front of him, his mind racing with thoughts about how it might all end. Each scenario was more awful than the last. He had put Rona's oxygen mask and harness on before he put on his own but gave her a quick glance. She hadn't squirmed out from under them. Good girl. He gave her a thumbs-up. She smiled and returned the gesture.

Another sound materialized. It made the sound of silence the *second* most terrifying one he had ever heard.

It was a ghostly, high-pitched keen, the sound of the wind skating across the skin of the aircraft, eerie and ominous like the Tibetan winds howling and wailing and hissing down from the ice-covered peaks of the Himalayan mountains. It made him long for the eardrum-rattling alarm. *Hello, tire iron.* It had filtered up to his consciousness and sneaked up on him like the new sound. The two of them worked in concert and brought him out of his fugue state into a level of trepidation that until then he didn't know existed.

According to Eden, the plane would slowly depressurize, but at the same time, it would descend toward the breathable air at ten thousand feet. He hoped the ominous sound wouldn't chase them all the way back down to earth. As if helplessly watching yourself crash into the ocean wasn't nerveracking enough.

The noise must have been there all along just waiting to make its presence known, first hiding in the shadows behind the dominant sound of the alarm, then behind the ear-splitting silence, and finally behind the noises that only he could hear: the steel hulls of his thoughts scraping against the craggy outcroppings in his mind.

He took another apprehensive look out the windshield. *You dirty, low-down son of a bitch.* A cloud had snuck up beneath them and blocked his view down to the ocean's surface. There could have been an entire continent below them, and he wouldn't have been able to see it.

"Wideawake Tower," Eden said.

He switched his attention to the conversation in his headphones. *Please give us a positive update.*

"Wideawake Tower," Eden repeated into the microphone in

her oxygen mask. "We have flameout in all four engines due to fuel starvation. We're going down."

"Airland 1219, I have you on primary radar," reported the now familiar air traffic controller's voice.

That's what I wanted to hear.

The controller added, "One-zero-four nauts from the threshold, Airland 1219."

She punched up information on her screens and did another series of quick calculations. "We have to conserve altitude. With empty tanks and factoring in wind direction and speed, we have about a seventeen-to-one glide ratio."

"Good news?" Quentin asked.

"I've seen worse. For every seventeen miles we move forward, we descend one."

You're a professional. Remembering Rona's words gave her the boost of confidence she needed. *A trained professional.*

If pilots had a zone, she was in it. She could see everything at once with microscopic clarity. Her focus was as sharp as a beam of light from a Fresnel lens. The world and everything in it ceased to exist except her and the Combi.

CHAPTER 37

A chill rippled through Le Blanc. Flying an aircraft that big, solo, with flameout in all four engines. He crossed himself and said a quick prayer for the pilot and the souls onboard AL 1219. They had been at 37,000 feet, but they were descending.

In minutes, one way or another, that aircraft would be down. On the ground or in the ocean. He crossed himself again.

John Hansberry crashed through the door in his robe and slippers, soaked all the way down to his DNA. The Royal Air Force station commander controlled everything but his receding hairline. "What's the status on that commercial plane?" he said, rushing over with his muddy, waterlogged slippers making little squishing sounds with every step.

Hansberry wasn't the type to be cat and moused about, so Le Blanc just got on with it. "Sir, it's no longer a commercial plane. It's a six-hundred-thousand-pound kite. Flameout in all four engines."

"All four?" The commander frowned as if he didn't believe it. "On a 747?"

"Yes, sir. The pilot's at the controls, but gravity's pushing all the buttons. No flaps, no thrust reversers, no spoilers. Only the emergency brakes."

Hansberry shook his head, and a few drops of rainwater flung from the tips of his matted hair. "Trying to land an aircraft that big ... without the controls ..." The color drained from his olive skin, leaving him ashen. He clapped a hand over his mouth as if he was going to keck, then regained his composure a mite. "If you stand that aircraft on its tail, it would be as tall as a twenty-story building. That runway out there is going to seem like a grain of rice to that pilot."

"And in a storm like this?" The aviator's voice filled his headset again. His attention snapped back to her. "Roger, Airland 1219. You're cleared to land on runway three-one. Heading three-one-four."

"Roger, Wideawake Tower. Runway three-one. Heading three-one-four."

Hansberry picked up one of the phones and gave a series of commands. Outside, the wind whipped blinding rain across Wideawake Airfield and the rain-slickened runway. An alarm wailed. It wouldn't take long for firetrucks to race out of the firehouse and rescue boats to hit the water. In the darkness all around Le Blanc, Wideawake Airfield emergency crews were in full scramble mode. Somewhere above the suffocating fog and the smothering clouds, the souls onboard the beleaguered incoming flight were in the same frantic state.

CHAPTER 38

The plane dropped closer to the clouds that carpeted the sky beneath it, creating a barrier that Quentin wasn't ready to go beyond or see what hellish fate awaited on the other side. With all the bad things they had found hidden inside other bad things, cursed nesting dolls gifted to Flight 1219 from an evil imp, he wasn't sure he wanted to know.

Eden now had the steely-eyed look of a robot. Laser-focused. She flew the aircraft and communicated only with the air traffic controller. Fine with him. He listened in on his headphones, for all the good it did him. Most of the communications floated above his head. He had never felt so insignificant and useless, a spectator sitting on the sidelines with a three-year-old. The ball had been in his hands all his life, and now he had become a silent cheerleader in a game where he didn't even know the rules.

Only God and the robot knew how much altitude they had lost. Or how far away from the ocean they were. Or how far from the island they were. When the clouds were still beneath them, he could at least gauge how fast they were dropping. Now they could be flying upside down for all he knew.

———◦◦———

Eden piloted the Combi between two worlds. Heaven above

with its quiet, crystal-clear skies, dazzling stars, and enchanting full moon. And hell below, an evil, chaotic world of dark gray clouds choking off the view of everything beneath them, of stabbing knives of lightning, of warring peals of thunder. She and her passengers were headed to the world of danger.

The bottom of the 747 sank into the puffy, gray floor. The paradise above powered down through a transient hole in the clouds here and there. Then the clouds took over again. No sky. No land. No ocean. No earth. Just swaddling clouds, thick and gray and dark. Visibility through the windows could only be measured in memories of what used to be there and aspirations of what she hoped was there. The giant aircraft jolted up and down, then smoothed out.

They dropped out of the bottom of the cloud into the open air, and Eden cringed. They were shockingly close to the teeth of the waves. She probed the churning, black surface where she had a clear view of everything.

And nothing.

Below, there was only endless water, roiling, angry water.

She peered through the torrential downpour. There was no island in sight. Nada. There was only uninterrupted pitch-black, and that was coming up much too fast for her liking. A cannon fired in her chest with every heartbeat.

Their plane was a helpless tin can above the gigantic, unending ocean.

If fear could make a sound, it would be that damn buzzer.

The hairs on the back of Quentin's neck stood at attention. The spinning tire iron was back. Everyone was supposed to be buckled in their seats, if they had one, even the lone surviving flight attendant, when they were about to land—or crash. Only bad news could have gotten her up at a time like that.

Until then, he didn't think things could get any worse. No doubt, as soon as Eden unlocked the cockpit door, it was going to be crazy on a cracker. The only question in his mind was just how bad. For anyone to be out of their seat at a time like that … On a scale of one to ten, with one being clogged-up toilet and ten being ass on fire … about eleven.

"We've got to get it right the first time," Eden said into her headset microphone, her priorities clearly where they were supposed to be, on coordinating with Wideawake Tower, not on dealing with whatever problem awaited on the other side of the cockpit door.

Quentin listened to the interaction in his headset. He surveyed the water outside the portside window, swept over to the windshield, and peered through the window on his side of the cockpit. His forehead rested lightly against the thick window as the chill of the multiple layers of high-impact glass and acrylic seeped in through his skin. Other than water, he didn't see anything. *Now I know how Noah felt.*

"Roger," the air traffic controller said. "Please confirm when you have a visual of the runway."

Eden said, "Negative. I do not have a visual."

No shit. All Quentin could see was an endless, inky black.

The cockpit door buzzer sounded again, followed by a jarring knock seconds later. Eden hit the flight deck door button without taking her gaze from the windows.

Sierra burst in. "It's coming up the stairs! Hurry!"

———————◦●◦———————

Quentin hotfooted it down the upper deck aisle. He could already hear metal straining and bending and heavy blows pounding beverage carts. He reached the lip at the top of the stairs and gazed down. He had to be still suffering from the lingering effects of hypoxia. There was no way in the hell that could be real.

Daniel charged up beside him and started playing with his zipper.

Ah, shit.

"It's built up a tolerance to the probetalamisol." Daniel leaned over and looked down the stairs. "Fuck!"

"How can that be?" Quentin asked. "I was just down there."

Daniel's zipper sang its same old one-note song, only with a faster tempo than ever. "It ... I don't ... Maybe ..."

At the bottom of the stairs, the mega-T's left hind flank, leg, paw, and two tentacles were all Quentin could see. The difference in them alone compared to the last time he had seen the creature made him pay close attention to his bladder. "You didn't say anything about this shit, Daniel. You said it changes ... but damn!"

"It must still have a food supply. And a pretty good-size one."

"The volunteers." Quentin felt nauseous. "All the angels in heaven. I've been trying to maintain the last embers of hope that they were still alive down there."

The stairs twisted and groaned. Then the same weird stretching and straining sounds Quentin had heard down on the main deck floated up the stairwell. They were louder, more aggressive. Unlike the first time he heard them, he knew that they were forewarnings.

What sounded like a herd of spooked buffalo stampeded away from the back of the cabin. He eased back himself.

Daniel flat-out hauled ass.

Quentin couldn't blame any of them. The mega-T was colossal. E-fucking-normous!

Its head slowly crowned through the stairwell hole. The mega-T stood on its hind legs as its hulking frame stretched and distorted from the floor of the main deck all the way up the stairs and into the upper deck cabin, bringing with it the smell of a mass grave. Its mouth opened and giant teeth lunged. Quentin ducked as the dingy whites ripped a chunk out of the galley wall behind him. The creature shook again, the kind of shaking that would shatter a human's spine.

Oh no! He knew what the beast was about to do. In a couple of minutes, the mega-T would break into the passengers' last safe haven. He had taken a beatdown when it was half the size. He had no clue how to stop it then and damn sure didn't have one now.

The rest of the creature's body ascended the stairs and settled into a gruesomely deformed mass in front of the galley.

Everything in Quentin wanted to get as far away from it as the aircraft would allow. Only a hayhead would stand there gawking at it like a fool. He might be able to buy the other survivors enough time for Eden to land. If it killed him, maybe it would stop the killing spree. There was no question the vengeful animal wanted to kill him.

Fine.

"Why don't you just swallow me whole, you big bastard? I bet I'll have better luck shooting you in the heart from the inside. Make that tough hide work in my favor. No green blood dripping all over the place then."

With its black eyes trained on him, the mega-T's body twisted, shook, and convulsed back into shape. Tentacles stretched forward and wrapped around seats at the back of the cabin. They were unable to support the strain and ripped out of the floor. The mega-T's body fit snug wall to wall. It stood on four stout legs with its head canted sideways.

"Hey! Over here! It's me you want!" Quentin hurled one of the ripped-out seats at the monster. The one metal armrest still attached clonked the beast square between its black eyes. It was another marshmallow.

The mega-T growled and lowered its head with its huge eyes focused on him. In them, he saw his own reflection, tiny and helpless. His heart was beating double, triple time. His nerves stretched so tight he could strum a song on them. Sweat pooled on his forehead.

The mega-T's head lunged. He dove out of the way and landed on the floor between two rows. A giant mouth opened, and the smell of death came rushing out. He looked up into the back of the behemoth's throat, then sprang up and bounded over the back of the seat in front of him. The animal's mouth crushed it, trapping him between the seat cushions and the back cushions like a taco.

The mega-T ripped the seat up to the ceiling, Quentin and all. He writhed and strained and pulled at the seat, but nothing he did freed himself. A giant glob of saliva slid down the seat toward him.

Daniel wasn't quite sure where she put it, and the marshal's life wouldn't wait for him to play hide-and-seek. His mind was a swirling vortex as he ran toward the front of the cabin.

The passengers spilling out into the aisle didn't move over. He hopped between two rows of seats on his right to gain a better vantage point. The bulk of the passengers were amassed like crabs at the front of the cabin. He couldn't blame them for getting as far away from the megateratoid as possible. The short, narrow hallway between the cabin and the cockpit door was definitely the most sought-after piece of real estate on the upper deck.

In the midst of the pulling and shoving, a group of hands working in tandem passed a young boy over the top of the other passengers and deposited him near the cockpit door. The humane act touched him.

"All … way to the … pit door … and please don't drop …'"
It was her voice.

He jumped up on a seat and scanned the faces. The flight attendant was trapped inside the biomass. Moses had an easier time parting the Red Sea than Daniel would have parting the passengers between him and her. He had to find it himself. And fast if he hoped to save the marshal. The last overhead compartment that he had seen the flight attendant clap shut was a good place to start. He made it to within two arms' lengths of it. From there, it looked like he wouldn't reach it at all. "Get out of the way! Move!" He pushed a tangle of bodies into the row of seats on the right, and the rest got the message. About time. They gave him the stink eye. He didn't give a shit. Milliseconds could mean the difference between life and death for the marshal. Daniel tore open the overhead bin. *There it is!* He was right. The flight attendant had stowed Dr. Speck's briefcase in there.

He yanked it out and blast-assed back to the marshal. The fell beast's putrid smell was an invisible wall. He laid the briefcase on the floor, filled a syringe with probetalamisol, and injected a tentacle that had grown to the size and fury of a gushing firehose. It thrashed and whipped around. He struggled to hang on. With one especially determined buck, he could find himself slammed against the wall.

Dr. Ross rushed over and filled one of the syringes. She handed it to him, and he stabbed another dose into the tentacle. She obviously had handled a few more syringes in her line of work than he had.

"Here. As fast as you can." He handed her the needles and bottle. She filled each syringe and handed it to him. They were a two-person assembly line, needle after needle, injection after injection.

Apparently, the mega-T had some plans of its own, and they didn't include getting jabbed with needles. The tentacle started to slither away. He tried to pull it back, but the tentacle acted like he wasn't there. "Help me!" he yelled toward the front of the cabin.

With all the infighting to get away from the creature, he was surprised when Kito and the two men who had been fighting earlier answered the call. They grabbed the tentacle and pressed it against the floor with their hands and knees.

Daniel reached over again and again. Then her part of the operation hit a lull. "Faster!" he said, his outstretched hand waiting for another syringe.

"That was the last one," she said. "What are we going to do now?"

"I hope we have injected it with enough." The tentacle beneath him was a bucking bull. "And that it starts to take effect any second."

The megateratoid showed no sign that the probetalamisol had *any* effect. Daniel's skin crawled with regret. If he could right this wrong—just this one—he might be able to look in the mirror without putting a fist through the face of the jackass that had the balls to stare back at him.

The marshal must have heard the disappointing news as well. "Look inside the black case," he yelled. "There should be one more in there."

Daniel ripped open the case. Sure enough, one lone warrior rolled around.

"Throw it," came the voice from above.

"But if you miss—"

"Just do it!"

Daniel tossed the syringe up to the marshal and held his breath. As Quentin reached for it, the megateratoid yanked him sideways. It had certainly been injected with enough needles to know what they looked like. The syringe bounced off the tip of the marshal's thumb, and his fingers closed around nothing but a fistful of air. The syringe sailed free.

The marshal lunged with his other arm and grabbed the prize within an inch or two before it fell beyond his reach. He pulled the cap off with his teeth, spit it out, then drove the needle into the giant's left eye. The creature's other eyelid blinked a dozen times while the one with the needle sticking out from under it only flitted.

Trying to hang on to the tentacle instantly became more difficult. That wasn't a good sign. A blow from the intensified thrashing would crack their skulls. Four grown men were helpless to do anything but go along for the ride. Daniel put all of his weight down on his section of the tentacle, fighting to pin it to the floor before it killed one of them.

Hey now. All right. All right.

If he wasn't mistaken, the tentacle showed a little less fight.

"Yes!" The thrashing was definitely slowing down. Growing less intense. Then the tentacle stilled beneath him. Finally. He let go and stood up. The other three men bounded to their feet, all smiles and hee, hee, hee. All too happy to be rid of the gator-green menace. But they didn't trust the probetalamisol enough to take their eyes off the tentacle.

"All right!" Kito shouted, pumping his fist.

"Stop it!" Daniel interrupted their premature celebration. "Look!"

They looked up from the tentacle for the first time.

All of their happy-happy, joy-joy bullshit stopped instantly.

The megateratoid was still on its feet, wobbling, and the marshal still hung in its mouth, swaying back and forth helplessly as the creature staggered. Claws ripped up the carpet with every wavering footstep. One after the other, the tentacles all flopped to the floor. Then the megateratoid's front knees buckled.

He couldn't believe the mega-T was still on its feet. A fraction of the amount of probetalamisol they had injected it with would have killed it when it was in the basement. *Go down. Go down and stay down.*

"Let go of him, you hateful son of a bitch." Kito chucked a broken armrest at the megateratoid's head, barely missing the marshal. It clonked the mega-T below the eye with the needle sticking out of it. The eyelid fluttered. Its face twitched.

A long, low growl filled the cabin.

Then the beast collapsed. The marshal and the folded seat cushion popped out of the animal's mouth and hit the floor.

"Quentin!" Daniel cheered his name.

Beyond the marshal, the creature plummeted down the stairs. The dead weight of the tentacle that he had injected slammed against his heels and almost knocked him off his feet. Hopping over it, he let the oversize jump rope slide by. One of its lifeless loops hooked the marshal and the seat and dragged them toward the stairs. Daniel rushed over. The marshal disappeared around the partition. "Quentin!"

Ka-thunk.

The creature hit the floor down on the main deck. Daniel listened for the air marshal, for the mega-T.

Nothing.

Non sum qualis eram and fuck this! Daniel shot around the partition as a bloody hand latched onto the edge of the landing. He clamped onto it and pulled. The marshal climbed back to the landing, bent over and huffing and puffing. Blood ran down from a fresh cut above his right eye. He had shed the seat.

"Help me find my other eye," the marshal said, panting, "so I can see how to kick your ass." He wiped blood from his eyebrow. "Looks like I've been yanked from death's clenched teeth once again."

"Damn good thinking, Marshal. Either the needle or the probetalamisol—or both—couldn't penetrate the megateratoid's hide anymore."

"Quick! If you can find a seat, get in it, and buckle in," the flight attendant yelled.

Daniel clutched the marshal's arm, but he popped up with the energy of a jack-in-the-box. His arm was solid. Muscular. He certainly didn't need any help.

"Look!" Kito yelled, gazing out of a window on the port-side, his voice urgent and drenched in fear. The entire upper deck cabin gasped.

Except for the ones who screamed.

A voice that sounded too deep to be a woman's and too high to be a man's cried out, "Oh my God!"

Daniel's mind created numerous theories, each one worse than the one before, about what had sent a wave of panic through the cabin.

Eden's voice came over the PA. "Brace for impact!"

The marshal blast-assed up the aisle toward the cockpit.

"Brace, brace, brace!" the flight attendant repeated. The passengers who had seats bent over and put their heads between their knees. Everyone else hung on to whatever they could.

Daniel raced to the first window. Nothing imagined behind his eyes was as bad as what was in front of them.

They were almost in the water.

CHAPTER 39

"Negative, Wideawake Tower."

Eden's gaze darted from one window to the next. "I cannot see the runway. I repeat, I do not have a visual." Runway? She didn't even see the island.

As she scanned the waters below, Quentin popped into the first officer's seat and jabbed the ends of his harness together. A feather of a cloud floated by below the aircraft. She wondered if the controller had made a mistake or if someone had made a mistake in giving him that position. *Come on. Where is it?*

"You should have it in sight!" the air traffic controller insisted.

She reached next to Quentin's left knee and lowered the landing gear. "Negative. I do not have a visual. Where is it? We're running out of sky!"

A blinding streak of lightning zigzagged down from the heavens. Quentin lurched forward and pointed through the windshield. "There! On your left!"

The island emerged through the dense fog, a lighthouse to a ship that would otherwise be lost at sea. "Yes! I see it! It's the most beautiful thing I've ever seen." Maybe they had a chance after all. She yawed the aircraft to the left. Creeping across the windshield was a tiny break in the heaving waters.

She lined the nose of the aircraft up with the landing lights in the distance.

Too much distance, by her estimation. They were plummeting. "I'm losing altitude too quickly!" she shrieked.

———◆———

Quentin heard panic in the robot's voice. Where was the "minor malfunction" dodge? The edge in her tone unnerved him. She had operated like a robot until that point. No cracks, no emotions, just a pilot reading her gauges, monitoring her screens, going through her checklists.

Eden's voice was a little higher in pitch than it was when he left the cockpit, far more assertive. He listened to both sides talk with pilot-speak in his headphones. He turned to study her face. The robot wasn't there anymore. Her eyes had a vacancy he hadn't seen in them before, as if she wasn't there anymore either.

"No room for error," she shrieked. "No room for error."

"Eden!" he shouted. "Snap out of it."

Her eyes stayed locked on the runway below as if she didn't know he was there.

———◆———

"No room for error" described Eden's current situation perfectly. Wideawake runway barely fit between the shores of the tiny island below. The approaching end of the asphalt appeared to be inches from the heaving Atlantic's shoreline. Up ahead, the far end appeared to be just as close to the ocean, eerily reminiscent of the deck of the USS *Abraham Lincoln* with a great body of water at both ends of the runway.

Her crippling fear of being surrounded by water with no room for error was no longer a specter in her past, something she didn't have to deal with. It was right below and coming up faster than she was prepared to handle. Fear had seized her in an iron fist like it had done on the bridge, like it had done when she crash-landed in the Pacific Ocean.

This could be worse than the first time. I could create a plane-load of Toppermans.

A chill came over her as if she were back in the ocean again. Her chest constricted. An invisible belt around it cinched down to a tighter notch with every breath. The same sense of impending doom she had when she crashed in the ocean rushed through her veins.

There's no room for error where the difference between life and death can be measured in inches. Riptide's relentless voice was a clump of thorns raking across her frayed nerves.

The runway below morphed into the deck of the *Abe*, and she was back in the cockpit of the Super Hornet coming in for a landing in her crippled aircraft, searching for the meatball in the dark, Riptide's voice warning her, *If you come in too low, you crash into the ocean. If you come in too high, you crash into the ocean.*

Her eyes scrolled over the water below. *Negative. I do not see the meatball. I don't see it. Where's the ball? Where is it?*

Riptide's voice played again and again in her head. *If you come in too low, you crash into the ocean. If you come in too high, you crash into the ocean.*

A small patch of land materialized around the *Abe*. The ship started to fade.

"For Rona!" The voice wasn't Riptide's; it was Quentin's. The deck of the aircraft carrier disappeared completely, leaving only the small patch of land in the South Pacific.

"Hey! Snap out of it!" He shook her arm.

"I have the meatball. I have the ball. I have it."

Perfectly aligned with what had been the stripe running down the deck of the *Abe* was now the stripe running down the asphalt of Wideawake runway. Lightning cracked the sky up ahead, and then—

That runway disappeared as well. The entire island below had turned to pitch.

No engines, no instruments, no visuals. Her chest constricted again, and the arctic chill returned. *Oh, no, you don't.* She took a deep, cleansing breath. *Not anymore. Never again. Pull it together. Stay focused. Follow the procedures. Concentrate on the protocol. Trust your training.*

The Combi had almost stopped its forward momentum in midair. *No, please. No.* She and her passengers were nearing the end of their glide slope, where there would no longer be any glide or slope. Only falling.

The island was gone again. It had to be there, but she couldn't see it. Without lights, it blended into the blackness of the ocean. Somewhere in that blackness lay their only hope, hiding from them.

The tail end of a lazy cloud glided by. *Wham!* Something punched the 747. It felt like a great fist from above had reached down and punched the shit out of them. As their altitude plummeted, her stomach climbed into her throat, and her ears popped.

"What was that?" Quentin asked.

"A microburst," Eden said. "It didn't do us any favors."

"It knocked us that much closer to the ocean. That *I* can see. If I had a good pair of night-vision binoculars, I could see a lot better."

Careful what you wish for, Quentin. Eden didn't think he'd like seeing how much closer to the ocean's surface the ferocious wind had shoved them.

"Pull up! Pull up!" the air traffic controller's voice shrieked in her headset.

Her heart started doing jumping jacks. Invisible talons sank into her chest. The tension in the controller's voice didn't leave much room for doubt. The darkness was a curtain, shielding their eyes from a horrifying sight.

Thunder boomed. Lightning cracked the sky from heaven to earth. For a moment, it pulled back the curtain, lingering long enough for her to get a clear view.

Holy Christ!

The ocean's surface was so close if there was anyone still alive down on the main deck, their feet were probably wet.

The roiling, black waves jumped up to pull them in. In the darkness, the black water had snuck up beneath them. The teeth of the waves gnashed at their underbelly.

The island sprang back to life, gifting her with runway lights from one end to the other. By her estimation, she wasn't going to reach either of them.

The controller's frantic voice pierced her headset again. "You're coming in too low and too slow. Pull up! Pull up!"

She couldn't pull up. She had done everything she could do. She was going to fail. Again. And everyone onboard was going to end up like Topperman.

"Brace for impact," she yelled.

CHAPTER 40

Above, an empty sky.

Below, the black waters of the Atlantic Ocean.

From horizon to horizon, nothing.

Silence.

No sign of the 747.

No sound from the 747.

There!

Its underbelly coming down from above as if dropped from heaven itself. Its four dead engines hanging from the underside of the wings. The main deck windows, dark. Then the upper deck windows, as dark as the ones that just plummeted by. A millisecond later, the tip of the towering tail fin, the last to go.

The aircraft, gone.

Disappeared as if dropped through a hole in the bottom of the sky.

CHAPTER 41

The little blip on Le Blanc's radar screen represented every living soul onboard the plunging 747. One way or the other, in seconds, that flight would be over.

The fingernails on his left hand sawed back and forth across his other forearm again. Hansberry leaned over his shoulder, fixated on the screen.

Suddenly, the symbol disappeared.

Hansberry gasped.

"Oh, mon dieu." Le Blanc tore his eyes away from the screen. "It's gone down."

Hansberry banged his phone down on the desk until it was reduced to fragments, then spun around and snatched up another one.

The commander raised it to his mouth and barked out an order. "Walton, get the rescue boats to the crash site. If there are any survivors ..." He paused, perhaps to realign his expectations with reality. "If there are any survivors, they're not going to last long in that cold water." His tone at the end was somber, matter-of-fact and devoid of any sense of urgency. Clearly, he didn't expect there would *be* any survivors.

Le Blanc resigned himself to the possibility that with a water ditch and nothing to slow their descent, all souls onboard may very well have perished on impact. He wiped his eyes and turned toward the window to keep Hansberry from seeing him weep.

A ghostly spectrum of pinkish-beige lights backlit the dense fog outside. He shot out of his chair. "Commander!"

Hansberry turned. And then turned white. The phone slipped from his fingers and landed on one of his squishy slippers.

The nose cone of a colossal aircraft punched through the massive fog bank just above the south end of the runway.

Hansberry beamed. "It slipped beneath the primary radar!"

"I guess that is why we try not to use it," Le Blanc said.

"Once the aircraft dropped close to the ocean, if the primary radar's signal had hit the aircraft at all, the returning signal could easily have gotten caught by the heaving waves and pitched back into the sky. Either way, the signal never returned, and to the primary radar system, the aircraft was no longer airborne."

The main landing gear slammed down on the runway. Smoke exploded from the screeching tires. Le Blanc couldn't pry his eyes from it. "That is a big aircraft."

Hansberry's smiling face morphed into a grimace. "No!" he shouted, looking through a pair of binoculars.

Le Blanc grabbed the wastepaper basket from under his desk and kecked up the Diet Coke.

<hr>

The brutal landing sent a shock wave of pain up Eden's spine. The 747 bounced, threw her against her shoulder harness, then slammed her back down in her seat.

We're on the ground. I didn't kill anyone. They're all safe. But that wasn't accurate. Only the back of the aircraft was down. A second impact loomed, promising to bring another round of punishment for them in the cockpit when the nose of the aircraft hit asphalt.

A bigger problem loomed ahead. *Our speed!* They were a hell of a long way from being safe. Their second impact looked like it was going to be a mother.

The windshield pointed toward the clouds. No way Quentin could see the ground through it at that angle. He looked through the side windows, whipped around, and checked on Rona, who turned from one window to another, eyes wild, fingers splayed.

"Sweetheart, it's okay."

After one look at Eden, he knew he had lied to a child.

The plane hurtled down the runway. Le Blanc clocked it at about two hundred miles an hour. The landing gear ground against the runway. Tires bursting. Sparks flying. Rims ripping away asphalt, clawing gashes into the rest. All happening in fractions of seconds, yet it seemed like it was unfolding in slow motion.

Slow down. Please, slow down. As the aircraft became more horizontal, Eden's view through the windshield progressed downward from distant clouds. Through the window on her left, the tip of something tall came into view, then took form as they ripped past it. A hill.

The nose landing gear slammed down, far less punishing than she had prepared for. Lightning bolts in the distance illuminated the sky and backlit what had been hidden in the shadows beyond the reaches of the island's lights. In the brief moments, Eden saw Ascension Island through the windshield for the first time. When she realized what she *didn't* see, fear sprouted two legs and started walking upright. There *was* no island.

Bolts forked down from the sky like giant, crooked party streamers, creating pools of white light on the surface where they hit the water. For a few seconds, the lightning bolts teth-ered the sky to the Atlantic Ocean and gave her an eyeful. Dead bang ahead, an abrupt horizontal line marked the very spot where land ended. She peered beyond the threshold into the nothingness where the island was no more, into the noth-ingness where land *should* have been, and beyond, into the lightning-streaked sky and spotlight-marked ocean.

Stop! Stop! They hurtled toward the edge of the cliff and the ocean below it, and there was nothing she could do to stop it. Just like on the *Abe*, she was desperately trying to come to a full stop before running out of real estate and ending up in the ocean.

The turbulent waters off the coast of Ascension Island pounded the hulls of the rescue boats. Walton's rescue team gazed up at the top of the cliff from six boats.

Hansberry's voice crackled through his phone. "Rescue Team Alpha. Heads up. It's coming your way."

"We're in position, sir," Walton responded from the flagship.

Johns touched him on the shoulder. "What does he expect us to do? The aircraft will never survive falling off that cliff."

The front landing gear chewed up the last of the asphalt and plowed into the dirt near the end of the runway. The grinding wheels changed pitch, becoming deeper, a single note hummed by the devil himself. Eden knew what dreaded sound they would make next.

The aircraft had slowed down significantly but was still moving forward when the front wheels went silent.

She felt the drop.

And heard Rona scream.

An outcry of gasps rose from the sea, so close together they could have emanated from a single source and included gasps from the members of Walton's rescue team who didn't have binoculars. Above them, the nose of the aircraft poked over the edge of the cliff. Then the two colossal, black tires of the nose landing gear sailed over it too. The bottom of the fuselage slammed down onto the dirt. A thunderous bang propagated over the waters. More of the aircraft skidded over the edge, creating one long screech as metal scraped against the earth.

------◀◆▶------

Everything was happening at lightning speed. Quentin pressed his forehead against the cold window next to him, and as he looked straight down, a shiver rippled through his body. He looked through the window behind him. There was nothing there either. No asphalt. No dirt. For him to find either, he would need a rearview mirror. The only thing beneath the cockpit was air. The front landing gear and cockpit had sailed off the edge of the cliff. Knowing that they were suspended in midair was more unnerving than the tire iron.

Below him, onyx waves crashed against jagged rocks. All the while, the aircraft was still grinding forward, crawling on its belly and on the main landing gear behind them. If it didn't stop pretty quick, the aircraft was going to tumble down the cliff and kill them all.

Quentin's body listed toward the steering yoke. He reached for his harness and rediscovered that he was already strapped in.

"Why's it doing that?" Rona screamed. "Make it stop!"

Fatherly instinct rose up from a place inside him he thought was dead and buried. He threw his hand back and braced Rona. "Close your eyes, sweetheart!"

"I want my mommy!"

"Hang on!" Eden yelled. "We're going over!"

The view through the windshield tilted downward. The sky shot to the top of the windshield and then disappeared altogether. The view continued to descend, and he could see the ocean waiting for them.

Lightning kept illuminating things he would rather not see. As the nose of the aircraft tilted farther over the cliff, the shoreline popped into view. More jagged rocks—everywhere he looked, saw-toothed and beckoning—ran down the face of the cliff all the way to the foaming shoreline. It was a long drop to the ocean.

———————◦————————

High above them, the nose of the aircraft tilted toward the ocean. The crew members of Rescue Team Alpha fired off a quick round of gasps and yelps.

Then they fell silent.

All eyes focused on the top of the cliff and watched the nose of the aircraft progress downward. A large rock dislodged from beneath its belly, tumbled down the cliff, and splashed into the ocean.

Johns shook his head and turned away. "I can't watch this. How can you all watch these people die?"

Walton reminded him, "We're here to rescue any surviv—"

Every team member—save one—either gasped or shouted something up to the heavens or cried out.

———————◦————————

The jagged rocks on the face of the cliff disappeared in the darkness between flashes, then disappeared from Quentin's view altogether. For some reason he couldn't explain, he was looking at the foaming waters of the shoreline, then the sky floated back down into view. Heck yeah, he was grateful, but none of it made sense. It defied logic. It defied gravity.

The nose of the aircraft continued to rise and became horizontal again, but only for a passing second. His view through the windshield tilted higher and higher, angling toward the clouds, further baffling him. He felt a big jolt like the back end of the aircraft had slammed down onto the ground. The 747 came to rest diagonally with the tail down and its nose pointed skyward.

Eden grabbed his arm, grinning like a damn fool and didn't care. "It's just like the Combi I saw during my walkaround inspection. There's no counterweight."

"I can't even pretend to know what you're talking about."

She unbuckled her harness. "All of the fuel tanks are empty. There's nothing to counterbalance the sixty thousand pounds of freight in the tail."

"You did it, Eden. You saved us."

"I-I did?" Minutes ago, she had been sure she was going to kill them all.

"You're a hero."

"No, I'm not." Nothing she did would ever bring Topperman back, but the passengers on Flight 1219 would get to go home to their families. Maybe her uniform wasn't veneer after all. *Sometimes the hardest person to forgive is yourself.*

Quentin tore open his harness and examined her. "Your eyes have improved to a hangover's pink. The warm color has returned to your face. How do you feel?"

"Better every minute. Rona, are you all right?" It was a dumb question if there ever was one. All Eden had to do was look at her. The little girl, with her eyes popping out of their sockets and her fingers splayed out, looked scared to death.

"I gotta pee!" she panted.

Eden and Quentin chuckled.

"That's understandable," Eden said.

Quentin dashed over to Rona and picked her up. "I have to find out if Hercules and the volunteers down on the main deck survived."

———◄○○►———

Quentin rushed down the upper deck aisle with Rona in his arms. Passengers sailed down the emergency chutes one after the other through the exit doors on both sides of the cabin. When the last one cleared the bottom of the chute from the starboard doorway, Quentin handed Rona to Sierra. The flight attendant jumped onto the slide with the child, landed feetfirst on the ground below, and popped back up. Thank God Rona's little feet were safe, back on the good earth.

He ran down the stairs to the main deck where he saw far more destruction than the last time. More seats were crushed; more overhead compartments had been destroyed. Carnage and destruction stretched all the way to the back of the main deck.

The crew rest was gone. It had been reduced to a pile of rubble. He saw no sign of Hercules or his men or the mega-T. He looked at the wall of bodies and realized that his feet were moving the rest of him closer to it, though he didn't need to.

Hercules's face and his unmistakably large frame had been cocooned into the wall of bodies a little lower than Quentin's waist with the other volunteers all stacked above him, all covered with the mega-T's webbing.

I should never have let them volunteer. I should have gone with them. "Damn it!"

Hercules's eyes sprang open. Quentin jumped and stumbled backward over a chunk of what had been one of the crew rest's walls.

"I thought you were the lusus coming back to finish us off," Hercules said. The other volunteers came to life as well.

"This stuff is strong as steel." Gaston pried a knee free.

Hercules tumbled to the floor first. Quentin charged toward the wall. Working feverishly, he and Hercules ripped away the webbing and freed the other four men.

Hercules said, "It's the last place it would look for us."

"But the saliva is poisonous," Quentin said as he helped Kinley to the floor.

Hercules pulled a clump of webbing from his hair. "Once it dries, it's harmless."

"How do you know that?" Quentin asked.

"When I reached for the oxygen bottle that I had dropped, my hand got tangled in some of it. It was dry and nothing happened to me. We ripped some from the bodies and tied ourselves in."

"It's been tracking me like a bloodhound ever since I shot it." Quentin showed them the hole where his pocket used to be.

From a distance—the front of the aircraft, by his guess-timation—came a great roar. "It's caught wind of me. The chutes back here didn't deploy. Hurry! You're going to have to hide behind—"

Hercules gave him a look of derision. Obviously, he was too big to fit behind anything shy of an eighteen-wheeler.

"Sorry. Run up the portside aisle. I'll keep it occupied in this one."

The other men sidled across the middle rows of seats and reached the other aisle. Quentin ran to the curtains and popped his head into the forward coach section. He pulled his head back and held up a hand for the men running up the portside aisle to stop.

They had no way of knowing that they were on a collision course with the mega-T. They would never make it to their exit door in time, but old Quentin Kane would have something to say about that. He took a deep breath and charged through the curtains into the forward coach section, yelling and screaming like a raving lunatic. The mega-T was ten or eleven feet from the other men's emergency chute. In all of its unleashed rage, it tore a diagonal path across the seats in the middle.

"Go now! Hurry!" Quentin yelled at the men still behind the curtain. He outran the beast through the last set of curtains and up the stairs to the upper deck. When he reached the top of the stairs, Eden was coming out of the cockpit. They were the last two in the upper deck cabin but were about to be joined by a third.

"Get out! Get out! It's coming!" Quentin yelled.

The crown of the creature's head popped into the upper deck cabin.

Eden ran down the aisle and reached the starboard exit door a split second before the air marshal did, barely avoiding a head-on collision. The passengers on the ground below sent up an explosion of cheers and applause to greet her. She jumped down the chute. The instant her feet hit the ground, she cleared out of his way. When he jumped, a smile warmed her face. His body abruptly stopped in midair, hanging there in the scant airfield lights, suspended above the upper deck emergency chute like a skydiver.

The intermittent lights coming from the fire trucks made the scene look that much more surreal. Many of the passengers gasped. She could only hold her breath.

He retreated back up to the door without ever touching the emergency chute. His hands latched onto both sides of the doorframe in what could only have been an attempt to yank himself back down toward the chute or to keep himself from going back inside the aircraft. Even in the wanting light, she could see him grimacing in pain.

She jumped back onto the bottom end of the chute. "No!"

Two firemen pulled her off and held her back.

"Help him!" she screamed. "It's going to kill him."

Each time the intermittent lights landed on him, more of him had disappeared back into the aircraft until only his fingers, fighting to hang onto the doorframe, remained.

"No! Let me go! He's going to die!"

His fingers slipped from the doorframe, and he was gone.

CHAPTER 42

The tentacle that was lassoed around Quentin's waist yanked him back into the upper deck cabin and dragged him down the aisle on his back with a grip so tight, he struggled to breathe. He reached for his handgun and found that the tentacle wasn't just crushing it against his body; it was blocking it too.

The leg of one of the few remaining aisle seats that hadn't been torn to shit was coming up fast. He placed the heel of his shoe against a loop in the tentacle and rammed it against the steel leg. The grip loosened. He yanked his sidearm free, aimed the nozzle at a point in the tentacle he hoped was far enough away to avoid back spatter, and squeezed the trigger. *Blam!* The tentacle severed. He ripped the end of it from his body and stumbled back to the doorway.

When he reached the exit door, his legs buckled, and he tumbled down the emergency chute. He didn't really mind the couple of strawberries he got on the way down, although they burned like a bastard.

Finally! He was off the plagued aircraft.

Eden stood near the bottom of the chute with both hands over her mouth and a fireman latched onto her arms. When his feet hit the ground, he couldn't help but smile.

She flew into his arms. "I thought you were dead."

"That remains to be determined." Damn, she fit perfectly in his arms like the last piece in a jigsaw puzzle. And she wasn't pulling away.

She cleared her throat, maybe coming to her senses, then slipped out of his arms. If he read the situation right, and oh, how he hoped he had, it felt like she had pulled away reluctantly.

His arms already yearned for the missing piece. "Hey, it stopped raining." The thunder and lightning put up a weakened fight. "The men down on the main deck. Did they … ? Are they … ?" He looked around. There was no sign of them, and he could have spotted Hercules easily. "They should have gotten off the aircraft long before I did." He turned to the firemen. "Did a really tall man and a group of men get off the plane?"

"I haven't seen anyone matching that description," the one with the mustache said. The baby-faced one shook his head.

Screams erupted from everywhere. Quentin looked around. All of the passengers were looking up at the aircraft. He followed their gaze up to the exit door, where the creature stood, filling the doorway with its grotesque features.

"What the devil is that!" Baby Face asked.

Quentin shook his head. "I'm still trying to figure that out."

The mega-T turned to its right, left, and stopped when its eyes locked onto Quentin. A roar blasted across the airfield.

"That thing's got a hard-on for you," Baby Face said.

Quentin patted his sidearm. "We need something serious."

"Well, this *is* a military base." Baby Face ran over and spoke with another firefighter, who promptly made a phone call.

Quentin looked back over his shoulder as a soldier trotted over with a rocket launcher. "Now, that's what I'm talking about."

The mega-T roared again. The soldier looked up to the top of the emergency chute and froze. Quentin took the rocket launcher from the man's unresisting hands. The soldier never took his eyes off the mega-T.

Quentin checked out the weapon and smiled. "Yeah, baby." From above came a loud crash. The mega-T was ramming its body against the doorway. It took a brief recess, and that troubled him more. The others may have thought their worries were over. Not him.

The mega-T shook violently.

"Shit on fire. Get the pilot out of here," he said to the two firemen.

Mustache asked, "Why? That thing is far too big to fit through the door."

"The hell it is. I don't have time to explain. Everybody, run!" He waved a hand, directing them down the runway and away from the cliff. "Get as far away as you can. Now!"

The deformed mega-T stepped out of the doorway, and its sharp claws ripped into the emergency chute with a great whoosh. It crashed-landed on the asphalt, where it reformed to its regular shape and enormity. When it dropped down on all fours, Quentin took off.

In the open space, the mega-T moved like a guided missile. It headed straight for him, and he headed straight for the cliff. Quentin had already fitted it for a through-and-through hole in its chest.

Somewhere behind him, a dog barked and growled, obviously pissed off to the highest degree.

A cool wind blowing in from the ocean met him at the cliff. He spun around and faced the charging beast. It lowered its head, a living bulldozer intent on bulldozing him off the cliff, no doubt. In a flash, he doubled back and rolled into the tiny crevice under the belly of the aircraft. When the mega-T zipped by, he rolled back out, popped up on one knee, and took aim. "I've seen the future, and you're not in it."

He shot the beast in the chest. It disintegrated into pieces—chest, ass, and all—that rained down from the sky and plummeted off the cliff. A Rottweiler shot past him and ran to the edge, barking and growling over the threshold.

"It's okay, boy. It's dead."

He laid the weapon on the ground and ran back to the cluster with the Rottweiler trotting alongside him.

"Vicious!" Rona yelled.

The Rottweiler took off. When Quentin caught up, the dog was licking Rona's smiling face. The two were a tangle of hugs, wagging tails, and giggles.

Through the flashing lights that swarmed the 747, the silhouette of a group of men appeared. In the middle was an imposing figure. Quentin met them near the tail of the aircraft. Lightning cracked, followed by a mean peal of thunder. Hercules seemed to no longer even notice.

"What happened to you guys?" Quentin asked. "You should have beaten me out of the aircraft."

Kinley slapped a hand on Gaston's shoulder. "Who knew that Gaston here is afraid of heights? We'd still be on that plane if I hadn't shoved his ass down the chute."

"Who knew that Kinley here is an unsympathetic asshole?" Gaston said.

"Are you all right?" Hercules asked.

"I will be. Just give me a minute." Quentin struggled to catch his breath. "Okay, maybe a week ... or two." He saw Eden coming and declared himself healed.

TR charged past her. "I want you to know nothing has changed. I still plan to pursue—"

A colossal fist smashed into his jaw. TR dropped to the ground. Lights out. No switch necessary.

Victor had finally shut the senator's mouth.

While the passengers milled around the runway, and firemen doused the flames on the landing gear, the sooty terns called out *wideawake-wideawake-wideawake.*

"We are all wideawake, wideawake, wideawake," Quentin assured them. He pointed toward the asphalt. "Look."

Eden looked back at the skid marks left by the nose landing gear. They lined up with the dashed white line running down the middle of the runway.

He flashed an approving smile. "A perfect landing."

She returned the smile and said, "I hate sushi."

"Italian then? Chinese? Indian? Mexican?" The sun shined through each word. He leaned down and kissed her.

When their lips parted, Eden said, "Why not all of them? Airland Airlines flies to all of those countries."

"It's a deal." He kissed her again.

Wideawake-wideawake-wideawake.

ABOUT THE AUTHOR

Teretha Houston has followed other career paths but never strayed from writing. She had the pleasure of singing background for some of her favorite artists including Whitney Houston and Stevie Wonder on award shows, *Good Morning America*, *Saturday Night Live*, and at a Super Bowl. Before the bright lights were cool, she was often working on a story.

After receiving her master's degree, she worked for the federal government while writing novels, plays, short stories, and screenplays with the help of a voice recorder during her three-hour commute. She is a film school graduate with directing and screenwriting credits.

Equal parts nerd and adrenaline junkie, she is a science geek who loves to learn about the latest discoveries, especially if they can be categorized as strange but true—which is how she describes herself—and a sports fanatic who played full-contact football and was on the martial arts competition team in college.

Find out more about her on her website, www.teretha.com.

Made in the USA
Coppell, TX
10 October 2022

84364637R00194